THE BLUE PERIL

*The Scientific Marvel Fiction
of the French H.-G. Wells*

THE BLUE PERIL

by
Maurice Renard

translated, annotated and introduced by
Brian Stableford

A Black Coat Press Book

Visit our website at www.blackcoatpress.com

ISBN 978-1-935558-17-0. First Printing. April 2010. Published by Black Coat Press, an imprint of Hollywood Com-
ics.com, LLC, P.O. Box 17270, Encino, CA 91416. All rights
reserved.
Printed in
the United States of America.

Introduction

This is the third volume of a set of five, which includes most of the "scientific marvel fiction" of Maurice Renard, and some related works. It comprises a translation of the novel *Le Péril bleu* (Louis Michaud, 1911).

The first volume of the series, *Doctor Lerne*, includes translations of the novella "Les Vacances de Monsieur Dupont," first published in *Fantômes et Fantoches* [Phantoms and Marionettes] (Plon, 1905), the novel *Le Docteur Lerne, sous-dieu* (Mercure de France, 1908) and the essay "Du Roman merveilleux-scientifique et de son action sur l'intelligence du progrès," first published in the sixth issue of *Le Spectateur* in October 1909.

The second volume, *A Man Among the Microbes and Other Stories*, includes translations of the novel *Un Hommme chez les microbes*, the first version of which was written in 1907-8, although no version was actually published until Crès released one in 1928, and the entire contents of the collection *Le Voyage Immobile suivi d'autres histoires singulières* (Mercure de France, 1909).

The fourth volume, *The Doctored Man and Other Stories*, includes translations of four stories from the collection *Monsieur d'Outremort et autres histoires singulières* (Louis Michaud, 1913), the novella "L'Homme truqué," first published in *Je Sais Tout* in March 1921, and a miscellany of later articles and short stories taken from various sources.

The fifth volume, *The Master of Light*, comprises a translation of the novel *Le Maître de la lumière*, which first appeared as a *feuilleton* serial in *L'Instransigeant* between March 8 and May 2, 1933.

The introduction to the first of the five volumes includes a general overview of Renard's life and career in relation to his scientific marvel fiction, which I shall not reiterate here,

5

confining the remainder of this introduction to the specific works featured in this volume.

Because Louis Michaud, the original publisher of *Le Péril bleu*—here translated as *The Blue Peril*—did not put dates on his publications, some confusion has arisen regarding the actual date of publication of the novel. Pierre Versins' *Encyclopédie de l'Utopie et de la Science Fiction* (1972) and bibliographical lists derived therefrom give the date of publication as 1910, while the version reprinted in the Robert Laffont ominubus *Maurice Renard: Romans et Contes Fantastiques* and lists derived therefrom give the date of publication as 1912. There is, however, no reason to doubt the catalogue of the Bibliothèque Nationale, which gives the date as 1911. Although the story is explicitly set in 1912, thus giving some license to the latter error, it is clearly futuristic, and although the internal evidence of the text suggests that the novel was probably written in 1909-10, the customary lag between delivery of a manuscript and publication supports the supposition that it was not actually published until the following year.

Le Péril bleu is widely regarded by aficionados of speculative fiction as Renard's masterpiece in that genre, and the judgment is certainly correct with regard to his published works, although Renard might not have endorsed it himself. He had intended his masterpiece to be the novel he had written immediately before it, and probably rewrote immediately after it, *Un Homme chez les microbes* (tr. as *A Man Among the Microbes*), but that novel had probably been reduced to a shadow of its former self by the time he compiled a version—the fifth—that was acceptable to a publisher, by which time its startling originality was no longer so evident. His experience in trying to adapt that text to the tastes and expectations of the contemporary audience—as construed by the editors who functioned as the gatekeepers of the literary world—might well have played a considerable part in the shaping of *Le Péril bleu* as a determined and ingenious compound of mystery and melodrama, augmented with a measure of comic relief. In that respect it follows the example of his first, and more successful, full-length work of scientific marvel fiction, *Le Docteur Lerne, sous-dieu* (tr. as *Doctor Lerne*), but carefully attempts to surpass that example in each respect. If it has the disadvantage, relative to its predecessor, of sprawling over a much larger narrative space, thus failing to reproduce the earlier novel's intensity of its focus, *Le Péril bleu* has the compensating advantage of contemplating far broader horizons of possibility.

What qualifies *Le Péril bleu* as a masterpiece is the adventurousness of its central premise, which is not far removed from the central premise of *Un Homme chez les microbes*, in the sense that it lends steadfast support the notion that there might be radically alien worlds—or, at least, invaluable heterocosmic narrative spaces ripe for exploitation by secondary creators—much closer at hand than the planets orbiting other stars, or even the planets of our own Solar System. Like its predecessor/successor, and several shorter scientific marvel stories by Renard, it attempts to impress upon the reader an acute sense of the fact that our own world might not merely be stranger than we imagine but stranger than we can imagine, at least at present.

Because the story is a mystery full of intended surprises and melodramatic flourishes I shall postpone a detailed commentary on its innovations until an afterword, but there is no harm in observing here that the novel's premise was not only strikingly original in its own day, but that it still provides a good deal of food for thought to the modern reader; in spite of the vast progress in the exploration of extraordinary ideas made by 20th century science fiction writers, very few have ventured into territories as exotic as the ones featured herein, and even fewer have done so with the same intellectual boldness and narrative flair. It is, in that respect, one of the classics of speculative fiction—and that respect is surely the one that matters most in the context of the genre.

This translation was initially made from the version contained in the Laffont omnibus, but the second draft was checked against the 1920 reprint edition issued by L'Edition Française Illustrée, which facilitated the identification of a small number of typos in the Laffont version.

Brian Stableford

THE BLUE PERIL

To Albert Boissière[1]

*"For one may say this, Madame: for birds and
philosophers, the Earth is merely the bed of the sky,
and men drag themselves heavily across it,
with the forbidden azure ocean above them,
where clouds pass as well as surges."*
Parthenope; or, the Unforeseen Port of Call[2]

Preface

Six months ago—at 9 a.m. on Monday June 16, 1913, to
be precise—I saw a young chambermaid who worked for me
at that time come into my studio. As I had just started an exciting work, and as I had given orders that I was not be disturbed,
the words that sprang to my lips were three or four choice
blasphemies, but the girl paid no heed and continued to ad-

---

[1] Albert Boissière (1866-1939) was a prolific writer whose
career ran parallel to Renard's, beginning with contributions to
symbolist periodicals and ending with the production of popular crime fiction; he experienced similar problems with name-
sakes; there was another Albert Boissière (1843-1912) who
was a mining engineer of some note.
[2] "Parthénope ou l'escale imprévue" is a story by Renard that
first appeared in *Le Voyage immobile suivi d'autres histoires
singulières* (q.v.). A translation appears in volume 2 of this
series, *A Man Among the Microbes and Other Stories.*

vance. She was carrying a lacquered tray bearing a visiting card, and her face was exultant with a triumph so striking that she appeared to be miming, with fortunate accessories, the celebrated choreography of Salome parading the head of John the Baptist on a silver platter.

I abused her benevolently. "What's this you're bringing? Is it the card of the Eternal Father that you're lugging around? Give it here. Oh, my God! Impossible! Show him in! Presto! Presto!"

I had read the name, the occupation and the address of the most illustrious of illustrious men: the man of 1912, the man of the *Blue Peril*!

JEAN LE TELLIER
Director of the Observatory
202 Boulevard Saint-Germain

For several seconds I contemplated the cardboard slip, evocative of so much glory, science, misfortune and courage. Very often, in the course of the terrible year 1912, the popular press had reproduced Monsieur Le Tellier's features, and I anticipated the appearance on the threshold of the room of a visitor at the height of his powers, with a broad smile and large bright eyes beneath a broad and clean-cut forehead, standing up to his full height and stroking his silky brown beard with his ungloved hand.

The man who was suddenly framed in the doorway resembled my vision as an old man resembles his younger self.

I ran to meet him. He tried to smile and contrived a grimace. He walked with a stoop, his stride uncertain, and had great difficulty carrying a voluminous portfolio. Now, alas, his black frock-coat hung loosely about his thin frame. The red rosette ornamenting his buttonhole was now neighbor to a grey beard. His eyelids remained timidly and gladly lowered. In short, all the emotions, sufferings and terrors of 1912 were now legible on his pale and exhausted forehead, tormented by dolorous wrinkles.

We exchanged formularistic greetings. Afterwards, Monsieur Le Tellier needed to sit down. He placed his swollen portfolio on his knees, and said to me, while tapping it: "This is the work I've brought for you, Monsieur."

"Really?" I said, in an amiable tone. "And...what's it about, Monsieur?"

He raised his eyes to meet mine. Ah, his eyes hadn't changed. They were the eyes that I had expected to see: large, intimidating eyes, accustomed to the spectacle of suns and moons, which were deigning to look at me...

"I have here," the astronomer replied, "all the documents necessary to the history of what has been called, more or less accurately, *The Terrors of the year 1912*."

"What!" I cried, overcome by surprise. "You want it..."

"...To be you who will write that book."

"You do me a great honor...but in truth, Monsieur, have you considered...it's an...enormous thing. The subject isn't the sort of thing..."

"Monsieur, what I'm asking you to tell is *the story of a family* during the Terrors of 1912. It's the story of *my* family."

At these words, which awoke memories of such superhuman catastrophes and told me exactly what the grandiose mission was that was being offered to me, a breath of enthusiasm lifted up my entire being. "What, Monsieur! You'd consent to deliver to the crowd...in detail...the vicissitudes...intimate...poignant..."

"It must be done," said Monsieur Le Tellier gravely, "because it's the only way to make the world understand *everything* that happened last year, and because such an informative task *has to* be undertaken."

"Quickly, Monsieur," I cried. "Show me the document! I'm dying to get to work..."

The papers were already on my desk. All sorts of information were to be found in the heaps—letters, newspapers, sketches, notes, legal transcripts, reviews, affidavits, photographs, telegrams, etc.—carefully arranged in chronological order, numbered from 1 to 1046 and indexed.

Monsieur Le Tellier leafed through this chronicle, reading items one by one, bringing back for me the phantoms of doom-laden hours. They surpassed in horror and bizarrerie that which the vulgar notion of the crisis had permitted me to suspect.

As an amateur of the unusual and a scribe of miracles, I had known and divulged the strangest of destinies. I had been acquainted with the physicist Bouvancourt, who had penetrated into the image of the world reflected in mirrors. One of my oldest friends was Monsieur de Gambertin, devoured in our own time, in the middle of Auvergne, by an antediluvian monster. I had consulted the testament of poor X***, who had been seen hurrying to an amorous rendezvous with his dead mistress. I had glimpsed the existence of Doctor Lerne, who interchanged the brains of his clients—or his victims—and thus falsified their personalities. The engineer Z*** had confided to me the task of explaining how he went around the world by remaining in the same place. I was there when Nerval, the composer, died after hearing the sirens sing in the hollow of a shell. I also possess—along with others just as fine—the memoirs of Fléchambault, the unfortunate who lived among the microbes.[3] In sum, my records contain quite a few

---

[3] The works referenced are, in the order listed, "La Singulière destinée de Bouvancourt" (tr. as "The Singular Fate of Bouvancourt"); "Les Vacances de Monsieur Dupont" (tr. as "Monsieur Dupont's Vacation"); "Le Rendez-vous" (tr. as "The Rendezvous"); *Docteur Lerne, sous-dieu* (1908; tr. as *Dr. Lerne*); "Le Voyage immobile" (tr. as "The Motionless Voyage"); "La Mort et le coquillage" (tr. as "Death and the Seashell); and *Un homme chez les microbes* (tr. as "A Man Among the Microbes"). The last-named remained unpublished until 1928; although its first version had certainly been written much earlier, evidently before *Le Péril bleu*—presumably in 1907-09. Apart from "Les Vacances de Monsieur Dupont," which first appeared in *Fantômes et Fantoches* (1905, signed Vincent Saint-Vincent), the short stories cited were all col-

curiosities, but—and I affirm it with my heart and my soul— all of that is nothing by comparison with the events that Monsieur Le Tellier continued to enumerate, while his gnarled finger riffled through the archives of the *Blue Peril*.

I must say that he had a gripping manner of story-telling, like all those who have lived their narration. Sometimes he even trembled with retrospective anguish, at the sight of certain pages that he had traced with his own vacillating hand immediately after some new incident—red hot, so to speak— and in the grip of despair.

That day, we both forgot dinner time.

Such are the circumstances in which I was called to write this history of the year of disgrace 1912. In order to do so, I have followed chronological order—the only one that the historian may adopt if he scorns effect, as is his duty. Every time that an item in the dossier has permitted me to do so, by virtue of its conciseness, its brevity, its accuracy and its comfortable manner of writing, I have inserted it into my story. This results in a rather disparate collection, many of whose morsels are denuded of literary style; this is regrettable—but should the slightest opportunity be missed to substitute pulsating life for the discourse of a reporter?

In this regard, I shall doubtless be accused of abusing the liberal hospitality granted in my book to the correspondence of Monsieur Tiburce. It is of scant interest, I admit, and its part in the action is minimal, but it completes so neatly the portrait of a person whose deadly type is becoming too frequent. It shows, with considerable humor, where certain excesses may lead, and it seems to me to be natural and moral to disseminate it in the places assigned to it by chronology.

---

lected in *Le Voyage immobile suivi d'autres histoires singulières* (1909). Translations of all these stories appear in volumes 1 and 2 of this series, in order of their publication— although the order given above might well be more accurately reflective of the order of their composition.

One more word. A large number of people have the excellent habit of following the march of events and the displacement of characters on a map. To situate the phases of the Blue Peril in this manner, I recommend the General Staff maps of Nantua (no. 160) and Chambery (no. 169), or the Ministry of the Interior map of Belley (XXIII, no. 25). These topographies combine the strictest exactitude with the merit of being drawn on a scale sufficient for one to be able to stick in minuscule indicative flags or pins with colored heads. As for a street-map of Paris, any will suffice.

Now, let us turn our eyes to the past and return mentally to the month of March 1912.

Part One: Where? How? Who? Why?

I. The Entrance of the Mystery

On what date is it necessary to place the first manifestation of the Blue Peril? This is a problem that has never been resolved, but about which it is necessary to say a few words. Let us first do justice to a singularly tenacious popular belief that is rightly called "the legend of the Auvergnian woman." No, the woman found on February 28 in a field near Riom, lying face-upwards on her back, has nothing to do with the origin of what interests us. It is truly extraordinary that such a fable is still accredited, when that woman's murderer, arrested six months later, confessed his crime and was sentenced to 20 years hard labor by a jury at Puy-de-Dôme, as is established by items 1 and 2 in the Le Tellier dossier (a witness-statement regarding the discovery of the body and an extract from the judgment). Given that, how is it that idiots still accuse the *sarvants* of having committed the murder? Fear reigned during the parliamentary session and it was necessary that public attention be distracted; I see no other excuse for such an aberration.

Let is return to the dossier. The third document is a series of five newspaper cuttings. On seeing them, readers are bound to recall the incident that forms their subject, which Monsieur Le Tellier now believes that he recognizes the initial mark of the sarvants. It is a presumption, nothing more—as will be appreciated.

LE JOURNAL
Under the headline: *COLLISION AT SEA*
Le Havre, March 3
    The steamship Bretagne, *in transit between New York and Le Havre, which was expected this evening, has made it known to its company headquarters by Marconigram that on*

the night of the first and second it was struck a ship that it was unable to identify, and which fled thereafter. The collision occurred in the aft section to starboard. The hull is badly damaged, fortunately above the water-line. There are five dead and seven wounded. The accident will not delay the progress of the steamship significantly.

Le Havre, March 4

The Bretagne *arrived yesterday, three hours late. There is no news of the ship that ran into it. The latter drew away with such rapidity that the* Bretagne*'s electric searchlights, immediately activated, were unable to discover it. It is true that the sea was rough and that rain blinded the observers and limited the field of illumination. The collision occurred while the Bretagne was lifted up by a large wave.*

(Followed by a list of the dead and wounded.)

Le Havre, March 5

The relevant qualified persons have no knowledge of any vessel that might have been in the vicinity of the Bretagne*'s course on the date and at the time indicated by the captain of the liner. The era of piracy being past, it is therefore necessary to revert to the hypothesis of a warship on a clandestine mission. This supposition is further supported by the fact that the enormous breach in the* Bretagne *seems to have been made by the spur of an armored prow. Is it a matter, then, of an accident or an attack? It is important to note that the* Bretagne*'s lookouts did not see any navigation-lights.*

Wilhelmshaven, March 6

The destroyer Dolch, *of the German fleet, went into dry dock yesterday afternoon for repairs. It has suffered damage, on the subject of which the orders are apparently to maintain secrecy. Might there not be a connection between these mysterious repairs and the no-less-mysterious accident of the* Bretagne?

LA LIBRE PAROLE
(Leading article of March 9, final paragraph.)

So, gentlemen, do you have faith in the words of the German commandant when he maintains that when his destroyer was damaged "he was 35 miles north of the Bretagne*"? Do you not raise an eyebrow when he admits that "the collision nevertheless occurred a few seconds after the steamship's"? Does it not tell you anything when he declares that "when taking part in nocturnal maneuvers, it is necessary to navigate with all lights out"? When he cries—like the captain of the* Bretagne*—"I saw nothing!" do you believe him? In that case, if you please, is there some evil phantom vessel present everywhere at the same time? Or did the two ships bump into one another despite a distance of* 70 kilometers*? I read in the official Cologne Gazette: "If we maintain silence on this matter, it is to avoid people in France drawing a connection between the two collisions."* Two collisions! *Allow me to smile—sadly.*

II. The Haunted Countryside

That incident had been settled for more than two months, and "the *Bretagne* affair" had been forgotten, when Monsieur Le Tellier's attention was alerted by a news item in the *Lyon Républicain*.

Monsieur Le Tellier received that provincial periodical in Paris because he was greatly interested in the Ain region, particularly Bugey, which is Madame Le Tellier's native land. The latter's mother, Madame Arquedouve, owns the Château de Mirastel there, where the astronomer and his family spend vacations, and Madame Le Tellier's older sister, Madame Monbardeau, lives all the year round in the village of Artemare, near Mirastel, where her husband has a medical practice.

It was, therefore, with a perfectly natural interest that Monsieur Le Tellier read the following lines in the issue of April 17.

(Item 8)

STRANGE DEPREDATIONS IN THE DÉPARTEMENT DE L'AIN

Regrettable events have occurred in the Ain. Criminals, animated by stupid motives of pillage and degradation, commit misdeeds there on a daily basis, and not one of them, unfortunately, has been apprehended thus far. It was in Seyssel[4] that it all began.

On the night of April 14 and 15, a number of garden tools and agricultural implements, which had been left outdoors, were stolen. The first Seysselians who perceived this set

---

[4] Renard's narrator adds a footnote: "Seyssel *de l'Ain*, which is, by consequence on the right bank of the Rhône, not Seyssel *de la Haute-Savoie*, which faces it on the left bank."

18

off for the *Mairie* in order to lodge a complaint. On arriving at the town hall, they saw that the hands of the large clock had, absurdly, been removed during the night. A lantern hanging from a bracket had similarly disappeared. Popular opinion incriminated certain inhabitants who had been manifestly drunk the previous evening, but all of them, having given an account of their whereabouts, were exonerated. The court was advised.

The day of April 15 passed without incident. On returning to their homes at midday and in the evening, the Seysselians found no trace of thefts or damage. They went to bed without any anxiety. The following day, however, they observed further depredations even less justified and even less reasonable than the preceding ones. A flag fixed to the gable of a new building had been stolen; the yellow-painted zinc sphere that served as a sign for the Boule d'Or inn was no longer hanging from its iron pole; a quantity of tree-branches had been cut in the orchards; a boundary-stone at the corner of the main square was no longer there; blocks of flint had quite their heap for an unknown destination; and finally, the grocer's cat, which had been roaming the rooftops for some time, could not be found.

The Seysselians decided to keep watch on the following night, but it was futile. Nothing happened.

The universal opinion is that it is a matter of a gang of practical jokers, and that the actions are those of the village's coarse tricksters.

Such are the news items that reached us 24 hours ago, which we refused to insert before being convinced of their exactitude. Today that exactitude is indubitable, and we have it from a reliable source—which, in truth, it is not superfluous to mention—that on the night when the Seysselians mounted guard fruitlessly, it was the next village, Corbonod, which received a visit from the thieves. There, they attacked and robbed kitchen gardens in particular. And the following night, the wretched hooligans committed their acts of vandalism in

*the hamlet of Charbonnière, not far from Seyssel. A goat-kid
from that locality, which escaped, has not been seen again.*

*The gendarmerie is working on the case. There are several suspects. We await further details and will keep our readers informed. But this is an exploit of thieves worthy of the
region—for let us not forget that the ridge of the hills overlooks the Val de Fier, which displays to travelers the house
of...guess who? Mandrin.*[5]

These lines intrigued Monsieur Le Tellier, perhaps even
more than was reasonable. On reflection, though, the thought
struck him that the mystery probably resided primarily in the
way the information was presented, and that only the lack of
details produced the appearance.

As he had to write to his brother-in-law, Monbardeau,
the man, avid for enlightenment, took advantage of the opportunity to ask him for some clarifications with regard to the
above. This is his letter; I have reproduced it in full because it
deals with events and things closely linked to our story.

(Item 9)
To Dr. C. Monbardeau,
Artemare (Ain)
Paris, 202 Boulevard Saint-Germain.
April 18, 1912,
My dear Calixte,
*Great news! We shall arrive at Mirastel on the evening
of April 26—my wife, my daughter, my son, my secretary and
I. I am notifying the worthy Madame Arquedouve by the same
post. You have read "my son" correctly, Maxime is coming*

---

[5] Louis Mandrin (1724-1755) was one of France's most famous bandit chiefs, whose name became legendary after he
was captured and broken on the wheel.

with us; the Prince of Monaco has given him a month's leave between two oceanographic cruises.[6]

Now you are prodigiously bewildered! You're wondering why we're leaving Paris so early this year. Let's say...well, let's just say that I'm exhausted by the inauguration of the large equatorial. That will be the official pretext.

Oh, my poor Calixte, that equatorial! You wouldn't recognize the Observatory. One might think that Perrault's Observatory is now Soufflot's Pantheon![7] *I shall explain: in order to lodge the immense telescope donated by the millionaire Hatkins, it has been necessary to construct a veritable Basilica dome in the midst of the little cupolas. That's why I mention the Pantheon. The esthetics have suffered cruelly. If only science had gained! But how silly it is to establish so marvelous an optical instrument* in Paris! *In Paris, which is ceaselessly a-tremble! Paris, whose sky is laden with dust! And on a vibratile monument where radiant heat hinders observation! Nevertheless, the American being desirous that his telescope should be located where it is, one could only bow to his wishes.*

The inaugural ceremony of April 12 was successful in every respect. Many foreigners were in attendance, because of the exoticism of the donor—but I'll tell you about all that.

---

[6] Albert I, who was the Prince of Monaco in 1912, became passionately interested in oceanography after a stint in the French navy, and worked on various research projects in collaboration with many of the world's leading marine scientists. He set up an Oceanographic Institute in Monaco, incorporating an aquarium and a museum, and fitted out his yacht, the *Princess Alice*, with a research laboratory. Renard obviously expects his readers to know all this; later developments in the text assume that they do.

[7] Claude Perrault (1613-1688) was the architect of the Paris Observatoire. Jacques-Germain Soufflot (1713-1780) designed the Panthéon.

Another thing. You'll find here enclosed an article from the Lyon Républicain. *It piqued my curiosity. Can you, who are on the spot, give me any complementary explanations? Is it serious? I scent one of those almighty farces to which our peasants are accustomed.*

Regards to your wife—and to your son and your delightful daughter-in-law, since you have the honor of their company at present.

Yours sincerely,
Jean Le Tellier.

And this is the reply:

(Item 10)
To Monsieur J. Le Tellier
Directeur de l'Observatoire,
202, Boulevard Saint-Germain, Paris.
Artemare, April 20, 1912.

Let me first, my dear Jean, bless the causes of your hasty arrival in Bugey. The detached tone of your letter does scant justice to the gravity of these causes. Gaudeamus igitur, *then!*

As for the "strange depredations," they might, indeed, be no more than a practical joke—and a damnably bad one! Broadly speaking, it's something like a haunted house. A haunted countryside, what! And do you know what our villagers, steeped in superstition, call their mysterious tormentors? Can you guess? A local dialect term.[8] *Sarvants, of course. Phantoms! And, in fact, the perpetrators are ungraspable,*

---

[8] The inhabitants of the region where the story is set, Bugey, still spoke Savorêt, a dialect of Arpitan—a Franco-Provençal language overlapping both French and Occitan—at the beginning of the 20th century. On the rare occasions when Renard renders local speech in that dialect, he then adds a French translation, but I have usually translated the items directly into English, except where a particular term, like *sarvants*, takes on a special importance.

22

leaving no trace but the very evidence of their thefts. In conse-
quence of which, as you can imagine, a rather powerful ap-
prehension has grown up as the nocturnal pillages have mul-
tiplied. For it continues, as you must have learned from the
Lyon *Républicain, and the villages of Remoz and Mieugy,*
between Seyssel and Corbonod, have each been subjected, in
their turn, to their little nocturnal raids. By coincidence, when
I received your letter, I had just been summoned to a patient in
Anglefort. I went there with my "new horses," and took ad-
vantage of the opportunity to go on to the theater of Beffa, as
the Italians say.[9]

To be frank, the thefts are of small consequence, more
annoying than genuinely injurious—but they're no less bizarre
for that, and, being committed with a wealth of comic detail
that give them a supernatural air, are well-calculated to strike
the imagination of my fellow citizens. One remarkable fact:
they are thefts. Where the scoundrels' hands fall, without ex-
ception, something is missing. Not content with ruining a
clock's face, they steal the hands. One never finds the cut
branches, the uprooted vegetables, the unhooked sign—
nothing. They are thefts, often of useless things. What does one
do with an old flag? Branches scarcely in bud? Part of a bi-
cycle thrown on the dung-heap? It's true that spades, hoes,
pitchforks and, more seriously, animals—a cat and a kid—
have been stolen, but I have a presentiment that all of that will
be returned once the comedy is ended...or, if you prefer, once
vengeance has been exacted. Exacted by whom? No one he-
reabouts can guess. The local people have no known enemies.
Then, despairing of finding the cause, the possibility of some
vindictiveness from beyond the grave is admitted: a mass ris-
ing of revenants, an invasion of sarvants*! It's mad, but what*
do you expect? It is all perpetrated by night, with the puerile
refinements that one is accustomed to attribute to specters;
then again, no footprints are found in the morning—no vestige
of any presence whatsoever.

---

[9] Beffa is Italian for "mockery."

Furthermore, it was quickly observed that the majority of the thefts have been committed at heights where burglaries do not usually take place: at the top of a tree, the roof of a gable, the fronton of a Mairie; and as the malicious individuals take care to erase any trace of the feet of their ladders, two legends were born that are running around the region: one of giant specters, the other of climbing specters!

Now, where do the blackguards hide during the day? Where do they deposit the fruits of their larcenies? Many questions would be easy to resolve if the countrymen wanted to spend the night on sentry duty—but they lock themselves away. A few bold spirits maintain watch, though, and policemen with them. Unfortunately, every time they set up an ambush in one village, the depredations take place in another. In my opinion, the gang—for there are undoubtedly several of them—retreats by day to the depths of the woods on the Colombier, whose ultimate slopes extend as far as the marauded villages to the west. That's where they hide themselves and bury their booty, unless they bury it in the sands of the Rhône—which, as you know, runs alongside these communes on the other side, to the east.

One of the more difficult enigmas to decipher, of course, is the absence of any trail of arrival and departure. Oh, they're rogues! And they've sworn to drive the entire region mad.

I'm resuming my letter, briefly interrupted; it seems that Anglefort was plundered last night. No one expected that. The inhabitants were bragging when I went there. Well, there it is! A wheelbarrow has been taken, a cart, more branches, though not nearly as many, a scarecrow from a field of green wheat— a few old rags on a stick—and a statue from my client's garden. It's that lady's domestic who told me about it. I don't know why, but the last two thefts appear to have disturbed her more—her and everyone else in the neighborhood. I don't see what's so troubling about the theft of a manikin made of rags and an alabaster gentleman....

Poultry has been stolen too...but I'll tell you that story; it's amusing.

An old lady, whose house is adjacent to the church, heard a noise in the night. What noise? It was unidentifiable. She went back to sleep. She said that she woke up just as the noise stopped—but then she heard the crow of a cockerel quite clearly. The cock was crowing in the dark and its song was coming from above, and from the bell-tower! *It was not, moreover, a dawn fanfare—not the classic cock-a-doodle-do—but "the cry of a cockerel calling for help, which is in danger,* or which is being stolen." *And the next day—which is to say, in the morning—she saw, as everyone else could see, that the metal cock that had perched on top of the bell-tower for 100 years had gone!*

Immediately, instead of crying ventriloquism, they cried miracle, and refused to pursue an affair in which the Good Lord was mixed up. Fortunately, the police have opened their eyes—for, whether it is vengeance or a practical joke, enough is enough. They will keep watch, I hope, on the villages that lie in the direction followed by the raiders—to the south. They will mount guard in the string of hamlets that extends between the Rhône and the Colombier.

The trails so far followed have, however, been abandoned one after another. A tramp has been released, his innocence of any crime admitted—but there are, it's said, new suspects: two Piedmontese journeymen. They have not been working in the vicinity for long and have followed the same route as the bizarre occurrences. Bearers of picks and spades, they have possessed the necessary tools to bury their pickings from the beginning, before having dishonestly procured a surfeit of analogous instruments—which still suggests a gang.

Imagine how frightened my wife is! How curious that is, her being so intelligent! "I've always had a horror of macabre farces and uproars!" she says. "The worst of it is that, if it persists, one of two things must happen. Until now, the tricksters have followed both the course of the Rhône and the valley of the Colombier, but that stops abruptly at Culoz. Well, since there are villages along the river and around the mountain, it will be necessary for them to choose between the two directions—and if they take it into their heads to negotiate the bend that the Colombier describes, first Mirastel, and then Artemare, will be squarely in their sights."

That's looking too far ahead! All this nonsense will doubtless come to an end well before reaching Culoz, well before you arrive here yourselves on April 26. In the contrary case, your presence, and that of Henri and Fabienne, our dear lovers, will stimulate Augustine's courage. I am therefore looking forward to that presence with all my heart, both as a brother-in-law and as a husband.

All best wishes,
Calixte Monbardeau

After this letter, whose unexpected amplitude greatly astonished its recipient, the dossier abounds with newspaper cuttings. Like everything which appears to concern the supernatural, the misadventures of Bugey rapidly captivated the French press. These cuttings are, for the most part, mischievous paragraphs riddled with errors. We shall only note therein the adoption of the word *sarvants*, which, by its apparent novelty and phantasmagorical acceptance, seemed appropriate to designate these mysterious unseen creatures.

You will read below, however, a sequence of passages selected—so as to avoid repetition—from a very remarkable report compiled by the public prosecutor of Belley—a professional observer. Before being officially commissioned, this magistrate had undertaken investigations on his own behalf, on a freelance basis; the following fragments are taken from the official notes to which the results of those enquiries were consigned.

(Item 33)

At this time (that of his arrival, on April 24) *seven villages have been molested, all situated along the road from Bellegarde to Culoz, between the river and the mountain, running*

26

from north to south. The local populations are almost at their wits' end, seeing more things than are actually there.

They are shutting themselves away. The story of the Anglefort cock has provoked a great sensation. I went up the bell-tower. Nothing would have been easier than removing the golden cock without breaking it; it was only attached to an iron shaft by means of a socket, into which its feet were soldered and not pinned. It was, therefore, merely a matter of lifting it up. Even so, in their haste, the delinquents cut through the solder with the aid of a chisel. Was not the cock's crow sounded to mask the noise of the chisel?

The vanished branches are quite thick, by comparison with the trunks. Not sawed off, but cut, with shears of unusual strength. The ball at the inn was not unhooked, but had its chain cut, with a single stroke of those same sturdy shears. All the thefts were committed outside and in the dark. *There is no case in which two similar objects have been taken. If two branches from a pear-tree are missing at roll-call, one of them was in leaf and the other in bud. No two cabbages of the same species have been carried off. The birds stolen were not of the same species...*

No ladder-marks on the wall of the inn, nor on the façade of the Mairie at Seyssel. None, either, on the tiles of the steeple at Anglefort...

The method of removing, without leaving any trace, a cart, a wheelbarrow and other heavy and voluminous objects of crime, is also a problem. The employment of a dirigible balloon would explain everything, but that would be strangely disproportionate equipment for a simple joke. The most fantastic stories are circulating in the streets. The Devil has resumed playing his old role here. It's unbelievable that anyone...

The large-sized statue stolen from a garden in Anglefort has become a nightmare. It's rather beautiful, according to the peasants, and "painted in such a way as to simulate a person."

A local watchman, down from the forest, tells me that he has heard curt noises of some sort, like the cracking of a whip, in the woods, in broad daylight. *Because he found decapitated trees there, he imputes these noises, these clicking sounds, to the action of a chisel. He similarly attests that he has set his foot in a little pool of fresh blood, whose formation on the ground he is incapable of explaining, given that it was not found under a tree—where some animal might have bled—but in a clearing; that it was not mingled with any debris of feather or fur; and that it was not surrounded by any evidence of combat. The man seemed to me to be a nervous victim of the suggestiveness of the stories, further hallucinated by solitude. On my request to elaborate his story further, he did not wish to say anything more.*

Conclusion: we are dealing with an association of individuals armed with powerful means of execution, abundantly provided with capital, whose immediate goal is to terrorize their victims. (The two workmen who are being kept under surveillance can only be accomplices.) But is this terror being spread for its own sake, or as a sort of preliminary anesthetic? Is this the comedy, or merely a prologue? If so, is it the prologue to a drama?

In fact, it was neither one or the other—or rather, it was both at the same time.

III. The Flying Thieves[10]

The two Italian workmen could hardly be ignorant of the suspicions weighing upon them. As the only equivocal travelers and unknown guests, people were all the more determined to believe them guilty when that guilt was, so to speak, removed from the category of misadventure to the superterrestrial rank to which the rural imagination had guided it. "Those Piedmontese! Those foreign beggars!" They might have been lynched on the spot—but the presence of the gendarmes and a certain reporter from Paris prevented that summary justice. "Better to keep a close watch on their actions," they said to one another—and that was decided.

Elementary cunning advised providing the two fellows with work and continuing to shelter them, in order to lull their suspicions. Unfortunately, one by one, the local farmers refused to do so. The Italians received their final wages on the evening of April 23, from a farmer in Champrion—the village tormented the previous night—and lay down to sleep beneath the stars, on the edge of the nearby forest. A couple of gendarmes was set to watch them and, hidden according to the rules of the art, fell asleep to a man.

Champrion, however, was plagued for a second time. The sarvants appropriated a goose and some ducks, whose owners, confident of not being robbed two nights in a row, had neglected to bring them inside. The inhabitants had also to deplore the loss of a simulated bronze urn, garnished with geranium-ivy, which surmounted one of the pillars of an entry-gate. The vase on the other pillar, likewise equipped with geranium-ivy, was let alone. Still that spirit of spoliation and

---

[10] The French term *vol* refers to both flight and theft, so there is a good deal of casual but untranslatable wordplay in this chapter, whose French title is *Les Voleurs volants*.

teasing, characteristic of hobgoblins, gnomes, brownies, ko-
bolds, imps, korrigans, djinn, trolls—and sarvants.

When they woke up, the paired-up policemen who had
gone to sleep with such unfortunate accord found that the Italians were no longer there—but they maintained doggedly that
the latter were hidden by the branches, well enough to have
been able to have run through the woods without being observed, exercise their villainous prowess and get back to their
hiding-place.

It is, in any case, undeniable that the journeymen had
left early that morning, heading for Châtel. A young lad was
able to catch up with them by bicycle in that hamlet, situated—like all the others—on the road from Bellegarde to
Culoz, between the river and the mountain. There, the two
companions were seen going from door to door all day, beg-
ging for employment that was inexorably refused to them. The
Châtelois were counting on a continuation of the bizarre
events and knew that it was now their turn to suffer them.
They looked at the two pariahs as if they were the Evil One's
scouts.

This is how they were described by the diabolical newspapers: one of them, tall and blond, made a contrast with the
other, short and dark-haired. Large belts girded them, red for
the former, blue for the latter. Similarly costumed in disco-
lored beige, coiffed by soft felt hats molded to their heads,
they were shod in heavy knee-length boots, and each of them
carried his pouch and his tools tied in a bundle slung over his
shoulder.

Having been sent packing everywhere, even from the
inn, they ate bread taken from their pouches when dusk fell,
and lay down under a bush on the edge of the village, on the
Culoz side. The local inhabitants, frightened by the descent of
a dark night, imprisoned their livestock and bolted their doors.
The sun had not touched the horizon when a midnight silence
already reigned over Châtel.

The Parisian reporter and two replacement gendarmes
then took up position at the tiny window of a single-story

barn, from which they could see the Italians' bush. These three watchers had decided to divide the night up into four watches; only one of them would stand sentry duty while his companions slept.

It was Brigadier Géruzon who stood the first watch while in anticipation of theirs, his colleague Milot and the reporter snored in the straw. Géruzon was to wake them up at the slightest sign of trouble. The suspects were sleeping twenty meters away, lying under a sweet-briar bush. The road passed by on the left, not far away, soon disappearing around a corner of the wood. On the same side, the Rhône rumbled, and on the other, the Colombier massif rose up steeply in its overwhelming supremacy: an enormous heap of chaotic stages, studded with buttresses and pitted by ravines, rocky and verdant, dark by virtue of the hour, masking the houses of Culoz with one final outcrop.

A church bell chimed seven, and there was a fine interval of brightness in front of him when Géruzon saw the tall Piedmontese move, sit up and wake his comrade. They were conversing together in low voices, making gestures toward the hamlet in a discouraged manner, as if somewhat disappointed, when they suddenly seemed to come to a decision, threw their pouches and tools around their necks, and set off along the road again, marching in the direction of Culoz.

Brigadier Géruzon decided that waking his colleagues would take time and would doubtless generate some noise. As the Italians were about to go out of sight round the corner of the wood, he jumped down to the ground from the skylight and set off behind them. And he would have to run! Not following the road, of course, in view of the fugitives, but across the fields and straight through the aforementioned corner.

He had just reached it when a sort of exclamation—a kind of "hup!" he said—struck his ears. And just as he arrived at the roadway, emerging with a thousand precautions from the curtain of foliage, he perceived the two Piedmontese about 60 meters away, not *on* the road but *above* the road, *at an approximate height of five meters*, moving toward Culoz with surprising rapidity *in mid-air*. In the blink of an eye, Géruzon saw them vanish behind the first outcrop of the Colombier.

Having lived through that prodigious adventure, as rapid as speech, the brigadier was initially dumbstruck. Then, running fast enough to render him breathless, he went to wake Milot and the reporter, in order to relate the phenomenon to them as succinctly as he could. He endured their annoyance and reproaches for having kept all the glory for himself, but he riposted with an explanation of the motives that had led him to act in that manner, and made the most of his bravery, adding that he had not done it without experiencing a slight thrill of fear. On the basis of that confession, the others accused him of hallucination, and lamented not having been there. The night being as dark as could be, however, the newshound decided to put off his investigations until the following day. Until then, telling themselves that Châtel was logically designated for attack, the three sentinels kept watch in silence, with their ears pricked.

They heard no abnormal sounds.

At dawn, they natives observed joyfully that nothing had happened during the night. This informed them that the Italians were nothing less than sarvants of a particularly malevolent species—flying demons—and they shuddered at the thought of Culoz, toward which they had flown: Culoz, where people had not been on the alert. They were right to shudder; the first cart-driver who passed by, coming from Culoz, spread the news of its pillage. The sarvants had skipped Châtel, finding nothing there to steal.

This discovery provided an admirable explanation—in a manner as simple as a hello—of the absence of footprints following the thefts, that being the altitude at which the thieves flew, since they were flying thieves who remained suspended in mid-air while they were "at work."

Needless to report, however, some people treated this as an absurdity, and many pitying looks were directed at Brigadier Géruzon. The honest gendarme was unconcerned by that. He guided the reporter from the sweet-briar bush to the corner of the wood, and they both saw the tracks of the Italians; the prints of their hob-nailed boots were easily distinguishable in the soil of the field. When they returned to the road, however, they were no longer visible, the two pedestrians having marched on the grass verge. To judge by their trail alone, therefore, the Piedmontese could have walked in that manner all the way to Culoz, or even beyond. It might have been the case, after all, that they had not taken flight—in the case of a (probable) aberration of Géruzon—and even that they had taken no part in the sack of Culoz. The reporter took it upon himself to send emissaries there by bicycle, charged with establishing the present location of the Italians, without putting them on the alert. Then, while awaiting their return, he extracted Géruzon from a group of locals, to whom his tale was beginning to seem overly wonderful, and advised him not to delay any longer in making his report.

The patrols of cyclists launched in pursuit of the nomads came back to Châtel around noon, *without having found the slightest indication of their presence anywhere.* This news succeeded in convincing the journalist, at least sufficiently for one of the leading Paris newspapers to publish this sensational headline on the following day:

(Item 81)

AEROPLANES OBSOLETE
The advent of avianthropes
The bird-men of Bugey

After which followed an interpretation of the Bugist mystery, by means of the proven existence of a gang of prowlers in possession of the secret of flight without wings. Our journalist called them, pedantically, "wingless avianthropes." He trembled to see such an important discovery—doubtless effected by the "diminution of corporeal weight, a sort of physical emancipation from matter, conferring freedom from gravity"—in the hands of such rascals. And he concluded with a black-edged portrait of the terror of the Bugists, whom he represented as "flabbergasted by fear," wondering what would happen now that the sarvants, having reached Culoz, had to decide between going into the riverside villages of the Rhône and the villages distributed at the foot of the Colombier.

This article, vaguely impregnated with a residue of skepticism, was condemned as a lie even by the most gullible of fools. Proofs were demanded, and that was the cause of a swarm of reporters heading for Bugey, disembarking at Culoz—a railway junction—coming from Switzerland, Italy, Germany and other more-or-less adjacent nations.

Whether because the local combination of the river and the mountain was necessary to their exploits, however, or because they were reduced to honesty by the vigilance of the gendarmerie, or for some entirely different reason, the sarvants suddenly ceased their campaign.

The journalists went home, to their republics, kingdoms or empires; the peasants made fun of one another; Géruzon thought he had had a dream. That unexpected quietude did not deceive the wisest of men—by which I mean Monsieur Le Tellier—in the slightest, however; for, when he installed himself at Maristel on the evening of April 26, the day after the discomfiture of Culoz, he planned to spend his vacation making a rational study of the mystery. The partisans of the hoax hypothesis even claimed that the arrival of such a clear-sighted man was not unconnected with the cessation of hostilities.

IV. Mirastel and Its Inhabitants

The time has now come to describe the location at which Monsieur Le Tellier, his family and his secretary, had just arrived, and also to sketch a portrait of those who came with him and those whom he found—and finally, to reveal why Mirastel had received its annual guests at such a premature moment.

To anyone observing it from the south—a tourist sailing on Lac Bourget, for example—the Colombier seems a formidable peak, an isolated mount. From that direction, one might take it for a giant relative of those buttes which strew the country with their abrupt rotundities, and which the natives call "molards." That is an illusion. The Colombier has no peak. What makes it seem as if it has is the fact that it is the rump of a very long chain in which the Jura terminates. The Colombier extends a long way toward the north, raising up its tortuous spine for league upon league before stopping here, in a gradual collapse of hillocks and ravines: a magnificent descent of curt and thickset forests, a succession of abrupt gorges and undulating moors, like the apse of some superhuman cathedral, from which outcrops of rock and verdure radiate like mountainous flying buttresses.

The eastern slope of the Colombier dies out at the level of the Rhône, whose meandering course festoons its contours. The western slope does not plunge so low, widening out into the pleasant plateau of the Valromey. As for the rump, it limits a vast marsh traversed by the Rhône.

At the foot of that rump, the highway, wedded to its curve, turns from there towards Geneva and Lyon; passing through the sarvant-haunted region, it alternately encounters villages and châteaux. The communes are distributed along the road, and are named Culoz, Béon, Luyrieu, Talissieu, Amey-zieu and Artemare. Between them, but higher up on the flank of the mountain, manor-houses loom up in their various and more-or-less lordly superiority: Montverrand, feudal; Lurieu, a ruin; Châteaufroid, Medieval; Mirastel, Louis XIII; and Machuraz, Renaissance.

Among all these châteaux, Mirastel alone is of interest to us. It is easily recognizable. From the railway, which runs alongside the road some distance away, one sees it standing out from the green background of the mountain between Machuraz, which has white walls beneath red tiles, and Châteaufroid, whose two towers bear blue slate cones. It is made of bricks—bricks that have become pink, always illuminated by the bright sunlight—and flanked by four corner towers. Three are still coiffed with their old grey slate roofs in the form of pointed balloons, like Saracen helmets, but the forth supports the cupola of an observatory.

The garden of Mirastel, leaning over its far side as if on a pulpit, surrounds it with a fleece of foliage. Its terrace, planted with trees, forms a rocky plinth for its wall. It overlooks its two neighbors, and is overlooked itself by the mountain hamlets of Ouche and Chavornay, which are superimposed behind it to the left, marking out the stony path to the summit. Two cart-tracks climb in zigzags to Mirastel's main gate. One comes from Talisseu, the other from Ameyzieu. Both are thus connected to the highway, but in the middle of the vague triangle that their fork describes, a goat-track climbs up the steep slope, leading directly from the road to the threshold of the enclosure.

How did that castle, in the freshness of its youth, escape so totally the hatred of Richelieu? Why is it not, like so many others, a ruin that one might mistake from afar for a rock, among all those rocks that evening assimilates to its disconnected battlements? Legend holds that it sheltered in those days, not some bellicose predator, but a mild and inoffensive gentleman, doubtless afflicted by insomnia. Spending his days reading books and his nights reading the sky, he loved to take inventory of the constellations from the top of a high tower. That was the origin of the name Mirastel, which means "aimed at the stars" or "stellar observatory."

In truth, when the late Monsieur Arquedouve bought the residence, the north-western tower had never had a cover; it ended in a platform—but many antique astronomical instruments were unearthed from under the debris, in the form of a mass of copper objects engraved and embellished with allegorical figures: zodiacal and equinoctial spheres, azimuthal horizons, quadrants, sextants, celestial globes, astrolabes, gnomons and other ancient items recovered from the Chaldeans, to which it was convenient to add one of those interminable telescopes of whose agency Kepler was availing himself in the era when Mirastel had been newly-built.

Monsieur Arquedouve, a rich Lyonnais businessman, acquired the domain in 1874, 11 years after his marriage and on the insistence of his spouse, who was infatuated with the country and dreamed of nothing but astronomy. This superior woman, an emulator of Hypatia, Madame Lepaute and Madame du Châtelet,[11] wanted to build an observatory on the

---

[11] Hypatia (370-415) was a famous Alexandrian philosopher who was reputedly massacred by Christian fanatics. Nicole Etable de la Brière Lepaute (1723-1788) was an astronomer who made numerous significant observations of Halley's Comet during one of its periodic returns and improved the calculation of solar eclipses, although she figures in most reference books merely as the wife of the royal clockmaker (a prestigious position, in view of Louis XVI's lifelong fascination with the Clock Room at Versailles). Emilie, Marquise du Châtelet (1706-1749), was famous in her own day as the patroness of various radical intellectuals—she provided Voltaire, in particular, with the precious refuge in which he was able to work a 14-hour day and thus become the most prolific writer ever to wield a goose-quill—but she was an accomplished physicist in her own right and Isaac Newton's French translator; she died in childbirth. All three became feminist heroines: shining examples of female intellectual attainment tragically tainted by martyrdom in the form of male derision and existential misfortune.

platform of the tower; but the work had only just finished when Madame Arquedouve was struck by a double misfortune. An all-but-inexplicable amaurosis deprived her of sight permanently, and her husband died, leaving the poor blind woman with two daughters, Augustine and Lucie, aged ten and eight.

From that day on, Madame Arquedouve never left Mirastel. In spite of her infirmity, energy and habit made her a remarkable educator and an accomplished mistress of the house. She devoted herself as necessity demanded to the most various kinds of work, with an incredible skill—but when she left her park it was to go into darkness, and it was a great pity, on beautiful starry nights, to see her raise her extinct eyes to the splendor of a sky that she could not see, *but whose harmonious silence she could hear.*

Her ambition was to have a stepson who was an astronomer. She realized it. Four year after her elder daughter's marriage to Doctor Calixte Monbardeau, established in Artemare, the younger married Jean Le Tellier, then attached to the Observatory of Marseilles. It was Monsieur Le Tellier who benefited from the installation of the tower. It was equipped with a fine equatorial telescope, which permitted him to pursue some of his work at Mirastel, during the summer months.

Now Monsieur Le Tellier was the director of the Paris Observatory, and Madame Arquedouve was a grandmother four times over. Unfortunately, however, a further deplorable humiliation had crushed her. Suzanne Monbardeau, the eldest of her grandchildren, had allowed herself to be seduced by a man named Front, a rustic Don Juan from Belley devoid of all sentiment. He had abducted her. Monsieur Monbardeau never wanted to hear his daughter's name spoken again, so the sad Suzanne lived with her lover in a modest cottage some distance from the little town, no longer seeing any member of her family except her brother Henri—and he, in order to meet her, had to hide from both Front and their relatives. There was a good deal of misery, as you can imagine.

In April 1912, Suzanne was 30 years old and her brother 29. An exceptional individual, a doctor and biologist attached to the Institut Pasteur, already famous for his admirable treatment for arteriosclerosis, Henri Monbardeau had just married a charming young local woman, Fabienne d'Arvière, and the newly-weds were resting at Artemare after a rather tiring honeymoon voyage while the Le Telliers received Madame Arquedouve's hospitality. Their cousin, Maxime Le Tellier, was then in his 26th year. Having served on the *Borda*, first as a cadet and then as an ensign, he had recently left the navy to occupy himself with oceanography with the Prince of Monaco. Told that his entire family was about to meet up in Bugey, he had arranged things so that the month of independence to which he was entitled would coincide with that assembly. There was also, in all the seductiveness of her 18 years and the grace of her blonde beauty, his sister Marie-Thérèse Le Tellier, who would require a great poet to describe her golden hair with a silvery gleam, her fresh flowery complexion, her soft gaze of the sort that Greuze loved, her slender, rounded and supple figure. She was good, and polite—one would have to know her to know how much!—and one could not hear the child speak without adoring her mind; and yet, her appearance was so troubling that young men did not hear her at all; seeing nothing but her marvelous lips, they thought only of kisses to come and not of the speech of the present moment.

Suzanne and Henri Monbardeau, and Maxime and Marie-Thérèse Le Tellier had spent the best part of their childhood at Mirastel and Artemare, in summer. There, Fabienne d'Arvière had joined in their adolescent games; there too, a poor little orphan, to whom Monsieur Le Tellier served as tutor, had spent many beautiful vacations in their company before becoming his patron's faithful secretary. Artemare and Mirastel! What memories! The young Monbardeaus idolized their Aunt Le Tellier; the little Le Telliers swore by their Aunt Monbardeau, and in the season of the sun there was a perpetual coming-and-going between Madame Arquedouve's château and the doctor's villa. They lived in both. They boarded there, sometimes for several days at a time.

Madame Arquedouve presided merrily over the enjoyments of the château, and she was so lively, that thin lady with the near-blue blindfold, in her black alpaca dress cut in a monastic style, with a little cape and a collar and sleeves of linen; she was so alert and ever on the move, that spare damozel, that one forgot that she was blind—and she doubtless forgot it herself, from time to time.

Suzanne's sin, alas, had cast the purple shadow of shame over all that—but one is surely not bound to blush continuously because one daughter of the household has fallen prey to a seducer. Thus, it was in the midst of a sufficiently jovial reunion that Monsieur Le Tellier made his entrance to Mirastel, preceded by his wife Lucie and his daughter Marie-Thérèse and followed by his son Maxime and his secretary, Robert Collin.

The sarvants were then at the height of their glory, and the conversation during dinner inevitable came around to them.

As soon as the meal was over, the four cousins escaped. Every year, the same joyful ritual led the new arrivals to make an immediate tour of Mirastel. In the fallen night they sought the silhouette of the ancient dwelling, with its iron weathervanes pointing toward the stars; they roamed around the farm adjoining the château, the sloping park, the terraces planted with flowering chestnuts. A *gingko biloba*, a rare tree whose ancestors went back to the Deluge, greeted them there like an old vegetal uncle. Then all four of them went into the centuries-old hornbeam plantation whose path led to the main gate, and whose tenebrous cradle forged a more nocturnal night within the night.

They were four moving patches, two tall and somber and two small and bright, gliding over the gravel extracted from the river with the sound of shifting pebbles. They pronounced sentences in which the name of Suzanne recurred frequently.

But here comes something black, yapping and frisky, which hurls itself upon the strollers. It is Floflo, a Pomeranian with hair made glossy by stroking—yet another childhood friend, a contemporary of Marie-Thérèse, although he was already an old dog then. They make a fuss of him. Suzanne is somewhat forgotten. And they continue their sentimental round, in the moonlight that has just sprung forth above a crest.

Very good. And what about their parents?

Their parents are chatting in the drawing-room with Madame Arquedouve and Robert Collin. And while Madame Monbardeau, her head full of sarvants, is quietly worrying about the "children" going out—which she considers imprudent—the grandmother asks Monsieur Le Tellier: "Why have you come to Mirastel so early, Jean?"

The astronomer does not reply straight away. He looks at his wife with a troubled expression. The latter then looks the secretary up and down, with considerable arrogance. She gazes malevolently at the frail little man, so thin and so ugly, seemingly taking inventory of his physical disadvantages—his prominent cheekbones, his excessive forehead and his wretched downy beard—and fixes her stare on the huge blue eyes behind his gold-rimmed spectacles, which are immensely thoughtful, as if they were as unattractive as the rest.

Robert Collin has understood. He senses that he is superfluous to requirements. He stands up and stammers: "If you will permit, I shall....hmm...go and unpack." Then he withdraws, wiping the lenses of his spectacles.

"What a nice boy that Robert is," says Madame Monbardeau. "How you treat him, Luce."

"I don't like intruders," says Madame Le Tellier, in a languorous tone. "The fellow is always the odd man out—it's boring. And such a face, too..."

"Luce! Luce!" groaned Monsieur Le Tellier.

Now, the reader is fortunate. The two sisters could not have said anything to paint them more accurately in fewer words: the one indulgent and good, frank and unaffected; the other nonchalant and full of acridity, thoroughly hardened. Let us add that Madame Le Tellier tints her hair with henna, that she lies down for hours without any valid reason, that her fingernails seem oily by virtue of being painted with polish, and we shall have described her sufficiently.[12]

Meanwhile, Madame Arquedouve has repeated her question, and since only family members are now present, Monsieur Le Tellier replies. "Personally, Mother, I shall be returning to Paris within a fortnight—but I wanted especially to bring you Marie-Thérèse."

"Is she ill? Or is it something else?" The grandmother is alarmed, thinking about her other grand-daughter, Suzanne.

"No don't worry. But you know that, on April 12, we inaugurated the equatorial donated by Monsieur Hatkins. What's the matter, Calixte?"

The doctor had started. "Nothing," he says. "It's that name, Hatkins....go on, go on..."

"That celebration was magnificent, Mother. Illustrious individuals, notorious socialites and not a few notable foreigners took part. Our Marie-Thérèse, who made her debut there, was a great success...and since that afternoon—damn it!—I've received so many requests for her hand in marriage, so pressing, so flattering and even so...unexpected, that, one the one hand, not wishing to marry her off so young, and, on the other, not knowing how to respond to the indefatigable avalanche of letters and visits that the excellent reason in question has not sufficed to repel, we took the decision to run away! It was no longer tenable! No one will come here to hurl us back into it."

---

[12] Renard's narrator inserts a footnote here: "Madame Le Tellier and Monsieur Tiburce—who will appear in the story soon—have asked the author to treat them herein without benevolence. They nobly desire that nothing in the depiction of the errors they made should attenuate the lessons to be drawn therefrom. Such an attitude magnifies them more than the errors themselves have diminished them."

"The Duc d'Agnès," said Madame Arquedouve, softly. "You know—that classmate of Maxime's, the aviator who came to Mirastel last year; has he asked for Marie-Thérèse?"

"No."

"That's a pity. I would have liked that."

"Me too," affirmed Madame Le Tellier.

"Her too," concluded Monbardeau.

"My God," retorted the astronomer, disconcerted. "My God...the Duc d'Agnès isn't a scientist...nevertheless, I don't see anything inconvenient in that...but he hasn't asked for her."

"In truth, you've received a great many proposals?" said the doctor, admiringly.

"Some of them are priceless, you know," said Madame Le Tellier, languidly. "An attorney from Chicago. A Spanish cavalry officer. A Hungarian diplomatic attaché. Even a Turk, Abdul Kadir!"

"Ah, the Turk—that's the cherry on the cake!" cried Monsieur Le Tellier, bursting into laughter. "A Pacha, come to visit Paris with a dozen creatures from his harem! He parades them around relentlessly, hermetically veiled, in the depths of three hired landaus."

"Hatkins hasn't entered the lists?" asked Monsieur Monbardeau, his expression severe.

"No—why?"

"Oof! I can breathe again."

"But my dear friend, Monsieur Hatkins doesn't know Marie-Thérèse. Anyway, everyone knows that he maintains a fervent cult to the memory of his wife. Finally, Monsieur Hatkins is the humblest of philanthropists and never showed himself, even for a second, at the inauguration. He has never seen my daughter—I'll swear to it."

"So much the better, so much the better!"

"But in the end..."

"I have my reasons."

"Since you know him, do you know that he's about to leave with his friends on a world tour?"

"That's all right by me!"

At that moment, the "children" came back in, blinking in the lamplight. "Hey? Did you run into the sarvants?" queried Monsieur Monbardeau.

And everyone laughed, more or less heartily.

"Are you content?" asked Madame Arquedouve.

"Can you doubt it, Grandmother?" Maxime replied. "From tomorrow on, we resume the good life of yesteryear!"

"You'll find your laboratory and your old collections again, and your aquarium."

"It will be useful again, that aquarium. I'd like to attempt a few experiments here in connection with my oceanographic work. Old Philibert will furnish me with fish every week—and I also intend to do a lot of water-colors."

"And excursions, I suppose!" cried Marie-Thérèse. "All winter I've been thinking about the moment when I'd be able to touch the cross on the Grand-Colombier. It's so beautiful up there!"

"Ah, ever the intrepid climber!" said Madame Monbardeau, gaily. "Marie-Thérèse, will you come to Artemare soon to seek food and shelter with us?"

"I'd already thought of that, Aunt!"

"Oh, not right away!" protested the grandmother, blindly using her mobile and lively hand to pat her granddaughter's head.

"When you feel like it," Aunt Monbardeau went on. "No need to notify us in advance—your room will be ready. And yours too, Maxime."

The country doctor's modest "new horses" were snoring on the terrace in front of the château. The four Monbardeaus installed themselves in the automobile.

"Goodbye! Goodbye! See you soon! Until tomorrow!"

Moonlight bathed the superb mountainous panorama. The motor car raced down the zigzags on the hillside. Leaning over the parapet, the Mirastelians laughed and shouted: "Look out for the sarvants!"

The horn sounded at the corner of the road.

It was so calm that the purr of motor was audible all the way to Artemare, where it stopped.

V. The Alarm

A week later, May 5—still at Mirastel.

It is pleasant to imagine Monsieur Le Tellier going into his study on that morning, for there is no finer spectacle than the meeting of a happy man with a ray of sunlight in the middle of a large and noble room.

Monsieur Le Tellier goes across the large room, darting a glance at the books covering the wall, opens the window, breathes in a draught of pure and luminous morning air—dominical air, for it is Sunday and all is well—and finally leans on his elbows looking out.

Between the flowering chestnut trees aligned on the terrace he sees the successive planes of the majestic slope, the marsh, then the cliff, at the foot of which the Séran flows and the railway flees; then, on the cliff-top, a plateau wooded with stumpy trees, in the center of which the Château de Grammont culminates; then, in the distance, drowned in mist, peaks, spires, arêtes and mountains with a little snow on their summits still, soon melted: the Mont du Chat (Aix-les-Bains!), the Nivolet (Chambéry!) and finally, lost in the very depths of space, the Dauphinoise Alps, like foggy lace.

A train whistles along the cliff. An automobile purrs along the road. And Monsieur Le Tellier thinks, with satisfaction, that a long and glorious week still remains for him to enjoy, before the train or his large white car bears him away to Paris.

His face is one big smile.

The sarvant has vanished, like a phantom that never was, but Monsieur Le Tellier has found the means to recreate it nevertheless. Not by looking at the stellar world, to be sure—for, in order to come to Mirastel, he has interrupted his important work on the star Vega, or Alpha Lyrae, whose radial velocity he has measured, and similar enterprises requiring powerful precision telescopes. He has, however, discovered an archaic treatise on astronomy in the loft, in a dusty niche not far from dismantled gnomons, and he has been amusing himself deciphering it with his watch-maker's magnifying glass.

On the desk, the old quarto volume offers him its manuscript ages to be spelled out—but it is so beautiful this morning that Monsieur Le Tellier grants himself a little idleness. He daydreams. Today, the inhabitants of Mirastel are going to dine at Artemare, where Marie-Thérèse went ahead of them yesterday evening. He daydreams. Why, there's Madame Arquedouve and Madame Le Tellier passing by, wandering beneath the *gingko biloba*—that "graceful survivor of primitive flora," as the textbooks say. Ah! Here's the postman! And who's that breaking out into song? It's Maxime, in the southwestern tower, where his laboratories are. Yes, Maxime is singing a tune from an operetta while he studies the interior of his unfortunate fishes. Very pretty, that song...

"Life is beautiful," murmurs Monsieur Le Tellier.

And he turns round, to face the old book on cosmography. It is then—not later or sooner—that he hears a soft, stiff rap on the door. Believe me, it is as stiff as if some skeleton were tapping on the panel with its finger-bone.

"Come in!"

Is it really a skeleton that is about to enter? Yes, since it is a man. It is even a skeleton with very little flesh on top and not may muscles, since it is Robert Collin. He comes forward, dressed in his eternal little frock-coat, the pale down of his beard like froth on his cheeks. His myopia makes his gold-circled eyes very soft. He brings in the mail.

"Good day, Robert. How are you?"

The other chokes, take off his spectacles, and says: "No, Master, not very well. I have to talk to you...about serious matters....and I'm...ridiculously...upset about them."

"Speak, my friend. What? Are you afraid to talk to me? You know the high esteem in which I hold you..."

"I know how much I owe you, my dear Master. Life, first of all, and education, and instruction. You've given me a family, and a great deal of friendship...and that esteem to which you just made allusion. So I shouldn't...but you see, one has a duty to oneself as well...and I don't have the right to remain silent, even though I know with certainty that my audacity is futile... Just promise me, Master...not to hold it against me if my request seems to you to be too outrageous..."

Monsieur Le Tellier has an idea what it is about. He is more touched than surprised, and more annoyed than touched. "I promise," he says.

"Well, Master, I'm in love with Mademoiselle Marie-Thérèse, and I have the honor of asking you for her hand."

Bang! There we go! cries Monsieur Le Tellier, privately.

The other continues; it is obvious that he is reciting a prepared speech. "I'm poor, an orphan, awkward and ugly. I'm not unaware of how grotesque I seem. But when one has the audacity to fall in love, what can one do? One must have the audacity to declare it. And a man who perceives happiness, even if it be the height of folly, has a duty to launch himself toward it. Now, my dear Master, I've accomplished that obligation vis-à-vis my own person. I know your answer in advance. I've done what I had to do. Let's not mention it again."

"My friend, I too have duties. Mine, in his matter, is to consult my daughter...once she is twenty years old. In two years, therefore, I shall make your sentiments known to her. And I can tell you, my dear Robert, that they raise the value of Marie Thérèse in my eyes and that they honor us all. I not only love you, my friend; I admire you. You're a great scientist, and, what is even better, a brave man."

"She won't want me...I'm not sufficiently good-looking..."

"Who can tell?" said Monsieur Le Tellier, meditatively. "You're endowed with singular scientific qualities...a strange perspicacity...a sort of divination...which might take you to the most envied positions. Marie-Thérèse isn't unaware of that. I know, myself, that she appreciates you as you deserve..."

"There's your family, Master!"

"That's true—but Marie-Thérèse is free to choose..."

"Alas!"

"Come on! No sadness. I'm not discouraging you, though! Think about it. Don't weep! Come on! I'm making a hopeful speech to you, on a sunny day—to you, who are young, and you're weeping! Oh, the beautiful spring morning, Robert! It's so beautiful and so spring-like that one ought to be amorous, not in pain!"

"I'll be frank. Look, I fear that…that Mademoiselle Marie-Thérèse is already in love with someone. I recognized…on this letter addressed to you…the handwriting of Monsieur le Duc d'Agnès. Coming after all the solicitations with which you have been assailed—and which my heart apologizes for having discovered—this letter has…upset me. I wanted to get in ahead of it, this morning…so I have spoken…"

"Give me that."

Indeed, the letter is signed *François d'Agnès*, and begins thus:

(Item 104)

Dear Sir,

I have guessed why you left Paris so mysteriously, and that has decided me to take a step by which it is scarcely probable that you will be surprised. I had hoped to make my request not by letter, but in…

Monsieur Le Tellier no longer dares to raise his eyes from the letter. He recalls a certain affirmation by Madame Monbardeau regarding Marie-Thérèse and the Duc d'Agnès. He compares the two claimants: the sickly little scientist with nothing at all and the intrepid sportsman, boyish and magnificent, noble of heart and lineage, rich in gold and intelligence—adorable, to be sure. And there are Shakespearean voices in his head, whispering: "Hail to thee, Le Tellier! Thy daughter shall be a duchess!"

But someone knocks on the door, and he shudders. This time, it is a dull knock, as if some cadaver escaped from the

49

tomb has come to thump the panel with its soft and leaden fists...

And behold: the two conversationalists shudder...for it really is a sort of cadaver that comes in, before anyone says: "Come in!" He is a man of sickly pallor. His torn clothes are covered in dirt; his shoes have walked on pebbles for a long time. His haggard eyes are open wide and he stands there, in the doorway, shivering like a wretch.

At first, Monsieur Le Tellier recoils—the unknown man is frightening. Then, all of a sudden, he launches himself toward the diurnal specter and takes him in his arms, warmly...for the most terrible quality of the livid, trembling, maddened, sepulchral intruder, is that of being Monsieur Monbardeau, unrecognizable.

The latter's brother-in-law has but one thought in his head: Marie-Thérèse has been at her uncle's house since yesterday; something has happened to her.

"My daughter...speak! Speak!"

"Your daughter?" the doctor articulates, painfully. "It's nothing to do with your daughter. It's my children—Henri and his wife, Henri and Fabienne. *They've disappeared!*"

Monsieur Le Tellier breathes in.

Monsieur Monbardeau, collapsing in a chair in tears, continues: "Disappeared! Yesterday. We didn't want to tell you...but there's no doubt, now. What a night! Yesterday morning, they both went out for a walk...to the Colombier...joyful! 'Perhaps we'll have lunch up there!' they said. So we weren't worried about their absence at lunch, were we? And then, then! The day went by. At dinner, still no one! And no news! No messenger to say *accident, broken leg, etcetera*...nothing! Nothing! It was already very late when I started searching. Darkness... Went through the villages, but the people were afraid, treated me as a sarvant! Refused to open their doors and didn't reply... Went through the woods. Shouted like a madman, at hazard, stupidly... At dawn, came back home, hoping to find them at the house...but no! And Augustine in such a state! Then I decided to come here...I was

50

afraid I might frighten the women, so I came through the farm in order not to run into them in the park. It seemed to me that I glimpsed Madame Arquedouve and Marie-Thérèse..."

"Marie-Thérèse? Come on, old chap, let's pull ourselves together. You're all at sea. You have to keep your head, damn it! You know full well that Marie-Thérèse has been at your house for twenty-four hours. Come on, think! She had breakfast with you yesterday morning, and..."

"Breakfast? Marie-Thérèse? Yesterday morning? Never! We haven't seen her. But then..."

Monsieur Le Tellier feels himself go pale all over. He looks, without seeing him, at Robert Collin, whose expression is that of a man under torture—and he listens to the operetta tune that Maxime is still singing, and which he can no longer bear.

"All three of them have disappeared!" exclaimed the doctor.

"Let's search! We must start searching right way. Quickly! Quickly!" Monsieur Le Tellier seems to have lost his mind.

"Yes," says Monsieur Monbardeau. "Let's search. But not like me—methodically. Me, I've wasted the most precious time of my life!"

"You're right—let's not get carried away. Logically! Logically!"

"Should we alert Monsieur Maxime?" hazarded Robert Collin. "There can't be too many of us..."

"That's right," said Monsieur Le Tellier. "Anyway, this is no time for singing."

They go from room to room until they reach the singer.

Maxime appears, in the midst of his collections and his aquaria, in a rotunda garnished with glass cases and basins. He is singing, but his hands are all red and his white apron is blood-stained. He has just extracted the swim-bladder from the fish that is there; he is now dissecting it, and singing—but he is so red with blood that Monsieur Le Tellier, in spite of his haste and anxiety, takes a step back.

"Papa...Uncle...what's the matter?"

The doctor explains: Marie-Thérèse, Henri and Fabienne have disappeared; they must be found.

Maxime and Robert reach an agreement then. They sense they alone are capable of thinking clearly. The two fathers are incapable of anything but distress. They are not men of action, and grief is overwhelming their intelligence.

Robert and Maxime consider the situation. In sum, the task is twofold. Firstly, Henri and Fabienne left from Artemare; they must have left a trail that needs to be researched. Secondly, Marie-Thérèse left from Mirastel; that creates another trail. Given the simultaneity of the two departures, it is a fair bet that the two trails intersected, and that a common accident has caused the three disappearances. No matter! It is a matter of systematically revealing each itinerary. Robert Collin, the doctor and Monsieur Le Tellier will discover the trajectory of Henri and Fabienne; the astronomer's automobile will transport them. As for Maxime, he takes it upon himself to inform his mother and grandmother of the ominous news, then to reconnoiter the route followed by Marie-Thérèse.

The former naval officer coolly arranges the operations.

Robert Collin organizes the embarkation; he positions himself next to the chauffeur. The automobile moves off.

Prostrate on the padded yellow leather seat, Monsieur Le Tellier is a fearful sight. He resembles Monsieur Monbardeau, a brother in suffering. The peasants of Ameyzieu, coming back from mass, do not recognize that ashen, hardened, strange face. In front of the post office in Artemare, however, Monsieur Le Tellier is galvanized into action. He calls a halt, gets out, and disappears inside. Five minutes later, he comes out again. He is helped back into the car.

"Go!"

Through her window, the postmistress admires the comfortable limousine, which speeds away, rapid and furtive, as fast as its wheels can carry it, and transmits the telegram that has just been handed to her:

(Item 105)
Duc d'Agnès,
40 Avenue Montaigne, Paris.

 Marie-Thérèse disappeared. Come quickly, with profes-sionals accustomed to searches.
 Jean Le Tellier.

VI. Initial Inquiries

"She never arrived at Artemare? Oh!"

As Maxime tugged feverishly at his short beard, Madame Le Tellier repeated: "Marie-Thérèse never arrived at her aunt's? She never arrived?" Disturbed and distraught, holding her head in her hands, she turned away.

Madame Arquedouve, very pale but still impassive, attempted to calm her down.

"Listen, Mother," Maxime resumed. "Marie-Thérèse is obviously with Henri and Fabienne. That's a safeguard, in itself."

"Where do you think they are?" said the grandmother.

"On the Colombier! Something's happened to them during their walk—an accident..."

"But what? There are no crevasses..."

"How do I know? There are pot-holes..."

"Look what's happened!" moaned Madame Le Tellier. "I didn't want her to go out on her own! I never stopped telling her that!"

"Oh, Mother—to go to my uncle's! Two kilometers to walk in broad daylight, on one of the busiest roads or a constantly deserted path! But, I need to know, exactly—first of all, what time did Marie-Thérèse leave yesterday morning?"

"10 a.m.," his mother replied. "She said goodbye to me in the hallway. Oh, if I'd known..."

"Are you quite certain that she was going to Artemare?"

"Absolutely. Marie-Thérèse never lies."

"That's true. Which route did she take? Up the slope or down the slope?"

"Ah—that I don't know."

"Nor me," added Madame Arquedouve.

"What was she wearing?"

"Her grey dress and her black tulle hat."

"Her traveling costume, with the short skirt?"

"No—but she had no plans to undertake an excursion, you know…"

"Oh, with Marie-Thérèse one never knows. The clothes wouldn't stop her. She'd cross the Alps in an evening dress. You know how she loves walking—and if, going up the hill, she met her cousins on their way to the Colombier, she would undoubtedly have gone with them, in spite of her long skirt and her light boots. She was sure that her absence wouldn't worry anyone, since my aunt and uncle weren't notified of hr visit in advance and since we were all to meet up at dinner today. For some time she's talked about nothing but climbing the Colombier. We can't delay any linger, though—I have to begin my search."

"Have the pony hitched up," said Madame Arquedouve. "Your mother and I will go keep your aunt company. I don't want to leave her on her own while you're exploring."

Maxime made enquiries among the domestics as to which direction Marie-Thérèse had taken when she left the grounds. They could not tell him. Then he went out and immediately went to the crossroads where four paths met. To his left the ascendant path cut into the hillside. To his right, descending and diverging, were the three paths leading to the highway; the first joined it at Talissieu, the second went straight down—it was, you will remember, steep and brutally direct—and the third at the village of Ameyzieu. Marie-Thérèse had taken one of these four paths. If the young woman had preferred going downhill, it was improbable that she would have taken the path to Talissieu, which led away from Artemare, but she might have had some reason for making the detour.

Common sense suggested to Maxime that his sister would have gone uphill; to salve his conscience, however, he wanted to examine the contrary hypothesis, and set off downhill. He investigated the surroundings. No trace of footprints could be seen on the stony pathway, nor was there any trace on the declivities of the central path. At the damp spot where it opened out on to the road, however, multiple imprints were noticeable in the marshy clay—but there were so many of them that they were confused.

Maxime questioned some passers-by. No one had seen Marie-Thérèse the previous day. Having acquired the anticipated certainty that no vestige of any accident and no trace of his sister were to be found in the appearances of things or the memories of people, Maxime, a scrupulous detective, attempted a further experiment. He would doubtless have better luck following the uphill path; Marie-Thérèse had surely climbed up to Chavornay by that route. She would have planned on following it as far as that commune and taking a by-road from there to Don, where she would join the road to Artemare—which is to say, *the road that Henri and Fabienne would have taken, in the opposite direction, to reach the upper slopes.* Maxime mentally reconstructed his sister's meeting with his cousins, at the junction of the paths, just above Don, or somewhere between that point and Artemare. The rest was explicable naturally...until the accident.

So there was Maxime, in the process of climbing the path through the bushes. Now, convinced of the excellence of the trail, he was making progress, without intending to, more carefully. At Chavornay, one of those deformed and cretinous dwarfs that one sees every day crouching on doorsteps only understood half his questions and could not confirm that a young woman dressed in grey with a black hat had gone through the hamlet. Near Don, however, having reached the crossroads, Maxime perceived his father's large white motor car coming up the hillside toward him, followed by Doctor Monbardeau's car—and this coincidence confirmed his supposition that Marie-Thérèse had come across Henri and Fabienne a little lower down.

Monsieur Monbardeau was driving his own car, with Monsieur Le Tellier beside him. Madame Arquedouve had taken her place in the other vehicle, with her two daughters and Robert, who leapt down as soon as the vehicle came to a stop. The presence of the women astonished Maxime. Robert explained it: Madame Monbardeau had insisted on taking part in the search. While she was gathering information in Arte-mare, her mother and sister had arrived; it had been impossible to prevent them from coming too, so they had taken over the new car.

"Great—that's crazy!" Maxime complained.

"Have you any news, Maxime?" his grandmother asked him, excitedly. "We have—Henri and Fabienne came up this way."

"That's right," said Robert. "They were seen leaving Ar-temare shortly before ten o'clock, dressed for an excursion; she was wearing a walking skirt and they both had their steel-tipped walking-sticks. A road-mender saw them on the road to Don and specified the time as 10 a.m., on the basis that the little local train leaves Artemare at 10 a.m. exactly to go up to Don, and that the locomotive whistled to signal its departure while the Monbardeaus were greeting him as they passed by. At Don, several other people saw them. The local doctor told us that they arrived at the same time as the little train. He'd gone to meet one of his colleagues, coming from Belley, at the station. At that time though, Monsieur and Madame Henri Monbardeau were alone."

"Therefore," Maxime put in, "Marie-Thérèse met them between Don and the crossroads where we're standing; that stands to reason. It's there that they made common cause. To-gether, they would have gone as far as Virieu-le-Petit, as they always do; they would have bought food at the inn to eat in the woods, as usual. I can see them from here, climbing through the forest. Let's go, quickly—to Virieu-le-Petit!"

Their faces were hopeful.

They soon reached Virieu-le-Petit, at an altitude of 800 meters; it was the highest point to which vehicles could take people intending to walk on the Colombier. Maxime went into see the innkeeper, an old woman. Yes, she had seen Monsieur Henri! He had bought bread, sausage and wine from her at about midday, and had even borrowed a game-bag in which to carry it all, with the knives and three glasses...

"Three? Three glasses? Ah!" Maxime felt joy take him by the throat. "And who was with him?"

"Two ladies, who stayed outside, on the road. While he bought provisions, they continued walking slowly in that direction. He caught the up."

"Were they Madame Henri Monbardeau and my sister, Mademoiselle Le Tellier?"

"Oh, certainly! Now that you mention it, there's no mistake! At the time, though, I only saw them from behind...one of them was dressed like a little girl..."

"In a short skirt, you mean?"

"Yes indeed—and the other like anyone."

"In grey?"

The entire family surrounded the innkeeper, uttering exclamations of victory.

"It's certain—it leaps to the eyes!" said Maxime, laughing.

Then the awareness of the situation came back to mind. It was Sunday; the inn was full. It was easy to find willing young men therein to search the mountain. Bornud, a special constable, a short vulpine old man, wiry and tanned, winked a sly black eye and set off with his dog Finaud.

Madame Arquedouve, demanding that no one should worry about her, established herself in a primitive room while the troop of rescuers attacked the slope of the Colombier.

As soon as the battalion had reached the forest, numerous branching pathways obliged it to divide up into companies, then into sections, and finally into squads, for of all the possible excursions, they did not know which had seduced the three missing persons. As they contrived the first split, Bornud discovered some bread crusts and sausage-skins in the ground. He rummaged around in the vicinity and found the innkeeper's game-bag under a branch that hid it from view. After a frugal lunch, Henri had hidden the henceforth-useless and inconvenient bag, doubtless saying to himself: "I'll pick it up on the way back."

That find caused a chill.

One by one, the patrols peeled off at the bifurcations. The fresh air became lighter and cooler as they went up the mountain. Bornud told them that snow still covered the summit of the Grand-Colombier, about 1500 meters above sea level, but the fact was only verifiable from the very foot of the peak or a long way away from the mountain, because of the screen formed by the surrounding masses.

The ascent tired the women, who were ill equipped. Madame Le Tellier, usually so lazy, climbed the awkward paths doggedly. Winter had created them from the beds of streams, strewn with sharp stones that injured feet or twisted ankles.

It was, to begin with, a reasonably methodical hunt, encircling the Colombier. They kept a lookout. From time to time, one of them shouted out at the top of his voice. As the sun went down, though, a fever took hold of the unfortunate relatives. They descended to the bottom of sheer ravines that they only needed to skirt to be able to see in their entirety. Madame Le Tellier moved foliage aside to look underneath, unconsciously. They went to the right and the left without rhyme or reason. Soon they no longer ceased crying out. Monsieur Monbardeau howled a local song incessantly: a joyful rallying cry; a sprightly piece of music to which the valleys of the Colombier had resounded many times, which resonated bleakly and thinly today without anyone noticing its strange modulation.

A similar disorder inevitably imposed itself on the other platoons, spread far and wide. The silence filled up with clamors. The echoes multiplied them, and were mistaken for replies. Thinking that they were going toward the people they were searching for, some of them found themselves face to face; they had to retrace their steps and resume the paths they had quit. Time went by; night was falling; shadows accumulated indecisive forms and transformed everything. Patches of red leaves on the moss caused alarm at a distance. They trembled as they looked up at the spurs of rock at the tops of vertiginous slopes. The wind animated the funereal fir-trees and compact thickets with quivering life. One might have thought, momentarily, that they sheltered some convulsive wounded man or some uncanny presence. Madame Monbardeau lacerated her hands searching thorny bushes. Bornud kept a keen eye on the life of the forest, and his dog quested before him, its nose to the wind…

But there was nothing, nothing, nothing. Nothing visible on those accursed crags or the dryness of the earth. Nothing anywhere! Nothing but hoarse shouts rebounding from rock to rock, sometimes mingling with the noise of a cataract traversing the dark gorges into which the forest plunged, only to rise up again, sometimes deep and sometimes shallow, but always taciturn and secret.

Mist rose up from the depths. The sky blackened.

Madame Le Tellier, who was in company with her sister, her husband and Bornud, let herself fall on to a mound on the upper edge of the woods; she could go no further. From that place, they could finally see the summit of the Grand-Colombier. It was a gigantic bare saddle-back, carpeted by glistening grass. Its hostile slope prohibited climbing. Three humps undulated its crest; they were white with snow, and on the highest one—the middle one—a monumental cross loomed up, infinitesimal in the distance.

They raised their eyes.

A man was climbing up toward the cross, with frequent pauses and slips.

Monsieur Monbardeau made a visor out of his hands. "It's Robert Collin," he said.

A groan answered him. Madame Le Tellier, harassed by fatigue and hunger, was fainting. She came round, but they could no longer think of continuing the search. What good would it do, anyway? The light was fading. Clouds were heaping up overhead. And had they not completed their task? Had they not explored the entire mountain, from the bottom to the deserted crest where Robert was?

The return journey was difficult, accomplished in a silence heavy with thoughts. The Monbardeaus and the Le Telliers had not eaten for 12 hours; hunger increased their anguish. At the inn, where Madame Arquedouve had ordered dinner, the lamplight illuminated exhausted faces, which interrogated one another anxiously.

Nothing. No one had found anything—and everyone had returned, with the sole exception of Robert. He had said to Maxime: "Don't wait for me before going back. I can take care of myself. No one need worry about me."

"Well, my boy?" said Monsieur Le Tellier, with a discouraged gesture. "What do you think?"

"Me. Well…that it's necessary to inform the authorities…"

"You don't believe there was an accident?"

"My God…yes and no…but the authorities…"

A knowing smile creased the lips of the peasants.

"The authorities have already been alerted," stammered Monsieur Le Tellier confusedly, in a low voice. "I telegraphed the Duc d'Agnès this morning; he'll bring policemen with him…"

Maxime, amazed, saw him lower his eyelids.

"If it's not an accident," cried Monbardeau, "what can it be? A flight? That's unthinkable." He hesitated momentarily. "An abduction, then?"

"I'm beginning to believe so," said Monsieur Le Tellier. "I'm expecting to receive a letter demanding a large ransom in exchange for Marie-Thérèse…"

"Undoubtedly," Maxime agreed.

There were some forty mountain-dwellers there, forming a circle. They shook their heads incredulously. Madame Monbardeau did likewise.

Monsieur Le Tellier stared at them, one after another. "Do you have an opinion, my friends?" he asked. "If you do, tell us."

Bornud answered on behalf of all of them, in the soft accent of the region. "Oh no! Definitely not! We don't know anything!" But the terror of the sarvant was hanging over them.

Rain suddenly began to fall violently. It was like the patter of a thousand tiny feet dancing from tile to tile above the heads of the company. A few shoulders shuddered at the noise.

Monsieur Monbardeau went to his brother-in-law and whispered: "Do you understand now why the theft of a statue and a manikin had such an effect on them? Do you see the progression?"

"Let's be frank," admitted Monsieur Le Tellier. "Have we been thinking of anything else—you since yesterday, me since this morning?"

"How stupid!"

VII. The Wait and the Arrival of Reinforcements

The following morning, at 8 a.m., they met as usual in the dining-room at Mirastel. Monsieur and Madame Monbardeau were there; the horror of being alone had gripped them as soon as they got back to the house in Artemare, and Madame Arquedouve had given them shelter until further notice.

It had been a bad night. Extreme tiredness and anguish had prevented all of them from sleeping. The rain was still falling. They cursed it for coming too late and rendering the ground susceptible to footprints at the wrong time. There was no news. Robert Collin had not returned; the Duc d'Agnès had not arrived, and the post had not brought Monsieur le Tellier the ransom demand for which he was waiting—for which he was hoping!

They talked a great deal, for fear that silence would give too much latitude to imagination. Madame Le Tellier, to increase her chagrin, felt extremely annoyed that Marie-Thérèse had disappeared at the very moment when the Duc d'Agnès had solicited the honor of becoming her son-in-law. She became excited, sobbed, and said, in a tone which mingled despair and bitterness: "I'd rather...oh, I'd rather have married her off to the Turk than not know where she is at this moment!" And she wept more copiously, before proffering other extravagances.

Maxime, disturbed by Robert's prolonged absence and irritated by the unanimous indifference with regard to such devotion, retired to his laboratory in order to obtain a little calm there. The fish in his aquaria no longer interested him, though. Oceanography annoyed him. His brushes and paints seemed to him to be playthings, fit for children who had no worries. He ran a distracted eye over the display-cases of his collection, suspended around the rotunda, and despised himself for having once thought so much of them.

They contained some curious things, though. Once, he had diverted himself by capturing animals of all kinds whose form and color were so exactly adapted to their supports or their environments that their enemies could no longer perceive them. He had also trapped creatures that made every effort to resemble other creatures, either to frighten their adversaries or to deceive the mistrust of their victims. In a word, it was a collection of *mimicry*.

Wanting to ease his anxiety, Maxime tried to recall the difficulties of his puerile hunts, in which the prey was all the more valuable as it concealed itself more perfectly. He remembered, sadly, the joy he had obtained when he could place some new insect under glass, poised on the leaf, the branch or the stone with which it confused itself. Many a time, to give him pleasure, Marie-Thérèse had set forth in search of mimics. Poor, dear, pretty sister!

Come on! Solitude and inaction were decidedly worthless. Much better to buckle on his gaiters and set forth to find Robert.

Having informed Monsieur Le Tellier of his intention, Maxime set off up the mountain.

The rain had stopped.

At Mirastel, they waited, and the time passed with desperate slowness. Monsieur Le Tellier strode up and down the corridors of the château and the garden paths. Monsieur and Madame Monbardeau tried to read the newspapers, which covered the event from every angle. As for Madame Le Tellier, she went up to her daughter's bedroom with Madame Arquedouve, and one of them tried ingeniously to rediscover Marie-Thérèse in the sight of her intimate possessions, while the other lovingly breathed in the floral odor that lingered there.

A few visitors called at the main gate. They left cards with expressions of their sympathy. Only Mademoiselle de Baradaine, the sole relative of Fabienne Monbardeau-d'Arvière, was allowed in. She poured out her overfull heart in a prodigious tirade of abundance and banality. The general consternation increased.

At 4 p.m., Monsieur Le Tellier was on watch on the terrace, on the lookout for the arrival of the Duc d'Agnès by air or overland, when he heard Maxime calling to him from the window of his laboratory. Robert was standing next to him. Monsieur Le Tellier ran to join them.

"My friend, my dear friend!" he said, on perceiving his secretary overwhelmed by exhaustion. "How grateful I am to you…!"

Robert stopped him. "I spent the night and the early morning on the Colombier," he said, "but don't complain on my behalf—only a few drops of rain fell on the place where I was. And that was more fortunate than one might have expected."

"You know something!"

Robert and Maxime looked at one another.

"Yes, Papa, there's news. But waited to catch you alone in order to tell you, because the others, if they knew that, would not let up until they had heard every detail—and we're convinced that it's better not to *describe* what Robert has discovered."

"What? Why?"

"Oh, don't worry—his discovery isn't terrifying. Far from it, since it puts a trump card into our hand. But Robert and I prefer that the thing should be *seen* rather than listening to a description of it, in order that everyone can make up their own minds about it. You know how suggestive the most neutral language is; you know how a speaker's opinion betrays itself, in spite of him, in his choice of expressions. Every statement is a judgment, however impartial one supposes it to be; to express a fact is, at the same time, to offer a critique of it. Now, it's a matter of an indication so extraordinary and inexplicable, of a problem so arduous, that it's absolutely necessary to gather the greatest possible number of opinions, without any of them being subject to the influence of the others."

65

"So be it. Can you take me there immediately...?"

"It's on the summit of the Colombier," Robert said. "We'll go with the policemen tomorrow. I expected to find them here."

"Isn't François d'Agnès here yet?" asked Maxime. "That's surprising."

Monsieur Le Tellier was drawn out of the meditation into which this conversation had plunged him by the roar of a distant automobile. He went to the window and saw a racing car coming along the road like an engine of destruction. In a fusillade of crackling, the increasing thunder of a machine-gun, it rushed forward to attack the slope. It leapt up it, climbing the hillside in zigzags more rapidly than an avalanche could have hurtled down it. It skidded madly around the bends, with impetuous squeals—and through the splashes kicked up by its passage, four rubber-clad men were visible, crouched uncomfortably in two bucket-seats amid suitcases and spare tires.

Monsieur Le Tellier was dumbstruck with admiration. Every turn was an acrobatic feat. The Duc d'Agnès took the last of them on two wheels. A second later, the furious series of explosions filled the hornbeam plantation and the smoking steel monster, stained with muddy streaks left by its hectic journey, stopped in front of the perron.

Monsieur Le Tellier went down to greet the newcomers.

Relieved of the waxed blouse and the waterproof jacket that gave him the appearance of a sea-lion, the Duc d'Agnès appeared, slender and lithe. The squalls and deluges had reddened and swollen the skin of his face in vain; his windswept eyes had wept in vain; he was so young and handsome that one would have taken him for a fairy-tale prince newly delivered from some frightful metamorphosis.

He explained his lateness. "I would have liked to have left yesterday, immediately after receiving your dispatch, Monsieur, but the Prefect of Police wanted to send some of his men with me, who were not free until today. May I introduce Monsieur Garan and Monsieur Tiburce."

66

Monsieur Le Tellier offered his hand to the two men. The first shook it firmly, but the second seemed to belong to some secret society, for he stroked the astronomer's fingers and palm in a most indiscreet fashion. It was almost indecent. Monsieur Le Tellier, blushing, pushed the travelers in the direction of his study.

Without losing a moment, he told them everything he knew about the disastrous adventure, taking care not to omit the conversation he had just had with his son and his secretary. They listened religiously. However, when he started on a list of hypotheses, one of the strangers, Monsieur Garan, interrupted him.

This individual, of medium plumpness and a martial bearing, had a tanned complexion, bluish cheeks and short-cropped salt-and-pepper hair. A black moustache, much too threatening and infinitely too large for him, looked like two bison horns beneath his nose. Large eyebrows of the same color were reminiscent of another moustache gone astray above his eyes—and this quadruple kiss-curl turned up its ends toward the sky. "Excuse me," he said, "if I stop you there. At the prefecture, we're familiar with the story of the Bugeysian depredations, and I told these gentlemen about them on the way. As for the suppositions that you might have formulated, I prefer not to know them. Let me first take account of *what is*. It's necessary to elucidate the mysterious item on the Grand-Colombier. Afterwards, we'll discuss it. It's the most respectable method."

"Pardon me," said the Duc d'Agnès. "I forgot to mention that Monsieur Garan is an inspector in the Sûreté."

Monsieur Le Tellier, stung by impatience, pointed to the other unknown man, who was profoundly absorbed in studying the room, and said to Monsieur Garan: "Is that also the opinion of your colleague?"

The policeman smiled behind his horned moustache. "Monsieur is not my colleague. I have not had the honor…"

"Tiburce is one of my friends," explained the Duc d'Agnès, not without a certain embarrassment. "He might be useful to us...yes, really...useful. He's an old schoolfriend of Maxime and myself."

Enveloped in a huge checkered Inverness cape, the sallow-complexioned clean-shaven young man with rounded eyes and features as rigid as those of a classical statue — whose scarlet mouth was perpetually open, standing out within his face like a tomato on a white cheese—presented a typical specimen of anglomania. He would doubtless have made a genteel Frenchman, simply by letting his blonde beard grow and giving birth on his ultra-violet lips to the smile that constantly solicited them. Perhaps, if dressed like you or me, Tiburce might actually have been indistinguishable from you or me...but there it was; Tiburce played the Englishman. He surrounded his French presence with London cloth, covered his Parisian physiognomy with a Britannic mask. That was why, instead of being august, in the fashion of a lord, he had the appearance of a clown.

"My friend," the Duc d'Agnès went on, "is a..."

"I'm a *Sherlockist*, and nothing more."

Monsieur Le Tellier had eyes like organ-stops. "I beg your pardon?"

VIII. Tiburce

Tiburce attempted to attain the heights of phlegmaticism and to look his interlocutor full in the face. "I said that I'm a *Sherlockist*," he repeated—but then he blushed so deeply that his lips disappeared into the radiance of his entire face. "*Sherlockist*...or *Holmesian*, if you prefer...as one says *Carlist* or *Garibaldian*..."

At that moment, Monsieur Garan was the very image of irony, the Duc d'Agnès of annoyance and Monsieur Le Tellier of incomprehension. Seeing this, Tiburce went on: "Surely you must have heard mention of Sherlock Holmes, Monsieur?"

"Err...is he a relative of the Augusta Holmes who composes music?"[13]

"No. Sherlock Holmes is a virtuoso, but a virtuoso detective. He's a detective of genius, whose fantastic exploits have been related by Sir Arthur Conan Doyle."

"Eh? Monsieur, in the present circumstances, to the Devil with novels, and away with your Shylock Hermes!"

"*Sherlock*," Tiburce corrected. "Sherlock *Holmes*." And he continued, without turning a hair: "Well, Monsieur, I am the living emulation of that imaginary hero, and I apply his incomparable method to the difficulties of real life."

Perceiving that Monsieur Le Tellier was getting increasingly irritated, the Duc d'Agnès timidly hazarded: "I affirm...in truth...that Tiburce will be a great help to us."

"Listen to me for a few moments," Tiburce added. "If you lack faith, it's because you don't understand. Let me explain. You see, Monsieur, my vocation was decided in the era

---

[13] The Paris-born composer Augusta Holmes (1847-1903) was reputed to be the natural daughter of Alfred de Vigny, to which notoriety she added by becoming the mistress of Catulle Mendès.

when I was formulating my philosophy—not during the day, when I was poring over one of those scholars whose works I ought to have been cherishing, but one evening when I read Voltaire's story *Zadig, or Destiny*. One finds there, Monsieur, a certain passage that is a sort of prototype of all detective mysteries, in which Zadig, although he has never seen the queen's dog, nevertheless gives a striking description of it to the chief eunuch, thanks to the traces it has left during its passage through a little wood.

"Reading that opened my eyes, and I decided to cultivate my own disposition to perspicacity—which was, I felt, imperious and rich. I say that without any false modesty. Sometime after that, the tales of Edgar Poe fell into my hands. I marveled at the sagacious mind of the detective Dupin. Finally, in recent years, an entire genre has begun to flourish in the wake of *The Murders in the Rue Morgue, The Purloined Letter* and *The Mystery of Marie Roget* and my vocation became clearer and clearer. To tell the truth, Sherlock Holmes dominates this produce as Napoleon dominated the history of his era, but every one of these works nevertheless has its importance and forms a breviary for the investigator or mysteries. Their collectivity, reinforced by several treatises on logic, composes the library of the amateur detective—and that library, Monsieur, never leaves me."

As he pronounced these words, Tiburce opened a suitcase that he had hidden under his Inverness cape and extracted from its depths a set of sturdily rebound volumes. One by one and side by side, he deposited on the polished desk-top Aristotle and Maurice Leblanc, Mark Twain and John Stuart Mill, Hegel and Gaston Leroux, Conan Doyle and Condillac, juxtaposing *The Perfume of the Lady in Black* with the first three volumes of the *Spectator*, and *The Adventures of Arsène Lupin* with *Inductive and Deductive Logic*. "Here are my masters," he said, pompously. "But don't get the idea that the study of these books is my only labor. I slog away enormously, Monsieur, and in every genre, in order to acquire the universal knowledge of the great Sherlock Holmes. I only set aside a manual of algebra, carpentry, medicine or cattle-breeding to run to the criminal court, the boxing club, the gymnasium or the riding-school, and I employ my vacations in applied logic, in order to pass from principles to practice, from theory to active service. Well, what do you say to that? I am pleased to see, Monsieur, that you have taken back your first impression. Come on! Come on! I shall recover your daughter—and it's me who says so. Hold on—I want to convince you even further!"

At this point, Tiburce sat down on a sofa, crossed his legs, fixed his eyes on a corner of the ceiling, nibbled his fingernails and declaimed, in a rapid and negligent voice, sharp and blank—the voice, in fact, that the actor Gémier[14] adopts for the character of Sherlock Holmes: "Monsieur, you possess a dog of the breed known as the wire-haired pointing griffon. And you have made that setter into a household pet, for you are not a hunter—not a hunter, but a pianist; a very good pianist, even, or at least you like to think so. I will add that you have served in the cavalry, that you usually wear a monocle, and that one of your favorite pastimes is target-shooting. Shh! Please be quiet and don't interrupt."

Without ceasing to stare into space, he continued: "The bottoms of your trouser-legs are covered in hairs. Now, these hairs can only belong to a dog of the specified breed or a goat, but it is not our custom to let a goat lie down beneath our feet. Thus…draw your own conclusion. On the other hand, I know that your occupations do not leave you the time to hunt, and I deduce that your dog, in spite of its nature, is a household pet by destination. You play the piano, yes; while shaking hands with you I recognized at the tips of your fingers the professional calluses of pianists. They revealed to me that you play very frequently. Now, a man of your age and intelligence cannot show such assiduity in the exercise of so delicate and art

---

[14] Firmin Gémier was the stage-name of Firmin Tonnerre (1869-1933), who created the role of Sherlock Holmes on the Parisian stage at the Théâtre Antoine in 1907.

unless he excels therein, or believes that he excels therein. Because of Ingres and his violin, I dare to affirm your talent as a pianist in spite of your astronomical genius. You have served in the cavalry, for you walk with your legs apart and you descend staircases as if you were afraid of catching your spurs on the steps. Thus, you are accustomed to riding horses—and it's a habit of long standing, for you are never seen riding out in Paris. Your humble and studious youth did not permit equitation, so it follows, in consequence, that you have ridden government chargers. Silence, I beg you. You wear a monocle. Exactly. I discovered its trace in the crease of your orbit, along with that of a carbine, for your left eye is accustomed to squint in order to aim; it is slightly smaller than the other, and the wrinkle known as a 'goose-foot' is more pronounced on the left than the right. As you don't hunt, it follows that you practice target-shooting. That's all. I have spoken."

"If that doesn't satisfy you…!" cried Garan, in a mocking tone.

Monsieur Le Tellier, however, was in no mood for joking. Without saying a word, he took a goatskin foot-muff from the shadows under the desk and threw it into the middle of the room. "There's your wire-haired pointing griffon," he said.

Then he opened a cupboard to display his typewriter. "Here's the piano."

From a drawer, he took out his watchmaker's magnifying-glass, implanted it in his right eye-socket, and added in a cutting tone: "Here's the monocle."

Finally, he produced a photograph that depicted him in his professional pose, with his right eye to the ocular lens of a meridional telescope and his left eye closed, like that of all astronomers during their observations. "And here's the carbine or the pistol," he said, with a hiss of irritation. "As for the cavalry, I don't know what you mean. I might have bandy legs, but I've never been on a horse. At present, my young friend, permit me to tell you that you've chosen a bad time and place to play the fool, and that, if it were traditional to make use of canaries for the purposes of divination, you'd be a bird of exceedingly ill omen. That's all. I have spoken."

Garan burst out laughing at the last insult—but scarcely had Monsieur Le Tellier vomited forth these imprecations under the influence of anger than he repented of having done so. Tiburce, now, was no longer trying to duplicate Sherlock Holmes. Green about the gills and crestfallen, he stammered vague tremulous excuses. He seemed desolate—even more desolate than his discomfiture warranted, to the extent that the astronomer, taking pity on him, hastened to add: "After all, everyone makes occasional mistakes. You'll have better luck tomorrow won't you? Excuse my fit of bad temper. Come on, gentlemen—I'll have you shown to your rooms."

He rang; a domestic appeared—but the Duc d'Agnès let his two companions depart. "I want to talk to you," he said to Monsieur Le Tellier. "First of all, forgive me for Tiburce. This is why I brought him here: Tiburce has been my friend since college; I've known him for years—years in which I've witnessed his generosity and his great heart, compared with the months in which I've observed his stupidity, which is recent. He's the most faithful, the most devoted, the most…innocent…of poodles. Nevertheless, those qualities would not have been sufficient to make me decide to bring him to Mirastel, if it were not for the fact that Tiburce was present when I received your telegram. Upset by such astonishing news, learning at a single stroke of Mademoiselle Marie-Thérèse's disappearance and the tacit approval of my request—since you were asking for my help—I was dazed for some little time by having simultaneously gained and lost a fiancée."

"I beg your pardon, but…"

"Just a moment. In that interval, Monsieur, Tiburce swore to me that he would recover Mademoiselle Marie-Thérèse. I forgot, in my distress, the innumerable gaffes of which the pseudo-Sherlock had been guilty. 'Oh,' I said to him, 'if you recover Marie-Thérèse, you may ask me for anything you wish!' Immediately, I realized that I had been foolish. For two years, Monsieur, Tiburce has been in love with my sister, and Jeanne loves him too. Certainly, if it only depended on me, their marriage would have taken place long ago, for I know no finer individuals than Tiburce and Jeanne. On the other hand, you know that my little sister isn't beautiful...Tiburce, who has a colossal fortune, doesn't want to marry her for her dowry.... In sum, everything would all be fine..."

"But?" said Monsieur Le Tellier.

"But, Monsieur, I remember my late father, Duc Olivier, and my late mother, née d'Estragues de Saint-Averpont, and all my ancestors. What would it do to them, in Heaven, if an Agnès were to take the name of a plebeian?"

"What does Mademoiselle Agnès think?"

"My sister will bow to the opinion of the head of the family—mine. In our houses, these decisions are never debated. Except...hmm...when Tiburce said to me: 'Will you give me Jeanne in exchange for Marie-Thérèse?'...what do you expect? It seemed to me that in the depths of their tomb my ancestors were no longer thinking about anything much...and I replied: 'Yes—recover Marie-Thérèse and Jeanne shall be your wife.' An hour later, as I completed my application to the Prefecture of Police, I was stupefied by my folly. I wanted to take back my promise and not bring the useless Tiburce—but I no longer had the right. Certain as I was of his incapacity, it was nevertheless necessary for me to facilitate him in a task whose success I had sworn an oath to reward."

"I understand his discomfiture! Poor chap! It's a pity that this Monsieur Tiburce isn't more resourceful; he might have recovered Marie-Thérèse. With such an incentive, one might do anything. Love!"

"Ha! Love, Monsieur! If you measure the chances of success by the grandeur of the love, then would it not be me who would recover my fiancée?"

"Umm...your fiancée...which is to say that...ugh! Listen—I was a trifle distraught when I sent the telegram. There's another young man who, concurrently with you, has asked for my daughter's hand. I admit to you that for my part...er.... In the final analysis, she'll make the choice. She's free to choose between you and Monsieur Robert Collin. In all fairness, though, it's fairly certain that the one who gets her back..."

"But Monsieur," cried the Duc d'Agnès, utterly nonplussed, "don't you know that Mademoiselle Marie-Thérèse has done me the honor of falling in love with me?"

"It's you who's informing me of that, Monsieur."

"Oh! But...it seemed to me that everyone knew..."

I've definitely spent too much time among the stars, thought Monsieur Le Tellier.

IX. On the Summit of the Colombier

At critical moments, every newcomer appears to be a savior. Doctor Monbardeau and the wives greeted Messieurs d'Agnès, Tiburce and Garan like a trinity of messiahs—and there is no doubt that Maxime and Robert would have shared their sentiment if the former had not been a schoolfellow of Tiburce the simpleton, and if the presence of the Duc d'Agnès had been capable of exciting anything but jealousy in Robert's mind.

On the advice of Monsieur Garan, they abstained, that evening, from any conjecture relating to the disappearances, and limited themselves to preparing the next day's expedition to discover the secret of the Colombier. When everyone went to bed, the great hope awakened by the support of the professional searchers had already begun to fade. Tiburce had been exposed as the silliest of maniacs, and Garan had revealed, beneath the external experience of a bourgeois captain, the mentality of a town sergeant. Several people, however, took as a good omen the rather long and still-mysterious absence the latter had effected before dinner, on the subject of which no one, for reasons of discretion, wanted to interrogate him.

They were to leave at dawn.

By the time the Sun appeared, Garan had already been up and about for an hour. It was necessary to lend him an overcoat, a walking-stick and leggings, for he had brought none with him. Tiburce was late. He finally came running with a clatter of hob-nailed footwear and colliding objects. One could not help admiring his equipment: his boots, his alpenstock, his hooded cape, his Tyrolean hat and the profusion of bags, satchels, boxes, sheaths, cases and haversacks that were hanging around his body like fantastic fruits.

Monsieur Le Tellier shrugged his shoulders.

Madame Arquedouve and her daughters wisely decided not to leave Mirastel. All of them pale in the early morning light—having aged two years in two days—they watched the automobiles depart.

The investigators were seven in number.

After Don, Garan asked to be shown the crossroads where Marie-Thérèse had encountered Henri and Fabienne Monbardeau. At Virieu-le-Petit, the inspector reinterrogated the tenant of the inn, who stuck to her original story. Then the caravan started off again, and soon passed the spot where Henri Monbardeau had hidden the innkeeper's game-bag—the place where the trail of the three missing persons was lost.

After an hour and a half of climbing through the verdant woods, the narrow path having made several turns forced by sumptuous ravines, and traversed numerous meadows more beautiful than the best-kept lawns, they came within sight of the triple hump of the Grand-Colombier. In the last two days the three snow-caps had diminished somewhat. The giant cross seemed tiny, high up and still very distant; eagles were describing slow spirals above it. Under Robert's guidance, they began the difficult ascent to the calvary. The slope became steeper and steeper; it became more slippery as their soles polished it, and began to take on the appearance of an infinite wall in the eyes of its assailants.

Tiburce was breathing heavily. He had disposed of some of his cargo, to the advantage of various others, but his hobnailed boots were skidding in competition. They had to haul him up. The harsh wind scouring the slope carried away his Tyrolean hat. When he paused, he dared not look behind for fear of vertigo, and thus was deprived of the contemplation of the magnificent display, far below, of the Valromey and the Lilliputian roofs of Virieu-le-tout-Petit.

Monsieur Monbardeau and Monsieur Le Tellier, prey to an ardent curiosity, pinched their lips to prevent them from questioning Maxime or Robert. The latter, who took the lead—and whom the gravity of the situation had singularly sharpened up—reached the edge of the white sheet and stopped. The wheeling eagles rose up higher. The snow could be heard fizzing under the soil. Fifty meters higher up, the wind made the cross whistle.

"Ah!" cried Monsieur Monbardeau. "There are footprints in the snow!"

"Don't make any other imprints!" Maxime instructed. "Stay off it."

Robert put on his spectacles and said: "It's here that we pick up the trail of those we're searching for. There's no doubt that they followed the route that we've just traveled. The goal of their expedition was the Colombier cross. They were the first people this year to make that traditional excursion, and the snow has marked their passage, of which the dry ground, the grass and the rocks conserved no trace."

"Are you certain that it was them?" asked Garan.

"Absolutely. Listen to me and look. We're in the presence of three parallel tracks that dig into the carpet of snow about three meters apart, going up toward the summit. They're recent, and were made at the same time, for the thaw has deformed them slightly and similarly. Moreover, that three-meter interval is definitely that adopted by three climbing companions. Look at those we have adopted ourselves. Thus, three people came up together, not long ago.

"Very well—I say that the left-hand track is that of Henri Monbardeau. It's the only one, in fact, that was made by a man's shoes—walking shoes, large and nailed for mountain use. The two others were made by women's boots—but the middle one is that of sturdy knee-length boots with flat heels, equipped with studs, while the right-hand one clearly reveals the contours of light boots with Louis XV heels. One could not find vestiges corresponding more exactly with the pedestrian equipment of the three missing persons, and that is sufficient to convince us that these are the tracks of Monsieur Henri, his wife and Mademoiselle Marie-Thérèse—but that's not all.

"Take note of these little round cavities that follow each course and are much more pronounced for the two tracks on the left than that on the right. They are, on the one hand, the holes made by steel-tipped walking-sticks, and on the other, the puncture-marks made by an umbrella or a parasol. In addition, the right-hand track is accompanied by particular indications, as if the snow had been swept…"

"Of course!" exclaimed Monsieur Le Tellier. "It's the skirt—my daughter's long skirt!"

"As you say, Master…"

"Very good," Garan approved.

"Very good!" Tiburce opined, open-mouthed.

"That's an excellent discovery," the inspector added. "The direction of the tracks, as they exit from this revelatory zone, will serve to orientate us. Going around the hump, following the edge of the snow, we're bound to encounter them—there's no need to freeze our feet by following the prints."

"Perfect," said Robert. "That's the reasoning I formulated, word for word."

They set off along the border of the dazzling layer in Indian file. Clinging to the flank of the steep slope, they went around the hummock and arrived on the other side of the mountain, facing the Alps. Mont Blanc dominated the formidable horizon, silvery amid the clouds. On that face, the gulf was hollowed out more vertiginously. At the very bottom of its profound valley, the Rhône seemed motionless and derisory; human beings, reduced to microscopic proportions, were invisible.

"Look—more footprints. But are they going up or going down?"

"Take no notice of them," Robert replied to Monsieur Monbardeau. "They're mine and Maxime's. You'll understand, soon. Yesterday we walked in our own footprints for fear of multiplying the tracks."

They continued along the border of the snow, thus turning around the cross, which was always above them, and of which they could only see the upper part.

By virtue of making a complete circuit, they found themselves back at their point of departure ten minutes after having left it, having gone around the entire perimeter of the white snow-cap *without having seen the slightest descending trace.*

Monsieur Monbardeau and Monsieur Le Tellier exclaimed at the same time: "They're still up there!" The reflection of the snow increased their pallor.

"Naturally," said Tiburce, supportively. "Since they didn't come down, they must still be up there."

Monsieur Le Tellier shivered. "Robert, my friend, why didn't you tell us…?"

"Let's go up," said the secretary. "I ask you to make a detour, though, in order that these three tracks remain well-isolated and quite clear."

The crest of the Grand-Colombier is by no means spacious. Its flattened strip is no more than two meters wide by thirty long. Monsieur Monbardeau, climbing with a sort of fury, arrived there first, and remained mute with shock, pressed against the shaft of the cross. There was no one there, where his imagination had already laid the corpses of his son, his daughter-in-law and his niece. There was nothing at all.

Nothing? Oh, if only…

"Henri's walking-stick! His broken walking-stick! It's broken!"

"Don't touch it!" shouted Maxime, from a distance. "It's essential that you don't touch it!"

"But the tracks—what about the tracks?" demanded Monsieur Le Tellier. "There must be tracks. Oh, it's too much!"

It was, indeed, *too much.*

The three tracks went up as far as the crest, but they suddenly stopped. The missing persons had undoubtedly arrived at the summit of the Colombier, *but they had not come back down and they were no longer there.*

Maxime, seeing that his father and his uncle were incapable of observing and reasoning, took charge of explaining the situation to them, to study it on their behalf and to point out what it implied.

"Come on," he said. "Let's have a little attention and calmness. Let's examine things, starting from the tracks at the edge of the snow. They continued their climb, initially in parallel. Then the two outer tracks drew apart slightly from the middle one, with the effect that, when they arrived on the ridge, Fabienne was a meter to the left of the cross, Henri five meters away from Fabienne to her left, and Marie-Thérèse six meters away to her right. There, our walkers paused to admire the panorama; each track, in fact, presents the same slight trampling, the same superimposition of imprints, and one can see quite clearly that the walking-sticks and the umbrella—or parasol—were digging into the ground. Everything points to a short pause—but the resemblance between the three tracks doesn't extend any further.

"In fact, Henri's trail clearly concludes with the normal placid trampling of a tourist at rest. It's like a dead end. Fabienne's trail is different; we discover, departing from the trampled spot, four footprints heading toward Henri—and that's all. A second dead end. Let's take note, nevertheless, with regard to those four footprints, that the distance between them is evidence of long strides. My cousin Fabienne must have been running when she made those four prints—running toward her husband. Besides, in the middle of the stationary trampling, we discover the mark of a sole forcefully dug in, which testifies to an abrupt departure by means of an energetic leap.

"Marie-Thérèse's trail—the one on the right—is more complicated. Coming from the trampled spot, a sequence of precipitate steps heads for the cross—but suddenly, a meter away from it, they turn sharply to the right, and those steps begin to descend the slope on the Rhône side at top speed. We count six prints, which are veritable leaps. It's a hectic run down an awkward slope, which suddenly stops at the sixth print. The last dead end.

"There was, therefore a moment when Fabienne and Marie-Thérèse were running in the same direction, which was, for Fabienne, toward Henri, and for Marie-Thérèse, toward Fabienne and Henri. An unknown cause prevented the former from reaching her husband and made the latter change direction. It was doubtless the same cause that spirited all three of them away."

"It was certainly not effected without a struggle," aid Monsieur Monbardeau. "That broken stick...it's definitely Henri's stick; I recognize it."

"Whether it's Monsieur Henri's or someone else's," Robert replied, "The most important thing is that it's the walking-stick that Monsieur Henri was using on Saturday. Its steel tip can only be fitted to the imprints on the left."

"What I don't understand," muttered Tiburce, "is that it's so far away from Henri Monbardeau's tracks."

"Precisely," Robert went on. "Gentlemen, I beg you to take note of the significant position occupied by that cane: close to the cross, between the ascendant track of Madame Henri Monbardeau and the place where Mademoiselle Le Tellier's track changes direction—which is to say, about seven meters from the trampled spot that manifests, for the last time, Monsieur Henri's presence...his *calm* presence, I mean."

"He could have thrown it from there?" proposed Monsieur Monbardeau.

"No. I thought of that. It isn't possible—for then he would have thrown it in the direction of the two women, at the risk of hurting them, and your son is not a man to have lost his head to that extent."

"But how do you know that the two women were there when the cane was thrown?" Garan objected. "Perhaps they'd already moved away..."

"Let's be clear. I contend that they were stationary in their places while Monsieur Henri was at his, equipped with that stick, whose tubular mold is there beside the traces of his own pause, for it was in moving towards him that they left these tracks here, one of which stops dead and the other turns away before disappearing no less totally. But I also contend that did not throw his stick from the spot where he was standing, firstly because he might have hurt his companions, and secondly because the snow around the fallen stick does not present any scuff-marks—which proves that the stick did not strike the ground at an angle, but vertically. It was, therefore, thrown *from above*."

Tiburce, who was chewing his lip ardently, interrupted. "Henri Monbardeau could have thrown it up into the air, and it fell back..."

"No, Monsieur. Firstly, I repeat, he would not have risked any action perilous to his companions. Secondly, look at the break. It would have required a sharp blow to produce it, and the person who broke that stick in that fashion must have been *holding it in his hand*. Such an effort, on the part of a man, similarly requires a point of support, or at least wedging it underfoot. Now, you will find no trace of that among Monsieur Henri's tracks. That stick has been broken somewhere between the place whether its owner was standing and the place where you see it embedded in the snow, to which it is molded like the setting of a gem. And if we examine the stick at closer range we observe that the break, which is made almost at right angles, can only have been the consequence of a violent impact on an *extremely hard corner*. I point out to you that the cross is constructed from fir-wood covered with a sheath of white-painted sheet-metal, cylindrical at the top, but *rectangular* at the bottom. One might therefore suppose that the stick was broken on one of the four corners of the inferior section—but that is not so. There is no dent in the sheath, and the stick conserves not the slightest trace of white paint. See for yourself. It's conclusive. On what, then, was it broken? On something that was there at the time, but is there no longer—something suspended in mid-air."

"You're very good," said the inspector, with a mocking laugh.

The Duc d'Agnès intervened. "I'm wondering why we're bothering with all this intricate reasoning. Isn't it obvious that the missing persons have been abducted by means of a balloon?"

"Or an aeroplane," added Tiburce.

"Oh, not that!" retorted the Duc. "There is no airplane sufficiently advanced to pluck three people from ground level in succession, nor any powerful enough to carry them off, along with the equipment that such a complex operation would require."

"Abducted...abducted?" Monsieur Le Tellier said to himself. "But with what purpose? If someone has abducted them, we would already have received news, threats, offers of...how do I know?"

"It's not possible!" shouted Monsieur Monbardeau, raising his eyes heavenwards.

"It can only have been a dirigible," Tiburce declared.

Monbardeau, however, pointed to the soaring eagles. "You might as well claim that it was colossal eagles that took our children!" he said, in a bizarre tone.

Tiburce smiled.

"Don't laugh," said Robert. "Baroque as the idea is, it occurred to me. Certainly, the hypothesis can be ruled out *a priori*—but it would explain almost everything! For a dirigible, Monsieur d'Agnès, would be seen arriving; it's an object that attracts the eyes. And if the kidnapers had approached in an aeronef, our friends would have been alerted and their footprints in the snow would indicate movements of retreat—but none of that is the case."

"That's true," said the Duc.

"Eagles, on the other hand, are always to be seen around the summit of the Colombier. No one pays any attention to eagles. Now, I defy you to measure the size of a bird passing almost directly overhead, because you cannot estimate the altitude of its passage. It is necessary to know one of those factors to deduce the other, and if..."

"Quite right, Monsieur."

"...and if fabulous eagles, far from any object of comparison, were soaring 1000 meters above the three excursionists, the latter would have taken them for common eagles situated within rifle-range. Given that, let us suppose that one of these chimerical raptors let itself fall upon Monsieur Henri

Monbardeau. It takes him by surprise; it lifts him into the air. Madame Fabienne Monbardeau races to her husband's aid, but a second eagle dives and carries her off. Mademoiselle Marie-Thérèse runs forward to help her cousin, but perceiving a third eagle descending upon her, she takes flight recklessly, until that one..."

"Shut up!" whispered Monsieur Le Tellier, pointing to Monsieur Monbardeau, whose eyes were wide with terror.

"It's only a means of making my point, Master. Collect yourself, doctor, and forgive me. It's an absurd and fantastic hypothesis. I only formulated it to add substance to our reflections. If the conjecture were credible, the story of the walking-stick would prove it wrong. It would be necessary to imagine beaks of bronze sufficiently unbreakable to be able to break wooden staves. And there are no more beaks of bronze than there are vultures capable of carrying off seventy kilograms of human flesh."

Monsieur Monbardeau wiped his forehead, and said in a hoarse voice: "Birds, no...but...flying men? Look down there...Seyssel, Anglefort...and remember the statue stolen therefrom..."

"Hey, Uncle!" protested Maxime. "Please don't confuse the misfortune that's overtaken us with all that tomfoolery!"

Robert bade him be silent, though. "That's another apparently lunatic hypothesis—and yet that one too occurred to me, for I reckon that there is nothing better than the study of false hypotheses to lead the mind to the truth. In science, sometimes, as in grammar invariably, two negatives are equivalent to an affirmation. When I know than something isn't here, I suspect that it must be elsewhere. And then, by virtue of elimination, one ends up gaining ground. Console yourself, doctor. The thieves of men—if there are any thieves—are not airborne sarvants...if there are any sarvants. To bear away a single person into the sky would require the alliance of *three* individuals flying with the strength—proportional to their size—of the most vigorous condors. It would therefore have required *nine* accomplices to execute

Saturday's kidnapping. Now, although eagles, even enormous ones, would not be noticed because of the reasons I've given you, a flock of nine *ornianthropes* could not pass unnoticed! Our friends would have retreated as they approached, and once again, the tracks show no sign of any sidestep, recoil or flight before the attack on Monsieur Henri, who was the first to be assailed. No, no...the dirigible, the eagles, the flying men....none of those hypotheses stand up."

Monsieur Monbardeau clenched his fists. "What, then? They didn't evaporate! Nor did they dissolve in the air like sugar-lumps in water, I presume! No lightning-bolt has sent them to the Devil! They haven't escaped from the summit of the Colombier like an electric discharge from a spike. They haven't ascended to Heaven like the prophets, have they? What, then? What? What? It's idiotic, in the end!"

Robert made an evasive gesture. "There's nothing more for us to do here."

"I beg your pardon!" replied Monsieur Le Tellier. "The snow will continue to melt. I'll make a sketch of all these imprints."

In that regard, Tiburce announced that it would be better still if he were to take a photograph of the snow from the top of the cross—but the intrepid Sherlockist had over-estimated his agility. He could only get half way to the intersection, and it was Maxime, remembering the masts and yard-arms of the *Borda*, who succeeded in the enterprise.

While Maxime was sitting astride the arms of the immense gibbet—designed, it seemed, to crucify some Titan—the inspector asked him to check whether the zinc bore any mark and the coating any scratches that might be attributed to the friction of ropes.

"None," he reported.

Unfortunately, when Tiburce tried to develop the precious photographs on his return to Mirastel, he found that he had forgotten to put film in the camera.

X. Deliberation

That same evening, all those who had participated in the search gathered in the drawing-room at Mirastel to hold a council. Henri Monbardeau's broken walking-stick lay on the table, in the middle of the circle, and the diagram of the footprints made by Monsieur Le Tellier was set before Madame Arquedouve. Each item had been punctured by Maxime with the point of a pin, in order to render the representation of the astonishing and terrible event sensible to his grandmother's fingers.

Monsieur Le Tellier wrote a detailed account of the session (*item 197*), which we shall summarize.

Monsieur Garan, who made no secret of the fact that his mind was almost made up, recognized nevertheless that a discussion might be useful. "Before asking ourselves *where* the missing person are," he said, "*who* is holding them captive and *how* they were abducted, it's necessary to know *why*."

Logically, in any case, the abduction hypothesis could only be adopted after the elimination of the hypothesis of a voluntary disappearance. That elimination could only be made when the cases of the three absentees had been examined successively, and the conclusion reached that none of them could have removed themselves from the world spontaneously, nor allowed themselves to be abducted. In the course of the discussion, however, when Monsieur Monbardeau affirmed that his son Henri had no reason to go into hiding, Monsieur Garan asked him whether he was aware that the young man received *poste restante* letters at Artemare.

"I conducted a little enquiry there yesterday evening," he declared. "On the very morning of the incident, Monsieur Henri Monbardeau presented himself at the post office counter and took away a letter bearing the initials H.M."

Monsieur Monbardeau's astonishment gave way to anger when Maxime, in order to disabuse Monsieur Garan, was forced to reveal that the letters bearing the initials H.M. came from Suzanne Monbardeau, and that the poor girl corresponded secretly with her brother. When the policeman persisted, it was necessary to tell him, in front of everyone, the sad story of Suzanne Monbardeau. No one could take any pleasure in it, inasmuch as Doctor Monbardeau took advantage of the digression to rail against the sinner and reproach her—he who had exiled her!—for not having shown her relatives the slightest sympathy in the wake of the disappearances.

Then the abduction hypothesis was returned to the floor.

Who might benefit from the triple capture?

Here, Monsieur Garan put forward the suggestion that Mademoiselle Le Tellier might have been abducted by one of the numerous aspirants that her father had refused. Being responsible for the safety of foreign residents in Paris, he had attended the inauguration of the Hatkins telescope in that capacity. Nothing had escaped him at that celebration or in its aftermath—a circumstance that had led to his being chosen to follow the present affair when the Duc d'Agnès had presented himself at the Prefecture on Monsieur Le Tellier's behalf.

The latter declared that he had only received three formal requests for marriage and, in consequence, had only had to issue three categorical refusals: to Lieutenant Pablo de Las Almeras, the Spanish military attaché; to Mr. Evans, an attorney from Chicago; and finally—he excused himself for having to make allusion to such buffoonery—to the Turk Abdul Kadir Pacha.

Monsieur Garan knew all three. They were, in his view, three trails to be abandoned. The Spaniard had just got engaged, the American had gone back to America a week before the disappearances, and the Turk had embarked at Marseilles for Turkey with his 12 wives on the morning of the unfortunate incident, under the inspector's own surveillance—which had, in fact, been the cause of the Duc d'Agnès' delay, the latter being obliged to await the arrival in Paris of the Côte-d'Azur express before being able to set off for Bugey.

Once it was proven that Marie-Thérèse Le Tellier had not been abducted for herself, a similar conclusion was reached concerning her cousin Fabienne. No one had any interest in kidnapping her, except perhaps for her former suitor, Monsieur Raflin, who was incapable of such an exploit, in view of the fact that he had been confined to his bedroom in Artemare for six months with a compound fracture of the leg.

There remained Henri Monbardeau. Had he been the primary objective of the fishing expedition?

Suddenly inspired, Monsieur Monbardeau then claimed, to everyone's amazement, that if anyone had taken his son captive, that someone could not be anyone other than Mr. Hatkins. "Yes, Hatkins the philanthropist, Hatkins the telescope-donor, Hatkins the billionaire!"

Henri Monbardeau, in pursuing his bacteriological research, had recently isolated, cultivated and attenuated the *bacillus sclerosans*; thanks to him, a cure for arteriosclerosis was close at hand. Now, Hatkins had offered five millions for his discovery—five millions disdainfully refused. Although Monsieur Garan was sure that the billionaire had left on a world tour, traveling via New York, several days before the kidnapping, and although Mr. Hatkins' honorability was not in doubt for the majority of those present, Doctor Monbardeau did not want to eliminate him from consideration. And Tiburce supported him in this paradoxical belief, suggesting that Mr. Hatkins might only have left France to establish and alibi, after having instructed a whole gang of accomplices to carry out the kidnapping.

They returned thereafter to the more serious idea of an association of criminals, skilled in terrorizing their peers and extracting ransoms from them. At this point in the conference, however, a violent quarrel developed between, on the one hand, Maxime and Robert, and on the other, Monsieur Garan—who, letting loose the dogs, accused them both of having faked the footprints on the Colombier, given that they had been alone on the summit of the mountain for some time before taking anyone else there.

Monsieur Le Tellier calmed his son and his secretary down. Then, to create a diversion and cut things short, he asked. "In the final analysis, what have we decided, Monsieur Garan?"

"Oh," said the other, "I don't want to say any more."

"All right. What about you, Robert?"

"I *can't* say anything, my dear Master. Nothing more, at least."

Seeing the inspector smile at the evasion, Monsieur Le Tellier was quick to say: "What about you, Monsieur Tiburce?"

"Hatkins! Hatkins!"

"Bravo!" said Monsieur Monbardeau, provoking indignant protests.

"What?" retorted Tiburce. "Before anything else, let's look for simple, possible, *natural* explanations. Let's not go beyond the *natural*." Citing one of his authors, he continued: "*I have long held to the principle that, when you have eliminated the impossible, that which remains, however improbable it might be, must be the truth.* Now, 'that which remains,' in my opinion, is the brigand hypothesis and the Hatkins hypothesis. And the latter, being the less complicated, must be preferable."

"The impossible…" said Robert. "How can any man know what is *impossible* and what is *natural*?"

"For my part," said Madame Arquedouve, "I'm with Robert. I sense that he has brought all the force of his wisdom to bear."

"Me, I want someone to give me back my daughter!" moaned Madame Le Tellier, at the end of her tether.

"At the end of the day, what are we going to do?" asked Monsieur Monbardeau, impatiently.

Tiburce, his nose stuck in a railway timetable, announced: "I'm setting off on Hatkins' heels! There's a steamboat tomorrow evening. Tomorrow evening, I'll take my leave of you."

"Robert, Maxime, what are you going to do?" asked Monsieur Le Tellier.

"Think," said Robert.

"Wait," said Maxime. "Wait for the bandits' demands."

"And you, Monsieur?"

The Duc d'Agnès replied: "I shall set about constructing, in collaboration with my engineer, aeroplanes as fast and as stable as possible...good flyers...good enough to hunt aerial pirates."

"Ah!" cried Maxime. "You're of the same opinion as me."

"Do that," Robert added. "That might be useful."

"Mr. Hatkins, I tell you!" Tiburce repeated.

"You're mad!" snapped the Duc d'Agnès.

Meanwhile, Monsieur Garan leaned toward Monsieur Le Tellier. "I beg you to forget what I said just now. It was my duty to be sincere."

"We have nothing against you," Monsieur Le Tellier replied. "You've expressed your opinion frankly and, in the final analysis, I admit that it's defensible. Except, you see, that my son and my secretary are entirely above suspicion—you don't know them."

Monsieur Tellier concluded his record of the evening thus:

As the meeting broke up, I saw Monsieur d'Agnès approach Robert. The two young men conversed for a few moments and parted with a firm handshake. Those who were familiar with the situation understood that the Duc had just informed his humble rival of the scorn in which he held the inspector's allegations. Then they agreed to devote all their efforts to recover Marie-Thérèse, the one by means of science, the other by means of his wealth, both without any concern for the future.

XI. A Lesson in Sherlockism

Monsieur Garan, whose bedroom was adjacent to Tiburce's, was woken up early by muffled and rhythmic noises and cadenced exclamations coming from next door. He went in unceremoniously, dressed in his nightshirt, and found the Sherlockist in the middle of a sequence of Swedish gymnastic exercises, designed to encourage the suppleness of the body and the strength of the muscles. At the sight of him, Tiburce, who was naked, turned his back on him and continued his rhythmic movements.

They had bid farewell to everyone the night before, for their train was early and Monsieur Le Tellier's automobile was due to set off at 5 p.m. to take them to Culoz.

"Well, colleague," said Garan, "Are you still determined to set off in pursuit of Mr. Hatkins?"

Tiburce scrupulously completed the rotation of his torso around his hips. "More than ever!"

"You know that it's insane?"

Tiburce poured water into a tub and started splashing around according to his routine. "Admit that it might be inspired," he said, after a pause

The inspector examined the room. A calculated disorder, in the Sherlockian style, made it into a virtual glory-hole. There was a strong odor of Navy Cut tobacco. In the shade of his moustaches and his eyebrows, turned up like the roofs of a pagoda, Garan's mouth and eyes began to smile again. "I assure you that your method is defective," he declared. "You lack experience."

"This will be educational, then," Tiburce replied, coldly. "I've given it a great deal of thought."

"Not only does Mr. Hatkins' character give the lie to your accusations," the other retorted, "but his departure prior to the abduction provides proof that, even if he were the author or instigator of the crime, the three missing persons are

92

not with him. He must, therefore, have set them aside, in order to occupy himself with them on his return, mustn't he?"

At that moment, however, Tiburce, was rubbing his skin with a horsehair glove, whistling as he went, as English stable-boys do while grooming their favorite colts. Having observed that, Monsieur Garan pivoted on his velvet-slippered heels and went to shave.

They finished getting ready at almost the same moment, and Tiburce, observing that they were early, said to the driver: "We'll start off on foot. You can catch us up on the road."

They went down the narrow little path between the two broader ones.

"Seriously," the inspector resumed, "Will you take my word for it?"

"No."

"Listen—it's ridiculous, and everyone will tell you the same. It's true that 'everyone' includes two lascars who hold the key to..."

"Robert and Maxime, you mean."

"Yes, my dear chap."

"It's my turn to say to you: that's ridiculous."

"Oh yes? Supernatural tracks—for show! For show, because supernatural occurrences, like that business at Seyssel, are tricks intended to deceive. At the prefecture, we always suspected that it was a prelude to something. Although, mind you, there might be some other connection between those sucker-traps and the abduction..."

"Certainly—I agree with you about that. The two events are connected. But with regard to Maxime and Robert, you're wrong. D'Agnès knows them very well, and he guarantees their good faith. As for the tracks in the snow, they can't possibly be supernatural. All things considered, though, I can't accept that the abduction took place at the summit of the Colombier. The imprints are probably only a stratagem with two objectives: firstly to frighten people, and secondly to mislead people as to the place where the kidnap took place. Someone could have brought the stick; someone could have made the footprints with boots on the end of long poles, from the height of a dirigible balloon moored to the cross. I mention mooring because the perpetual wind would have prevented any flying machine remaining stationary..."

"But that's exactly what I thought!" cried Garan. "That's why I asked Monsieur Maxime whether he saw any scratches or rope-marks..."

"The fact remains," concluded Tiburce, "that *supernatural* equals *nonexistent*."

"Amen! It's a pity you don't always reason like that."

"Is my system so defective, then?"

"Yes sir! Firstly, you quibble. Moreover, most of the time, you extrapolate from clues that might have several possible explanations. Example: your gaffes regarding the foot-muff, the monocle and everything else you spouted about father Le Tellier. When a multitude of possible explanations presents itself, it's necessary to consider them all—for if one of them escapes you, it's always the best. And sometimes, confronted by that infinity of solutions, one doesn't know which to plump for. It's better, when one has a choice—as you have—to take the testimony of a single action, which only a single cause could have produced. One can risk assertions of that sort without fear. They're proven by the circumstance that no other interpretation accords with the acts—while you, with your procedure, see evidence everywhere that you've preconceived. Hold on, though—I can discover any proof anywhere, of anything! What do you want? Affray? Rape? Murder? I'll wager that here, at the junction of this pathway with the road, I can easily demonstrate a crime or a contravention. Here's a bush all roughed up; here are some deep holes in the soft soil. What are they, really? Doubtless some stray rustic with his cow, or a thousand other things! Look at the road, now: that double rut tells us that a heavy automobile has set off abruptly toward Artemare. It was hollowed out by two rear wheels, skidding in response to a sudden impulse. What does that establish? That an angry mechanic had to repair a tire and set off brutally, or that an apprentice chauffeur has been making his debut and has been practicing stopping and starting, or that a sentimental traveler wanted to pick some of that hawthorn, or that…how do I know? It could be anything, at the end of the day. Anything!"

Tiburce lowered his head. "You're right," he said. "But what do you want me to do? My life's at stake, Monsieur Garan! Don't tell anyone, but if I recover Mademoiselle Le Tellier, I can marry Mademoiselle d'Agnès."

"Ah! Good, good! Then, don't set off after Hatkins—for to suspect such a man is to fly in the face of the obvious. Instead, try to get the truth out of Monsieur Maxime and Monsieur Robert—especially the latter, who might perhaps have duped his comrade, since he went up the Colombier before him."

"Ah! Yes, I think so, Monsieur Garan; do you, perchance, suspect some complicity between Robert and one of the three missing persons?"

"Yes, indeed—that's the basis of my thinking. I firmly believe that, with or without the connivance of Henri Monbardeau, Robert Collin and Mademoiselle Le Tellier, who are in love…"

"You think they're in love! And that's what you're basing your charges on?" cried Tiburce, with a sort of joy.

"Certainly."

"In that case, Monsieur Inspector, you're on the wrong track. Please take the trouble to disillusion yourself. For two years, Mademoiselle Le Tellier has been in love with my intimate friend the Duc d'Agnès."

"Are you sure?"

"There's not the slightest doubt."

Monsieur Garan furrowed his horned eyebrows—and that was such a droll sight that Tiburce burst out laughing. "Poor dear Inspector! If that's all you have in your sack, it will be necessary henceforth to believe in the flying men!"

"Oh yes!" grumbled the discomfited policemen. "Flimsy manikins—little balloon-men filled with hydrogen! That's the Prefecture's hypothesis."

"Not so stupid!" said Tiburce, approvingly. "That would explain why they keep moving in the same direction—that of the wind. A search ought to be made of the little wood at Châtel—I'm sure that the real Italians are in hiding there while people are beating the countryside looking for them. That, at least, is *natural*."

At that moment, the automobile loaded with Tiburce's luggage rejoined them.

"Let's go—*en route!*" said Garan.

"*En route*—in pursuit of Hatkins!"

Mortified by his blunder, the inspector replied churlishly that Tiburce was free to take whatever action he pleased, and that he, Garan, would go his own way.

As they arrived at the station a number of travelers were coming out, having arrived on a night train from Paris. Most of them were armed with photographic apparatus. Garan recognized them as journalists. One of them came over to him.

"Ah! Monsieur Garan, isn't it? What a lovely morning! Permit me, for a second..." He was trying to obtain an interview, but the policeman refused and became cantankerous.

"In sum, Inspector," the poor man insisted, "is it really a case of abduction? Yes or no? Tell me, I beg you. Who has kidnapped these people?"

The interrogated man then began to rant. "They're devils, Monsieur. I've seen them. They have bats' wings, goats' ears and serpentine tails. Hairy all over, they spit fire from their mouths and instead of a backside they have a journalist's head, which resembles yours like a brother's! There—are you satisfied?"

Having said this, he disappeared into the waiting-room, threatening the heavens with the quadruple menace of his allied eyebrows and moustaches.

XII. Sinister Occurrences

The Duc d'Agnès was in a hurry to get to work with his engineer. He left Mirastel on the same day as Tiburce, and on the following day, May 9, Monsieur and Madame Monbardeau returned to Artemare. At the old châteaux, life then began to be a painful and mournful ordeal. Everyone was obsessed by thoughts of Marie-Thérèse. At times, they would have preferred the assurance of her death to the unbearable torture of uncertainty. When one fears for a young woman, one has so many things to dread, does one not?

Madame Le Tellier spent long hours shut up in her daughter's room. Then, a sudden need for action that afflicted them all overwhelmed her innate languor, drove her outdoors and caused her to wander at hazard, very rapidly, at a tumultuous pace.

Everyone had a portrait of the missing girl on his desk or mantelpiece, and everyone looked at it repeatedly and religiously, to the accompaniment of thoughts or memories, like an icon on an altar. Madame Arquedouve was deprived of that consolation; her dead eyes refused it to her—but there was an irreproachable bust of the Marie-Thérèse in the drawing-room, so ingenious that it evoked the young woman in her entirety, and the little old lady was seen palpating the marble for long periods with her subtle white hands, considering by that means the unique resemblance that she was able to distinguish. It was an occupation that caused her pleasure and pain at the same time. She smiled, and then she sobbed. Then her eyes, which had anticipated oblivion, unfortunately ceased to be useless, and wept all the more for being unable to see.

Whenever she heard Madame Le Tellier coming, she made an effort to interrupt the flow of her tears, and the two women diverted themselves by talking about a calamity of which everything reminded them. Everything—even the dog Floflo, which remained silent; even the house, which seemed desolate. Normally, it flourished, thanks to the efforts of Marie-Thérèse; she was able to arrange flowers in a vase with that Japanese grace that makes one forget that they have been picked and are dying—but the vases remained empty, like bodies without souls, and the irises by the *botasse*,[15] vainly mauve, decayed far from human ken.

It seems that the most depressed of all of them was Monsieur Le Tellier. The astronomer no longer left his study. Weary of contention, exhausted by thinking about the incomprehensible catastrophe, he no longer had the strength to reason; he daydreamed, looking out over the magnificent countryside. The spring scene, full of life and sunlight, seemed to him to be bleak and empty. The joy of the season aggravated his depression. He looked at the flowering trees in the orchards, and thought of skeletons in macabre fancy dress. His daughter had passed so frequently—my God, so very frequently!—before that spacious mountain scenery that he no longer saw it as anything but the background of a portrait from which she had disappeared: the very spectacle of her absence.

As for Maxime and Robert, they were working—the former in his laboratory, in order to combat anxiety; the second in his room, on clandestine projects whose objective no one could easily guess.

Until May 13, nothing troubled that cruel calm, except for a few exploratory expeditions made by Robert to Seyssel and the other molested communes, and one trip to Lyon by Monsieur Le Tellier.

The latter was an atrocious journey. He departed like a madman, having read that the cadaver of an unknown woman had been pulled out of the Rhône, whose death might have taken place as far back as the ill-fated May 4. He absented himself under a pretext, without anyone knowing, and came back that same evening, relieved of a heavy burden. The

---

[15] Renard's narrator inserts a footnote to explain that *botasse* is a dialect term for an artificial pond or, more generally, any standing water.

woman in the morgue was dark-haired, middle-aged and of Oriental origin. A dredger had extracted her from the mud, naked and tied up in a sack. All of that was so far away from Marie-Thérèse, so alien to Monsieur Le Tellier's preoccupations, that he finally perceived the excess to which his depression had led him. From that day on, he gradually grew stronger.

There were also reporters continually ringing at Mirastel's main gate and who, when turned away, set about taking pictures of the château and its surroundings. There were the arrivals of the postman, too, always eagerly awaited, always disappointing…and that was all that there was.

In the countryside too, tranquility had been re-established, when, all of a sudden, something happened.

On the night of May 13 and 14, the village of Béon, situated between Culoz and Tallisieu at the foot of the Colombier, three kilometers from Mirastel, was ravaged. Sacrilegious hands stripped foliage from the fruit-trees. Various small animals, sleeping in the open, disappeared without trace. Finally, and most importantly, *a woman, drawn into her kitchen-garden by an unusual noise, did not return, and suffered the same fate as the branches and the animals.* It was impossible to find her.

From Béon, a vague ripple of fear spread out in a circle through the region. The journalists flocked there—but from that moment on, sources of terror never ceased to multiply, for a new village received a visit from the sarvants every night.

Soon, in fact, people were being stolen away in broad daylight from out-of-the-way locations. Many of them were shepherds or cowherds going forth alone with their animals in the vicinity of the mountain. On most occasions, only one person disappeared, sometimes two, and occasionally three. It was noticed that the diurnal abductions were preferentially carried out on high ground, and that the abductors, for fear of being betrayed, took care to capture the witnesses to their actions.

On the night of May 14 and 15, Artemare was visited. The sarvants, for some unaccountable region, had skipped one hamlet, two villages and three châteaux, including Mirastel. The disappearance was recorded of Raflin, the former suitor of Fabienne d'Arvière. The poor man, still infirm, was limping across his back yard when he was apprehended. His aged mother was mad with terror, fearful that he might be cold because he had only been wearing a dressing-gown.

On the night of May 15 and 16, leaving the road and heading southwards, the sarvant raided Ceyzérieu, opposite Mirastel beyond the marsh. Then it came back to the road, mistreated Talissieu—where it took possession of a new-born foal—took the ornamental spire off one of the towers of Châteaufroid, and pilfered a few rabbits from a farmyard enclosure.

On May 17, Dr. Monbardeau received the following letter, which threw him into despair and, on the other hand, proved that the scourge had progressed further than it seemed—which is to say, as far as Belley. The letter was from Front, Suzanne Monbardeau's lover.

(Item 239)

Monsieur Monbardeau,

Although our relationship has always been strained, I find myself under the sad obligation of informing you of what has happened to me.

On returning yesterday from a fortnight's journey, I did not find your daughter at home. She must have gone off with someone else, since I know that she has not returned to your house, taking advantage of these pretended disappearances—for you would not want me to believe that she has fallen victim to that. I have not been able to obtain any information regarding her flight, the house in which I have had the honor of accommodating her being some distance from the town. That's how it is.[16] *But I thought it my duty to inform you, so that you know that from now on, even less than in the past, there is no connection between us.*

Regards,
Onésime Front.

The horror of the fact was reinforced by the triviality of the boor who announced it. Suzanne had certainly not sinned for a second time; everything affirmed that. She must, therefore, have fallen prey to the sarvant! And what corroborated that was the devastation, on the night of May 17 and 18, of Saint-Champ, not far from Belley.

Suzanne abducted! This final blow put the lid on the Monbardeaus' distress. Madame Monbardeau was out of her mind for a week, and then railed incessantly against the paternal rigor that had exiled the repentant sinner—to which Monsieur Monbardeau did not know how to reply, and bowed his head, weeping.

On the morning of May 19, the people of Artemare leaned that the night had been fatal to the village of Ruffieux, situated five kilometers beyond the Rhône on the road from Seyssel to Aix-les-Bains. The news lacked precision; there was vague mention of several people having been abducted, which required confirmation—but before that confirmation was obtained, the Artemarians heard of an event more sensational still. A reporter-photographer from Turin had set off well before dawn for the summit of the Colombier, in order to photograph the theater of the abduction in the splendor of the sunrise. This refinement is explained by the incalculable number of snapshots that he colleagues had already taken of the same place, in various conditions of time and temperature. In the same way that Marie-Thérèse and her companions had not come back down again, the reporter did not return.

---

[16] Renard's narrator adds a footnote to say that this sentence was crossed out by Dr. Monbardeau.

There was great consternation in Artemare, palavers and whispered discussions, the outcome of which was that a troop of courageous men—they could still be found at that time—set off in search of the lost envoy. They went up to the cross, and there they discovered the photographic apparatus on its tripod, *in the company of a sort of hideous, goiterous dwarf, clad in rags, sprawled on the grass, whom no one recognized.* There was not the slightest trace of the journalist, unless he had been magically transformed into that repulsive creature with the excessively large head and the excessively sort arms, who watched the rescuers approach with animal eyes.

The searchers paused, looking everywhere for the former appearance of the journalist, but there was nothing! Then they approached his new manifestation—I mean the impassive ugly creature—and soon perceived that they were dealing with an unfortunate deaf-mute cretin.

In time they became bold enough to touch him—for, until then, the fear of burning their hands had deterred them. They tried to get him to stand up, and found—the ultimate disgrace!—that he was paralyzed. So they picked him up, along with the tripod, and they started to go down the mountain. When they reached Virieu-le-Petit, though, with expressions in which bewilderment persisted, they happened to meet a cowherd who was getting ready to take some fir-trunks to the saw-mill at Artemare, and the man, catching sight of the dwarf, cried out in dialect, which translated as: "Hey! That's Gaspard! What's he doing there?" And he told them that the idiot was a native of Riffieux, that he spent his days and nights crouched on the doorstep of his father's house—which opened on to the road—and that all the cowherds, hauliers and messengers knew him by virtue of seeing him crouching by the roadside, motionless.

The story caused an uproar. An infernal substitution had taken place, of a journalist from Turin and an innocent from Ruffieux, on the top of the Colombier! Attempts were made to interrogate Gaspard, to obtain the slightest expressive gesture from him, but they were fruitless. Never had he been so deaf, nor so mute, nor more imbecilic, nor so paralyzed. His father, when he saw him again, regretted having done so. Such was the sole escapee, the only person who might have given any information on the subjects of the sarvants, and the only one they had elected to leave behind. The other reporter-photographers gave Gaspard's father money, however, in order that he would permit them to take photographs of the hero, and he was thankful for his child's return. Contrary to rumor, Gaspard had been the only human being that the sarvant had removed from Ruffieux.

On the night of May 19 and 20, it was the turn of Amey-zieu, almost beneath the walls of Mirastel—but the abundant precautions with which the country-folk surrounded themselves limited the damage and the material losses.

The guests at Mirastel told themselves that the hour had come for them to be tormented. The dangerous zone seemed to have narrowed around the château as it had expanded further away. Hazard alone could spare them from the sarvant's attack.

Monsieur Le Tellier rejoiced in that fact. Since the commencement of the depredations, persuaded like everyone else that their secret was identical to that of the abduction of the fourth of May, he had spent his time in various activities. At first, he had been heartily glad at the thought of all the hypotheses that the resumption of hostilities had eliminated. By virtue of that fact, the range of conjectures had been singularly restricted, and that circumstances seemed to support the Duc d'Agnès, who had predicted that other abductions would take place before any ransom demands were issued. The present number of hostages retained by the sarvant demonstrated that the latter had not had any special interest in Marie-Thérèse and her cousins.

Having understood that, Monsieur Le Tellier immediately telegraphed the Duc d'Agnès, so that he could stop his friend Tiburce from following his false trail. The Duc replied, however, that Tiburce had already set off after Hatkins, having embarked for New York in pursuit of the billionaire on May 8.

103

Monsieur Le Tellier lamented that enormous stupidity and returned to his personal preoccupations. With his son, his bother-in-law and his secretary, he visited the plundered locations. They made observations; they asked questions. They experienced a sort of perverse relief in establishing that other families were suffering from the scourge that had struck them—but they did not obtain any clues, and started again, even more fervently, stimulated by the three women—who combined their encouragement with recommendations of prudence. The women did not let them go out after sunset, and forbade them to separate themselves from one another when they ventured into lonely places.

One day, however, Madame Arquedouve, who was the first to preach confidence and zeal, and was known to possess an uncommon bravery, suddenly changed her attitude and showed herself to be exceedingly pusillanimous. Pressed to confess the cause of her alarm, she eventually gave way the day after the sack of Ameyzieu. That night, *as on the night of the sack of Talissieu*, she had perceived strange vibrations— perhaps not exactly sounds, but something of the same sort: something vibrant, which her blind person's senses had permitted her to appreciate.

They were perceptions analogous to those provoked by the passage of an airplane or a dirigible, or even a large fly, too distant to be *heard*, in the proper sense of the term, but neither one thing nor the other. It was a *somber* buzz, by virtue of being dull and deep, which impressed all her nerves, her entire body, rather than her ears. That anomaly had woken her up in the middle of both those nights, very apprehensive. The first time, she had been able to believe that she was the victim of one those delusions to which the infirm are exposed, but now she no longer doubted the authenticity of her sensations. That was why she had decided to speak.

In the wake of such a revelation, there was no one at Mirastel who was not profoundly thoughtful.

They were not the only ones to be meditative on May 20, 1912. By that time, all France and all Europe were taking an

104

interest in the Bugist problem. The newspapers of the old world were taking account of "the advent of a new terror." The majority opined that it was "surely by the aerial route that the sarvants came," and more than one "that they must belong to the flying species of which Brigadier Géruzon caught sight of two specimens."

The Middle Ages were revived. Legends slid from hearth to hearth. Some, forgotten for centuries, were mysteriously resurrected. They even infiltrated Mirastel, and mingled their chimeras with the logic of the rationalists.

There was, however, no more time for reflection; while mulling over his mother-in-law's story, Monsieur Le Tellier prepared to be vigilant, to see what might be seen. But the sarvants now appeared to have adopted the tactic of leaping from one place to another, randomly and capriciously.

He deduced from this incoherence—organized, after a fashion—that they would not fall upon Mirastel 24 hours after ransacking Ameyzieu.

Of all the mistakes that might have been made, that one was revealed, in hindsight, to be the worst.

XIII. The Sarvants at Mirastel

Since the resumption of the raids, Maxime had calculated the advantages that a searchlight might offer to the threatened dwelling. An excellent means of defense and observation, nothing was easier to improvise. At the instigation of his son, Monsieur Le Tellier had two remarkable powerful acetylene projectors sent from Paris, which two watchers were to maneuver continually every night.

Received at 1 p.m. on May 20, their installation was undertaken without delay, in the attic of the south-western tower—the one where Maxime's laboratory was—beneath the low cupola. The modern rectangles of two large dormer windows, diametrically opposed, one looking northwards and the other southwards, punctuated the Louis XIII roof. The pivoting searchlights only had to be set up there to be able to direct their beams in every direction, each of the two illuminable sectors taking up exactly half of the surrounding area.

As they were not expecting the sarvants until the following day, the work of mounting the projectors was executed, as one might imagine, with more care than rapidity. At dinner time, only one of the searchlights was in place. It had, however, been filled with acetylene.

After the meal, Monsieur Le Tellier—still thinking about the next day—gathered the household together and gave the servants a lecture on observation. He recommended calm, self-possession, notes to be taken as soon as possible, written on anything that came to hand—on a wall, if necessary, with a stick of charcoal or a pointed stone...

He intended to repeat it all, and to explain his theory, on the following day.

Night fell. Robert proposed that they finish setting up the second light. The objection was raised that it would be better to do that in daylight, and that they would have 18 hours of sunlight for that purpose.

Then commenced one of those evenings so painful to those with heavy hearts. Everyone tried to kill time. Madame Le Tellier attempted to play patience. Her mother did crochet-work, in which her industry surpassed the skill of the sighted. Not far away, in the billiard-room adjacent to the drawing-room, Monsieur Le Tellier, Maxime and Robert started a game of billiards.

The windows had been left open, for the weather was fine and warm. They overlooked the terrace. The interior light illuminated the chestnut-trees and the lower branches of the ginkgo, as flat and stiff as painted trees. Beyond the parapet, the countryside was confusedly visible, dark and blue. Nothing but the impacts of the billiard balls, the noise of footsteps on the carpet, and the sound of four voices coming from the direction of the servants' quarters disturbed the background silence. At intervals, a train streaked the profound darkness with a trail of sparks, resonated metallically on the Marlieu bridge, and left the scene. They could also hear—but only by pricking up their ears—slight movements of gravel; they were the comings and goings of Floflo, mounting guard like a good little sentry.

Such pleasant evenings should always be holidays...

But what's that?

What's the matter? Why is Madame Arquedouve running into the billiard-room, her hand extended in front of her, her face distraught, stammering with fright?

"What's wrong?" cries Monsieur Le Tellier.

She grabs her son-in-law's arm. "They're here! I can hear them...feel them, rather!"

Robert has already started running, precipitating himself toward the tower in which the searchlight is lodged.

"Close the windows!" moans Madame Le Tellier, who comes in as pale as a corpse.

"No!" retorts Maxime. "We must try to see...to hear...Shh!"

"Shall we go up to the tower?" says Monsieur Le Tellier.

"No...no time... Shhh! Shhh!"

107

They listen. They're like wax figures in a museum. They can hear Robert going up the stairs to the tower, four at a time; they can hear laughter coming from the kitchen...a train whistle...the lap-dog moving back and forth...

Except for Madame Arquedouve, no one can hear anything apart from these sounds—and yet, they interrogate the darkness with all their might. It is rendered more impenetrable by the contrast with the luminous foliage; they try to listen with their eyes...but the darkness is the same, for their eyes as for their ears.

"Listen!" whispers the blind woman. "They're very close now..."

They hear nothing.

Yes—a bellowing. Yes—a whinnying. The farm has woken up. The ducks set up a frightened quacking in the darkness, as if a fox or a weasel were approaching; and there go the hens, which give voice to a prolonged clucking, as if an eagle were hovering overhead... The sheep intone a chorus of heart-rending lamentations...

Anguish reigns among the animals—and Floflo, who has come to a halt, suddenly starts barking.

Madame Arquedouve lifts up a finger and says: "The animals can hear too. They understand."

There is a momentary silence then...and finally, in the depths of that silence, everyone hears the *hum*.

It is the arrival of a large fly, or a moth. Yes, it is the hum of a moth, hovering above a flower into which it plunges its long proboscis: a murmur that is simultaneously soft and robust, which seems strident even though it is very low; which is, in fact, curiously melancholy, and which shudders in your breast like a steamer's propeller-shaft.

Now the windows are starting to vibrate...

"It's coming from above!" they murmur. "No—it's coming from the marsh. From Artemare! From Culoz!"

"The mountain," says the grandmother, breathlessly.

Madame Le Tellier, with one hand on her quivering throat, whispers: "It's still very distant, mother, believe..."

But she does not finish, because a light, inexplicable breeze stirs the foliage; the leaves rustle, and a there is a sudden resonant *snap!*

They start at the abrupt sound that has just resounded somewhere outside, not far away, and seemingly in mid-air.

Floflo is barking furiously.

"Thunder?" asks Madame Arquedouve.

"No, Mother," Monsieur Le Tellier replies. "There was no lightning. We didn't see anything."

"It wasn't a spark either, an artificial discharge…"

"Evidently."

"Maxime, get away from the window," implored Madame Le Tellier.

"Keep listening!" commanded the astronomer.

The dog gives voice and runs to the far end of the garden. It's pursuing the sarvants, for sure; they're moving away. The humming has died away too…but Madame Arquedouve affirms that she can still hear it.

The dog falls silent. They breathe in. The blind woman's features relax…

A sharp cry!

It's nothing—just Madame Le Tellier, frightened by the unexpected sight of a broad beam of light, like a ray of sunlight piercing the night…

One might imagine that this auroral dart were completing the recent snapping sound, that it is a lightning-flash following the thunder, prodigiously…but the brightness persists and endures.

"Don't be afraid, Luce," says Monsieur Le Tellier. "It's only the searchlight."

A minute later, he rejoined his secretary in the little round attic.

Standing on a stool, Robert's upper body was invisible, projecting through one of the skylights, and he was making the dazzling beam—solar in its power, lunar in its whiteness—describe vast arcs, sometimes celestial and sometimes terrestrial. He was darting his shaft of daylight over the whole of the southern landscape that could be embraced from his position. The searchlight illuminated villages, mountains, woods and châteaux by turns; it seemed that their image was being projected on a black screen, in the fashion of a magic lantern—but Robert had to lean over and lift up the projector with its heavy support to extend his field of exploration toward the Colombier; he did not discover anything at all whose presence was not legitimate.

The sarvants were already out of sight.

"Did you see them?" asked Monsieur Le Tellier.

"I lost too much time," he secretary replied. "I had to start the generator, to light up...it took too long. They've gone—but they didn't do anything." War-weary, he abandoned the projector, which swung around, sweeping the expanse, and came to a halt pointed toward the ground, irradiating the terrace.

"Oh!" Robert exclaimed. "Look, Master!"

"What?" said the astronomer, sticking his head out of the window.

"The *ginkgo*. It's been cut!"

Monsieur Le Tellier was, indeed able to see by means of the acetylene light that the *ginkgo biloba* had been decapitated. From his high station, he could see the severed trunk, whose cross-section formed a pale disk.

With a single stroke the sarvant had cut that roundel, as broad as a man's neck and as hard as oak: with a single stroke of a chisel, so skillfully, so rapidly and so accurately applied that the tree had not even trembled; with a single stroke of the chisel whose click that the forester had once heard in the forest—the chisel to which no one had given another thought, but which was pitilessly pruning all the plantations in Bugey!

"They chose well!" remarked Monsieur Le Tellier. "Ah, the scoundrels! The most beautiful tree in the region. The only *ginkgo*! But how did they get away? Madame Arquedouve claims that they came from the mountain; they must have gone back the same way—but that's precisely the sector that you couldn't illuminate! Of course! The dog followed them as far as the end of the garden. Ah, he certainly got their scent. Brave Floflo!"

"Poor Floflo?" said Robert, who seemed extremely anxious.

"Why *poor*? Have they taken him away? Did you see him being carried off?"

"No—but he suddenly stopped yapping."

"Floflo!" called Monsieur Le Tellier. "Floflo!"

No Floflo.

They did not dare go out to search for him in the ominous darkness. The cook called to him all night long through the small panel in a door.

He had been taken.

It was thus that Mirastel was haunted by the sarvants, which were still called "flying men," *ornianthropes* or *anthropornix*.

The witnesses of the event remained perplexed, however, not only by the promptitude and dexterity of the marauders, but also by the breath of wind that had blown through the foliage. It had blown for scarcely a second, that wind—the time of a wing-beat; as if it really had been a wing that had stirred the leaves—and when they thought about the awakened and alarmed animals, and the hens clucking as if at the approach of a bird of prey, the crazy hypothesis of eagles regained all its force.

Monsieur Le Tellier admonished himself in vain and recalled that the eagle-hunters recruited by his brother-in-law had returned empty-handed. He shivered no less with fabulous terror when he learned, the following evening, of a further strange and breathtaking event.

XIV. The Eagle and the Weathervane

The sarvants were not content with visiting Mirastel. They had also violated the village of Ouche, above the château. Alerted in the morning, Monsieur Le Tellier went there with Maxime and Robert. They were shown two squares of cabbages and one of carrots, completely harvested by the enigmatic prowlers, and the place where, the previous day, an irregularly shaped stone had stood, of which nothing now remained but a hole in the ground.

"Still the same old refrain," said Maxime. "The gentlemen mimic phantoms. They elect to take rare but useless items for the sake of effect: a kind of menhir; a branch from a *gingo*; a pet Pomeranian dog."

Robert folded his arms. "Do you think," he said, "that cabbages and carrots are useless rarities? Have you noticed the eagerness with which our enemies have recently been devastating marketable crops? That the individuals who never appropriated two identical objects to begin with are now putting their hands on all sorts of vegetables?"

"Come on! All of that is to annoy the citizens—to make them pay dear for their tranquility!"

"Do you see any trace of tools or footprints?" asked Monsieur Le Tellier. "I don't."

"Nothing, as usual," replied Robert. Then he added: "Think about it, all the same Monsieur Maxime—when it's a matter of animals and human beings, the sarvants aren't very particular in relation to the quality. Do you see? They carry off any woman or man, the first cat that comes along, and heaps of worthless rabbits, save for exceptions that seem due to chance. Admit it. Doesn't it seem that way to you, on reflection? That's the way it is?"

"Yes, that's right," the doubter confessed, after a moment's thought.

"Well then," Robert went on, in an almost gleeful tone, "in that case…"

"What are you getting at?"

"You might be making a mistake, that's all." And he cut any discussion short by moving away from his companions. He asked Monsieur Le Tellier to excuse him if he were not back in time for dinner, and set off downhill towards Artemare.

The father and son took the pathway back to Mirastel. "As long as he doesn't do anything reckless," murmured the astronomer.

"He's stubborn," said Maxime. "Impenetrable and stubborn—but brave! It's not the first time he's gone off on his own. I know that. He slips away…"

"He'd give his last drop of blood to recover Marie-Thérèse…"

"She's worth it," muttered Maxime. "She's worth the blood of a Duc!"

"All the same," Monsieur Le Tellier continued, without picking up the thread, "I'll be glad when he comes back…I want to talk to him about the searchlight."

"The searchlight? What should we do with it? It's quite simple—dismount the projector and install it along with the other one at Machuraz. Since the beginning of their campaign, your jokers have never gone back to the same place; they won't come back to Mirastel, but they haven't plagued Machuraz yet. We need to ask the owners for permission to set up our lights there. Let's go right away."

That was what they did.

The two Le Telliers did not want to entrust the task of dismounting the lamp and packing up the lenses and mirrors to anyone else. They devoted such unaccustomed attention to the handiwork that they decided they ought to finish the job after supper. The previous day's events had convinced them no longer to put off until tomorrow what could be done today. Consequently, they went back up to the attic of the tower with a lantern and got down to work, mute and preoccupied—for Robert Collin had not returned.

They worked for some time in that fashion, without saying anything, listening for someone climbing the stairway and crying: "Here I am!"—but only the rustle of wrapping-paper filled the twilight, while, overhead, the weathervane grated intermittently.

Finally, someone came up the stairs.

"Here I am!" said Robert.

"We were getting worried about you, my friend!" exclaimed the father.

"Where the Devil have you been?" asked the son.

"To the summit of the Colombier."

Maxime looked the secretary up and down and quipped: "You're very neat for a man who's come back from the mountain. What a careful fellow he is! He's as spick and span as he was this morning, with his frock-coat brushed and his boots shiny…"

"That was a grave imprudence!" complained Monsieur Le Tellier. "You know how dangerous that place is!"

"I wasn't afraid," said Robert, quietly polishing his gold-rimmed spectacles. "I think I've found a means of protection against the…sarvants. No, no…don't ask me anything. To tell you my method would put you on the track of my hypothesis…and I beg you to give me credit. Anyway, I have to tell you about something that I've just witnessed. I'd like your opinion about it. You mustn't be annoyed if I limit myself, at present, to revealing this fact to you, without saying what I think of it myself. Besides, what I think is so vague and so…no one would believe me. They'd confuse my ideas with objections. And at the end of the day, I have a…particular interest…in finding the solution by myself, haven't I? Because of…in the end, it's a matter of recovering Mademoiselle Marie-Thérèse, isn't it?"

"Get on with it!" roared Maxime, impatiently. "What have you seen?"

114

The little man replaced his spectacles on the bridge of his nose, tugged at his wretched downy beard and said: "I've seen an eagle." He looked each of them in the eye, one after the other.

Monsieur Le Tellier shuddered. "Ah!" he said. "I've thought about that a great deal today. But it's so extraordinary…"

"I've seen an extraordinary eagle," added Robert Collin.

"Extraordinary in what way?" Maxime asked, pressingly. "Enormous?"

"That I don't know. I lacked a point of comparison by which to estimate its size. I had been leaning on the upright of the cross, for about an hour, when I saw it pass by a long way to the east, above the Rhône, at high altitude. It was flying from the south-east to the north-west. I hadn't noticed it before, because there were others around, here and there—but they were normal eagles…as it had been itself, until the moment when…

"In brief, what I noticed about it was the disordered and very extravagant beating of its wings. I had a pair of binoculars; quickly, I aimed them—and I observed that the raptor was surrendering itself to a sort of mad incantation, while flying at a speed that seemed to me to be average—although there also, the lack of reference-points prevented me from determining the animal's velocity.

"I followed it easily.—but all of a sudden, it disappeared from my instrument's field of view. Then, with the naked eye, I saw it climb rapidly into the sky, at a near-vertical angle and with considerable rapidity…except that it seemed diminished, as if it had become smaller. I was lucky enough to be able to catch up with it with my binoculars, and before it plunged into the clouds, I recognized the cause of that apparent diminution. *It was because the bird had folded its wings.*"

"What?" Maxime protested. "It was climbing *without flying*? Without even soaring?"

"That's odd!" added his father.

"Without flying," Robert confirmed. "Without soaring. With no more movement than a stuffed eagle on a perch!"

"Are you sure of what you saw?"

"Yes, Monsieur Maxime, I'll answer for myself. Now, what do you think of the phenomenon?"

"Let's see," said the astronomer. "Of what nature were the movements that preceded this fantastic flight?"

"Brutal wing-beats, in every direction, which must have required all the creature's strength."

"And which maintained it at a good speed and at the same height?"

"Yes."

"In sum," Maxime proposed, "they were similar to the contortions that discus-throwers go through before launching a weight or a quoit?"

"My God…yes."

"In that case," Monsieur Le Tellier continued, "your eagle was bracing itself, before heading straight upwards…it might have been a means of storing energy?"

"I'm asking you, Master. But it's certain that a carnivorous bird, flying in that manner, could disappear in no time, after having snatched its prey…"

"And what color was it?"

"Tawny…rather like the plumage of an owl."

"Hold on!" said Monsieur Le Tellier, not quite able to gather his thoughts. "After all, this eagle might perhaps have been gigantic, since you weren't…*listen! Who's that coming up the stairs?*"

They fell silent. The wooden steps resonated dully. Someone was coming upstairs, bumping into the steps in their hurry…

Monsieur Le Tellier picked up the lantern and went to the door, just as Madame Arquedouve emerged from the darkness. She had a deathly expression, and she launched a cry of alarm in a hoarse voice: "The sarvants! Again! They're coming back!" It was a strange and terrible sound, like a whispered howl.

116

"They're coming…" repeated Monsieur Le Tellier.

"Holy thunder!" Maxime swore. "We no longer have the searchlight!"

Without losing a second, though, Robert had snuffed out the lantern, and the two skylights now cut out two rectangles of sky, which seemed to brighten gradually. Maxime understood the stratagem; he leapt upon the box containing the generator, put his upper torso through the window, and set the widow-frame back against the roof. Robert cleared the other skylight in the same manner. Each of them was covering half the expanse; everything was therefore accessible to their gaze. It was dark, but within a radius of 100 meters, a man—or anything of similar dimensions—could not escape their notice.

Between them, behind them, in the obscurity of the attic, they could hear Madame Arquedouve trembling; behind them and between them, at the pinnacle of the cupola, the wrought-iron weathervane creaked periodically.

The moth-like hum had just begun. Where? Everywhere, it seemed—to the right to the left, in the sky, in the recesses of their breasts. As on the previous evening, they stared into the darkness as hard as they could, with the feeble eyes of diurnal animals…

The stables, the cowshed and the henhouse awoke. The sheepfold sobbed…

The half-light seemed to them to alternate between dazzling brightness and opaque darkness…

In the distance—or was it?—the sarvant hummed.

Robert felt a slight breeze caress his forehead, and he redoubled his vigilance.

Maxime also felt the breeze…

And the weathervane creaked…*but instead of creaking just once and stopping, it commenced the admirable prodigy of no longer ceasing to creak, turning around and around without pause, in imitation of a rattle!*

The breeze, which was still blowing, died down. Mechanically, the two watchers had turned their heads to look at the weathervane. They saw it come to a halt as the wind eased—and they resumed their surveillance of the plain and the mountain.

Suddenly, behind them, between them, at the pinnacle of the cupola, there was a dull *snap*.

An instinctive recoil brought both their heads back into the shelter of the roof, and they distinguished the fall of a hard and heavy object, which rattled loudly on the slates as it tumbled...then nothing more...and then the arrival of the object on the gravel of the terrace...

The hum had vanished.

"Damn!" gasped Monsieur Le Tellier, mopping his forehead.

"Disappeared! Flown away!" said Robert, having resumed his observation-post. "Damn! No luck! The weathervane's not creaking any more. Ah! *It's no longer there!* It's fallen down! That's what fell down!"

"They've knocked it down," Maxime completed, from the other opening. "This time, though, they've carried nothing away. They've let go of their prize. It must have slipped out of their hands..."

"What about the searchlight?" added the astronomer. "One might say that was unlucky."

"I didn't see anything!" muttered Robert. "Behind our heads! What bad luck! And not to have been able to resist the movement that made us pull back our heads in that cowardly fashion, stupidly!"

"Ahem!" said Madame Arquedouve, slumped on the top step of the spiral staircase.

"What is it, grandmother? Are they renewing the attack?"

"They're...only just going away....there! They've gone."

"Yes?" said Monsieur Le Tellier. "They're *really* gone this time? Finally. We can go out without danger! It would be as well to go search for the weathervane. We might perhaps learn something from its examination. It made a dull thud..."

They went down—but they found no sign of the weathervane-rattle save for a depression of the relevant size and

118

shape hollowed out in the gravel, beneath the laboratory windows, where it had struck the ground.

"That's a bit stiff!" groaned Maxime. "They came back to get it! Grandmother was right—they hadn't gone! That proves that they're only audible at close range. Oh, if only someone had seen them from my laboratory, from which they must have been visible when they picked up the weathervane! We'd know what kind of noses they had!"

"Noses...or beaks..." ventured Monsieur Le Tellier.

Meditatively Robert thought aloud: "That weathervane...rotated on its axis...it seemed to be in the middle of...it seemed to be caught up in a whirlwind...a little cyclone...helpless... Hey, Monsieur Maxime, what about the breeze? Naturally, you felt it moving from left to right, since we were back-to-back, and I felt it moving from right to left?"

"But no—it was blowing from my right..."

"Aha! Then it really was a *circular* breeze..."

"Damn!" cried Monsieur Le Tellier.

But Robert hastened to ask: "Given all this, what do you think of my eagle?"

"Several contradictory things. That even if eagles sometimes carry off young animals and children, they're not accustomed to stealing weathervanes...but I also think that the manner in which your eagle was agitated bears an astonishing resemblance to the sort of flight employed, it's said, by the men of Châtel, and that, perhaps, some sort of...disguise... Are you with me? A man costumed as an eagle...to deceive... There's always been an element of burlesque in all this..."

Maxime laughed sardonically. "Costumed? Why not metamorphosed, as the journalist from Turin was mutated into a dwarf? My dear father, I no longer recognize you..."

"It's you that isn't recognizable. I know perfectly well that my inferences are fragile, but for want of better, I'm obliged to deliver myself to conjectures that might be stated in the scientific form: *everything happened like this*. Besides, you interrupted me, and I hadn't finished. We might be in the presence of a new, or recently-discovered, force—or rather a

119

buoyancy—which living beings are able to acquire, and acquire without wanting to, against which their bodies struggle…"

"Ta ta ta! We're afraid, and that's all. What have we done thus far, not counting gaffes? Prevarication and poltroonery. With so many precautions, we'll never see the sarvants! Nothing prevents one from seeing one's adversary like an overly large shield. Look, it's ridiculous only to go out of the villages in numbers. That's exactly what's needed to catch a glimpse of the enemy. Personally, I've had enough of all your cowardice. From tomorrow, I'll do as Robert does, and go out alone wherever it suits me."

Seeing that Maxime was getting angry, Monsieur Le Tellier wished him goodnight. Once he had gone back down to the hallway, Robert said to Maxime: "Listen. You're being rash. Trust me: *if you go out alone, dress like one of the missing persons; make yourself a copy of one of them.* If need be, dye your hair and beard. Shave, if necessary. Don't forget the walking-stick and gloves, and go as far as to reproduce the gait.

"Today, before climbing the Colombier, I went to Dr. Monbardeau's house and there, according to his indications, I dressed in a khaki costume belonging to his son, similar to the one he was wearing on the day of his abduction. Monsieur Monbardeau helped complete the resemblance; we covered a black felt hat with chalk to turn it white, and I put on yellow boots. That's why you found me looking so neat on my return—I'd just returned my borrowed clothing. It's a useful trick—at least, I think so. In any case, it seems to have succeeded, since here I am. But be discreet, won't you?"

"Are you cracked?" asked the other, simultaneously amused and disconcerted. "If the stratagem works, why keep it a secret?"

"For various reasons, but most of all because there presently exists another means of immunization, which is the fruit of empiricism, and is certainly more reliable than my procedure, which is the result of calculation. That means is precise-

120

ly the one that you've rejected, which consists of gathering in force away from habitations. That's well-known; everyone accepts that temporary obligation, and those who refuse to submit to it—imbeciles, hotheads or braggarts, meaning no offense—won't want to use my system either."

"There's some truth in that..."

"Except...except that...will the first of the two procedures, the more popular, always be efficacious? And is the second—mine—reliable? Is it by chance that the sarvants didn't carry me off during that first experiment? Might it be that they didn't see me? Paradoxical as it might seem, you know, *I desire that wholeheartedly*. For, if that one part of my theory were to be verified, the entire theory would be true, and then..." He passed his hand over his forehead, as if he were facing frightful apparitions. His hand was trembling and beads of sweat were forming on his brow.

"...And then, my dear chap, you haven't had dinner," Maxime finished. "You're hungry. Empty stomach, hollow head. Hunger is leading you astray."

"Monsieur Maxime," said Robert, "I would give my life to be mistaken."

XV. Other Contradictory Facts

The period that followed was truly terrible, for the sole reason that some people were still incredulous. The neighboring populations retained a suspicion of trickery, and those of the inhabitants who admitted the epidemic of disappearances did not realize how far it might extend. In their view, it was a local calamity. Some merely passed for St. Thomases, who had not seen anything themselves—but in the heart of Bugey, in the neighborhood of Belley, more than one wit or churl persisted in refusing to take it seriously. That is what is incredible! That is what provoked more and more misfortunes!

The audacity of the enemy increased with the number of its successes. Its field of operations eventually became an immense circle that took in Saint-Rambert, Aix-les-Bains and Nantua. Within this province, which continued to grow incessantly, the sarvant levied its incomprehensible tithe, and those who did not believe in it became its unfortunate victims.

What about those who believed in the sarvant, though? The unfortunates were living in fear. Did they want to go out? An escort was necessary; they rendered the service reciprocally, and one saw cohorts of villagers going abroad, looking at the sky, which had become equivocal. Ah, the sky! An enigma had been added to its numerous mysteries, and its depths retreated even further from human eyes. Dwellings were locked up well before dusk, and when the hostile night had fallen, people listened carefully, for it has been agreed that an alarm bell would be sounded in any commune where the sarvants had been detected. They only ever heard it, though, in the depths of feverish ears where the blood rang its own unhealthy bell. Well after dawn, they would open a door-hatch, a ventilator, then the windows, and finally the door.

Some remained sequestered. Others, less timorous, forced themselves to go out—but it only required a tremor for them to tremble, a door to be moved by a draught for them to go pale; the wind, most of all, was able to frighten them. Rumor had spread of the breeze agitating the chestnut-trees at Mirastel and preceding the frightful snap, with the result that a zephyr passing through foliage seemed to them to be something malevolent watching them; its caress sent frissons running over them. They wanted to know the origin of the wind and exactly what it was—questions they had never asked before.

What they feared, to tell the truth, was being grabbed from behind, in crushing hands that were always perceived too late. That is why they turned round continually. Tapping a comrade on the shoulder, taking him by surprise, was a deadly game. On the avenue in Belley, during a game of boule, a citizen with a weak heart dropped dead because his partner had touched him in that fashion.

One Wednesday, near Talissieu, the corpse of the rural policeman was discovered in a mulberry hedge. In the course of a twilight patrol, his shirt had been caught on the thorns; certain that he had been harpooned by the sarvants, the poor devil had lashed out, but the brambles had wrapped their claws around him and fear had killed him; his expression clearly showed that he had died of fright.

Although every dwelling was full of occupants, most of the villages seemed to have been evacuated. The streets resonated here and there with the passage of a group. Sometimes, in their oppressive silence and emptiness, one brave and bold individual would slide along the walls with the face of man in perdition—and like everyone else, he lifted his eyes to Heaven, not to pray but to maintain surveillance, for everyone had less expectation of salvation from the Heavens than of peril.

The countryside was deserted. A few flocks, guarded by groups of children, were still in the meadows; at distant intervals, phalanxes of laborers worked the fields. A lugubrious meditation overhung the faint songs and strained laughter. To complete the misery, the month of June was overcast, interminably rolling clouds intercepting the sunlight. Every day, though, processions flowed out of the churches, composed of crowds in mourning-dress, and prayers were said imploring God to put an end to a scourge that could not even be clearly defined. As usual, terror encouraged conversions. One priest, having researched the old Medieval formulas, carried out exorcisms.

The further away one went from Bugey in any direction, the more the emotion was attenuated, as might be expected in frontier regions. The region was a hearth of dread, which radiated over the land and whose intensity decreased with distance. Outsiders, whose were still not anxious on their own behalf, were living in perfect tranquility, and in many distant States people still took the sarvants for a hoax.

One unimaginable thing is that Maxime—a guest at Mirastel, so severely tested in his affections by the general misfortune—was in the ranks of the skeptics, as unmoved as if he were living at the antipodes. His firm common sense, as a mariner and soldier, baulked at the supernatural. He refused to admit it—and as the supernatural seemed to be the only explanation of the facts, Maxime was not far from denying the facts themselves, if not in their reality at least in the appearances they presented. He remained convinced that everything would be explained *naturally* when the bandits demanded money to return the captives safe and sound. In his view, the sarvant's only martyrs were the nervous individuals slain by fear. He had tried hard to take the stories of flying men and eagles no longer flying seriously—stories of a world turned upside-down and a saturnalia of creation—but he had not succeeded, and privately considered them to be theatrical trickery, the machinations of some of illusionist, or tall tales.

In spite of everyone's remonstrations, and in spite of his mother's anxiety, he often went out on the mountain alone and painted water-colors from nature. He said that he needed to practice in order to execute the color plates for a treatise on ichthyology. He showed off his confidence with extraordinary insouciance, and never missed an opportunity to get away, no matter how briefly. When there were journeys to be undertaken, he took responsibility for them, and it was he and the mechanic who took the big white motor-car—which he delighted in driving—to fetch provisions.

Maxime took the vehicle to Belley on the second Thursday in June, the stocks of calcium carburate being in need of renewal—for they had decided to remount the two searchlights, and every night, for the present, their double beam shine from the top of the tower, making it resemble a fantastic windmill with capricious fiery sails. He was on his way back to Mirastel as dusk fell. As he emerged from Ceyzérieu—which stood on a ridge facing the château, on the far side of the marshy plain—he was suddenly carried away by the beauty of the view.

A sea of mist submerged the depths. Villages—even their bell-towers—had disappeared. The vapors elevated their imponderable felt as far as the line of manor-houses. The setting sun, monarch of gold and shade, silhouetted the Colombier superbly, making its ridges stand out and carving out the hollows of its ravines. The mounting darkness had already conquered the base of the rump, but the high crags were still flamboyant. A heavy cloud plumed the summit, making it resemble the crater of a volcano. There was something antediluvian about the landscape.

Maxime imagined that he was living hundreds of thousand years earlier, when the waves covered the plain and the mountains jetted flame. The Moon was rising to his right from the heights of the Chautagne, enormous and deep red in color, like a lukewarm prehistoric Sun—and he thought about primitive humans, prey to the multiple anguish of a world they did not know, unfortunate victims of inexplicable elements, every manifestation of which must have seemed supernatural to them, who were doomed to die convinced that they had lived amid prodigies.

The Moon spread carmine tints across the surface of the fog.

The automobile went down the slope and plunged into the stagnant mist.

The fog was quite dense. The road vanished from sight ten meters in front of the hood. He changed down into second gear, passed over a small bridge, made a left turn and went alongside the invisible meadows of Ceyzérieu. After the bridge at Tuilière, he was forced to slow down even further; the winding road was full of hazards.

In the whitish half-light, the spinneys loomed up as a succession of indistinct masses, which distance blurred accordingly. The little marshy clearings were fuming gently.

Suddenly, Maxime braked hard and seized the mechanic's wrist in a tight grip.

"Look! What's happening down there?"

In front of them, in the depths of the fog, very close to ground level, a monumental elongated shape—a sort of large spindle, like the silhouette of a dirigible balloon—was gliding sinuously along, briskly and rapidly, between the clumps of trees. It disappeared into the mist, which its passage had disturbed, and which moved in its wake in nonchalant swirls. It was merely a glimpse.

"Did you see it?" demanded Maxime, overcome by surprise.

"Yes, Monsieur Maxime. It's a big balloon. How rapidly it moves! Ninety, at least!"

"For sure…ah, we have the truth!" cried the young man, as he set off again. "I know it now!"

"Ah! Perhaps that was how Mademoiselle was abducted…"

"What? You didn't see, then? You didn't notice anything odd?"

"No, Monsieur Maxime."

"Come on—the gondola? *There wasn't any gondola!*"

"Does Monsieur Maxime think so?"

"I certainly do think so."

"Didn't see—moving too fast…"

"Didn't you hear anything? Me neither. Mind you, the car's motor was making a racket, and shaking."

"Right! Monsieur Maxime let it race when he declutched so quickly. Finally, we're coming out of this cotton wool—which is no bad thing…"

Indeed, the automobile was climbing the slope toward Mirastel and soon emerged into the evening light. Maxime was able to observe things at his leisure.

The sea of fog was quite motionless. No wake disturbed it. The risen moon, reduced and paler, now imparted nacreous streaks to it. The immense atmosphere was only haunted by bats. As far as the eye could see, there was no balloon in flight. The furtive aeronef, which seemed to be steering without a crew, like a phantom dirigible, was doubtless still gliding beneath the vaporous expanse, which extended as far as the eye could see.

Maxime reached Mirastel and pulled up in the main courtyard. He was astonished to find his relatives and all the domestics gathered there around a four-wheeled cart, furnished with a massive box, whose owner was speaking animatedly. Maxime recognized Philibert, who held the fishing concession at the Lac du Bourget. Every Thursday, the man went from house to house bringing the Friday fish, and he was he who supplied the ichthyologist-oceanographer with the subjects of his experiments and the models for his plates.

Philibert was making a speech, and Maxime observed the serious and attentive expressions of Robert Collin and Monsieur Le Tellier, who were listening to him. No one, moreover, took any interest in the return of the automobile. Having advised the mechanic to keep quiet about the dirigible, the son of the house went over to the fisherman and asked him to begin his story again. It was not ordinary, and dated from the same day.

Philibert's house was situated close to Conjux, on the shore of the lake. He had come out that morning at about five o'clock to go "furnish" his mare, and had paused by the lake momentarily, for he liked to contemplate his fishing-ground.

The water, sparkling in the dawn light, was smooth and transparent. The fish were swimming close to the surface.

Suddenly, though, the mirror-like placidity had been broken. Some distance from the shore, Philibert saw something forming in the water like an instantaneous, fugitive hollow…and from the bottom of the hole leapt the most magnificent pike imaginable. The fish sprang up with a formidable bound, out of its element, *and did not fall back*. While the navel in the lake closed up again beneath a wave, it commenced surprising contortions. For three or four seconds, it lashed the air with its tail and its fins, and then it shot off, *flying above the waves*, as kingfishers do. It doubled the promontory on which the Château de Châtillon stood, and was lost to sight behind it.

Such was the story that Philibert told, much less succinctly. The domestics were hearing it for the second time, but they exclaimed in amazement again.

"You can imagine," the fisherman said, "that I rubbed my eyes! And it seemed quite frolicsome, that devil of a fish!"

"It was making violent contortions, though, wasn't it?" said Monsieur Le Tellier.

"Oh, yes—then. Writhing like a mad dog, damn it!"

Monsieur Le Tellier made a sign to Robert. "This bears a curious resemblance to the men at Châtel and the eagle of the Colombier…"

Maxime interrupted. "Come on, Philibert. You were seeing things. Did you really see it? Cross your heart?"

"I swear it."

But the oceanographer told Philibert that he knew the species of fish better than anyone, and assured him that no fresh-water fish was capable of flight.

"Well, Monsieur Maxime, is there any marine flying fish that can do what the pike did?"

"That, no—and their length never exceeds 30 or 40 centimeters."

"Well, I'm telling you that it was a pike! And I know them as well as anyone. A first-rate specimen. An old diamond, green and glorious, at least 40 pounds!"

"Lord Jesus!" cried the cook.

"Anyway," Maxime retorted, "in what fashion do you claim that it flew? Flying fish can only stay airborne for about thirty meters; they dive back into the water then take off again."

"No, no—mine *flew*. It made little jumps as it drew away, zigzagging briefly to the right and the left, and it stayed at the same height. If it dived back in, it was the other side of Châtillon, because I can certify that it stayed four or five meters above the water all the time."

Maxime laughed sarcastically. "And did you stay on the bank for a long time afterwards?"

"My word, no! I went to harness up right away, and empty the keep-nets into the fish-well." He changed his tone to say: "Except, ladies and gentlemen, that I told everyone about my adventure along the way—that's why I'm late. Night's fallen, and if you'll be generous enough to let me, I'll sleep here, because...it's not that I'm afraid, but..."

"That's understood," said Madame Arquedouve.

"I've brought you some lavarets, Monsieur Maxime."

"Thanks—put them over there to the left, please."

Having taken his father and Robert Collin aside, Maxime told them what he had seen in the fog. He maintained that the dirigible was the pirates' craft, by virtue of the original disposition that did not permit the gondola to be seen, and because of the skill required to travel so quickly through the fog, avoiding obstacles."

"How quickly was that?" said Monsieur Le Tellier.

"So quickly," his son replied, "that the balloon hardly had time, so to speak, to mask the trees in front of which it glided. It was like an express train, you understand: you can see the things behind it, and never cease seeing them, in spite of the opacity it interposes between you and them for the blink of an eye. Well, that was what it was like."

"What rapidity, indeed! But then, you were unable to make out any details, especially in the fog."

"A veil of thick muslin surrounding me would have had the same effect. One couldn't see anything but silhouettes at

129

the distance at which the autoballoon passed. I noticed...I thought I noticed the absence of a gondola. It was a colossal cigar, which scattered the mist around it."

"Larger than an ordinary dirigible?"

"Oh! No, I don't think so. In sum, it's definitely an improved aeronef, which flies away a top speed once a theft or abduction is accomplished. It entrusts itself to the mist in order to pass unnoticed, making use of fog as it makes use of darkness. The fact of having seen it here is a certain guarantee that it's the corsair, for me. You're convinced, I imagine."

"What about the fish?" said Monsieur Le Tellier.

"And the flying men?" added his secretary, with a caustic smile.

"The fish and the flying men? The fancies of naïve peasants! Brigadier Géruzon and Philibert the fisherman are superstitious, visionaries. Take note, furthermore, that Philibert thought he saw his pike wriggling as if contorting itself, as was said of the men at Châtel, Suggestion! Pure suggestion!"

"And the eagle?" Robert objected. "I saw that so-called vision myself."

"Agreed. You saw it, through your spectacles—gold-rimmed spectacles, even. Your sight and your imagination are overly rich."

"Don't joke, Maxime," his father went on. "Nothing's certain, to be sure. What I'm about to say is doubtless only a means of translating my thoughts, nothing more...in any case, it's by expressing the same idea in different forms that one succeeds in making it more precise, so as to judge it...but at the end of the day, everything is happening *as if* entities of every sort were being endowed, to put it bluntly, with the ability to fly, under the influence of some force or other, probably natural. I say *natural* because that force, having acted upon a bird—which scarcely had any need of it, since it could fly already—can only be a blind force of nature. Given that, what is astonishing in the fact that human beings, animated by evil instincts and pursuing some unknown objective, might profit from that suddenly-acquired faculty? What is astonishing about evil designs being engendered in the souls of honest men suddenly promoted to the status of lords of the air?"

"With your theory," Maxime replied, with a snigger, "you could explain the triple disappearance on the Colombier by Marie-Thérèse and my cousins flying off, without recourse to the hypothesis of kidnappers…"

"No," replied Monsieur Le Tellier, patiently. "In that case, they would have come back. Besides, the footprints in the snow reveal a drama, an abduction. No, that would be absurd—but I reply to you, even so, because it is scientific to examine all the arguments that present themselves."

"What do you make of my dirigible, then?"

"It's a balloon like any other. You aren't familiar with all the models…then again, you didn't see it clearly enough, because of the fog and its speed. In my opinion, it was piloted by one of those daredevils, those road-hogs who think the aerials routes belong to them. And that's it. What do you say, Robert? You seem perplexed…"

"Master…do you think, then, that my eagle was a veritable eagle?"

"Yes, because Philibert's pike was a real pike. From a distance, in the sky, a giant eagle or someone dressed as an eagle might, strictly speaking, be sustainable…but someone dressed as a pike? That's lapsing into absurdity. But it's getting dark now. Are you coming, Maxime? We're supposed to be on watch with the searchlights. Have you got the carburate?"

That night, the two guardians of the tower lighthouse, saddened by their lack of knowledge, meditated long and hard on science and ignorance…and the full Moon, at the height of its arc, seemed to them to be the mouth of a well of Babel, in whose depths human beings were agitating confusedly.

XVI. The Dirigible Again

"Come in! Oh, it's you. Robert! Good day."

"Good day, Monsieur Maxime."

"Your lordship in my laboratory—that's an event! What's brought you here this morning?"

Robert, visibly distraught, repeated listlessly: "An event!" And he added: "Quite a temperature, eh? Hot, for the season."

"There's going to be a storm."

Maxime, who was seated in front of a mechanical diagram, resumed drawing, wondering what the secretary's visit might signify.

The three windows in the rotunda were wide open, but it was so hot that they did not succeed in creating the slightest current of air. A chaotic mass of leaden clouds encumbered the sky, which was as tumultuous as an aerial battlefield, as immobile as a sky in a painting. Beneath it, earthly things took on an ashen reflection. The plain, bristling with poplars, seemed to be bearing arms, awaiting some memorable event or important person. It was a fine stage-setting for a tragedy.

Inside the laboratory, an unhealthy daylight whitened the glare of the aquaria and the glass cases. The fish—which were brightly lit, in order to enable Maxime the painter to capture their multitudinous nuances—maintained their positions in the water somnolently.

Robert went to the glass cases in which mimicry displayed its bizarreries. From a distance, some of the cases seemed to be full of branches, grasses and shoots; at closer range, one perceived that a certain twig was a cunning caterpillar, a certain patch of bark a wily moth, or a certain exotic leaf an ingenious bug. But there were not only animals disguised as vegetables; there were also animals costumed as other animals. Other cases, in fact, lodged butterflies pinned in pairs; each member of each pair resembled the other sufficiently to be mistaken for it, and yet one was poisonous to small birds whereas the other, being inoffensive, owed its survival in modern times entirely to its resemblance to its venomous double. Unfortunately, it must be said, because Maxime had been occupied with other pastimes since childhood, and had lost interest in these, time had greatly modified his preparations; all the greenery had faded, and many of the little corpses had been infected by mould. Now, many of the similar creatures were beginning to differ.

Robert pointed this out to the young man, and continued: "They're droll, all the same, these identities—a sort of zoological masquerade. The chameleon, in order to remain unperceived, can make itself red or green, according to whether it is set against a red or green background!"

"Oh, yes. It's the story of the lion, tawny against the tawny desert sands; it's the story of the bear, white against the white snow of the pole. All of that is mimicry. But why should these tricks interest you, the spectator of constellations?"

"Why not? There are presumably fish that dedicate themselves to mimicry?"

"Nature is full of examples," Maxime said, laughing. "Man himself cloaks the color of walls...but I see that you're quite attentive, Robert. Do you, perhaps, suspect the sarvant of donning a night-blue costume in order to..."

"What stupidity!" the secretary put in.

"This little museum provided me with a great deal of diversion once...it determined my vocation as a biologist. Today, I've got other cats to skin..."

"Is your work on the water-color plates going well?"

"Not bad," said Maxime, taking several of his works out of a box. "Oh, it's not Van Ostade or Jan Steen[17]...it's suffi-

---

[17] Adriaen Van Ostade (1610-1685) and Jan Steen (1626-1679) were Dutch masters contemporary with Rembrandt, whose work is in much the same vein. It is an odd comparison to draw, in this instance.

cient, that's all. For the moment, though, I've given up painting fish."

"Ah—dissection!"

"A certain amount of dissection, yes—but accessory to another, more captivating study. Am I boring you, Robert?"

"Not at all."

"You'll understand. It's for the museum of oceanography in Monaco. I'm trying to design an aquarium in which deep sea fishes can live *normally*. Our trawlers can easily catch them at a depth of more than 9000 meters, but decompression and the abrupt change of temperature damages them and causes them to burst. I'm trying to construct an enclosed living-space, in which the pressure and temperature are maintained. As you can see, I'm in the process of scribbling a plan involving pumps—but it's not easy...the invention will have many consequences. Think about it! To reconstitute the vital environment of such different creatures! To be able to observe their *authentic* habits. To see them light up with multicolored phosphorescence in the darkness in which the tank will remain plunged, as in the eternal night of the submarine regions!"

"Ah—that's what you're trying to do," said Robert.

Maxime, however, misinterpreted the excited tone of this interjection. He imagined that Robert was reproaching him for not employing himself with other, more urgent work. "Yes that's it," he replied, blushing. "And it's forgivable. I've also tried to penetrate the mystery of the disappearances—except, you know, I have my own idea about that. It'll be settled before long by the kidnappers themselves—the people in the autoballoon."

"Really? Really?" said Robert, completely absorbed in a reverie.

"Oh, come on, Robert, be frank! You're beating about the bush, talking about everything and nothing. What do you have to say me?"

"I beg your pardon...ah, yes...you were saying? Exactly, exactly... I've...taken on a mission, as you've deduced." He smiled. "A mission on behalf of Madame your mother. She's frightened by your temerity. For some time, you've been going out every afternoon on to the mountain, with your painting equipment. And, being unable to do anything herself, she's delegated me to come and see you…"

Maxime put his hands on Robert's shoulders. "You're very kind, old chap," he said, "but I'm *certain* now that it's a matter of a dirigible, and I reckon that in broad daylight, a man on the alert would be stupid to let himself be taken, just as he would be cowardly and contemptible to stay at home like a hare in its lair."

There was a silence, which Robert broke. "At least, then, follow my advice—dress in such a manner as to reproduce the appearance of one of the missing persons…"

Maxime burst out laughing. "But that's yet more mimicry! Honestly, Robert…"

"I assure you that it's necessary to be careful."

"Really! You're wasting your time, old chap. A student painter like me has too much need of practice—and the mountain is too beautiful! Sumptuous and ever-changing; at every hour of the day, on every day of the month, one would think it the canvas of a different master. I have an exquisite little model up there: a twelve-year-old shepherdess, who poses for me in a stunning setting in a magnificent location. Oh, she's not frightened, that one! She doesn't spare a thought for the sarvants. Besides, her brother César, a clear-headed young herdsman, stands guard during the sittings…look here, of chap—I present to you Mademoiselle Césarine Jeantaz. Not lacking in juice, eh?"

In the pale light he brandished a half-finished watercolor, which was, as he claimed, genuinely "full of life". In the middle of a herd of cows and a few goats, a young girl, sitting on a frock, was playing the accordion. Her delicate mouth, wide open, was suggestive of a song emitted at full volume.

"It's very pretty," Robert said, appreciatively. "But Madame your mother is extremely worried…"

"Tell her...oh la la! What a curse it is to have all these hens clucking! Well, tell her that I'll finish this pastoral study tomorrow, and I'll be well-behaved thereafter!"

"Why not today? I'm not a clucking hen, though, and I'm not joking. You know full well that I have an idea..."

"Spit it out, my dear chap—spit it out!"

"Alas, you wouldn't believe it any more that the flying men, the flying fish or the eagle flying without wings."

"You have no proof, then?"

"I only have good reasons. That won't be sufficient for you."

"In the end, though, Robert, if you know where my sister is...and the others...it would be criminal to remain silent. We have to go after them. Where can they be? Obviously, for my part, I haven't the slightest idea. Where is the bandits' lair? If only we had a means of seeing them flee in one direction or another! But they hide in the midst of dark nights, fogs, clouds. Look at that impenetrable vault of cloud—above that, the sarvants are free to fly around as they wish...*great gods, Robert! What did I tell you?*"

Standing up, his eyes shining and his arm extended toward the sky, Maxime pointed to a dot in the clouds.

Robert looked, excitedly. In one of the swirls of a large, sluggishly-moving, slate-grey cumulus cloud, an oblong shadow was discernible, diaphanous and phantasmal.

"The dirigible!" murmured Maxime, very quietly—as if he were afraid of frightening the vision away.

Robert shielded his eyes from the livid daylight. "Is that really the thing that you encountered?"

"It's definitely the same one—the gondola's invisible. And if it isn't the same one, what is it doing there, without moving, lying in ambush behind its cloud?"

"Hmm," said Robert, extremely interested.

"For it's definitely *behind* the cloud," Maxime continued. "What we're seeing is the shadow it casts. It's nothing but a shadow on a swirl of cloud. They think they're invisible.

They have no suspicion that their shadow is betraying them. Come on—admit that I was right!"

"Yes...yes, indeed," said Robert, with more politeness than sincerity.

"Ah! There's the shadow growing paler, because the wind's getting up and the swirl of cloud's disintegrating...there's nothing left."

A tempestuous gust of wind blew into the rotunda. The papers scattered, caught up in an eddy. The sudden shaking of branches was like the sound of the sea. The trees, becoming pallid as their leaves were inverted, bent before the force of the wind. Shutters clattered loudly. Dust-devils ran along the pathways. A vertical flash of lightning split the sky, and the clouds began to break up.

Maxime, with his hair blowing in the wind, was on the lookout for the flight of the cumulus clouds to expose the aeronef—or for the corsairs to throw off ballast in order to climb above the storm...but the dirigible had departed, without employing that means.

And the scenery became tragedy itself. The magnificence of the unleashed elements further magnified all the mysteries that were sensible there. The thunder rumbled, seemingly the din of the clouds racing pell-mell toward some unknown goal—and to complete the scene, a second lightning-bolt raced a zigzag course: the flourishing signature of the storm.

XVII. Assumption

Although the sky was still ominous and seemed to be keeping a further storm in reserve for the afternoon, Maxime—as much for the sake of bravado as personal inclination—took up his landscapist's apparatus and set off for the mountain, in spite of unanimous reprobation.

An hour later, wearied by the heat and his own diligence, he perceived the herd of ruminants and their young guardians in the distance.

The pastureland was both grandiose and cheerful. The hemmed-in meadow formed a vale, gracefully hollowed out like the curves of a garlanded hammock. One of its edges rose up in a rocky wall, launching forth to continue the mountain; cyclopean crenellations, mingled with brushwood, cut out its crown. The other side, much less steep and bounded by the edge of a wood, inclined almost immediately in the other direction, its plane of rocks, green oaks and giant box-trees declining all the way to Mirastel. Innumerable narcissi perfumed the luxuriant pasture. It was strewn here and there with grey outcrops of rock, and on one of them, where her brother César had just perched her, Césarine Jeantaz had already taken up her pose and was fingering her accordion, chanting a waltz— for everything that peasants sing becomes or remains a chant, whether it be *Viens Poupoule*, the *Marseillaise* or the *Dies Irae*. She interjected her "Bonjour, Monsieur!" between two notes, and César bowed to the *Moncheu*.

Maxime was soon installed on his camp-stool, in the shade of the first trees of the wood, with the boy by his side.

"Keep a careful lookout!" he said, to salve his conscience.

"Have no fear!" replied the indoctrinated César, in Savorêt. "I'll see them coming!"

The exquisite girl let her tiny feet dangle, in their coarse clogs with lime-wood soles. An old straw hat shaded the blonde shock of her hair. Between her red hands, the accordion stretched, and then folded up, marking out with the same lively rhythm the indefatigable sequence of monotonous songs. Around her, the cows and the goats dispersed, sounding their bells—and the bells of the narcissi pealed out their perfume.

"Keep a careful lookout!" Maxime repeated, astonished by his own suspicious unease.

César's eyes never quit the cloud-laden sky, which seemed to slide by in a single piece, under the pressure of a furnace-wind. Sometimes the crenellations of the wall were confused by a cloud lower than the others.

At the sound of a violently-agitated cow-bell, Maxime looked away from the singer.

"Hey!" said the herdsman. "What's got into Rodzetta?"

Rodzetta was a russet goat, which, having drawn some distance away, came back at a gallop, bounding and bleating. Did it not....did it not have the appearance of fleeing? Of being pursued?

Maxime raised his eyes, and was reassured. The sky was deserted; it was still flowing uniformly, like an inverted river of molten lead, low and warm, but deserted. Césarine sang competitively...but her chant was abruptly transformed into a piercing cry. The accordion fell silent, and dropped...

Standing up on the rock, gesturing madly, as if convulsed by an attack of epilepsy or a sinister attack of St. Vitus' Dance, the little girl struck out at the air in every direction, uttering frightful howls. Her cries and the panicked tintinnabulation prevented Maxime from hearing the sarvants humming, but he sensed their proximity by the vibratory disturbance of his rib-cage...

The sky, the vale, and the wall were deserted, however! He was about to hurl himself forward to assault the rock and rescue the child when an unexpected spectacle petrified him, mouth agape with terror and surprise. A sibylline delirium still possessed the girl. Horribly pale, a frail pythoness maltreated by rapture, fighting against the sudden malaise that was brutalizing her, *she was now lifted up several centimeters above the monolith, with nothing there to hold her up!*

Then, all of a sudden, she stopped screaming, doubtless due to the effect of fatigue; her voice was no longer audible. She was still trying to make herself heard; she seemed to be howling, but no sound emerged from her mouth! And as the herd had fled, the velvety nocturnal hum droned at its leisure.

Maxime drew upon all his muscles and all his strength in an effort to master the fright that was paralyzing him. Alas—a lamentable marvel!—before he could move. Césarine Jeantaz, projected with incredible force, rose up into the sky like a ball, and disappeared.

The opaque continuously-flowing cloud continued in its course. A tumult was produced therein, and then died down— and that was all. The misfortune had unfolded with such promptitude that the accordion released by Césarine was only just coming to a stop among the narcissi.

Maxime recovered from his stupor then, but fear still gripped his entrails. Confronted by that prodigious outrage, he—the naval officer, hero of many a skirmish with the Tuareg, who had fought with a smile on his face against murderous water and deadly fire—ran away with his hands over his eyes, leaving behind his camp-stool, his canvas, his palette and little César fainted on the grass.

He fled directly through the sloping wood, for the best path was too much of a detour, in his view. The wretch hurtled down the precipitous slope, stumbling, rebounding, grabbing hold of trees, sliding over flat rocks and provoking falls of stones—which preceded him, accompanied him and followed him, with the result that his flight became a landslide.

Beneath him, however, the roofs of Mirastel grew visibly larger.

He arrived soaked in sweat, livid and shivering, with bloody scratches, bare-headed, and his clothes in tatters. He ran into a room where his relatives and Robert were gathered around a samovar, and while they all ran to meet him, he collapsed and started sobbing, mortally ashamed to have been so conceited and so cowardly.

He was sat down in an armchair. Madame Le Tellier put her maternal arms around him—but he could not distinguish anyone.

He made gestures of powerlessness and pity, and repeated hectically, in the midst of his tears: "Marie-Thérèse! Oh my God! What have they done to her? Where is she? Oh it's frightful!"

His father made him drink a cup of tea generously laced with rum.

"Come on, my lad—what's happened? Tell us."

Maxime told them. He finished up by admitting his cowardice—and then gave way to despair, as before. He struck himself on the forehead with a feverish fist, saying that he wanted to go out again, to rush to the aid of the little Jeantaz girl...

Monsieur Le Tellier forbade him, and ordered that five peasants and four servants should be sent to accomplish that duty.

"We were hidden...hidden by the foliage," gasped the piteous Maxime. "That's why we weren't attacked!" Then, under the combined influence of rum and sadness, he said, tearfully: "She was gone, my God, like a popped cork! A poor little cork—my God! And her poor little voice, which was strangled...and suddenly broke off, so abruptly! And I did nothing! Oh! Nothing...!"

Above his head his parents exchanged anxious glances.

Finally, Monsieur Le Tellier came to a decision. "This is no time for weeping," he said, severely. "It's a matter for discussion and understanding. This disappearance is identical to that of your sister and your cousins—let's work on that basis. Firstly, are you certain that it was an abduction?"

"Yes, yes! She fought. She resisted. And if it had been a blind force, César and I would have felt it too..."

"Good. But you mentioned a cork just now. Was the child really launched by an impulse originating on the ground?"

"No, no…it came from the air."

"Indeed, the snow on the Colombier revealed nothing of that sort…"

"She was lifted up," said the young man, mollified by alcohol and compassion. "She was lifted up like a poor terrified little holy Virgin, like a poor little puppet extracted from a Punch-and-Judy show by a string…"

"Yes, but you didn't see any string…any cable…?"

"There was nothing. Not even a thread."

"Very well…hmm! Strictly speaking, everything might be explicable… The sarvants' balloon must have been hidden in the clouds, where we know it likes to float without being seen. It's not difficult to imagine that they possess a means of seeing through them, probably with the aid of a tube—a simple tube piercing the layer of cloud beneath them, which must be too narrow in diameter to be seen from below… As for the capture *at a distance…*"

"I wonder, Papa, whether it *breathes* its victims in? I noticed a great tumult in the cloud, which might well have been caused by a vehement breath…a current of air traveling vertically upwards…"

"Did you feel it?"

"No, you're right. I didn't even feel the breeze, this time. I don't get it…oh, when one's seen such a…!" He became emotional again.

Monsieur Le Tellier hastened to occupy his son with other more or less fantastic possibilities. "The arrival of a projectile as large as a human body suffices to explain the tumult to which you alluded. It isn't that. It's better to suppose, not that the sarvants *suck up* their victims, but that they *attract* them by means of a special kind of magnet, in the same way that a true magnet attracts iron. *Animal magnetism* means something, after all! Moreover, there's something about the property of magnetic attraction—an occult something-or-other, and a tyrannical, active will—which always troubles the mind. They employ this method to draw up people, animals and anything that isn't fixed to the ground, you see. For the rest, they make use of the chisel, and they make their descents by night."

"Wasn't there a forester who claimed to have heard the chisel in broad daylight?" recalled Madame Arquedouve.

"Yes, mother—but it was in a solitary location, on the far side of a curtain of fir-trees."

"In any case," said Madame Le Tellier, "the mysteries are cleared up now, or at least reduced to one: all the abductions, including that of the unfortunate flying men, who were among the tormented rather than the tormentors...and the eagle and the fish too!"

"Exactly," Monsieur Le Tellier went on. "Géruzon and Philibert must have mistaken what was happening, the former to his Piedmontese and the latter to his pike. Otherwise, they'd have seen them rise up more steeply into the cloudy sky. Our adversaries possess a special electromagnet, and they maneuver it above the clouds—that's what's happening. But they're not imbeciles, damn it! To have found the animal magnet..."

"Accursed clouds!" cried Madame Le Tellier. "Without them..."

"Without them," the astronomer replied, "we would have seen even less than we have, for the sarvants would only operate by night."

Robert was pacing back and forth, maintaining a stern silence. Monsieur Le Tellier searched his secretary's physiognomy in vain for some sign of approval; he found nothing there but concern.

"But *why*?" said Madame Le Tellier, taking her head in her hands. "Why are they carrying out these abductions?"

"And what becomes of the prisoners?" Today it was Maxime who moaned that.

"Where are they?" added Madame Arquedouve.

Without taking his eyes off Robert's face, her son-in-law hazarded: "Oh, they can't be far away—doubtless in some retreat in the Alps or the Jura. The relative narrowness of the haunted zone seems to indicate that the sarvants don't stray far away from Bugey."

"We must find it!" said the blind woman.

"But how do we track them down? They're ungraspable, transient; one hardly even hears them…"

"*Listen!*" cried Maxime, haggardly. "*Listen! The hum!*"

A similar frisson ran along everyone's spine.

"My poor child!" said the grandmother. "It's a hornet you can hear through the open window."

Madame Le Tellier mopped Maxime's brow with her handkerchief. "Talk about something else, I beg you," she implored. "It's impossible to rest taut nerves…"

"We must find it!" repeated the secretary, as if in a dream, marching furiously.

Madame Le Tellier stopped him in his tracks and woke him up, saying: "Doubtless, with his airplanes, Monsieur d'Agnès will be able to catch sight of these bandits and pursue them to the entrance of their cave or their fortress! We've just received a letter from him, and…"

"That's true!" said the astronomer, with feigned joviality. "The letter even encloses an indescribable telegram from that Monsieur Tiburce… Here, read this, my boy. That will change your mind. My word! That Monsieur Tiburce is the silliest Nigaudinos[18] there ever was!"

Maxime read.

---

[18] Nigaudinos, whose name is a derivative of *nigaud* [simpleton], is a character in the farcical drama *Pied de mouton* [literally "sheep's foot," but more familiar as the name of a kind of mushroom] (1806) by Alphonse Martainville and Louis-François Ribié, which became an archetype of French theatrical *féerie* [fantasy]. The most famous scene in the play is one in which Nigaudinos fights an absurd duel with Gusman, his rival for the affections of the heroine Leonora.

XVIII. A Letter and a Cablegram

(Item 397)
Letter from the Duc d'Agnès to Monsieur Le Tellier
40, Avenue Montaigne.
June 9, 1912.
Dear Monsieur,

It was a month ago, to the day, that I left Mirastel, leaving you so desolate. I have worked hard since then, but it was not until yesterday that I finally became sufficiently hopeful to have the courage to confide in you.

Assuredly, I am not without anxiety on the subject of this legendary dirigible that Maxime has, you tell me, seen in the fog and which does not seem to require aeronauts. Your description reminded me of telemechanical torpedoes: those little vehicles of catastrophe that can be successfully steered from a distance without wires. Why, indeed, should there not be analogous balloons, whose various mechanisms are controlled at a distance by a captain above suspicion? That would complicate our task—for, assuming that we might take possession of the deserted balloon, what indications would such a capture give us as to the identity and domicile of the sarvants?

Fortunately, nothing is certain. Besides, the machine that we are about to build—our hunting airplane—will, I hope, *be quite remarkable. It is, alas, no more than a hope. This is how things stand, though: yesterday, my chief of construction, the pilot Bachmès, had a meeting with an engineer who claims to have discovered a motor powered by atmospheric electricity. To capture this potential of nature, to extract the all-powerful volts from its vast source, is a chimera that has been pursued for a long time, as you know; it would reduce fuel consumption almost to zero, the machinery to a negligible weight, and would, above all, produce a* miraculous velocity.

If the invention is not a hoax, and if it is really sufficient to turn a propeller and stabilize a current-transformer, we shall buy the patent, and we shall construct it immediately. That will be done quickly, I think—but what is "quickly" when one is anxious? What is happening to the missing individuals? Thirty-four days! *Where is Mademoiselle Marie-Thérèse? Oh, my dear Monsieur, how I wish I were at my post as an aerial scout, to find out* where, how, who *and* why?

What a terrible thing waiting is. I spend my day in the workshops of Bois-Colombes, where I have made so many fruitless experiments—and I stay there, pawing the ground, conscious of the time wasted. Would you believe that I sometimes envy the fate of Tiburce? He, at least, has a precise goal, vain as it might be, and he is ceaselessly employed in trying to attain it. He has the solace of action...but the cruel disappointment that is waiting for him will drive him mad! I enclose herein a cablegram from him, which I've just received. It's not the first news he has sent me; he sent me a Marconigram from mid-ocean, the day after his departure, simply to notify me of it. Since then, I've received nothing. Perhaps seeing so much foolishness packed into in so few words will plunge you into an astonishment that will make you forget momentarily the precariousness of our situation. It is, unfortunately, the only advantage we can obtain from the enclosed dispatch.

I beg you, dear Monsieur, to give my good wishes to Madame Le Tellier, etc.

François d'Agnès

P.S. A considerable effervescence is rife in all the airplane construction-yards, especially those of the State. There is a search going on for an apparatus appropriate to this new mission: the pursuit of aviators uncatchable by virtue of their speed. Rumor has it that some of them are departing on reconnaissance flights over Bugey with presently-existing, entirely inadequate machines—famous names are cited. We shall do better than that. Have patience and courage.

F.A.

(Item 398)
Cablegram from Tiburce to the Duc d'Agnès
San Francisco, June 6, 1912.

All well. Have not yet caught up with H but am certain M-T is with him. Have learned that H accompanied only by men. Deception. Crude stratagem, anticipated. Besides, indisputable calculations prove M-T with H, as is HM. New fact: evidently went with him voluntarily. Why? Mystery. Clarification soon. Have departed for Nagasaki. Am embarking this evening for Japan. Their precipitation suspect. Your stupid sarvant stories have reached here. Are making San Francisco smile. Respectful homage to your sister.

Tiburce

XIX. The Tragic Hornbeam

The discovery was made about three hours after dinner.

It was June 19. Madame Arquedouve and Monsieur Le Tellier had gone to visit Dr. Monbardeau in the automobile. Robert Collin was in Lyon, making purchases that he considered to be urgent. Madame Le Tellier had stayed at Mirastel with her son.

Maxime's nervous state still required a good deal of care; he refused, moreover—with an unhealthy obstinacy—to leave the grounds. In the beginning, he had not even wanted to go out of the château, and now it was only on the insistence and the prescription of his uncle that he consented to take a little fresh air and exercise. Twice a day, at 10 a.m. and 2 p.m., he went for a walk on his mother's arm, taking 100 paces beneath the hornbeams. That way, he said, they were sheltered from the Sun. The truth was that they were sheltered from the sarvant, the vault of foliage hiding the strollers from any sky-based gaze. Such precautions might have seemed childish, since there was no longer any cloud, and since the walks were also taken in the broad southern daylight in a populous place—but those who laughed at Maxime had not seen the Assumption of the little Jeantaz girl.

And so it was that Madame Arquedouve and Monsieur Le Tellier were returning from Artemare, having raised the canopy for reasons of prudence and traversed the deserted countryside in that fashion. They arrived home. The automobile turned, went through the gate, and was engulfed by the gallery of verdure, shady and pinpricked by sunlight.

It suddenly came to an abrupt halt, with a squeal of brakes and a skidding of locked wheels.

"Eh? What's up?" said Madame Arquedouve, huddled in the back seat.

Thrown forward by the sudden stop, Monsieur Le Tellier saw Madame Le Tellier collapsed on the ground in the middle of the avenue, two meters from the front bumper, staring at him with the eyes of a madwoman. She looked like a simple-minded beggar-woman. Hatless, her bodice ripped beneath her arm, she had not budged as the automobile approached; nor did she budge as her husband got out. When she was lifted up, supported by him and the chauffeur, she remained limp and tremulous.

Monsieur Le Tellier carried her to the car.

"It's Luce, Mother," he said. "She was there. I don't think she's hurt, but she's extremely upset…"

From the sound of his voice, although he attempted to keep it level, Madame Arquedouve grasped the gravity of the situation.

"Who are you?" stammered Madame Le Tellier. "Max-ime…is no longer here, you know. I have no more child-ren…no more, no more…"

Until they reached the perron, no one had the strength to speak. They were devastated by this new disaster and by its effect on the mind of the unfortunate mother. The astronomer sent someone to fetch Doctor and Madame Monbardeau, and then the invalid was put to bed.

Prostrate as she was, Madame Le Tellier soon became painfully overexcited. She babbled incoherently, made incom-prehensible gestures, and spoke continuously about her son and an inexplicable "calf." From time to time, she put her hands to her sides or threw them out in front of her, as if to escape from a grip or defend herself against an attack.

"The calf! The calf that glides!" she murmured. "Ha! Don't squeeze me! Don't squeeze me! Who's squeezing me? Who's squeezing me, then? Let me go! Maxime, get away! Ah! Aaaah! We have to get away. This is what we have to get away from! Quickly! We're covered up here…yes, my child, well-covered beneath the hornbeams… Like Marie-Thérèse… He's with her, in the sky. It's the calf that carried him off. It's not an angel—it's a calf!"

Monsieur Le Tellier, bewildered by this wandering, and fearful of the disturbance that must be fomenting in the mind that was giving birth to it, tried to obtain at least a semblance of rational progression. He asked questions, but one might have thought that Madame Le Tellier did not hear them. God only knows, however, how desperate the astronomer was to discover something, for this abduction from beneath a hornbeam plantation, in broad daylight, from a cloudless sky, in a busy park, and the subsequent salvation of Madame Le Tellier—a favor granted or attempt failed, so contrary to the sarvants' habits—were veritable phenomena.

"Come on, Luce—what calf are you talking about?"

"It's gone! It's gone!" the crazy woman moaned.

"You say that it was gliding, this calf. How?"

"Let me go!"

"Yes, you've been rudely grabbed…your blouse is torn as if by fangs, to the right and the left…but there's no one here any longer. Calm down. Don't keep making that gesture, my dear Luce—there are no more sarvants."

"Maxime! Maxime!"

"Well, how did Maxime go? Through the leaves of the arbor, wasn't it? As if drawn into the sky? Did the foliage prevent the dirigible balloon from being seen? How did Maxime go?"

"It's a calf!"

Monsieur Le Tellier stepped back, alarmed for the first time by the problem of the madwoman confronting him. Alas, there was nothing more of his wife in the bed than a poor soulless body, a miserable half of a human being.

The scientist looked at her from the depths of his thought, and said to himself: *Science knows no more about the minds of the insane than it does about the prisoners of the sarvants. They are both atrocious disappearances. And yet, since human beings have souls, they accept, with neither fear nor blasphemy, that—by one means or another—one of these souls might be stolen by an immaterial thief, just as those of my children seem to have been. In the same way that every day brings further abductions in Bugey, every day brings new psychic abductions to the world. Where are they all? Some of them might come back. Where is Lucie's? Where are Marie-Thérèse, Maxime, and all the others...and will they ever come back?*

The doctor arrived, and quieted his sister-in-law by means of some drug. Madame Monbardeau took up a position beside her. Before replacing her for the night at the invalid's beside, Monsieur Le Tellier was able to discuss the event with Robert Colin, who had just come in, bringing back several well-wrapped packages from Lyon, about which no one thought to interrogate him.

Shattered by the double abomination, the secretary opined: "Any significant items of information we can get from Madame Le Tellier will be precious. At the risk of tiring her slightly, we must try...in everyone's interest. The hypothesis of some sort of magnet, which you advanced the other day, wasn't implausible, but the place occupied by Monsieur Maxime and his mother, under the hornbeams, has just falsified it. They were invisible to individuals situated above them...individuals of any sort, it seems to me...unless..."

"Let's be clear, Robert. Your behavior, in all this, remains secretive. I don't doubt for a moment the excellence and the purity of your speculations...but in the final analysis, do you *know* anything? Have you *deduced* anything? If so, for pity's sake tell me—has today's frightful episode confirmed your hypotheses or not?"

"I can't say that it has crippled them. It has no bearing on the essential question—which is to say, the identification of the sarvants—whose solution I have glimpsed very vaguely. Given that my knowledge is even vaguer with respect to the *method* of abduction, I wouldn't be at all displeased to acquire supplementary indication on that matter. As for the sum of my conjectures...it's so nebulous that I lack terms specific enough to explain it. It's so terrible, too, that I dare not say anything until I'm certain...and in order to be certain, it will be necessary to go and see. I'm sure, too, that such an experiment will bring many surprises of the nastiest sort. In any case, Master, even if it's to the detriment of her health, try to obtain some precise information from Madame Le Tellier..."

"If you think it's so important...I'll ask Monbardeau whether it's a superfluous cruelty. She's asleep now."

"Leave it until tomorrow," Robert conceded.

Before dawn, however, he knew what there was to be known.

Monsieur Le Tellier is watching over his wife. By the attenuated glimmer of a candle, the astronomer observes the malevolent sleep that shakes the invalid with the effects of nervous discharges.

Two o'clock sounds.

She turns over, wails, utters inarticulate noises, stammers the ghosts of lugubrious speech-acts that are the soliloquies of nightmare. Her eyelids open on dilated pupils. She tries to get up, and does so, haggard and tremulous, sitting upright though still asleep.

Monsieur Le Tellier goes into action. He tries to make her lie down, to make her rink a spoonful of medicine. She looks at him, and says: "Maxime!"

"Come on, my love—it's me, Jean!"

"Maxime, are you coming for a walk in the hornbeam plantation?"

"Lie down and go to sleep, dear Lucette. It's time, it's night..."

"It's time for your walk, yes, Maxime—two o'clock chimed just now. We'll be fine in the shade. Give me your arm, and let's go for a walk in the wood while the wolf—oh, no, not the wolf!—while your grandmother and your father are at Artemare."

She seizes her husband's arm. She tries to get up again. In spite of the violent suffering he is experiencing, Monsieur Le Tellier would like to take advantage of the odious opportunity that is offered to him to *find out*—but he does not want the somnambulist to suffer at all.

She is still trying to get up.

Then, an inspiration leads him to say to the unfortunate, whose voice is choking: "Mama...it's me, Maxime—and we're underneath the hornbeams..."

Now, there is nothing more to do than listen.

"It's nice to go for a walk," says the sleeper, moving her legs beneath the bedclothes. "Here we are at the end of the lane, near the gate. Let's go back. Half a turn...look, Maxime, how pretty it is, that green nave, so cool and vast, with that dazzling hole at the end, that portal 'mad with brightness.' Yes, you're right, 'tunnel' is more accurate than 'nave.' The hornbeam grove has the dimensions and the shade of a tunnel.

"Ah! What's that, at the far end, in the sunlight, coming toward us? A calf? You say that it's a calf? Hey—how quickly it moves! But Maxime, its feet aren't moving...in fact, they're not touching the ground. It's gliding through the air. Oh! It's coming toward us at top speed, this calf! There's no need to be afraid? You say that, but you're as white as a sheet. Here it comes!

"It's charging us! Without moving! It's frightful! Aaaaaah! Let me go! Something's got hold of me, Maxime! From behind...it's squeezing me... Oh, it's let me go...what's got hold of you? What's wrong with you? It's that calf, that motionless calf! Oooooh! Don't scream! Why those disordered movement? No, no, don't scream, my little one, my little one...!

"Finally, you're not screaming any longer...finally. Thank you. Why are you hanging on to that creature? Aaaaah! It's lifting you up! The calf...! Fleeing backwards under the hornbeams...stop! Stop it! Scream, then, Maxime! Scream! Call for help...! Nothing...ah! Down there in the sunlight, he's turning round... Help! Help!

"Disappeared...like Marie-Thérèse!

"Who are you? You know, Maxime...he's no longer there. I have no more children...no more, no more, no more...

"The calf! The calf that glides!"

Madame Le Tellier struggled desperately. The noise she made brought her sister and the doctor, who had stayed at Mirastel, running to her bedside. Monsieur Le Tellier left it to them to watch over the lamentable delirious creature, who could no longer do anything but repel phantoms as she saw that frightful scene again in disconnected fragments. Without losing a moment, he went to Robert's room.

In order not to be surprised to find his secretary still awake at such an hour, as the light of dawn filtered through the shutters, Monsieur Le Tellier truly had to be sunk in the uttermost depths of his being. At the time, he scarcely noticed that Robert hurriedly closed a glass-fronted cupboard, or that the cupboard was full of objects that presented the appearance of an optician's equipment, or that that floor of the room was buried by a profusion of recently-undone wrapping-paper.

Robert turned to him with an embarrassed expression. Uncomfortably, he stroked a large red ledger with copper latches, which was brand new.

Already, though, Monsieur Le Tellier was telling him how his wife had just re-enacted the abduction.

The little man heard him out without saying a word, then collected himself for a few minutes. "What incomprehensible things!" he said finally. "The sarvants are never inconvenienced for long! At 2 p.m.! That's impudent. The domestics must have heard them…"

"They say that they didn't—but I'm convinced, myself, that they're lying. Fear must have petrified them, when their duty was to go to the aid of my wife, who was crying out. That's what they refuse to admit, and that's why they deny having heard anything at all. We'll never get anything more out of them."

Robert Collin reflected again, and asked: "Was there anyone in the fields who can tell us what the state of the sky was at that precise moment?"

"No one. On the other hand, in Artemare, I took note of the extraordinary sight of the deserted road and the abandoned crops. We were the only ones outside—but Madame Arque-

154

douve no longer has her sight, and the extended canopy completely blocked the view of the sky, for the chauffeur as well as me."

"That's regrettable. Ah! Which dress was Madame Le Tellier wearing?"

"A black one, very simple, with no pattern," the astronomer replied, slightly taken aback.

"No hat?"

"No."

The secretary took out his notebook, consulted it, and said: "Master, everything's clarified with regard to the abnormal liberation of Madame Le Tellier. She has hennaed hair, and she was dressed as if in mourning; her appearance was therefore similar to that of Mademoiselle Charras, abducted on the eleventh of June in Chautagne, who had reddish-blonde hair and had just lost her mother."

"What do you mean about the similarity? For the love of God, tell me what you know. All this confusion! This calf that carried off my son! I'm losing my mind too!"

"Well," said Robert, compassionately, "I suppose…but then again, hold on! Really, I can't! Put yourself in my place: I only have vague suspicions. I told you that, Master: I won't speak until I'm certain of everything. But then, it's more than probable, other considerations might well prevent me from speaking…for fear of spreading panic…"

For fear of spreading panic? Monsieur Le Tellier said to himself. *Lucie's appearance confirms to the description of Mademoiselle…Something? Ah! This is a supremely incoherent discourse, damn it! Is it, by chance…hang on! What about that arsenal I glimpsed in the cupboard? And all this activity at three o'clock in the morning? Damn! Damn! Is he going mad in his turn…?*

He left the room in the midst of these disagreeable reflections—and we have to recognize that Robert's actions were increasingly giving him grounds to think that he might have lost his mind.

XX. Insanity

Two days later, Doctor Monbardeau—whose medical skill is justly renowned—certified that his sister-in-law's recovery was a mere matter of time and patience. Madame Monbardeau took up residence at Mirastel again in the capacity of nurse; and, although Madame Le Tellier manifested excessive sensitivity, although the slightest surprise electrified her and although five minutes could not go by without her making reflexive gestures as if to push someone away or talking about the inexplicable calf, a gradual but evident amelioration justified the doctor's prognosis.

It was an unexpected stroke of luck; the cerebral disturbance had been the final violence. Supplementary proof of that was obtained when, the invalid's hair having grown slightly, it was perceived that the new growth was white. All of her hair must have turned white, but until now the dye had prevented anyone from noticing. To accelerate the patient's convalescence, it was necessary that she, too should get some fresh air. While admitting that she needed it, however, no one would have permitted it during those detestable days—for, since Maxime's abduction, which had been perpetrated with a boldness, cynicism and skill as yet unrevealed, the Bugists no longer went out in the open without taking infinite precautions.

Even Monsieur Le Tellier forbade his relatives to go out. He was subject then to a second loss of morale, and abandoned himself to interminable meditation, less occupied with penetrating the mystery than considering his own distress. Once, when Madame Arquedouve asked him if he had discovered anything, he replied: "I've discovered that one should always love one's nearest and dearest as if they were destined to die imminently."

Robert's extravagances had ended up exhausting him. He was showing incontestable signs of mental alienation. By this time, fear had already disturbed his mind considerably. Was a contained and concealed terror beginning to ruin that splendid intelligence? One might have thought so.

His insanity had begun with an explosion of joy, an expression of constant and singularly inappropriate gaiety. After that, he visibly buried himself in somber recollections. Under the influence of an obsession, he undertook another journey, not to Lyon but to Geneva, and came back from Switzerland, on one of the hottest days of 1912, carrying a heavy fur cloak under his arm. From then on, nothing prevented him from going out every morning for long and alarming walks, which kept him out of doors until nightfall. He came in at 7 p.m. precisely, but the monomaniac vanished again immediately after dinner, then reappeared the following day.

And how he dressed! A burlesque equal to that of Tiburce himself! Clad in the costume of a tourist, with an extremely warm woolen fleece, with knee-length boots of thick leather, he set off with all manner of portable apparatus of the sorts carried by explorers. A little hunting-knife was suspended at his hip. A revolver-holster comprised a belt and a polished leather shoulder-strap. Crossed over his breast, the straps of a water-bottle and a game-bag overlapped those of a Kodak and an imposing pair of prismatic binoculars. On his back he had a green canvas rucksack, stuffed with mysterious objects, and an intriguing elastic band hung down from the sack. An otter-skin cap topped off his hairy sweat-suit, and the fur cloak only left his right arm in order to warm his left.

Thus harnessed, the pitiable weakling left Mirastel dressed as if for a polar expedition, and strode along the dusty roads beneath a Sun that might have pumped the ocean dry. The roads were no longer being maintained. Robert ceaselessly roamed their pot-holed terrain, only encountering a few carefully-sealed carriages and a few automobiles in a hurry to be elsewhere. Sometimes he had to jump over columns of ants, which were crossing the Republic's macadam, and sometimes he had to go around stony debris fallen from the mountain, which had been left in the middle of the road.

He often went to climb the Colombier and to wander there like a soul in torment or a stray poet, a lover of forests and summits. He seemed particularly careful to admire the views. His gaze went from one to another with remarkable celerity; none of the beauties of time and space escaped him. The Colombier had been the mount of snows, then of narcissi; soon it was the mount of strawberries. It was also that of grasshoppers, and Robert's footsteps prompted their strident leaps, like fugitive gymnastic vaults from here to there, this one red and this one purple. But the strange wanderer did not like that buzzing stridulation, which covered the meadows with a musical carpet, and he muttered periodically: "Oh, my God! Nothing but grasshoppers! A plague upon grasshoppers! Accursed grasshoppers!" Or some other monologue of that sort.

Impenetrable and serene, punctual and smiling, he came into the château's dining-room at the second stroke of the bell. At table, he made no reply to remonstrations and seemed quite happy about his pranks and whims. He was not seen again until the evening meal.

Monsieur Le Tellier noticed that he also went out at night, and wanted to confine him to the house—but the other warned him respectfully that he would escape at the first opportunity, never to return. Monsieur Le Tellier gave in. The poor man had begun to doubt his own judgment; he no longer knew whether he or Robert was the more reasonable, or whether duty compelled an incessant patrolling in search of the sarvant, however madly and randomly, with a thousand ridiculous, burdensome and theatrical—in a word, Tiburcian—eccentricities. The astronomer had to limit himself to quaking with fear during his secretary' absences; and he would have quaked even more if he had known that Robert possessed a method of deceiving the sarvants by means of a certain similarity of dress, but that his comic-opera costume bore no analogy with any of those that he would have been able to imitate!

Every time Robert went out, Monsieur Le Tellier wondered whether this would be the evening when he would not return—and the evenings were very slow in returning, although they returned just the same...as did Robert.

On Wednesday July 3, however, at 7 p.m., they started on the soup without him. His place remained a dramatic void between the blind woman and the madwoman. Monsieur Le Tellier, the doctor and his wife were exchanging taciturn glances when the butler gave the astronomer an unstamped letter.

Monsieur Le Tellier frowned, and went very pale. "Robert's handwriting!" he said, in a strangled voice. "Hold on...let's see.... *My dear Master, don't expect me for dinner. I've gone to the sarvants' lair. I'll bring you news of your daughter, whatever the cost. Count on me. Robert Collin.* The poor fellow! He's got himself abducted!" Then he asked the butler: "Who gave you this letter?"

"It was Monsieur Collin, Monsieur, a week ago. He told me that the first time he was late for dinner, even if it were only for a second, I was to give it to Monsieur."

The letter shook in Monsieur Le Tellier's fingers. "He's got himself abducted—voluntarily!" Madame Le Tellier began to get excited. Madame Monbardeau instructed him to be silent with a gesture. "He wasn't mad," he went on, paying no attention.

"What about that cloak, then?" asked Dr. Monbardeau. "Those furs?"

"Perhaps he thinks that the sarvant's lair is in the glaciers," suggested Madame Arquedouve.

"Undoubtedly," said Monsieur Le Tellier, thoughtfully. "The sarvants..."

The visionary stood bolt upright. "The sarvants!" she cried. Oh, who's squeezing me? Maxime!" Horrified, she strove to extract herself from the remembered hands that had gripped her under the hornbeams. She clenched her own arms in the places where the grip had bruised her through the torn fabric.

"There!" said Madame Monbardeau, reproachfully. "What did I tell you? Shut up, Jean."

But as he saw his wife indefatigably reproducing the scuffle of June 19, Monsieur Tellier reminded himself with a shudder that Robert had run into unparalleled danger of his own accord. Oh, the brave man, the hero! He had thrown himself, gladly into the grip of the formidable mystery; day after day and night after night he had had the superhuman courage to persist in his heroism and wait *patiently* for the infernal attack!

"He has no family, has he?" the doctor asked.

"No," said Monsieur Le Tellier, with a tear in his eye, "He only had ours...or rather, he only had a dream. Alas, I'm already talking about him in the past tense!"

Two days later, the Bugist postmen having been on strike since the visitation of Orges, the two brothers-in-law went to fetch the mail from the Artemare post office.

Monsieur Le Tellier unfolded the *Nouvelliste de Lyon*, addressed to Madame Arquedouve, and read:

(Item 417)

Members of the Alpine Club, who set out yesterday to climb Mont Blanc, discovered a long streak on the side of a long wall of snow, which seemed to be due to the friction of an enormous and resistant cylindrical object. One might have thought, they said, that a metal-clad automotive aerostat of the Zeppelin type had passed that way, brushing the wall in question. Might it be the track of the famous sarvants? Might it be the imprint of the mysterious dirigible twice sighted by the unfortunate Maxime Le Tellier? It is permissible to suppose that it might.

"There it is," said the doctor. "That's where they're based, Jean."

"But Calixte, how the Devil did Robert deduce that?"

"I hope they'll mobilize the Alpine troops and search the crevasses. No one's doing anything for us! What a lousy government!"

XXI. The Blue Peril

The mobilization of the Alpine troops had been an accomplished fact for some time. Under the pretext of maneuvers—in order, it appeared, to avoid a fresh outbreak of public panic—the administration had ordered military searches, and each garrison had taken up arms in turn. Bugey had been explored from top to bottom, without awakening any suspicion. The officers' reconnaissance missions were in accordance with the Sûreté's inquiries; the army and the police operated in parallel. Inspector Garan, putting his errors behind him, had cooperated many times in the shrewdest strategies. Neither in the Alps nor in Bugey, however, had any glimpse been caught of the sarvant.

The hovels of the suburbs, the cellars and sewers of the towns, the subterranean workings of old dungeons, the quarries, the chasms, the caves, the forests, the crypts of ruins and the catacombs of abbeys were explored without result. The robbers' lair remained an enigma. The dirigibles and airplanes ready to launch themselves in pursuit of the phantom balloon remained inactive, and those which patrolled the atmosphere above the bleak solitudes came back from the wild goose chase empty-handed.

At the moment when Dr. Monbardeau was demanding the mobilization of the Alpine forces and fulminating against the government, therefore, the work to which the State had devoted itself in Bugey and the surrounding areas has been under way for some time, with a discretion motivated not so much by the need not to alarm the citizens—it seems to us, on the contrary, that the sight of troops would have reassured them—as by the fear that it might all be a monumental joke. The Camelots du Roy,[19] for example, were capable of any

---

[19] The Camelots du Roy was a youth organization founded in 1908 as an auxiliary to the Monarchist movement Action

impertinence, when it came to making the present régime look ridiculous.

In truth, it had been decided that this State endeavor would continue to the end—but it produced several suggestive disappearances of advance sentinels and solitary agents, and they were obliged to cut the phenomenal hunt short in order to avoid refusals to obey orders and defections.

The existence of the sarvants was not officially recognized; the researches carried out throughout France, and even beyond, were even more carefully hidden—for, without knowing why their field of action was restricted to the Bugist regions, and extended so gradually, it was suspected that the brigands went a long way to deposit their captives. The frustration of local searches seemed to establish that.

Powerless to discover what was going on, and fearing the extension of an evil whose gravity became increasingly clear from day to day, the government threw away its mask and attempted to organize a protective system, with the aim of circumscribing the scourge. It decreed preventative measures—prophylactic dispositions, so to speak—applicable throughout the territory. The populations that had not been subject to the tyranny of the sarvants then began to fear it. It could only augment its empire insensibly, of course—but within it was the abomination of desolation.

The administrative services and social life were no longer functioning. The region was gradually being emptied of its inhabitants. Since the kidnapping of Mademoiselle Le Tellier and her cousins, every abduction had provoked further departures. Trains crammed full of peasants arrived in Lyon and Chambéry, and the Swiss border saw an exodus of French refugees. Panic suddenly took hold of them; to subsist, moreover, they sold their livestock at a knockdown price, some of

---

Française, initially—as its name implies, a *camelot* being a newspaper-seller—to hawk its propaganda-sheets in city streets, although their role soon expanded far beyond that service. The organization still exists.

them surrendering their fields and farmhouses, and they fled, glad to have found buyers. They were rich; others had not the means to get away—fifteen thousand, perhaps. The latter lived on nothing, barricaded in their houses as if in the depths of animal-dens. No one communicated with his neighbor; but news reached them somehow, transformed and magnified, redoubling their anxiety. Robert's eagle was the giant bat known as a "vampire" and Philibert's fish took on the form of a flying shark, a dragon or a tarasque of Gothic times.[20]

Around the condemned villages, the crops that no one harvested were going yellow. The grass in the meadows grew tall and thick; the vines became entangled with long flexible stalks and grass turned the surfaces of the white roads green. A deathly silence was everywhere.

Sometimes a vagabond risked a robbery. Bands of thieves also came forth in the hope of looting abandoned properties. Suddenly, though, horrible screams went up from inside houses or in the distant countryside: battles of men against mad dogs, or forgotten cats, or against rival gangs, against fear, or even against...no one knew what. After a while the looters no longer came. From that day on, the only human beings to be seen wandering in the fields and woods were wretched lunatics, whose number grew by the hour. They emerged from their voluntary jails under the domination of puerile ideas, products of fear and claustration. Half-naked, at a loose end, the unfortunates wandered randomly, nourishing themselves on grains and roots. The sarvants, rumor had it, chose some of them; the majority committed suicide.

It was not rare, in fact to find hanged men dangling from trees and signposts at crossroads, having fled from fear into death. Across the valley, a succession of pylons sustained the electric cables from Bellegarde to Lyon; almost all of them

---

[20] A tarasque is a mock-up of a monstrous creature paraded through the streets at Pentecost and on St. Martha's Day in a number of villages in the south of France, most notably Tarascon, from which it takes its name.

had served as ladders for desperate individuals who electro-cuted themselves by touching the cables. Charred mummies twisted in simian postures at the summits of these miradors, seemingly playing the fool between them. The rivers carried floating corpses, heralds of the plague of fear. The railway was a rendezvous of crushed bodies, over which a great stink hung. Thanks to the flocks of crows that descended upon the region, however, the charnel-house quickly became an ossu-ary.

Posterity will be astonished by such a debacle, because it will forget how human beings understood the calamity. It was no longer a persecution by bullies, no longer a stratagem of pirates. It was the end of the world. In anguish, people evoked the beasts of the Apocalypse that had been seen in the sky: a calf, an eagle, a pike. For them, the sarvant became the Exter-minating Angel, and they believed that Jehovah was beginning to depopulate the Earth, starting with Bugey.

Ten centuries before, the same alarm had spread. The ter-rors of the year 1912 were equal to those of the year 1000—and if they were less generalized, at least they had a *raison d'être*, while the others were the offspring of ineradicable fan-tasy.[21]

---

[21] Renard's narrator inserts a footnote here, which translates as: "On the night of May 18 and 19 1910, the end of the world was supposed to accompany the return of Halley's comet. Is it necessary to recall the number of suicides engendered by that prediction?" The panic in question was whipped up by the newspapers in anticipation of the Earth's passage through the comet's tail on May 18, when journalists given to wild conjec-ture recklessly wondered whether the atmosphere might be poisoned by a massive infusion of cyanide gas. Edgar Allan Poe had earlier written "The Conversation of Eiros and Char-mion" (1839), in which life on Earth is annihilated as a result of the planet's passage through a comet's tail, and the 1910 scare apparently inspired Arthur Conan Doyle to write *The Poison Belt* (1913).

It seemed that an epidemic was infesting that fraction of humankind. Indeed, the persecutors might carry you off unexpectedly, without anyone being able to do anything about it, as is often the case with cholera. As in times of cholera, the survivors maintained the expressions of pursued slaves, in which fear as forever imprinted. They did not even wonder where the missing persons had gone. No one doubted that they had been massacred. The women wept a little whenever they thought about them; that provided a fortunate trigger, and they found a momentary relief in their tears. Laughter was no more than a vague memory in the utmost mental depths of paradise lost. All hearts were constructed, especially by night.

The nights were spent listening, on the lookout for the notorious hum. All of them thought they could hear it. They perceived it by autosuggestion. And when dawn broke in its canicular splendor, roasting the innumerable carrion outside, then, through a gap in the door, a crack in the wall, or between two dislocated tiles, the poor folk would stare at the imperturbable sky, limpid and blue, streaked with swallows: the untrustworthy sky, with its mask of serenity. All day long, they contemplated that blinding azure. Their dazzled eyes saw colorless little undulating worms appear, which disappeared when you tried to look at them. They were frightening themselves with the blood-vessels of their own eyes.

The murmur of the season disguised itself as a redoubtable hum. Sixty times a minute, they thought they could distinguish something or other. Many claimed to have glimpsed the ascension of various creature and objects, climbing alone and vertically into the atmosphere—but they would not have sworn to it, strongly suspecting that they were poor sentries.

Mirastel was the last château still to be occupied. Madame Arquedouve and her daughter Lucie were hardly transportable, and Monsieur Le Tellier clung on to the idea that he would find his children there, where the sarvants had captured them. The departmental representatives took advantage of the circumstance and demanded a detailed report on the situation from him.

165

In the wake of that report, they wanted to apply a new defensive tactic, but the official delegates in Bugey only stayed there for a week. That hell tested the strongest wills, the worst ambitions and the most hardened braveries.

The entire Earth was then keeping watch on Bugey. It was a gangrenous patch whose horrid spread was fearfully tracked—an invasive ulcer so incurable that the entire world, with sweat on its brow and brooding eyes, kept an incessant check on the progress of the French cancer. The international press turned into a sanitary bulletin.

San Francisco was no longer smiling.

As the whole Earth kept watch on Bugey, the whole of Bugey kept watch on the sky. From one end of the region to the other, that was the only thing that mattered. People made light of everything but that. No one was interested in the fattening of pigs, the impending vintage, the withering hay, the flourishing rye, the propitious or unfavorable temperature, and any municipal quarrels. Fortune and poverty no longer counted for anything; politics had lost its importance. A war might have broken out, an invasion might have threatened the old world, or the yellow peril might have descended upon Europe—what would it have mattered?

Only one concern merited anxiety. Only one danger was worthy of being avoided: *THE BLUE PERIL.*

Part Two: Where. When. Who. Why.

I. The Square Patch

The Blue Peril! *Die Blaue Gefahr! Le Péril Bleu! El Peril Azul! Il Perile Azzuro!*—that journalistic term enjoyed the same success as its cousin, the word "sarvant." Its employment became universal, and it exercised a most curious influence upon the world's thinking.

The power of words knows no limits. The new evil had been designated as the Blue Peril because the aggressors came from the sky; soon, though—as if to verify the inanity of worldly investigations—by virtue of continually reading, saying and hearing "Blue Peril," people were no longer inclined to believe merely that the villains took refuge in a terrestrial stronghold after having utilized the sapphire highway, but that that the enemy was the sky itself.

A reasoning process was required to bring matters to this point. The immense difficulty of the searches was observed; attention was called to the myriads of explorers in the process of hunting the sarvants' hiding-place; and the number of places on the vast globe that might escape their perspicacity was calculated. Virgin forests, unclimbable mountains and caverns whose opening were almost imperceptible were considered, as were subterranean fortresses and submarine bases—but the idea of water led back to the idea of the air, and once again the calmest minds found themselves examining the sky as one keeps watch on a brigands' lair. It was a singular mistrust, and it was singularly widespread, since the astronomers allowed themselves to be drawn into it.

Yes, it is scarcely credible: the familiars of the ether, the confidants of Elohim, no longer envisaged the object of their study as it had previously been and should reasonably still have been. It did not matter that nothing had changed in celestial mechanics; more than one Laplace confessed the emotion that he had felt in considering the firmament, and the calculations of observatories overflowed with errors in the year 1912.

Monsieur Le Tellier followed the example of his colleagues. It is not that the sky had retained its former charm for him, nor that the astronomer felt obliged to work for the moment on professional projects; misfortune had brought his attention back to the affairs of this world, and since his departure from Paris, Monsieur Le Tellier had not directed the smallest optical instrument at any planet whatsoever. Sometimes, however, in the course of an enfevered evening, he leaned on a windowsill in the fresh air, looking out into the night, and meditated, not as a physicist reflects but as a desperate dreamer. He no longer saw the stars with a scientist's eyes, as universes about which he knew everything that a man of today could know; he saw them as brilliant points that had a magical aspect. The moons, the suns, Mars and Venus, Saturn, Aldebaran, Cassiopeia and Hercules were no longer, for him, objects of analysis and mathematical reasoning designated by letters of the Greek alphabet; they were auroral seeds scattered in the darkness—and now, most of all, he stared at the blackness between the stars.

The images of his son and daughter no longer quit his retina. Their memory filled his soul. He imagined them in the heart of Africa, in a citadel surrounded by impenetrable lianas, then in the bosom of Mont Blanc or the Himalayas, prisoners in dungeons deeper than mines, then held captive under the sea, in bizarre steel cells. Finally, succumbing to the contagion, he interrogated the sky with a terrified gaze and whispered: "The Blue Peril!"

With an effort, though, he shook off the absurd obsession, rebuked himself harshly for having yielded to it, and, in order to chase it away and sanitize his ideas, he forced himself to choose a star in a constellation, to rehearse the history of its knowledge, and to recite its spatial and temporal numbers. As you might guess, the star that most frequently solicited his gaze in these scientific moments was Vega, or Alpha Lyrae—

the Vega whose observation he had suspended in order to come to Mirastel, leaving behind the work that he had intended to continue a fortnight later, but still had not resumed after two months. Monsieur Le Tellier contented himself, therefore, with the spectacle of the beautiful white star toward which the Sun is taking us. It seemed to be waiting for him, and he admired its striking pallor for a long time.

On July 6, at about 1 a.m., fleeing a bed-alcove haunted with nightmares, he went on to the balcony and sought out the star Vega. It had reached the culminating point of its orbit; it was about to pass very close to the zenith, a few degrees to the south. To see it, he had to tilt his head back and look almost at the very center of the sky. It was gliding from left to right, innocent and serene.

As it cut across the meridian, though—which is to say, having reached the summit of its course—it suddenly went out.

Monsieur Le Tellier stood bolt upright. He had not recovered from his stupor when the star shone again, more beautifully than before, and continued its rotation around the Earth, sinking toward the west.

The astronomer's eyes no longer left it. Intoxicated with energy and curiosity, he followed it passionately until the morning, which effaced it. He had watched unfailingly for the recurrence of a phenomenon that his expert eye had not had the opportunity to observe again. He then attributed it to an optical aberration caused by fatigue and enervation, and went to sleep.

When he woke up, however, he reconsidered the matter. Hmm! A hallucination? Perhaps—but he doubted it. In any case, the apparent extinction had not been produced by a scintillation of longer duration than usual; he was sure of that. The star's disappearance had lasted too long for that—an interval that his long experience estimated at five seconds. Then again, no, no—he really had witnessed the momentary disappearance of Vega, and nothing known or anticipated could explain it. The most reasonable explanation was to suppose that an asteroid had passed the star, provoking its occultation—but a *dark* bolide? Hmm...hmm...

It is important to specify that Monsieur Le Tellier possessed an absolute assurance that no bird or aerostat had interposed itself between Vega and his eye. To mask a first magnitude star for five seconds would have required the intervention of a bird or aerostat so close to the spectator that it would have been clearly observable in the luminous night.

This little stellar incident, observed by such a man, took on a capital importance. Monsieur Le Tellier ruminated over that detail, which another man would not even have perceived, all day long. The result of his deliberations was that he repaired at dusk to the tower observatory, carefully took an inventory thereof, tested the movement of the clockwork and the equatorial telescope, cleaned the lenses, opened a crack in the dome to expose an arcade of void, and then—thus having revealed the band of space in which Vega described its curve—set his watch to sidereal time and aimed his telescope at a point on the horizon. That done, he waited impatiently for the rise of the star: the dawn of that enormously distant sun, which had mingled *ex abrupto* with his gravest preoccupations, engaging his interest from thousands of kilometers away at the precise moment when he was asking himself: "Where are the sarvant's victims?"

That thought was burning in his brain. And when Vega appeared—when he saw the blinding star in the middle of the nocturnal disk cut out by the objective lens—he was obliged to stiffen himself.

"Come on, then, weakling!"

With a flick of the thumb be switched on the clockwork mechanism, and the obedient telescope accompanied the star in its course.

It was a fine astronomical telescope for an amateur. It was a meter long and magnified a modest fifty times—but the magnification was of no importance with regard to Vega itself, dazzling as it was; the best telescopes cannot make the stars seem any closer, because they are too far away, and only serve to make them clearer. In any case, Monsieur Le Tellier was beginning to suspect was only playing a walk-on part in the drama, for time went by without his observing the slightest anomaly in the star's conduct.

Midnight sounded.

Monsieur Le Tellier did not leave the ocular lens. Anyone but as astronomer would have grown weary of it, but he maintained clear sight and an alert mind. The star and he examined one another. The clockwork, regulated in accordance with the movement of the heavens, hummed discreetly, and the little telescope reared up with a uniform and gradual progression, neutralizing the rotation of the Earth and constraining the observer to change position continually.

Soon, the tube was almost vertical, aimed seven degrees to the south of the zenith. Vega passed its culmination once again, and Monsieur Le Tellier, lying down with his head laid flat on the ground, shivered.

The star had disappeared again. At the same instant, it seemed that the blue background darkened...

One. Two. Three. Four. Five. Vega reappeared, and the field brightened.

"It's an eclipse!"

In no time at all, the clockwork was switched off. The astronomer seized the chronometer whose button he had pressed at the moment of the star's disappearance; the occultation had lasted four point nine seconds. He noted the time, and consulted the *Connaissance des temps*;[22] the eclipse had occurred within a minute of the same time and at the same place as the previous day. The screen that had interposed itself between the Earth and Vega was therefore *an object moving with our planet: a body associated with our world, remaining motionless above Bugey, situated seven degrees south of the zenith of Mirastel.*

---

[22] *Les Connaissance des temps et des mouvements célestes*, first published by Jean Piccard in 1679, is the oldest astronomical ephemeris.

But at what height?

The astronomer set out to estimate it. In fact, since it had been stopped, the telescope had been subject to the rotation of the Earth, re-entering the general order; it sufficed to reverse it slightly to fix it upon the mysterious point permanently. A rotating knob brought it back by a millimeter, and within the telescopic field, traversed by other stars, the sky darkened again, and the stars went out one by one as they progressed.

That dark vapor, Monsieur Le Tellier said to himself, *isn't in focus, that's all.*

Two turns of the milled control-button caused the ocular tube to sink into the objective tube, and the diffuse cloud gathered together, condensed, solidified and became *a strange square black patch.*

What's that? With the naked eye, looking directly upwards, absolutely nothing could be seen; the object was much too distant—but in the telescope, it was as clear and definite as Vega had been a little while ago. And that fixity intrigued Monsieur Le Tellier. *Without any doubt*, he thought, *this is the aerial island where my children are held captive by rogues. But how the Devil is that titanic balloon moored? It holds firm in the atmosphere, like a rock beaten by waves! Its nature, in any case, is not the question. It has to be an aerostat...or something similar. It's an invention of human beings, whose interest is not in meteorology. But it must be devilishly high up to be invisible in broad daylight without a telescope! Ah, we were just saying: how high is it? A simple problem.*

Having ignited a small cigarette-lighter, he checked the extent to which he had shortened the telescope in order to bring it into focus. Then he made a calculation, and his face darkened in amazement.

"Fifty thousand meters!" he murmured. "What! That machine is at an altitude of 50 kilometers! So there must still be breathable air at that altitude? One can live more than a dozen leagues above the ground, then? I'm delirious. That's contrary to all accepted theory!"

172

A bleak dejection succeeded the pride of his discovery and the almost-joyful thrill he had experienced. Already, he had been dreaming of a squadron of aeronefs blockading that accursed buoy—but 50 kilometers! No balloon could climb so high. The sarvants were out of range!

But in that case, what was that patch?

He put his eye to the ocular again. The patch had not changed in its form or its color.

It's not very large, thought Monsieur Le Tellier.

He measured its dimensions, made more calculations, based on the coefficients of size and height, and deduced that in reality, the sides of the black square were 60 meters long.

When he had stared and calculated all through the rest of the night, his knowledge had not increased by an iota. He realized that the sensible thing to do was to wait for daylight and study the patch once it was illuminated—a good resolution that proved impossible to keep. He finished the night at the end of his telescope, mulling over conjectures and talking to himself.

"A buoy, damn it! I can always come back to it, in spite of everything. It can't be anything but a buoy, of which I can only see the bottom…a sort of ultra-perfected balloon, which maintains itself in rarefied air. That it might be unconnected with the abductions is unacceptable. Everything's in accordance…and yet, I don't understand. What reason do these scoundrels have for lodging their victims at such a height? Half-that distance would be amply sufficient to protect them from any incursion. Why, too, that apparatus of terrorization—the stolen minerals and vegetables? Why make us wait so long for their letter of extortion? What new and furtive machine do they use to lift their victims up to that balloon-buoy? And where did they obtain that marvelous science? In sum, who are these people who work miracles of audacity, genius and wickedness?"

Monsieur Le Tellier had not voiced one in four of the questions pressing upon his lips. A cock crowed. The rising Sun struck the patch from above. It was quite obvious that it

173

was a vague entity, a solid sheet composed of brown rectangular pieces with very thin colorless lines between them.

Almost unthinkingly, "to see what would happen," the astronomer interposed a lens between the objective and ocular lenses, in order to set the image—which astronomical telescopes invert—the right way up. That metamorphosis of the telescope into a long-distance terrestrial eyeglass had no noticeable effect.

The astronomer was irritated. Occasionally, he tried without success to perceive the patch directly. The turquoise sky had a virginal purity, exempt from the faintest suspicion of brown, the most infinitesimal molecule of blond, or even of any darker blue. Too far away! Too far away! Thus, the patch could not be perceived, even if one neglected to take account of the thickness of the air, which is never totally lucid in spite of its appearance, and is tinted with ever-darkening blue.

Monsieur Le Tellier, returning to the ocular lens of the telescope, discovered nothing new. Without becoming weary, he observed the underside of the enigmatic object. He examined the edges of the square more carefully, especially the northern one, which ought to have been the most convenient for observation, given the slightly southward displacement of the object relative to Mirastel. He wanted there to be some sort of balustrade, guard-rail, bulwark or more-or-less baroque banister around the patch, along the edges, and he anticipated the appearance of some infinitesimal and adored head leaning over the abyss, as tiny as a pin-head...

In the end, he pulled himself out of that exhausting contemplation. Three hours of patience had taught him nothing new. The angle was awkward. It was necessary to observe the thing in profile, not from underneath; thus, it was necessary to observe it from a greater distance. Yes, but in that instance, an amateur telescope would no longer suffice. Larger telescopes would become indispensable...

Suddenly, he had a flash of inspiration. The Hatkins equatorial![23] The dream! A magnification of 6000 diameters! Six thousand instead of 50! Much better. But would it be possible to see the *thing* from Paris, more than 500 kilometers from Mirastel? Wouldn't the rotundity of the Earth prevent it from being seen? Wouldn't the *thing* be below the Parisian horizon, with respect to the line of sight? Quickly, a pencil, paper, a table of logarithms...it was all right! It *would* be visible, 20 kilometers above the horizon...

That same evening, Monsieur Le Tellier caught the Paris express at Culoz.

---

[23] Given that Bugey is much closer to Nice than Paris, M. Le Tellier might have thought of using the equatorial at Nice Observatory had Renard not taken care to equip the Paris Observatory with an imaginary instrument of even greater power; indeed, the idea of the gift from an American millionaire might well have been inspired by the example of the Nice Observatory, which owed its foundation in 1887 to a philanthropic donation of that sort.

II. Sequel to the Square Patch

"Chauffeur! To the Observatory!"

Monsieur Le Tellier is leaving the PLM station. He does not look well this morning. All night long, in the carriage—his second night without sleep—he has labored doggedly to understand; he has filled his notebook with geometric diagrams, algebraic equations and arithmetical operations...and he understands less and less. The mystery has never seemed so mysterious as it has since he has begun to clarify it. He has also begun to have doubts about the Hatkins equatorial. It is certainly powerful, but its situation is deplorable. The patch is visible in theory, but in practice? Will the telescope be able to pick it out, through an atmospheric mass of more than 50 kilometers, stuffed with clouds and mists, where variations in temperature produce innumerable refractions? The dust and smoke of Paris constitute a serious barrier in themselves. To obtain anything clear, it will surely be necessary to reduce the magnification...

But here, at the end of its avenue, is the Observatory, with its cupolas. Here is the Saint-Sulpice of science, with its terrace, which seems to be seething. Here is the Sainte-Geneviève of astronomy, with that huge preponderant bubble, which is the dome of the great equatorial. Here is the Sacré-Coeur of Montparnasse!

"Ah! Monsieur le Directeur!"

The porter, surprised and respectful, hands over a bunch of keys. In the courtyard, the director evades a few astronomers who have just finished their night's work and are going home. He goes up to the second floor on the beautiful stone staircase. He goes into the housing of the great equatorial and comes to a halt, involuntarily, in admiration.

Leviathan! Goliath! Polyphemus!

The dimensions of the telescope are so colossal that Monsieur Le Tellier cannot remember them. One might think that one were inside the turret of a fortress or some monstrous suit of armor. The enormous concavity of the zinc vault takes on the appearance of an armored skull-cap, and the equatorial is a prodigious cannon, inclined toward the world's axis, menacing the sky. Its gun-carriage, a tower of masonry in the center of the rotunda, is enveloped by light metallic structures—stair-heads, ladders, spiral stairways—and an infinity of precision mechanisms is visible there, some slender and others Herculean, as one might expect to find around an instrument that is simultaneously a lady's watch and a crane for heavy lifting. The equatorial rests on the pivots of the howitzer. It stretches forth: a Colonne Vendôme that is a bombard, a bombard that is a telescope; a mastodon of a cylinder, an elephantine leaning tower of chrome-steel, grey and mat. Perspective tapers its extremity; it hardly shines at all. Its ocular lens, complicated by a mass of tiny machinery, genuinely looks like the breech of a gun. And is it loaded, this artillery piece? A layman would fear so, and dread its deafening detonation, and wonder what phantasmagorical projectile it might launch at the Moon...

It is warm under that bell. The meditative silence is almost that of a basilica. The rumor of Paris, distant and oceanic, murmurs incessantly. From second to second, the ticktock of the sidereal clock echoes from the arches of the cupola, redoubling the accumulated gravity of passing time.

To work!

Monsieur Le Tellier maneuvers a capstan. The dome pivots, rolling on its castors with a rumble of thunder and brass. Cords are drawn out. A large opening is uncovered to the south-east: the direction of Mirastel. The optical artillerist aims his "Long Tom," which slowly declines toward the horizon. By means of the little secondary telescope stuck to the large one, known as a seeker, he tries to pick out the square patch.

God, how small he is beneath the equatorial! One might take him for Gulliver beneath a giant's microscope.

But the patch? Where's the patch?

Wait! He gropes about, turns wheels, aims lower, then to the left. He remakes his calculations...changes lenses to reduce the magnification and increase the clarity...

Ah! There it is at last, that accursed patch. Here it is in elevation, instead of being seen from underneath—but it can only be discerned at a magnification of twelve hundred, no more, and is unsteady, disturbed by the atmosphere, vibrating because of the great city that makes the Observatory tremble. It has not moved; that is the only conclusion of the entire session. As for saying exactly what it is, that is equally impossible for various reasons.

It's stifling in here!

Exasperated, Jean Le Tellier goes out on to the terrace. He strides back and forth furiously, going around the domes whose hemispherical domes protrude there, like half-inflated balloons in an aerostat park. He bumps into items of recording apparatus, staving in a pluviometer that gets in his way with a blow of his fist.

It's idiotic—all these machines which only serve up stupidities! Science, science, science! Oh, it's in its infancy, is science!

Paris extends beneath the feet of the irritated astronomer. The human ant-hill extends before him the convexity of its vale of tears between all the vales of misery constructed as far as the eye can see. It descends from Montparnasse to rise again at Montmartre, and in the distance, facing the Observatory to the north, as if it were its own distorted reflection, stands another crumple of cupolas. By a strange symmetry, Sacré-Coeur and the Sacred Brain dominate Paris, each to one side. They are two parallel but dissimilar temples, both built to extend toward the heavens and which, jealous of one another, seem to be challenging one another above the heads of an entire people. Which will prevail? Which of these two temples on the two hills ought to prevail? The astronomer sways momentarily. Rather than being here, should he not rather be there, in the ecstatic observatory of Heaven? A Heaven so constellated that it no longer contains any darkness?

Ah! Courage, you crazy fool! It's not yet time to give up. Nothing is lost! About turn! Confront the enemy: the sarvant!

With a determined tread, Monsieur Le Tellier crosses the platform and recklessly stands on tiptoe, leaning on the balustrade. Down below, in the garden, the housings of the photographic meridional telescopes round out their mosque-like roofs. Further away to the south, toward Mirastel and the patch, is the Montsouris Observatory, and further away still, better placed than Paris in certain respects…Saint-Genis-Laval, near Lyon. That's it! That's it!

It's to Saint-Genis-Laval that it's necessary to go now. Patience and perseverance! I'll be there before nightfall. Let's go!

Monsieur Le Tellier never found out how the journalists got wind of his presence in Paris. Still, there was a group of gentlemen with pens on the alert, waiting for him at the Observatory's main gate. He did not think he ought to conceal his discovery of the patch from them, nor his recent disillusionment. Sensational news! The reporters, no longer feeling joyful, immediately dispersed with an inconceivable rapidity and, while each one ran to his editorial offices at top speed, Monsieur Le Tellier—who had a couple of hours to kill before the departure of his train—took a cab to the Duc d'Agnès's house in the Avenue Montaigne.

The young sportsman had just come back from Bois-Colombes. He was radiant. He had the highest hopes of the airplane under construction; the apparatus capturing atmospheric electricity was a marvel. No, he had no further news of Tiburce. But how did it come about that Monsieur Le Tellier was in Paris? A patch? At an altitude of 50 kilometers? Inaccessible to any airplane? Too high? Ah, damn it! That was upsetting…but this patch must be the sarvants' lair, mustn't it? There was still, in consequence, the phantom dirigible, which could be pursued, captured…the *Epervier*—as he had named his hunting aircraft—would therefore be useful for something. Ah, damn it! He had been afraid for a moment! But all would go well, very well! Mademoiselle Marie-Thérèse, oh, my God, he swore that he would save her...and to marry her, damn it! Oh yes, yes, that Robert Collin—smart, very smart, damn it!

The Duc d'Agnès needed to talk a great deal and blaspheme a little when he was very content. He was still jabbering away and cursing when he arrived on the station platform with his future father-in-law. There were special editions of the newspapers that the astronomer had informed on sale there. The latter bought a few gazettes. Alone in the carriage that bore him away, he had the leisure to study the various interpretations that had been put on his words. But what did these ornamental flourishes matter? If the language varied, the core of the information remained faithful and accurate. At that moment, millions of intelligences were being updated. Tomorrow, the universe would know about the existence of the enigmatic patch. And then...oh, the stimulation of thought! It would produce such an effort on the part of humankind that the patch would be brought down, no matter what the cost, my friends! Ah! It would be brought down! It would be unhooked, flung on to the ground!

As Saint-Genis-Laval, though, the view of the sarvant patch he had was from below. It seemed to be constituted by an aggregation of indistinct elements. It formed a sort of brown pavement without overmuch regularity, with rays of light shining through between the rectangles.

As large telescopes could not be mutated into terrestrial telescopes, all manner of expedients were employed to straighten the image of that square logograph. It was projected on screens. Variations of shade and clarity were observed in the intermediary rays, in places...new points of interrogation.

Fifteen astronomers surrounded Monsieur Le Tellier, succeeding him at the ocular of the telescope or in front of the projection. They aimed every telescope in Saint-Genis at the same visual target, fruitlessly. And could one ever count the number of people who were imitating them? Hundreds and thousands, making use of everything from hand-held binoculars to equatorial reflectors. There were people gazing in places from which it was impossible to see the patch, through kilometers of terrestrial arc. There were many, relying on the indications of the newspapers, who could not identify the point at which to aim. The majority saw nothing—and yet, a simple pair of opera-glasses was sufficient to make that little russet patch emerge from the sky-blue.

Eyes, and yet more eyes, were searching out the dark star in the azure firmament—but all those gazes laying siege to the sky were no more than a prelude to the superb movement that was about to hurl humankind to assault the clouds.

III. The Assault on the Sky

The announcement of the Le Tellier discovery ran along the telegraphic wires and crossed the oceans on Hertzian waves or in submarine cables. Immediately, the mass of explorers disseminated everywhere in quest of the sarvant stopped searching. Caravans in the desert, missions in the pernicious forests, regiments among the Barbarians, chains of climbers on the flanks for needles of ice, all set out on return journeys. Horses turned their noses toward the stables, boats headed for port. The word was for aeronauts alone.

For a long time—since the possibility of an aerial pursuit had been recognized—aircraft construction-yards had been working zealously, but when it was averred that the bandits had elected to base themselves *in excelsis*, their activity redoubled and the workshops were swarming.

The problem had become complicated. At the outset, it consisted solely in establishing speedy machines, stable and controllable, appropriate to the pursuit of pirates. Now, the question of altitude had abruptly and completely changed everything. And what an altitude! Fifty kilometers! They were admirable, these pirates who maintained their den 50 kilometers up in the air, in an environment reputed to give hardly any lift, in an atmosphere so poor that science recognized it as a near-vacuum as good as any that could be obtained with a pump! Admirable, in truth! But who could match it? Who would be equally admirable? Who would duplicate their work and permit honest men to rise up to where a few scoundrels of genius had perched their hideout?

While awaiting the solution of that problem, it was judicious to employ observation balloons and airplanes to get closer to the patch, and to apply all the latest improvements to them. Equipped in that manner, they would at least be able to evade the phantom dirigible, or—according to some—attack it.

Unfortunately, prudence was lacking. The reader will remember the bold professionals going up in aerostats, biplanes or rudimentary monoplanes, having already committed the generous recklessness of circling around the suspect regions. From July 9 on, their number increased day by day. The atmosphere had never been so dangerous, and never had so many machines been seen confronting the Great Deep. Wooden hangars surrounded Bugey with a girdle of barracks. At every moment, a new searchlight shot up. Flights of balloons rose up into the sky like bubbles of gas in a champagne-flute. The aeronauts and aviators took expensive binoculars with them. Some of their names were famous. Notorious foreigners left their homelands and withdrew from the most attractive competitions in order to come and explore the air above Mirastel. Highly paid individuals, wishing to honor their own glory, took to the air incessantly with sublime determination. Day and night, the State's finest units—its military aeronefs, as yellow as pointed silkworm-cocoons—passed back and forth, policing the skies and mounting investigations in the house of Uranus.

All things considered, it was no more than an altitude contest dramatized by the circumstances. The winner would be the person who got close enough the square patch to distinguish it more precisely. And they climbed, and climbed....and climbed...as far as the frightful regions in which they had to inhale provisions of oxygen and live an artificial existence, with the assistance of chemical artifice. Thanks to strange helmets and breathing-apparatus, they passed the limits at which illustrious martyrs had met their deaths. They surpassed 10,800 meters. That was the record.

The most skillful, therefore, had remained more than 39 kilometers from the patch; they had only made out a vague square, dark and checkered, formed of opaque rectangles and transparent lines, which were simply breaks in continuity between the parallelograms. Occasionally, these lines were partially sealed by a dark point...

All that was already known.

It was also known that climbing higher could not be done—but such is the ardor of sportsmen that they try to realize the impossible performance anyway. It required the catastrophe of the *Sylphe* to cool it.

The *Sylphe*, a large spherical balloon belonging to the Aéronautique-Club, departed from the camp at Valbonne and was driven toward Bugey by a rather brisk wind. It immediately gained a considerable altitude; nevertheless, it was followed for some time. With binoculars, it was possible to see the four voyagers—two astronomers and two aeronauts—busy with their observations. Night fell. The balloon disappeared. It was never seen again. It did not land anywhere. Impetuous automobiles scoured the frightened zone, where it might have come down. They did not find the *Sylphe*. The reclusive Bugists, interrogated through closed doors, reported that nothing terrible had happened for days. As they no longer went out, the sarvant, for want of prey, seemed to have given up hunting.

The automobilists might have been surprised at this juncture that the sarvants had not extended their circle of havoc beyond the depopulated territory...but they were only concerned with the *Sylphe*. The day after their return, several ascensions were cancelled. An amazed consternation weighed upon the hangars. Orders were posted by committees prohibiting the use of free-floating balloons and instructing that people were only to take to the air in airplanes, helicopters and aeronefs whose maneuverability, endurance and speed had been proven.

In spite of the authorization required by dirigible machines, four or five daredevils ventured forth. You will still recall the *Antoinette 73*, which suddenly fell out of the sky in the twilight, like a javelin, and ended up floating in the Saône with its wings extended. Its pilot had not bailed out. He was one of the kings of space. Immobile in his bucket-seat, his straps still buckled, with the legendary cigarette stuck in his bloodless lips, he was dead, with a big hole in his skull and two savage claw-marks, one on his throat and the other on the nape of his neck.

In the midst of the despondency, however, exchanging blow for blow, two other news-items burst like bombs of enthusiasm. The Duc d'Agnès and the pilot Bachmès, his chief mechanic, had just "brought out" a marvelous monoplane: a lightning-fast aircraft furnished with an atmospheric electricity captor and a stabilizer as ingenious as was imaginable. Simultaneously, the State's aerial squadron was enriched by a new unbreakable cruiser, astonishing in its agility and submissiveness.

The French public is always the same. An abrupt turnaround directed its attention to these two actualities. It enveloped them with uniform admiration, and uniform pride, even though it regarded them as rivals—rivals because one was heavier than air and one lighter than air; rivals because one was publicly-owned and one privately-owned; rivals because they were two conquerors of the same element, two candidates for the same victory by the same means: speed. In the mind of the public, it was indispensable that one would defeat the other; a contest was inevitable.

The government seized the opportunity to channel the popular excitement towards the sporting contest, and thus to create a diversion from the anguish of the Blue Peril. It instituted, for the month of September, a prize of 400,000 francs for a race between an airplane and a dirigible, over a distance to be determined—settled in advance by the two champions that everyone recognized. It begged the journalists to whip up excitement until the day of the race. Covertly, meanwhile, it gave orders to its engineers and the council for special enterprises to study how it might be possible to get up to the sarvants' lair. It secretly promised fabulous prizes for altitude, and solicited the experts of every nation and race by means of personal letters.

These letters reached the most diverse destinations, under roofs white with snow or scorched by the Sun; some received them in autumn, some in spring. After having read them, everyone set to work. Little yellow men bent over silken pieces of paper and painted delicate geometries; tall blond men went to their blackboards, chalk in hand. And all of them drew the same figure in the same fashion: a circumference representing the Earth, and then another circumference, larger than and concentric with the first, which delimited the atmospheric layer above which there was nothing but vacuum. Above that second circle the brush or the chalk placed a point—the patch—then drew a straight line from the patch to the Earth, in the direction of the center: the distance to be crossed.

Fifty kilometers! thought the scientists. And then, recalling the tenor of the letter, and what they were required to invent, they shook their heads. This one said something curt and hoarse, that one something long and soft, another something melodious—but all these speeches had a single meaning, and there was no jargon so mediocre that it did not contain the relevant term—for in every language, no matter what proverbial wisdom may say,[24] the adjective *impossible* has its equivalent.

---

[24] A popular saying in France alleges that "the word impossible is not French." The original statement is generally attributed to Napoleon, although opinions vary as to when he is supposed to have said it, and one anecdote gives the credit to his slippery minister of police Joseph Fouché.

IV. A Message from Tiburce [25]

(Item 502)
Duc François d'Agnès,
40 Avenue Montaigne, Paris
France, Europe.
Nagasaki, July 20, 1912.

Ante-scriptum. Before anything else, be reassured; I conserve the greatest optimism with regard to catching up with the fugitives. That being well-established, I shall render an account of my work—succinctly, for I shall soon be taking the ferry to Singapore, via Canton.

My dear friend,
        I am out of prison. I spent a week there.
        Before my last cablegram, I had crossed America from New York to San Francisco in pursuit of four individuals who were several days ahead of me. In these four individuals—four men, according to the information given—I had easily recognized Hatkins, Henri Monbardeau, Madame Fabienne Monbardeau and Mademoiselle Marie-Thérèse Le Tellier, traveling in disguise and in drag.

---

[25] Renard's narrator inserts a footnote here: "As I insert this letter in its chronological setting, in spite of the promise I made to follow M. Tiburce to the conclusion of his divagations, in order to edify young readers, I experience some scruples. The apparent irrelevance and erratic quality of the missive is an affront to my sense of order and homogeneity—but I have hastily repudiated such stupid preoccupations, in view of the interest of the task to be fulfilled. I even anticipate that M. Tiburce's errors, abruptly recalled in this fashion, without the shadow of a transition—like a trapdoor opening up over an abyss—will be all the more striking for the reader."

In San Francisco I learn that the steamboat to Nagasaki had raised anchor on the eve of my arrival. I scent something, I bribe an employee of the company, and as best I can—for I can only speak French, alas—I work out that a group of six passengers has embarked on the aforementioned steamer. None of their names corresponds to any of those of the quartet for which I am searching, but of these six individuals, four have descriptions diametrically opposed to those of my fugitives. Are you with me? It. is, therefore, them, too well disguised. It is them, with a pair of additional accomplices.

There is no hesitation; I embark in my turn.

I arrive in Nagasaki. I visit all the hotels, one by one, and after a thousand difficulties, occasioned by my ignorance of Japanese and English, I succeed nevertheless, by an accumulation of dearly-bought confidences, in acquiring proof that a French couple resembling the Monbardeaus is staying in one hotel and that another couple, who must be Hatkins and Mademoiselle Le Tellier, is in the hotel next door. The scent continues to guide me. I take a room in the hotel where I suspect that Hatkins and Mademoiselle Marie-Thérèse are hiding under the aliases of the Reverend James Hodgson and his daughter. I reserve a table near to the one they are due to occupy at dinner, with the aim of making certainty of their identity, then I put on my own disguise.

At the first stroke of the gong, Tiburce was no longer anything but an old Italian priest—you will not be unaware that this is the favorite disguise of my master, Sherlock Holmes; I have brought a dozen complete transformations, but that soutane seemed to me to be appropriate. Ah, without flattering myself, I may say that my wrinkled face, my aquiline nose and my white wig created an illusion. Fine make-up!

As I was going down the staircase leading to the restaurant, however, a respectable lady who was coming up looked at me with a dumbfounded expression. Other people did the same and, on the threshold of the dining-room, the manager of the hotel, alerted by one of these imbeciles, asks me to go into his office.

My disguise has been penetrated—I have no idea how! I try, in spite of everything, to counterfeit Italian speech, but I don't know any Italian. Then we go up to my room. My luggage is searched. Because of my unusual wardrobe, I'm initially mistaken for Fregoli in the process of doing some impression.[26] *In the depths of my fifth trunk, however, they discover the burglar's kit that no serious detective is ever without. I am no more than a crook. Procedures are instituted; I am locked up. Thanks to the French consul, my detention only lasts a week; everything is cleared up—but I have all the trouble in the world avoiding being repatriated under guard.*

In this interval, I am informed that the day after my release, *the pseudo-Reverend Hodgson and his so-called daughter departed for Singapore,* via *Canton.* Subito—*as the old Italian priest would say*[27]—*I make arrangements enabling me to follow them this evening, unfortunately leaving behind, in the hands of the authorities in Nagasaki, my tool-kit, my costumes and my make-up: all my precious Sherlockery!*

I wonder whether the Monbardeaus are accompanying the fake Hodgsons. I shall find out in Singapore. At any rate, this series of precipitate departures is indicative of flight; *and since they're on the run,* it must be them.

Adieu, my friend. Don't forget to mention me to Mademoiselle d'Agnès. Regards,

Tiburce

Post-scriptum. Busy, never ceasing to plan my tactics, I can't write often. Forgive me. I'll do so whenever I can. Above all, remember me to your sister.

---

[26] The pioneering impressionist Leopoldo Fregoli (1867-1931) became famous as a "quick change artist," relying as much on costume as the imitation of mannerisms to make his caricatures plausible.

[27] The Latin *subito* [sudden] is most commonly encountered in musical notation; the reference to the likelihood of it being used by an old Italian priest is a joke.

V. It Rains... It Hails

Let us return to Mirastel.

Monsieur Le Tellier, having returned from his trip to Paris and Saint-Genis-Laval, found no other change among his relatives but a sustained amelioration in his wife's condition, and from July 8 to August 3—which is to say, from the day of his return to the day that we have now reached—existence at the château was depressingly uniform. The observation of the immutable and impassive patch was the principal business: a sterile task, and a source of irritation.

Some days, it is true, the spectacle of Lebaudys and Clément-Bayards, Libellules and Demoiselles[28] competing on high amused the gaze in spite of the conscience. In the wake of the misfortunes of the *Sylphe* and the *Antoinette 73*, however, the atmospheric arena seemed to change its role. Despon-

---

[28] The Lebaudy brothers, Paul and Pierre, were among the first commercial airship designers; their chief client from 1907 on was the French Ministry of War. The Ministry also commissioned Clément-Bayard, a firm of automobile manufacturers founded by Adolphe Clément, to build military airships in 1908, and the same firm was commissioned to build aeroplanes on the Demoiselle [damsel-fly] design originated by Alberto Santos-Dumont—who had been the first aviator to make a heavier-than-air flight authenticated by the Aéro-Club de France in 1906. The Libellule [dragon-fly] aircraft was originated by Santos-Dumont's chief rival, Louis Blériot, in 1907, but crashed during testing and the design was abandoned. By the time Renard published *Le Péril bleu* in 1911, Santos-Dumont had given up aviation after crashing a Demoiselle in 1910 and the Ministry of War's airship program had suffered a dire setback when its dirigible *République* crashed disastrously in 1909. There is, therefore, a hint of irony about this supposedly-celebratory image.

dency descended again. Monsieur Le Tellier felt an urgent need for diversion.

While Madame Arquedouve and her elder daughter devoted themselves to domestic responsibilities and took care of Madame Le Tellier, Dr. Monbardeau bravely went out to bring succor to suffering and sequestered unfortunates. Monsieur Le Tellier decided to accompany him. They were the first Bugists to resume regular circulation in an automobile. It was claimed that "there was nothing so very courageous about that, given that no automobile had ever been attacked and that the sarvants had taken no more prisoners for some time." Agreed—but please remember that before the *Sylphe*, no balloon had ever been attacked either, and no airplane before the *Antoinette 73*. You will note, too, that if the sarvant was no longer taking the earthbound, it was only for lack of finding them within its range, out of doors and within the incomprehensible cabalistic circle whose outline it did not seem to want to cross. There was, therefore, on the contrary, a good chance that it might hurl itself upon the large white automobile that emerged every day from Mirastel, and stopped at every door, thus offering itself to the strikes of an aggressor that impatience must have been emboldening.

One day—it was August 3—the doctor and the astronomer were chatting beneath the sunlit canvas canopy. The car, coming from the château, was about to go into Talissieu. The physician was complaining about the unrelenting heat and drought, and the pestilence that one breathed in without cease; he was expressing his fears on the subject of a probable epidemic when he interrupted the conversation in amazement.

"Look! It's raining! That's hard to believe!"

Large drops were falling on the canopy, visible through its translucency. Monsieur Monbardeau put his open hand outside but uttered a cry of alarm when he brought it back moistened with red liquid.

"Stop!" commanded his brother-in-law. "Are you hurt, Calixte?"

"No—it just fell!"

191

"What? That's not possible!"

They got out in front of the first houses in the village, facing the cross and not far from the stream. Several droplets were bloodying the canopy and the footplate. Others were reddening the dust at the place where the automobile had passed through the crimson downpour.

The mechanic's eyes widened. "Is it birds fighting in mid-air?" he asked. "That's been seen before."

"No," his master replied. "Look!"

All three of them had instinctively raised their heads. One might have taken them for three of the damned escaped from Hell. There was nothing to be seen: nothing but the blue, the blue of the Peril; nothing but a few small birds—sparrows and swifts—all of whose blood combined would only have made one of those droplets.

"Is this the phenomenon known by the name of the *rain of blood*," asked the doctor, "which is produced by particles contained in the water?"

Poor doctor? Why was he playing the encyclopedist, while his lips were trembling? To reassure himself, or to reassure Monsieur Le Tellier? And why did the poor astronomer feel obliged to reply, between his chattering teeth: "No, no, there's no cloud; it's not rain. Besides, a shower wouldn't be limited to such a small area…"

Through his folded-up pince-nez, serving as a magnifying-glass, Monsieur Monbardeau examined the madder-red stain that was drying on the back of his hand. "It's definitely blood," he said, after a minute. "Really blood. It isn't coagulating normally, I admit…but it's blood all the same. Let's go back; I'll analyze it and…I'll tell you if it's…human or animal blood."

"I don't have the slightest doubt that it's blood!" murmured Monsieur Le Tellier. "Before going back and carrying out an analysis, though—which will be interesting—I want to put a few remarks on the record here, with both of us as witnesses. Look at the drops on the canopy; they're elongated, in the form of exclamation marks. That's explicable by the movement of the automobile while the shower was falling on it. Now come here—look at these drops on the ground; they're star-shaped, like the rowels of spurs. If you consider that there isn't the slightest wind, you'll easily conclude that the blood has fallen to the ground perpendicularly, from an immobile location situated at the zenith of its point of arrival."

"From the square patch!" declared Monsieur Monbardeau.

"No, it's not from the square patch, because that isn't directly above the place where we're standing. Mathematically, it's at the zenith of Ceyzérieu, since it's seven degrees to the south of Mirastel. Above us there's *nothing*. Do you understand, Calixte: NOTHING. Then again, think about this: at a height of 50 kilometers, *there can be no liquids*, given that it's an almost perfect vacuum, unless science is in error.

"There's another thing: how do we explain that the blood isn't desiccated, if it's covered 50 kilometers in free fall? These drops would inevitably be a residuum. All the blood of a man, reduced to a few tears...of a man, or a woman...or an animal..."

"Let's go back, I tell you. In half an hour we'll be able to verify the species that had bled. Let's go back; this splash is turning my stomach—I'm in a hurry to analyze it, to be able to wipe it off."

The bloody hand contracted with horror—and yet, that might well have been Monsieur Monbardeau's own blood: that of his son or his daughter...

They got back into the car. A ballistic whistle, increasingly loud and sharp, became audible above the canopy, and ended with the *plop* of an object falling in water.

They turned their heads. A second whistle scored the sky and ended with a sound of breaking branches.

"Aeroliths?" said Monsieur Monbardeau.

Behind the walls of Talissieu, the sounds of fortification were audible, then that silence of silences, which is that of a crowd that one cannot see and which is keeping quiet.

The automobilists went to the edge of the stream that ran through the wood and moved along the bank, following the current. The clear water was suddenly disturbed, and swept along a cloud of mud, which had just been lifted up by the impact of the fallen object. The waited for the mud to settle, then were able to distinguish, embedded in the stony mud of the stream bed, a human head—which stared at the three anguished faces leaning over it, with one lidless eye and one eyeless orbit...and saw the three recoil in fright.

The mechanic's recoil was so forceful that he sat down in the middle of a bush. He sprang out again with a single bound, as if he had touched the Burning Bush, and pointed to something that was lodged there: the second aerolith. It was a man's leg, flayed, red and bleeding.

"But...but..." stammered the doctor, "that's been done by...by someone professional...someone used to handling a scalpel...it's a preparation! Ugh! What's that, there?"

He bent down over something small that had, at that very moment, flicked his hat, and picked it up. Lord! It was a meticulously-severed little finger.

"Watch out!" howled the mechanic. "It's starting again!"

More whistling...a confusion of whistling sounds...

Around them, as they stood there sick with repugnance, fell a horrid hail of viscera, feet, arms and legs: an entire dissected cadaver, each fragment of which was a hideous but remarkable anatomical preparation; an entire body worked on by virtuoso medical students, coming from a part of the sky where nothing existed.

"Will you stand by your allegation?" stammered Monsieur Le Tellier. "That it's a dissection!"

The doctor made an expert examination of the debris. The horrible head was pulled out of the mire. The two fathers resembled the poor fellows of the times of the alchemists and Gilles de Retz who, having lost their children, trembled at the thought of finding them with their throats cut on some philosopher's workbench.

"Yes," Monsieur Monbardeau asserted, "they're limbs and organs that have been dissected...if not *vivisected*! This forearm might well have been prepared while still alive."

"Oh!" cried Monsieur Le Tellier, on the point of fainting. A terrible apprehension gripped his heart. Who was the dead man?

"The head's unrecognizable," said the doctor. "It's that of a man, of course, but how can we identify...oh, my God! My God!" He moaned, madly. "One might think...no, I'm mistaken, aren't I? No! Look at the teeth: It's no one. I mean...it's not one of ours...."

The astronomer stared into space with a fearful expression. "So," he said, slowly, "there must be criminal experimenters up there, refugees beyond the reach of ordinary folk, in an impregnable fortress where some ignominious research is being carried out?"

"I'm not sure. When all's said and done, these are simple preparations, very skillfully executed, but not in conformity with the classical rules of dissecting-theaters..."

"Think—these probably aren't the first wastes to have fallen in the vicinity. We might search the surrounding area..."

Having buried the debris, they set out on the investigation, each of them by himself—and each of them made a further discovery.

Monsieur Le Tellier found the branches of an ash tree, oddly split and bizarrely decorticated, with strips and cross-sections *botanically* excised.

Monsieur Monbardeau found the bones of a calf or a heifer. The bones were dispersed, but in a particular manner: here the vertebral column, there a shoulder, elsewhere the pelvis. He counted them; the skeleton lacked a left hind leg. The doctor called Monsieur Le Tellier and told him that the animal had been thrown from the sky in pieces, like the dead man they had just buried. "Insects and carnivorous animals have undertaken to clean the bones, with the result that we cannot discover, under the remains, the bruises that they must have inflicted on the moss in falling from such a height. The moss, after all, is a shock-absorbing cushion that recovers promptly."

The astronomer claimed, however, that these remains might be quite old, that the country was covered with similar carcasses, and that it was not necessary to see sarvants everywhere, just because…

The mechanic's voice interrupted him. Having finished his tour, which he judged sufficient, the servant had been coming back when he had looked more closely at the crown of the sycamore at the foot of which the two brothers-in-law were holding their discussion. "What's that moving up there?" he asked. "If the gentlemen care to stand aside, God willing, I'll shoot it down!"

He pulled a revolver out of his pocket and fired.

The tree lost a few leaves and crows took flight, leaving visible the leg of a white heifer—or a white calf—caught in the topmost fork of the sycamore. Such was the mechanic's find. It was revealing. The calf—or the heifer—had fallen out of the sky quite recently, and one of its pieces had stuck in that elevated spot, where animals were not accustomed to go to die, entire or in lots.

Monsieur Monbardeau formulated his judgment in the following fashion: "You see, Jean—let's not try to delude ourselves. Above us, in his impregnable belvedere, a biologist with neither faith nor law is devoting himself to ferocious experiments in comparative anatomy." After a pause, frightened by what he had dared to say, he went on: "If the sarvant is the biologist in question, of course, he must have been somewhat short of human material for some time—listen to this desert!"

Their search had drawn them away from the village and close to the railway. The only sounds they could hear were the rustling of foliage, the buzz of mosquitoes, the chirping of birds and—most of all—the cawing, croaking and yapping of all the feathered and furry undertakers that held sway over the province. By the evidence of the ears, one might have thought that the sons of Adam no longer reigned.

As if to protest, a locomotive and its carriages filed past, with a particularly ostentatious blast of its horn. That breathing and whistling iron hydra had at least 400 heads, of both sexes; 400 traveling faces ornamented its windows, on which the fear of passing through Bugey, in tow behind a boiler susceptible to breakdowns, was clearly legible.

The Mirastelians went back.

"What's odd," said Monsieur Monbardeau, "is that *they* don't go beyond that circle..."

"What's odd," said Monsieur Le Tellier, "is that the things *they*'re throwing away aren't being thrown from the patch, since it's not overhead..."

"Bah! The patch is a floating dock, which can be moved at will!"

"I can't admit that."

In fact, the brown patch had not moved. It was still in the dead center of the blue circle, in the telescope in the tower.

At the zenith, there was nothing.

Monsieur Le Tellier went down to Maxime's laboratory to confer with Monsieur Monbardeau, who, for his part, had been getting to grips with the red stain—but the astronomer, who expected to surprise the doctor, was petrified by what he was told.

The analysis of the blood revealed animal corpuscles mingled with human corpuscles. The blood might be the blood of a hybrid creature similar to the centaurs, satyrs and sirens of fabulous Antiquity! Was the sarvant, then, called Dr. Lerne or Dr. Moreau?

During the following week, the whistle of falling objects was heard many times, by night. The objects made holes in the ground. There were stones, neatly sawn through or bearing evidence of chemical attack, branches excised by the knife of an experienced naturalist. There was also the flesh of birds, fish and mammals, all very carefully butchered, and many humans in little pieces...many dead people, who were difficult to identify...

197

VI. The Bait

In the midst of troubled sleep, Monsieur Le Tellier thought he felt a hand touching him. He woke up suddenly. Madame Arquedouve was standing next to his bed in the light of dawn. The château was asleep. The chiming clock, that nightlight of silence, was the only thing making a sound. It was 4 a.m.

"Jean! They're here!"

They, pronounced in such a tone, were the sarvants.

Monsieur Le Tellier leapt out of bed; hastily putting on a dressing-gown, he asked the blind woman: "Can you hear them?"

"The hum, yes. I've been hearing it for a quarter of an hour. I was in doubt...fearful of being mistaken...but it's them."

"A quarter of an hour! What are they doing, then? Where are they?"

"I think they were circling the château, at first. Now, it seems, they're no longer moving. Don't open your window— it's futile. I think they're on the other side of the château, behind."

"That's odd—I can't hear anything at all. You're right: from here, one can't see anything at all in front of Mirastel."

"Come into the gallery," advised Madame Arquedouve. "You'll be able to see from there—but take great care going past Lucie's door; remember that the slightest alarm might provoke a relapse!"

They went on tiptoe to the gallery. That was what they called a broad corridor that ran along the rear wall on the first floor.

"The hum's getting closer," the blind woman murmured. "Or rather, we're getting closer to it. Can't you hear it, Jean? It's very soft, though."

"Yes, I'm beginning to," whispered Monsieur Le Tellier. "It's like a little fly imprisoned in one's heart. Let's stop here." They were about to reach the first window in the gallery. "Don't show yourself, Mother—I'll go on, on the sly..."

The window-panes were quivering imperceptibly. Monsieur Le Tellier carefully stuck out his head. He imagined the landscape that would appear—the sloping lawn, girdled by woods, the upper slopes of the Colombier—and he was greatly excited by the expectation of finding some individuals or some machine inhabiting that landscape.

Behind him, Madame Arquedove held her breath, waiting for him to speak.

Through the window-frame, he saw the trees of the farm, the slope of the mountain, the woods, the edge of the lawn-clearing...a quarter of it, a third, half...

"What's out there, Jean? You're shivering...so tell me..."

"Oh, it's joy, Mother!" Monsieur Le Tellier cried, delightedly. "Maxime—Maxime's there! He must have escaped. Ah, Maxime, my boy! I'm coming!"

"But Jean—is Maxime alone?"

"Yes, alone in the middle of the lawn. He's sitting in the middle of the lawn. Let me go down, run...I think he needs someone to take care of him..."

"Go! Go quickly!" the grandmother repeated, joyfully. "Maxime has come back!"

And she went through the whole château, waking her daughters, the doctor and the servants, telling them the wonderful news: "Maxime's come back! He's escaped from up there! Come! Come!"

Meanwhile, the astronomer went out on to the perron and shouted to his son: "Why aren't you coming in, my boy? Are you ill? You should have called us..."

At the sight of his father, though, Maxime stood up, and from afar, with a voice and gestures redolent with catastrophe, he shouted: "Don't come any closer! In the name of God, stay in the house!"

Monsieur Le Tellier stopped. It was not the sarvants that frightened him, but his son. He could see him more clearly than he had from the window, being much closer.

Maxime was standing up. His expression was sad, so very sad...he was thin and dirty; his torn waistcoat hung in tatters; he had no hat—and on top of all that, the expression of terror that seemed to be invading his horror-widened eyes...all of it bathed by the returning light of the rising Sun.

Maxime is mad! thought Monsieur Le Tellier. *This adventure has completed the work of insanity that the story of the little Jeantaz girl began...Maxime is mad!*

Without taking a further step, in order not to upset him, he spoke in a calm voice: "It's all right; I won't budge. But come here, then—come! We'll wait for you. You can't stay there..."

The young man made a gesture of despair. Large tears ran down his emaciated cheeks. "Papa! I can't come! I can't!"

"Come on, my dear boy—pull yourself together. Is your sister with you? Where were you? What about Suzanne? And Henri? Fabienne? Have you seen Robert?"

"I've only seen Robert. And more!"

Above him, there was considerable agitation in the château. All the people Madame Arquedouve had woken up were emerging in front of Maxime, half-dressed, with delighted expressions: his grandmother, his mother, his uncle and his aunt, the old servants...and he, convulsively and imperiously, howled: "Don't come any closer! No one! Go away! Go back inside! They'll take you too! They're lying in wait for you. Can't you hear the hum!"

Halt! The hum! That's right! Everyone heard it then...but what was making it? Their eyes scanned the surrounding wood; that was the only hiding-place where the sarvants might be lying in ambush.

"But there's nothing to be seen!" said Monsieur Le Tellier. "Are they in the woods, Maxime?"

"You don't understand—but do as I say. We've no time to waste in explanations. Do as I say—don't come any closer.

200

There's nothing to be seen, but they're holding me just the same. I'm here as bait…a lure to attract people…because they haven't been able to capture any more for some time. Do you understand? Don't come any closer, then. If you love me, let them carry me off alone."

A muffled scream greeted that plea, and Madame Le Tellier ran back into the château, *madly*. Several servants followed her, very frightened. Their fearful remarks and the unfortunate mother's exclamations were audible as they fled: "They're going to carry him off again! They're going to carry him off again! Oh, they're going to carry him off again! Oh! Oh!"

Monsieur Monbardeau was more rational. "Listen, Jean: I think your son's exaggerating. Think! There's nothing to be seen, damn it! And there aren't any clouds! Maxime must be trapped by some electromagnetic fluid, whose production causes the hum—a fluid controlled from the height of the patch. It's one of your own hypotheses, remember—the animal magnet. Only, follow me carefully—the sarvants have never abducted more than three people at a time. I'm sure that if five of us stay together, and rush Maxime—you, me, the gardener, your chauffeur and the coachman…yes? Are you in, Jean? Are you in, Célestin? Clément? Gauthier? Get ready, then—I'll count to three. At three, we'll charge Monsieur Maxime, and bring him back to the château. One…two…*three!*"

The doctor's calculation was correct; the sarvant was not able to take five people at a time. The rescue party was half way to the prisoner without a prison when an enigmatic force, lifting Maxime up, set him down again 20 meters further away, on the edge of the wood. The hum, now more high-pitched, resumed in the darkness. The runners had stopped.

What a scene! It would have required something akin to the sardonic pencil of Jean Veber[29] to describe that château

[29] Jean Veber (1864-1928) was a political cartoonist, primarily associated with the satirical periodical *Gil Blas*; his grotesque

behind that lawn: the terrified faces of bonnet-less housemaids in night-shirts at the windows; in front of the perron, a few male servants gathered around Madame Monbardeau, who was rigid with fright beneath her night-gown, and Madame Arquedouve, whose blind eyes were enlarged with the desire to see. On the lawn, the five men—the doctor's pyjamas, the gardener's apron, the astronomer's dressing-gown, the coachman's striped waistcoat and the mechanic's blue overall—were all huddled together, making calamitous faces. Then, all alone confronting all those gazes, there was the lamentable object of so much emotion, collapsed in the grass and weeping like Jesus falling down for the third time. All of that was in an atmosphere in which the legendary and the quotidian were juxtaposed, and hence burlesque.

"But what can we do? What can we do?" bleated Monsieur Le Tellier. "Tell us, Maxime—what should we do?"

"Alas! If they catch one of you, they'll carry me off! And if they don't catch anyone, they'll carry me off just the same! Let's try to make it hard—it's so terrible up there! There are tortures!"

Suddenly, Monsieur Le Tellier cried out in alarm: "Who's there? I saw someone sliding through the woods. Who's there? A shadow, I tell you, which…ah!"

A spark flared up among the branches; a detonation resounded in the wood, very close to Maxime, and white smoke appeared. The young man fell down heavily. His mother emerged from the smoke, rifle in hand. A woman made of snow could not have been paler.

"That way, he won't suffer any more! He's no longer suffering! I love him more than that!"

"Unfortunate woman!" shouted Monsieur Le Tellier. "Don't come out! Hide! Hide, then!"

The madwoman recoiled into the undergrowth, then disappeared.

---

caricatures sometimes caused offence—as they were, of course, intended to do.

At that moment, Maxime's body was seized by a violent somersault, then fell back. The stupor of the witnesses was prolonged. Like a serpent's hypnotic gaze, the sarvant's hum exercised a magnetic influence on their ears. Then that deep and obscure sound suddenly seemed to weaken, drawing away from the depths of their breasts, and they could hear nothing but the natural sounds of the morning.

Monsieur Le Tellier spoke sharply to Madame Arquedouve. He was so upset that he blind woman could not make out what he said.

"Mother, I'm asking you whether you think they've gone...or, at least, whether...the force is no longer there....if the fluid has risen up again...if the action of magnetism has ceased..."

"There's nothing more, so far as I know."

"What!" said Monsieur Monbardeau. "They've abandoned Maxime? Oh! It's because he's dead, then! Quickly, let's go see! He must be dead. They've only made a corpse of him, those vivisectors! That's why they've released him."

All together, they walked to the prostrate form.

"Oh, damn it! Damn it!" said the physician, in a low voice. "Full in the head. Straight into the skull! Oh, damn it!" Then he exclaimed: "No! Not dead! He's breathing! Alive, but he looks like a dead man. Oh, the blackguards! They can't see that from up there, with their telescopes! That's not surprising, from 50 kilometers!"

"Alive?" Madame Le Tellier came out of the wood. "Alive? Maxime? He's still with us, and I haven't killed him?" The dear, benevolent lady burst out laughing; she kissed her son's inanimate face—and her unbound hair, part-red and part-white, spread out bizarrely.

Already, without any distinction of sex, the old manservants and the young housemaids were drinking the alcohol the follows emotional experiences. And it was on that day, on August 11, that the south-east wind[30] began to blow.

---

[30] The reference is to the annual mistral.

VII. From August 11 to September 4

To shoot her son, Madame Le Tellier had made use of an old hunting-rifle that had belonged to her late father, Monsieur Arquedouve. In the moldy game-bag she had only found a single live cartridge, with a round bullet. That the shot had actually gone off, therefore, was only of those catastrophic misfortunes that one would not dare to put in a novel; it is the only implausibility in this actual history.

The antiquity of the weapon and the deterioration of the powder had ensured that, instead of transpiercing Maxime's head, the lead bullet had lodged in the bony thickness of his skull, behind the ear. They were able to extract it from the wound that same evening. It would take a long time to heal, though; and at that time the victim had not recovered consciousness. They could not count on him to unveil the mystery of the square patch. The doctor, anticipating the young man's awakening, forbade any over-exciting conversation.

Madame Le Tellier promised to keep silent, along with the others. It was she who looked after Maxime—and it must be said that she acquitted herself admirably. She had recovered her reason. A fright had caused it; another fright had suppressed it. Sometimes, it seemed that the madness had departed *before* the rifle shot, and that Madame Le Tellier had taken that action quite consciously. She spoke without remorse about what she had done, and said that she was ready to do as much for Marie-Thérèse if the opportunity should present itself, declaring that death was preferable to "such shameful treatment." It was a defensible theory, and Madame Le Tellier would not have hesitated to sustain it even more heatedly if she had know about the "rain" and "hail" of August 3 in all its atrocity. Her husband and brother-in-law had, however, kept that secret, and they hoped to keep it longer, although such dissimulation became more difficult every day.

More difficult? Why?

Because often, in the middle of the night, in the darkness warmed by the south-east wind, sinister whistling sounds were heard, which the doctor and the astronomer recognized. Madame Arquedouve was violently disturbed by them. She was told that they were falling aeroliths. The fact that St. Lawrence's Day marked the beginning of a season of shooting stars supported the lie.[31]

At dawn, Monsieur Monbardeau and Monsieur Le Tellier went out, with heavy hearts, to search for the fallen objects—they no longer fell in daylight—and never left the environs of Talissieu without having discovered as many objects as there had been whistling sounds. They found carefully-worked detritus belonging to all three realms of nature. The animals and humans sometimes bore singular stigmata, significant of total or partial asphyxia, compression and decompression, or more refined tortures.

After having identified the cadavers negatively—that is to say, after acquiring the certainty that they were not those of Marie-Thérèse, Henri Monbardeau, his wife, Suzanne or Robert—they consigned them to their graves. When they recognized a torture-victim as someone from the neighborhood, common sense advised them to keep quiet about it. Rumor of the truce having spread, however, other helpful Bugists began, like them, to go from town to town in motorized ambulances, serving as nurses and food-suppliers. They also perceived that it was hailing dead men in Talissieu, and spread the news. Soon, the terror was renewed in that lethargic region, where a near-tranquility had gradually been restored to the negative life of the country folk.

During their morning investigations, Monsieur Monbardeau and Monsieur Le Tellier encountered men and women

---

[31] St. Lawrence's Day is August 10; the annual Perseid meteor shower—resulting from debris left behind along its orbit by Comet Swift-Tuttle—peaks during the following week. In the Middle Ages, when the cause of the phenomenon was mysterious, it was known in Christendom as "St. Lawrence's tears."

who were undertaking similar funerary labors. They were the relatives or friends of missing persons. Intolerable anguish had driven them from their fortified hovels, at the risk of being abducted in their turn. Some came from far afield. Reclusion had made them jaundiced; broad daylight made them blink their eyes continually. They wandered unmethodically, and sometimes aimlessly. Strong sunlight struck their ivory-white heads, shaded for so long; sunstroke killed them, or made them kill themselves. The ardent south-east wind set other hanged men swaying.

Because of this, and rabid dogs, foxes and wolves—even a few bears, it was said—and because of diseases of every sort, there were even more deaths in Bugey between August 11 and September 4. It is proven, however, that the sarvants did not contribute to that in any fashion, even though the contrary has been maintained by a host of obsessives.

Monsieur Le Tellier did everything he could to oppose these murderous excursions, which died out of their own accord. The era of their cessation coinciding with a sensible improvement in his son's coma, the astronomer decided to accept a pressing invitation that the Duc d'Agnès had made in the course of a letter dated August 22 (*item 618*) and to spend a few relaxing hours in Paris—which, incidentally, allowed him to express a little sympathy and gratitude to the Duc.

We shall not reproduce that letter; it is rather long. Monsieur d'Agnès informs Monsieur Le Tellier therein that the contest of speed between his airplane and the State dirigible has been fixed for September 6. He reiterates the name of his machine, the *Epervier*, and gives that of the aeronef—the *Prolétaire*—furnishes technical information about the race, and urges Monsieur Le Tellier to come and watch the contest and judge for himself the modern hippogriff on which his daughter's kidnappers are to be pursued. He says that his monoplane can do more than 180 kilometers an hour, but that its rapidity is nothing compared to its stability. It is not yet automatic equilibration, but already "something roughly similar...based on the principle that, if an aviator could see the vagaries of the wind in the same way that a navigator can see the waves of the sea, it would be easy for him to steer against them—Bachmès has devised a stabilizing apparatus whose purpose is to render aerial waves perceptible to a pilot; light antennae radiate around the aircraft; by means of electrical sensitivity, they respond to the slightest moment up to thirty meters away from their points, and communicate their indications to a gauge set before he eyes of the interested party."

The start of the race was to be in the heart of Paris, above the Esplanade des Invalides, where the finish-line would also be located; this measure was intended to avoid the displacement of an excited multitude. The two competitors were to double the cathedral at Meaux and come back, covering 24 kilometers.

Monsieur Le Tellier left on September 4, at 10:29 p.m. as before.

VIII. The Red Notebook

The day of the race arrived. The weather was fine. Monsieur Le Tellier perceived that when the concierge came to open the shutters and serve his chocolate. The worthy scientist detested hotels, which he called "fussy," so he was staying in his own house, without a manservant.

The weather was fine. The sun illuminated the apartment, stripped of its curtains and carpets, with its chandeliers and its furniture swathed in dust-covers, filled with a odor of camphor, vetiver and pepper. The window-panes were coated in Spanish white and envelopes hid the renowned water-colors in the drawing-room: the Harpignies, the Fillards and the Le Nains.[32]

The weather was fine; the race would be excellent.

As he got dressed, Monsieur Le Tellier went over what the Duc d'Agnès and he had agreed. The starting-gun would be fired at 10 a.m.; at 9:30 a.m., an automobile belonging to the Duc would be waiting at Monsieur Le Tellier's door, would take him to the Invalides to witness the first act of the trial, and would then immediately set out to take up a position at the entrance to Paris, in order that he might see the vicissitudes of the final kilometers. A special insignia would serve as a priority pass for the vehicle.

---

[32] Henri-Joseph Harpignie (1819-1916) was a landscape painter numbered among the precursors of Impressionism. The second reference is presumably to the rather obscure Ernest Fillard (1868-1933). The surname Le Nain was a signature used indiscriminately by three brothers who shared a studio, Antoine (1588-1648), Louis (1603-1648) and Mathieu (1607-1677); like the Dutch masters cited earlier in the text, they were best-known for painting peasants, but it does not seem at all likely that Le Tellier would have even one painting by them on his walls, so I might have mistaken the reference.

The weather was fine. A crowd of people was walking along the Boulevard Saint-Germain, part of a black host moving in the same direction, from the left bank to the right. For the moment, the entire swarm of the capital was heading for the line of the course, which the newspapers had advertised.

Well, it's nearly time, thought Monsieur Le Tellier. He took up his watch in order to put it in his waistcoat pocket. *Exactly nine-thirty*.

Just then, the sound of a bell resonated in the antechamber, as if to sound that half-hour, for want of the clocks that had all stopped. Smiling at the coincidence, Monsieur Le Tellier opened the door himself—and the smile vanished from his suddenly colorless lips.

Monsieur Monbardeau was standing there, in traveling costume, looking at him sadly.

"What's the matter now? Is it serious?"

"Don't worry. All those you left at Mirastel are well. However..."

"Marie-Thérèse...?"

"No, no! Robert is dead, old chap!"

"Ah! But how do you know? And why have you left Maxime, who is still so ill, alone with the women? Couldn't you have written to me or sent a telegram?"

"I have my reasons, believe me. Listen: the night before last—that of your departure!—I was woken up by the whistle of a fall. As usual, I went out the next morning—yesterday—in the required direction. Madame Arquedouve had said to me: 'An aerolith fell last night between Aignoz and Talissieu.' That's in the marsh.

"After three hours, aided by a few men, I was able to recover it...it was in an extremely muddy spot; we went forward on planks, which we had to take up behind us and extended before us. At the bottom of a kind of puddle hollowed out by the violence of the impact, a shapeless mass was slowly sinking into the mud. We pulled it out, at the expense of incredible efforts. Something told me we shouldn't give up...

"I saw immediately that he hadn't been killed by the fall, but well before. The impact had only crushed a cadaver. He had died of asphyxia...*primarily* of asphyxia. His face was swollen, his lips thick and black, like the rest of his face, his eyes extraordinarily dull, his mouth full of coagulated blood. I thought I could also see that he had been subjected to various pressures. When we subject animals to a vacuum, by way of experiment, they suffer the same effects as Robert. A brief autopsy demonstrated to me that his body had swollen up and become bloated, that blood had come out of the epidermis like spurting sweat...that he had, in a way, exploded. Certain anatomical remains had already borne analogous marks, but much less accentuated. He hadn't been vivisected—no, no, that hadn't been done to him."

"What an abomination! But that doesn't tell me why you've come."

"I came to carry out his last wish." From his pocket, Monsieur Monbardeau took a red notebook with copper clasps, which the astronomer remembered having seen before somewhere. "I've come to give you this manuscript. Robert carried it beneath his clothing, secured by a belt, next to his skin. Read what's written on the label."

To be delivered as soon as possible to Monsieur Le Tellier, Director of the Observatory. If he is dead, to Doctor Monbardeau of Artemare. If he is dead, to the Duc d'Agnès. If he is dead, to the Head of State.

On seeing Robert Collin's handwriting, Monsieur Le Tellier could not hold back his tears. He opened the clasps with a hand made clumsy by impatience, and said: "Dear, dear victim of his devotion! Poor boy! Alas, it's two months since he was abducted. Two months of captivity for love of Marie-Thérèse! Alas, for the beautiful dream that he had! And to think that that dream would never have been realized!—that Robert, undoubtedly, would never have had that which is reserved for the Duc to recover...if my daughter is ever returned to us! For him, is it not better to be dead? Let's see what he has to say to me...eh? Who's there?"

"Excuse me, Monsieur," said the concierge, who had just come in. "There's some gen'men downstairs who say they're waiting for you."

"Ah—the car! That's true! You see, Calixte, that I'm absolutely forced to go to this race...and I'm already late...hold on! You can come with me. I'll take you. We'll read the notebook on the way. Come as you are—come on.... My poor little Robert! What a loss! What a loss!"

Amid the crowd of pedestrians, a hundred idlers were forming a circle around the automobile. The sumptuous four-seater intrigued them, being so long and so low-slung, painted mouse-grey like a torpedo-boat, manned by two chauffeurs in khaki livery wearing tricolor ribbons on their arms, and having two flashes in the colors of the Aéro-Club—the sporting organization of the day—in the guise of headlights.

The chauffeurs doffed their caps. One of them gave Monsieur Le Tellier the white armband of an official steward. "Let's hurry, Monsieur," he said, in a respectful tone. "We'll miss the start, and no mistake."

But Monsieur Le Tellier, for the moment, judged the race to be of secondary importance. While the car set off briskly with the brio of a 90-horse-power engine, driven by a mercenary who had no pity on the tires, he began to read to Monsieur Monbardeau what Robert had written for him in pencil—in a neat and regular script, at least in the first few pages.

He had reached the fifth line when one of the men in khaki turned round.

"I don't think it's worth the trouble of going to the Esplanade. The crowd's mad, and no mistake...we'll never get there. If Monsieur wishes, we could take the Concorde and the Rue Royale, then go along the great boulevards. That way, we'll see them pass over, and we'll arrive all the sooner at the exit from Paris...and no mistake."

"Do as you wish," said the astronomer—and he resumed his interrupted reading.

IX. Robert Collin's Journal

What we shall read in Robert Collin's journal is what
Monsieur Le Tellier read to Monsieur Monbardeau in Mon-
sieur d'Agnès's automobile, in the midst of the population of
Paris:[33]

July 4, 3 p.m. *Twenty-four hours have gone by since my
abduction. Until now, I've had too many things to observe to
be able to write. I intend to make a daily record of what I've
seen, and to get it to whoever might be able to make use of my
information to free the prisoners. To get it to them! How? I
don't know... So, it was yesterday (Wednesday July 3), at 3
p.m. that I became a victim of the sarvants, voluntarily. I had
already been exposing myself, alone, for some time. It seemed
that they did not want me. Finally, yesterday, as I was crossing the Forestel—a meadow half way between the Grand-
Colombier and Virieu-le-Petit—I heard the customary hum
approaching, descending toward me.*

*The trilling of grasshoppers was as loud as the hum. It
seemed distant. I looked up into the air, but saw nothing. My
heart was making more noise than the sarvants and the grasshoppers. The long-awaited moment frightened me. I had an
idea about what to expect, but it was vague. I knew that I'd be
taken up into the air, very high—I was entirely dressed, in
consequence, in garments of the warmest sort. I was expecting
a sensation of suction or attraction, which would lift me up to*

---

[33] Renard's narrator inserts a footnote: "*Item 657.* Will the
reader forgive us for reproducing it word for word? We dare to
hope so. The incorrect form given to this primitive document
by its feverish author appears to us to be sacred. We would
have reproduced it in facsimile, were it not for the obligation
that were are under to publish a volume at 3.50 francs (not
including surcharges)."

a balloon or some other machine hiding in the distance, when I felt myself seized brutally from behind, about the torso, and lifted as if by a gigantic, hard and violent fist.

Mad gestures. Attempt to turn around to face the aggressor. Waste of effort. I struggled. During this time whatever was holding me drew me backwards, to itself and released me—except that I did not fall. There was a gap of several centimeters between my feet and the ground. An inexplicable click resounded. The hum became louder, and was confused with other sounds, but that was all I could hear—no more grasshoppers, or anything else. I tried to save myself then, cursing my temerity, mad with fear. Incontinently, though, I encountered a resistance, a rigidity without appearance. I bounded in the opposite direction: the same rampart. It was as if a hypnotist had ordered me to believe that there was always an obstacle in front of me; as if the air had solidified around me while remaining as transparent as ever. I thought about the power of suggestion, especially as a cause of levitation, which reminded me of experiments in spiritualism, previously assessed as fraudulent.

All of that took a second.

Then, suddenly, an incalculable force originating from below launched me into the air: an inexorably hectic rise due to some unknown pressure whose action I felt abruptly beneath my feet. One might have thought that the Earth had hurled me into the sky. I was projected like some sort of cannonball...

And I was alone in mid-space, rising up vertically, faster and faster. Below me, the pastureland of Forestel was already no more than the paltry center of an immense, incessantly-growing circle, and the Colombier appeared to flatten out to the same level as everything else. Because of my rapid ascent, the circle—the Earth—was like a moving funnel, all of whose points were being precipitated toward the middle, breathed in by a central cupping-glass. Sensation of nausea above that vertiginous basin, atrociously gut-wrenching. Vertigo paralyzed me. At first, I had gesticulated like the men at Châtel,

213

trying to escape. Now, the terror of the gulf petrified me, the fear of falling back into it, if the mysterious force were to be switched off.

I perceived that I was in a crouching posture. Crouching? On what? On an immaterial and yet solid platform—immaterial, and yet real; unreal and yet material: a flat surface that did not exist, and which, even so...yes, which was vibrating! Impossible to move to check the instruments I was carrying—a barometer among others. Impossible.

Nevertheless, I succeeded in reasoning in my immobility. I managed to listen. The hum persisted in the vicinity. There was also the noise, the wind, of my ascension: ssssssss.... But I felt no breeze. Then I thought of being in an ascending air current, in the bosom of a vertical column of artificial wind, which was lifting me up as rapidly as it flowed toward the zenith itself...but that did not explain the solid contact of my point of support.

At that moment, I still had the conviction that the ascent was only the first phase of the voyage, that I would soon reach the machine where the pump or magnet was located, and that that machine would carry me through the ether, doubtless to some heavenly body—for my default assumption was still that the sarvants were the inhabitants of some other planet, their actions having seemed to me to be extraterrestrial: marvelous, one might say. So I watched out for the appearance on high of that machine, which did not show itself.

And I continued to rise. The Earth's disk comprised an immense extent of regions, already much less rich in colors, and blurred. Mont Blanc was a dazzling projection leveling off increasingly. I had far surpassed its height.

What? *I thought.* Here I am at more than 4810 meters, and I'm not cold!

I estimated the altitude I had reached at 6000 meters. Temperature declines by approximately one degree per 515 meters, so I should have been covered in ice; my respiration should have generated a thick vapor; I should have been shivering; I should have been suffering mountain sickness, to combat which I had brought an oxygen cylinder. Probably, all that was about to happen. I observed my breath, which would become awkward, accelerated, labored, and my heart, which would beat precipitately. I watched out for a sensation of plenitude in the vessels, the pulse of the carotid. I expected my nose to start bleeding at any moment. My head would ache, certainly; I struggled in advance against sensory numbness, somnolence, mental prostration. It seemed to me that I already felt the characteristic thirst, the desire for cold drinks— nauseated, tongue dry, belches, aching knees and legs, as if after a long march, exhaustion...but, save for the stomach- ache due to vertigo, there was none of that—none of the symp- toms that I had studied carefully in books.

And yet I was still rising, and I was certain that if I had been able to pick up the thermometer and look at it, I would have seen that it stood at between 16 and 18 degrees below zero. In sum, it was quite comfortable—and yet I was at least 9000 meters above ground—higher than Gaurisankar, where the thermometer would have marked 35 below zero! I remem- bered, with amazement, that without oxygen, no human being had ever attained those regions without losing consciousness. Berson and Süring had reached 10,500 meters, but with oxy- gen respirols.[34] Besides, was I not higher now? It was a dream! I had to check...

---

[34] Arthur Berson and Reinard Süring broke the previous alti- tude record in the balloon Preussen on July 31, 1901, but near- ly died in the attempt. Like Robert's, their oxygen-supplies were only equipped with mouthpieces, not masks, and became useless when they lost consciousness; fortunately, they had already begun to descend and recovered when they reached 20,000 feet. Robert's account of the symptoms of hypoxia are presumably derived from a publication by their collaborator, the Austrian physiologist Hermann von Schrotter. The impro- vised term "respirol" is considerably older in its origin; it is used to describe the hypothetical breathing apparatus em- ployed in Henry de Graffigny and Georges le Faure's scien-

I made an effort, which succeeded; the vertigo was diminishing as I drew away from the Earth. I was able to grab the oxygen cylinder behind my back and hold its mouthpiece close to my lips, in case of emergency. Then the thermometer: + 18°C! And the barometer: 760 millimeters! Exactly the same pressure as that at ground level! The mean pressure of terra firma*! Was I really still on Earth? I thought I was an idiot. My state of mind was somewhat different from the heroic one that I had anticipated!*

Naturally, one page of this notebook represents one minute. I listened harder. It seems that I perceived... and I perceived quite clearly a soft double flapping sound, which made a muffled clip clop, clip clop, *and so on. Being alone—and what solitude!—I attributed the noise to myself. Was it not some effect of altitude on my physiology?*

By means of my watch, and assuming that I was still rising with the same velocity, I made approximate calculations of height. Soon I was certain of having reached 30,000 meters— and the record of unmanned balloon-probes! But there I had the illusion of being motionless, because my continued movement away from the too-distant Earth was no longer sensible at a glance. On lifting my eyes, however, I could see the sky losing its blueness, darkening. Then, suddenly, above me and to my right—which is to say, to the south of the point toward which I was rising—I perceived a blackness that was visibly growing. It seemed to me that it was falling, but it was me who was rising toward its fixity.

I was about to look through my binoculars, but an unexpected sick feeling took hold of me. A buzz in my ears beat an incessant drum-roll. It seemed that the clip clop *had stopped abruptly. I was gripped by an intense cold; my arms and neck-muscles stiffened, spontaneously and progressively. I expe-*

---

tific romance *Aventures extraordinaire d'un savant russe* (1888-96; tr. as *The Extraordinary Adventures of a Russian Scientist*, Black Coat Press), and might well have been coined by them. The term is used nowadays as the name of a drug.

rienced incredible difficulty in breathing, my eyes clouded over and I was scarcely able to observe that the thermometer had dropped, plunging terribly to -22°, and that it was continuing to fall. I was unable to search for the barometer in one of my pockets. Even so, my failing eyes thought they discerned a form that was emerging everywhere, on all sides at the same time. It seemed to me that the air was growing dark... but was that not a result of the onset of fainting?

The instinct of self-preservation found me the mouthpiece of the bladder full of oxygen; then, immediately, I recovered my senses. All weakness was dissipated,

I was imprisoned in a tall and vast cylinder of ice, a kind of sealed turret. I was crouching on the bottom of a jar of ice whose thickness was increasing continuously, gradually attenuating the daylight. And it was snowing inside the cylinder. My clothes were covered in frost, my breath condensed into sleet; it was as if I were imprisoned in a frosted-glass jug.

Suddenly, the soft flapping resumed, with greater rapidity—should I say liveliness, or even eagerness?—as if to make up for lost time. I think it was behind my back. That magical sound was accompanied by a sort of draught of warmth and dryness. The temperature rose again; the light brightened again; the refrigerated jar melted. Soon, no more remained of it than a thin cylindrical sheet of frost, and that sheet—that tube—disappeared in its turn, as if wiped away. With it went the last hint of sickness, as if it too had been wiped away...

I found myself alone in the midst of immensity, still rising. The mirage had lasted a few seconds. The sky was visibly less blue than before, however, and the black dot, increasingly large, had become a square spot.

It was then that I tried to take up my binoculars in order to observe that spot—but I recalled that they had slipped out of my hands in the first moments of my fainting fit. I felt a keen irritation when, to my profound amazement...

At this point, Monsieur Le Tellier ceased reading from the red notebook. An immense clamor had distracted his attention.

The automobile emerged into the Place de l'Opéra. A cannon-shot had just announced the start of the race, and it reverberated around Paris in glorious and enthusiastic echoes.

X. The Famous Friday, September 6

For the first time, the sky of old Lutèce was about to serve as the arena for an aerial regatta.[35] It was a festive blue.

The entire city was seething, half its people having invaded the roofs. Since early morning, its edifices had been crowned by a swarming mass of human beings. Skylights had been rented out like the front seats at a première. Overloaded with spectators, several balconies had already collapsed. Certain houses seemed to have come to life, so extensively covered were their façades and terraces with agitated humankind. The thick tide of the crowd moved in slow eddies through the rivers of the streets, the pools of the squares, especially in the quarters cut through by the course of the race. That imaginary line, drawn between the Invalides and the Cathedral of Meaux, traversed the Carrefour de la Rue Louis-le-Grand, the Rue de la Chaussée-d'Antin, the Boulevard des Italiens and the Boulevard des Capucines; there, more than anywhere else, the buildings half-disappeared beneath a living carapace. The prodigious city served as a grandstand for everyone. It was filled by the infinite rumor of a titanic Coliseum. A menagerie odor mingled with cooking smells rising from the ground dulled the warmth of the fine late-summer day.

No one was talking about the Peril anymore; people were only talking about the race. The two competing machines gave rise to intense chatter. No one had seen them as yet, and yet everyone had his favorite, some preferring the lighter-than-air craft to the heavier-than-air craft, others wagering against the

---

[35] In fact, by September 6, 1912, "old Lutèce" (i.e. Paris) had served as the starting-point for one of the most lavish air races of the period: the Circuit d'Europe, which involved 52 competitors and began on June 18, 1911. Renard had evidently completed his text before that event took place, or had even been advertised.

State or against Capital, while many others based their opinions on the more-or-less irresistible sympathy they felt with regard to the pilots.

The pilots—the gods of the moment—were the Duc d'Agnès, the jockey of the *Epervier*, and Captain Santus, mahout of the *Prolétaire*. News-vendors were selling their portraits and biographies. They held them up on the ends of poles to the curiosity-seekers on the balconies, and jumped aboard carriages that were trying to reach the suburbs in the direction of Meaux.

As time advanced, the heaped-up public quivered with excitement. Circulation in the main streets increased, as in the arteries of a fever-victim. At the Carrefour Louis-le-Grand, the effervescence attained its maximum at about 9:45 a.m. From then on, those lower down, not being able to see anything, shouted to those higher up, behind the monstrous letters of billboards, among the advertising-hoardings and the chimney-pots: "Can you see them? Have they taken off?"

From the balcony of the Pavillon de Hanovre, the roofs of the Vaudeville and the summit of every roof, the reply came back: "No!"

Gibes followed. That produced a jolly confusion of invective—and those lower down continued to gaze at those higher up, who were all gazing at the distant dome of the Invalides, where the sunlight gilded, even more than its bronzes, two shining granules: two little captive balloons, maintained at an interval of 100 meters, determining the starting-line, which was also the finish-line.

Down below, underneath the little balloons, there must have been a considerable deployment of rostrums, bands and flowers. The national pomp draped its crimson velvet there upon golden rods. The *Marseillaise,* inevitably...

But at 9:50 a.m., the audience on the roofs became agitated, like a crop-field stirred by the breeze. It was like a profound, tremulous and gigantic sigh of delight, and the same phrase was repeated hundreds of thousands of times: "There's the *Prolétaire* going up!"

They could see it. It was a long tapering cigar, yellow and red. It rose up, glossy with reflected morning light. The propeller, rotating with a lightning glimmer, was visible through opera-glasses.

"Here's d'Agnès! Here's the *Epervier* now!"

"Eh? So small? That little thing flying back and forth?"

"It's him—but you can see that it's describing spirals around the dirigible."

"Ah! They're level!"

"Level with the little balloons!"

"Beyond the little balloons!"

The evolutions of the airplane and the aeronef were followed excitedly. The *Prolétaire* came about majestically and directed its prow toward Meaux. It was no longer seen in profile, but head on. It resembled, thus, a sphere of paltry dimensions. The *Epervier*, next to it, extended its rigid wings, in order that they would pass the starting-line together; that was understood.

Then the cannon-shot thundered, a signal fired by one of the Invalides' pre-Montgolfierian culverins, now twice historic. The pathetic, sumptuous, solemn cannon-shot was met with the response of an immense popular clamor, which reverberated around Paris in glorious and enthusiastic echoes.

Santus and d'Agnès were off.

An enormous joy filled the leaden terraces. They came straight toward the Carrefour. Parasols snapped shut and, higher up than anyone else, the cinematographs picked out their expected silhouette. Opera-glasses rigged out the people with the long eyes of black lobsters, showing them the *Prolétaire* and the *Epervier* side by side, growing larger and larger, the *Prolétaire* yellow and the *Epervier*...ah! *blue!* The *Epervier* was blue! The news ran through the crowd like a sonorous *ignis fatuus*. Blue! The monoplane was blue! They had not expected that, and they were not pleased to discover that the bird was blue, the color of the Heavens and the Peril, like a little bit of sky elegantly materialized. The bird was blue! It was like something from the *Thousand-and-One Nights*, with a suggestion of fairy-tales!

"Fly to me promptly!" said the multitude, laughing incontinently.[36]

The cinematographs began to function, zoom lenses came into play...

They were flying at an altitude of 100 feet. In the calm air, they approached silently, in a whirlwind. The airplane, equipped with its electricity-extractor, was not making the usual racket. Its two propellers were visibly turning, like two nebulous suns, and their double throb was audible, like two high-pitched sirens, setting up a sort of irritating resonance, that grated on the nerves like the highest-pitched strings. The *Epervier*'s slender stabilizing antennae became visible, as slender as a cat's whiskers—or the legs of a giant gnat—all around the apparatus.

A trail of ovations followed them. When they reached the Carrefour, there was an explosion of cheers so frantic that it was comparable to a firework display. It was a concert of shouts, in which everyone cried out the name of his favorite at the top of his voice, concurrently: "Bravo, Santus! Bravo! Go on, d'Agnès! Go on, then!"—because the *Prolétaire*, to the right and above the *Epervier*, had a slight lead.

Hearts palpitated to a chauvinistic rhythm. The crowd waved handkerchiefs and hats frenetically. Captain Santus raised his kepi; his aides gave military salutes; the Duc d'Agnès gestured with his hand.

You might have thought you were seeing a copper shell pursued by a steel eagle. The two tempests that they provoked shook the oriflammes at the tops of the flag-poles. A gust of pride and intoxication swept over the pale faces, and on the

---

[36] The members of the multitude are quoting from Madame d'Aulnoy's famous 17th century fairy tale, "L'Oiseau bleu;" the full line is *"Oiseau bleu, couleur du temps, vole à moi promptement"* [Blue bird, color of the sky, fly to me promptly].

roof of the Vaudeville a well-known actress, addressing the universe, proclaimed in her beautiful voice: "It's chic, all the same, to be French!"

Suddenly, though, the great crowd became alarmed; the ocean of human beings swelled with anxiety.

Just as the rivals were passing over the Pavillon de Hanovre, the *Prolétaire*'s poop had dipped. Its cruciform fins jerked downwards, and further downwards, and its unbreachable envelope suddenly caved in, as if someone were pulling at it obstinately from the interior of the balloon itself…

Slowing down, the dirigible reversed its engines desperately…but the gasbag reinflated in the same way that it had deformed, unexpectedly; the aeronef pitched, leapt up, restarted…and…

And it was the *Epervier*'s turn-which, without any apparent cause, heeled over in an alarming manner, its left wing lifting…

The Duc d'Agnès could be seen operating his controls at top speed, veering in spite of his best efforts and unable to straighten up. The monoplane listed; it was about to fall into the gulf carpeted with living beings. The army in the gulf moaned in agony…then howled victoriously! The *Epervier* was on the move again; a diabolical roll swayed its blue wingspan—but it was no longer listing. A second swerve righted it, and launched it into the contest again, in pursuit of the *Prolétaire*.

The acclamation that they had sewn as they passed by died away. People turned round to follow them until they were lost to sight. The women, however, were breathing in their smelling-salts. God, what a fright they had had!

The automobiles were roaring, sounding their horns, sirens and whistles, impatient to get beyond Pantin.

What had happened? Had the backwashes of the propellers interfered with one another? An atmospheric current?

The comments were in full flow when muffled and sinister sounds broke out: groans, collisions; a tumult of horror. All eyes turned toward the terrace of the Pavillon de Hanovre. A

223

commotion there was throwing people into one another. Frightened eyes were upraised; telegraphic cables had broken spontaneously, and their fall had provoked the disorder. The stone balustrade held back the mob, while the sculpted groups that decorated it supported clusters of panic-stricken individuals in search of a refuge. The left-hand sculpture suddenly collapsed with its howling cargo. The block fell on to the pedestrians on the pavement, amid blood, fear and amazement. There were too many people on the statues, damn it! The others were also about to fall...

But no. What fell was rubble, which continued to crumble away from the wall at the same place, showering the breathless wounded with further blows. Emerging from the breach in the gallery, an infernal stream of ruin and demolition descended along the old grey wall: a slow thunderbolt worked its way along the masonry, eating out a white, deep and cruel crack...

And the crowds that thronged the area, seized by panic, watched that frightful fraying extend. It continued to descend, stripping the rotunda, splintering its façade, shattering the windows, fracturing the ironwork, stoning the dead and the dying. As it reached the height of the nearby chestnut-tree, the tree shuddered and split...that flameless, noiseless, lazy thunderbolt crumpled the leaves and broke the branches from top to bottom...

And then the indescribable itself occurred.

A terrible crash like two colliding trains was abruptly heard, in the very center of the crossroads, and a catastrophe unfolded unequalled in the centuries of history: a fantastic tohu-bohu of telescoped carriages, stricken horses, livid coachmen, demented chauffeurs and bloodied individuals fleeing insanely in every direction, howling: "The Blue Peril!"

Lined up on the steps of the plaza, the surrounding crowd had started as one man. Here and there, people were gesticulating like fanatics, but the others, breathless, remained rooted to the spot by fear and stupefaction. None was in mortal terror, but even so, a groan ran through the multitude like a simoom through a forest of baobabs. From further away, feminine lamentations arose.

What did they think was happening? Nothing, for the moment. After a few seconds of panic, a number of witnesses had the curious impression of a "hardening of the air" or a "magnetic barricade", or a thick wall of crystal—superlatively pure crystal—slowly descend across the boulevard, as a theater curtain descends. To either side of it, the circulating traffic was colliding with that strange portcullis, which flattened against the wooden pavement those unlucky enough to be directly beneath it. What they were able to imagine—the certainty—was that some diabolical sluice-gate had blocked the way.

In spite of the cataclysmic debacle which then ensued, in the name of the Blue Peril, rescuers ran forward—but the hypocritical object stopped their charge. They ran into it with considerable violence. They were crashing into emptiness, into nothing at all. They encountered an insurmountable *absence*. The air, on the attack, staved in their skulls.

The police, with great difficulty, regained control. An officer intervened, had the two ranks of carriages cleared away, and set up a cordon of his men around the perfidious region, whose isolation was required. Thus was established a broad interval, which started from the Pavillon de Hanovre and extended for a dozen meters into the Chaussée d'Antin. The sight of the uniforms engendered confidence and released tongues. A revolutionary assembly would have been quieter. No one was talking about the race any longer; they were only talking about the Peril.

Amid the impetuous chatter, ambulances and stretchers cut through the swarming crowds, and fruitless attempts were made to reach the unfortunates who were crushed against the ground by the now-impassable atmosphere.

The Prefect of Police, who had just arrived, began to lose his assurance when a well-dressed gentleman, having elbowed his way through a veritable crush of his peers, was brought to him by an agent. The gentleman had an imposing appearance.

He wore the white armband of an official steward and was clutching a red notebook to his breast. He was followed by another gentleman, in traveling costume. Someone recognized Monsieur le Tellier; his name sprang from mouth to mouth while the Prefect of Police, taking off his hat, placed himself under the newcomer's orders.

The astronomer exercised a kind of dictatorship. The fearful masses, sick with worry, had scented his competence and adopted him as their protector. He calmly riffled the pages of the red notebook, then stuck it in his pocket. Afterwards, escorted by a general staff of various personages, he set out to accomplish a tour of the impracticable space, striking it with the flat of his hand.

At each slap, the air rendered a dull sound.

A policeman imitated him. His comrades, reassured, similarly began to rap the impenetrable atmosphere, to the extent that the entire cordon was tapping away, seemingly undertaking an exercise in simulated riot control. The box in space, however, made a noise like a washboard. Monsieur Le Tellier hastened to put an end to it. The brief collective demonstration had sufficed, however, to reveal *visually* the presence of a large *invisible* object and the shape that it adopted at the height of the policemen. The public on the upper steps had grasped this at a glance, and, as the inexplicable cracking of the Pavillon had not been forgotten, imaginations took flight and the events changed shape.

A large, invisible, oblong object had just fallen from the sky, after having collided the *Prolétaire* and tipped the blue bird over.

Monsieur Le Tellier continued his round, still feeling his way, but at the two ends of the object he needed a stool to reach it; the extremities were raised; one of them, moreover, corresponded to the termination of the graze in the Hanovre's rotunda, and that graze ended two meters above the pavement. The other extremity, in the Chaussée d'Antin, was the object of sustained attention on the astronomer's part. A taller stool was passed overhead, from hand to hand, until it reached him.

Monsieur Le Tellier gave a few orders, which were immediately transmitted. Bicycle couriers drew away.

The examination of the object continued. According to the gestures and manipulation of the feeler, it seemed that it was terminated by two points, like a torpedo. It can be assumed that such a word cannot fail to give rise to apprehension. "Meteor" and "shooting star" had already been mentioned; that was nothing—but "torpedo" signified something *manufactured*! An explosive device! A *bomb*, in sum, and an enormous one! Were the sarvants anarchists? Nihilists determined to obliterate Paris?

The central brigades and a battalion of the Republican Guard requested by Monsieur Le Tellier arrived at the appointed place in order to contain a confusion as dangerous as any riot. The troop regulated the flow of the citizens, pushed them back without any violence and cleared the Carrefour. The way was clear for the appearance of three scarlet automobiles, full of firemen with shiny helmets, which turned the corner of the Rue de la Michodière to the lugubrious tocsin of their two-note horns.

A short time afterwards, more firemen arrived. These were carrying ropes and jacks. Monsieur Le Tellier asked them to form a circle and delivered a brief harangue, in a voice that his friends would not have recognized.

"Gentlemen, the Prefect of Police has brought you here to carry out a task that is scarcely banal. A little while ago, a voluminous object fell on Paris. It is up to you to clear the public highway. This object *you will not be able to see*. It is there, within the closed cordon of policemen surrounding it, there on that layer of stricken unfortunates—it is what has crushed them.

"I tell you that it is invisible; don't be afraid—for scientists, that's perfectly natural. Simply tell yourself that the object has the benefit of *absolute transparency*; that will help you to understand. What is it, exactly? We don't know—and it's very important that we find out. So I've decided, with the agreement of the authorities, to have the object transported to the Grand Palais, where we shall be able to study it at leisure.[37]

"It's large—but I have every reason to suppose that it isn't as heavy as one might think. It's shaped like a weaver's shuttle the size of a dirigible balloon—without a gondola. It's a spindle, which is square in the middle and whose ends are two tapering, pointed cones, exactly like a *de luxe* Havana cigar. I call your attention to the end that is in the Chaussée d'Antin; it is...ornamented...with a...contraption...with which it is necessary to take care.

"I think I can assure you that there is no danger. However, although the object is made of a substance very solid to the touch, I beg you to act with a great deal of prudence, as if your cargo were as fragile as glassware and as if death might emerge from the slightest crack...

"Let us go closer. It is stuck cross-wise, obstructing the Carrefour, as you can see. I'm now on the other side, and have to shout to make myself heard—it stops sound waves, but not rays of light.

"Let's get to work!"

The officers distributed the men to the left and right of the invisible object. Fifty ropes were slipped underneath it, between the victims of crushing. Each sapper grasped the end of a cable, and a captain ordered: "Heave...ho!"

The ropes stiffened, lifting up their mysterious burden, but each one adapted to the profile of its point of application, so that the fifty ropes displayed the boat-like form that weighed upon them. Nothing could have been odder than those lines, taut but not rectilinear.

The firemen made an adjustment that prevented an inextricable convulsive tangle, then, in collaboration with town

---

[37] The Grand Palais was still a relatively recent monument in 1911, having been built to house the Exposition of 1900; it was a deliberate attempt to emulate the Crystal Palace constructed half a century earlier to house London's Great Exhibition.

sergeants, sustaining the invisible load like Atlas and shrugging their shoulders—which effort perpetuated the support of the nothing—their two parallel files started marching in the direction of the Opéra.

A squadron of municipal guards flanked the grotesque convoy. The infantry of the garrison formed a line along the route, holding back—with difficulty—the flocks of street urchins and shop-girls, office-workers and hooligans which accumulated pell-mell. A legend was propagated through the groups, born of the misinterpretation of Monsieur Le Tellier's speech as much as his title of astronomer; it was said that a dirigible balloon made of rock-crystal had arrived from the Moon, manned by Selenites, which could not be seen by the naked eye. Presented in these terms, the adventure provoked guffaws of laughter; the fear of being duped gave rise to the suspicion of a hoax, in which some of them would believe until their dying day.

From the heights of the mezzanine floors in the Rue de la Paix an efflorescence of clothes-fitters and models, and a babbling host of couturiers and milliners, leaned out of windows to watch the passage of…whatever was passing by. Bewilderment silenced them. "Well, what's all this? Oh, a funeral procession! Where's the hearse?" The notion of the invisible was beyond their reach.

In the Rue de Rivoli, an errand-boy threw a marble over the ropes "to see whether they were pulling his leg". The marble ricocheted off a helmet. The scamp was arrested for the edification of the plebs.

The cortège advanced. In the Place de la Concorde, six generations of Parisians, provincials and foreigners surrounded it, like shifting sand amassing in dunes behind the ranks of soldiers with their weapons grounded. The crowd gave the impression of humankind entire. Monsieur Le Tellier and the Prefect of Police marched at the head. When they had completed their route, the former consulted the red notebook. He was overheard, in front of the obelisk, sending guards on horseback to the nearby Ministry of Marine, to the naval dockyard at Grenelle, and to the school of advanced aeronautics, with instructions to gather as many naval officers as possible at the Grand Palais.

Questions were raining down on the rope-bearers, but their orders rendered them mute. They had the impression that they were transporting a vast apparatus, relatively light but offering a great deal of resistance and inertia, which they privately attributed to its cubic capacity.

Between the Chevaux de Marly, the hurrying column hesitated. Beneath visors of metal or leather, faces petrified with alarm turned away. An increasing murmur was audible in the distance...

But it was not the advent of a second disaster—it was the race! The competitors were coming back! They had forgotten all about them...

Two atoms were emerging from the depths of the sky: two chimerical and authentic dragons, offspring of human beings and science, fighting graciously and with gusto, arriving amid a wake of cheers more beautiful than any symphony.

The *Epervier* had pulled ahead of the *Prolétaire*! It sank toward the finish-line, an arrow in its speed, a crossbow in its appearance. The cannon gravely consecrated the victory of the blue bird.

By virtue of an exchange of destinies, Captain Santus retired into obscurity, and Monsieur Le Tellier replaced him on the podium of renown, next to Monsieur d'Agnès—but Paris did not know that both these idols, apparently so different, had but one thought in their heads, one love in their hearts and one name on their lips: Marie-Thérèse.

XI. Continuation of the Journal

Busy with the guidance of his apparatus, the pilot of the *Epervier* had not noticed any sign of the general commotion. He learned of the miraculous event after landing his aircraft in the midst of a sparse crowd. The agglomeration had ranged in the direction of the Grand Palais, where the centripetal star of Parisian movement was now converging. The Pont Alexandre drew out the marching crowd; the Duc d'Agnès took the same route.

Not everyone who wanted to could enter the strictly forbidden edifice. The 131st line regiment was guarding the entrances against a shameless and innumerable crowd. The aviator presented himself to the colonel door-keeper at the same time as three naval officers. Having had their entitlements validated, they passed through.

The tranquility of the deserted, excessively cathedralesque hall, scarcely cheered up by chirping sparrows, contrasted bizarrely with the forced gathering outside. At that time of the year, the temple of exhibitions and horse-shows was liberated. At the center of its immense floor was a huddled group of infinitely small gentlemen. To one side, pygmy agents and insectile foremen were sitting on the ground, seemingly resting.

The Duc d'Agnès knew perfectly well that it was a matter of some invisible object; he was not in the least surprised not to be able to see anything. Within the group, he recognized Doctor Monbardeau and Monsieur Le Tellier, chatting to the Prefect of Police.

"Well," said the latter, "if you're absolutely determined, read it."

"It's indispensable," Monsieur Le Tellier retorted. "I demand, urgently, that no one should touch the *object* until we have acquainted ourselves with the entire contents of the journal. That will surely enable us to avoid snags, and perhaps accidents."

"So be it," agreed the Prefect of Police. Addressing his officers, he said: "Let your men have a meal, gentlemen."

The voices, initially shrill, were amplified by cavernous and thunderous echoes which burst forth from the angles of the architecture.

"Ah, Monsieur!" said the astronomer, on seeing the Duc. "Come in! Congratulations! Let us tell you a story!"

The young victor welcomed the congratulations with a smile, and did not weep at the story which apprised him of the death of Robert Collin—but what intrigued him most of all was the invisible object—the thing that had shaken him so rudely above the Pavillon de Hanovre. "Where is it?" he said. "Where is it?"

"Walk straight ahead," instructed Monsieur Le Tellier, "toward that cast-iron pillar; you'll run into it." Then, in a secretive murmur, he added: "There's some kind of propeller at the rear, you know."

Monsieur d'Agnès walked forward, holding his arms out in front of him, like someone moving in the dark, or a blind man, and came up against something hard, smooth and cold, which did not exist so far as his eyes were concerned. Monsieur Le Tellier showed him an imprint in the dust, shaped like a boat, like a prelate's ogival seal. He told him that it was caused by the base of the strange object, and showed him the poor little sparrows lying all around it, which had flown into it and broken their heads on the invisible rampart.

"Notice that the draught we were able to feel is no longer perceptible," he concluded. "The object is intercepting it. On reading Robert's journal, we shall marvel at the shelter provided by this singular screen…"

He opened the red notebook. His audience gathered around. Monsieur Le Tellier leaned back casually into the void, and resumed his reading from the beginning. He revisited the formation of the cylinder of ice around the bewildered Robert, rising toward the zenith, then the disappearance of the unexpected jar. Finally, he repeated the memorable passage at which he had been interrupted by the popular clamor:

It was then that I tried to take up my binoculars in order to observe that spot—but I recalled that they had slipped out of my hands in the first moments of my fainting fit. I felt a keen irritation when, to my profound amazement, I perceived them nearby, lying in a circular pool of water, in which I had collapsed myself—a large liquid disk about four meters in diameter, exactly like visible water in an invisible tub. That round puddle was carrying me like the flying carpet in the Persian fable. I was taking an obligatory hip-bath therein, but I was grateful for the illusion of support that gave my eyes something to rest on, thus delivering me from vertigo. Beyond it— for it was clear and calm—the blurred Earth was growing paler.

I understood that the water came from the melting of the cylinder. And since it was there, as round and flat as a mill- stone, there had to be an invisible floor underneath it that was supporting us—the pool, me and my binoculars. The ice—dear Lord!—had formed on the interior of a material cylinder, permanent but invisible: a turret-elevator with the aid of which the inhabitants of that square patch brought their pris- oners up to them! I was neither in a column of aspired atmos- phere nor a magnetic fluid, but in an invisible elevator po- wered by an unknown force: a sealed vase in which the pres- sure and temperature were maintained equal to those down below, and where, in consequence, the barometer and the thermometer always indicated the same figures. And a little while before, when the ice had made its appearance, when I had fainted—what had caused it? A breakdown! A simple breakdown of the machinery!

I was stunned for some time. We astronomers are long used to marveling at various invisible objects,[38] however, so

---

[38] Renard's narrator inserts a footnote: "This phrase repro- duces an idea that Monsieur Le Tellier has already expressed, albeit rather differently, in Chapter X, and which might sur- prise the reader. What follows with clarify this temporary con- fusion."

how admiring could I be of a box that was, after all, no more for my eyes than a real elevator had always been for my nose—which is to say, imperceptible—no more than oxygen, for example, had always been for them, but which was for my hands well and truly hard, polished, rounded and cold, and which, tapped with a finger, sounded for my ears. That did not prevent me from drying my binoculars with my handkerchief, in order to look at the square patch where the ingenious skip was doubtless going to deposit me. The skip was certainly being hauled up, for there could be no question of aerostats at such altitudes, even ones inflated with pure hydrogen and much less heavy than air. Invisible halyards? Hertzian currents? Magnetic attraction? One or the other. It was the spot that would transport me to another planet...

I reasoned in that manner, but I was mistaken. The higher I climbed, the more accentuated became the southward displacement of the spot, which presented itself in the form of a brown square checkered with colorless lines. I was therefore heading somewhere else—and that annoyed me.

The terrestrial horizon had appeared in the course of my ascent. To the south, the west and the north it was tinted with a characteristic blue-green. The seas! I must be prodigiously high up! Having made approximate numerical calculations, I found that we must be 40 kilometers from the ground. Another ten kilometers and I would reach a zone...

Damn it! I thought. It's there that science situates...let's see, then, what does science have say about the atmosphere that is relevant to me? The atmosphere: a gaseous layer that envelopes the Earth and follows it in all its movements. Its thickness is not known with certainty. All that is known for sure is that it does not vanish into the void. Its theoretical limit is 10,000 leagues; estimates vary from 70 kilometers to 40,000!

What is known from reliable evidence is that there are two distinct layers in the atmosphere. One, the lower, in contact with the ground, measures about 50 kilometers in depth. It is rich, unstable, traversed by clouds and tormented by winds.

234

It is the environment that supports terrestrial life, and it is what people mean when they talk about "the atmosphere." This layer rarefies as it becomes more distant from the Earth and it becomes a vacuum at about 50 meters—not an absolute vacuum, nor the ether, but a relative vacuum, such as one can obtain with a pump.

It's the relative vacuum that constitutes the second layer of atmosphere, whose thickness is problematic. It is an etherized atmosphere, according to Quételet:[39] a vacuum scarcely seasoned by air; a slightly aerated vacuum in which human beings could no more live than in an absolute vacuum. A stable and serene zone, it is superimposed on the first— insensibly, the meteorologists say, but certainly somewhere around 50 kilometers—and gradually becomes an absolute vacuum.

So, if my ascent continued much longer, I would penetrate that layer, as terrible for me as the bottom of the sea! And the milieu that I was traversing must already be extremely rarefied! What, then, was the spot?

I studied the spot. Set against that extraordinarily dark blue sky, it was almost level with me. I was thus easily able to see it. As was logical, it had changed shape. But my eyes were mediocre, and I raised the binoculars to them. At the same time, I unbuckled the strap of my photographic apparatus in order to make use of it.

Thud! *A violent shock threw me down full length in the suddenly-splashing puddle. Bad luck!—my spectacles fell off and I dropped my binoculars! Simultaneously, it seemed to me that darkness abruptly fell* above me. *I heard metallic sliding sounds* around me, *dry clicks*...

---

[39] Adolphe Quételet (1796-1874) is now best known as a mathematician and statistician, but he was also a professional astronomer who also used his observatory in Brussels to make meteorological observations, which he attempted to integrate into his more general interest in geophysics.

235

The horrible rigid grip that had lifted me from the Colombier seized me again and, at the very instant when I took
my spare pair of spectacles out of my pocket, I felt myself
lifted vertically upwards, and then stop. I heard a metallic
scraping beneath me; the grip lowered me by an inch, then
released me, and I found myself standing on another invisible
support—which had to be at the height of the cylinder's ceiling, if I recalled the icy apparition correctly. Five meters lower down, though, the round pool became calm again. To complete my misfortune, my photographic apparatus had also
fallen; I saw it floating, out of reach, next to my binoculars
and my spectacles. It was a major disaster for me, but...

[At this point, a few words were crossed out.]

The sky had suddenly become as black as ink, even
though it was day-time. From the height of the new cabin into
which, I deduced, I had been transported after it was superimposed on the first, this is what I discovered:

A horizontal surface extended into the distance in every
direction, absolutely bare and calm. It described around me,
to the horizon, the immense circumference of the open sea,
and above it the firmament was a black cupola in which the
stars shone excessively, all of them, and all fixed. And in that
ultra-nocturnal sky, like that one would see from the Moon or
any world without an atmosphere, the ray-less Sun was declining, a large, precise disk. The snowy surface of that slivery sea
shone toward the horizon, but the nearer it was to me, the less
it shone and the more it became diaphanous, unreal, phantasmal, finishing up by disappearing. Beneath me I had nothing
but a 50,000-meter abyss, without anything interposed between its depths and my eyes, and that abyss was full of light.

I found myself on the surface of an ocean of light, or rather of atmosphere—an ocean whose bed was visible: the
Earth, with the algae of its forests, the shoals of its mountains.
I had just emerged into a deadly milieu, on to the surface of an
atmospheric sea; and that sea was nothing other than the first
layer, the famous first layer, which did not conclude gradually, by progressive rarefaction, as science had every right to

suppose, but concluded suddenly and neatly, like a true sea. Contrary as it was to the expansive properties of gases, the two atmospheres were superimposed like two liquids of differing density—and now, the horrific vacuum surrounded me.

In my new receptacle, the same temperature and the same pressure as before; the same flapping sound. I palpated the invisible case experimentally, and found it cubic and narrow; I could touch the ceiling. As I devoted myself to this occupation, innumerable grinding sounds became audible in the walls of my cell and perhaps in the roof: the rattle of iron components, the clicking of hooks. None of that could have made any noise externally, in the vacuum, a poor medium for sound, but within my cube the air conducted sound as well as light and I could hear everything that touched the walls.

Suddenly, I felt myself forcefully lifted up—me and my capsule. Thanks to my three lost objects, which suddenly seemed to sink downwards and describe a plunging arc, I deduced that I was being made to describe a rather complicated ascending arc, analogous to that of goods moved by a steam-powered crane when they are unloaded. The water in the pool down below had disappeared; doubtless the departure of my cabin had put it in contact with the vacuum, and everyone knows that in a vacuum, there can be no liquids.

Immobile now, higher than before, I gazed stupidly at my lost binoculars and detective equipment. I turned round abruptly in the direction of progress, beside myself at the thought that some accident might put me in contact with the void, and wanting to know where I was going...

The spot was coming toward me.

It appeared to be situated four or five kilometers to the south—the stars gave me better information than the compass, which was functioning poorly. To the extent that my spectacles permitted me to gauge it, it was a kind of lattice-work house. The sole characteristic of which I could be certain—and easily—was that it was not posed like a pontoon on the quiet phantom sheet, but that it seemed to be hovering in the void, at a considerable height—about a dozen times its own height—above the atmospheric sea.

I think I'm describing this badly—but if one knew the situation I was in!

And my invisible vehicle, too, was not moving at the level of the aerial sea. It was following an undulating course at a variable height, tracing sinuous curves vertically and horizontally, climbing and descending slopes, slowing as it rose and accelerating as it descended, but continually approaching the lattice-work house. One might have thought that it was rolling along an invisible road, on an invisible terrain set upon the surface of the air like a floating island. One might have thought that, having reached a certain celestial harbor, after a gaseous journey, lifting-tackle had deposited me on a quay, on a truck waiting there, and that the truck was transporting me along a winding road, through an invisible landscape, to the destination of that latticed building, visible itself but constructed on an indiscernible hill...

I was finally about to meet my kidnappers and see the person for whose sake I had come once again.

Vertigo, however, made itself felt again, more powerful than ever, aggravated by the roller-coaster movement of my wagon. (Was it a wagon?) I had to lay my cloak on the floor in order to solidify it for my eyes and hide the view of the Earth-bed abyss.

What a situation!

I tried to make myself to believe that the strange ground in question, unbreakable and invisible, sustained by the atmosphere at its periphery, might well be an artificial creation, a fabrication of engineers. I would have liked to believe it, to reassure myself that the fear generated within me by the idea that such a thing might be natural and unknown, an unsuspected attic of the Earth...an attic of Damocles...

I was greatly overexcited. That idea fluttered in my skull like a panic-stricken butterfly in a box—the idea, in that puerile and morbid form, that certain savants, having taken to the air, had become the sarvants! But I had great difficulty; I

238

felt in my bones that I was in a natural world. *The best, most agreeable thing was to suppose that its inhabitants were the same human beings who had discovered it...perhaps men made invisible, or perhaps men as visible as me, whom I was about to see, finally, in their château of palisades.*

Of palisades. It still seemed to me that they were palisades. It was getting close, that château; I was climbing the hillside that led up to it. I was climbing the invisible mountain, in the midst of the void. I was climbing above the Air now, toward the construction. Again I felt a need to express the joy that came over me at the thought of the person that I was about to rejoin here...who was probably contained in that prison...

[More words were crossed out here.]

Ah, that prison! It reserved the most atrocious heartbreak for me...

As he read these final words, Monsieur Le Tellier could not help experiencing a great emotion. The red notebook trembled in his hands as if it were a living creature on the point of death. The reading concluded with a croak that was all the more harrowing for being slightly risible.

Seeing that, the Duc d'Agnès, who was listening with his eyebrows furrowed, took possession of the journal and continued reading in the same fashion...

XII. The Journal, Continued

The visible mass toward which I was being ferried along a serpentine upward path, the steepness of which inclined my floor and made the wheels groan under a more forceful effort—the mass, the spot, the prison—was not a lattice-work house. It was not a good, solid and visible house, like those on Earth. Soon, my defective eyes saw that the mass was dispersed in a quantity of distinct small masses which, by the raw light of the black sky, seemed to me to be starkly white and black. These small masses were arranged on steps in horizontal rows, like things set on an invisible stage...

And, obviously, that was what they were. *How stupid I was not to have guessed it at the outset. It was the invisible warehouse of everything that the sarvants had brought up from the Earth!*

My imperceptible delivery van went alongside the ground floor of the imagined monument. That ground floor was occupied by a veritable wood, very low, planted in squares of earth that had surely been brought from down below, one load at a time: brown soil, thickly disposed in unequal squares—squares separated by empty bands; or, to put it another way, by walls that could not be seen.

It was a nursery set in a pancake of humus, which resembled a huge chessboard. And beneath it, the invisible ground thickened as far as the atmospheric sea on which it rested. And above that meager wood, where I recognized the various species of Bugist trees, I perceived a suspended *expanse of dry branches, stones and rocks. It was easy to see that they were posed on the first floor, in rooms corresponding to the rectangles of earth, but they occupied a smaller surface area.*

Above these minerals, on the invisible parquet of the second floor, I saw all sorts of animals arranged in a space equal to that of the stones.

While moving along that fantastic façade, I glimpsed fish swimming in the bosom of parallelepipeds of water whose receptacles could not be distinguished.

Noah's Ark, after a fashion.

Finally, higher still, beneath a final floor reserved for birds, there were men and women. Were our tormentors also there? I was about to find out.

Mademoiselle M-T LT... I searched for her with all my might...

The men and women suspended in mid-air seemed very interested in my arrival. I clearly saw those who were disseminated along the façade leaning against the invisible wall to look at me more intently. The light of the void rendered them as white as clowns, with black shadows in their faces. The others—those who were not on the façade—were spaced out over the entire surface area of the story, like soldiers untidily arranged for drill exercises. They were looking at me through the sparse layer of animals below them. On seeing them thus isolated from one another, like pawns carelessly arrayed on the squares of a chessboard, and seeing them stay there instead of running toward the façade, I understood that each of them had a small separate room.

I was brought to a halt almost in the middle. There was the sound of something hooking on to the top of my cabin; grinding sounds became audible all around, and I was lifted up again, past the level of the plants, then the rocks, then the animals.

On the human floor, I came to an abrupt halt. My cell was slid on to the floor of that story, and I deduced that it would now be incorporated into the mass of the building, and that it was no more than a cube filled with air, juxtaposed with other similar cubes, each containing its man or its woman. Very close to me, in the next compartment, a young man was studying me, and all my Terran brothers had turned toward me: apparitions supported by nothing, it seemed, camped paradoxically in the void, pale and somber at the same time,

241

dirty and repulsive, with faces from an asylum, hospital or prison.

I looked for Mlle. LT in the dispersed crowd. I didn't recognize any of those nightmare physiognomies. There was definitely no one there but victims. The sarvants, too, were invisible!

That's where I am now.

My neighbor is obviously a young Englishman, beardless, haggard and dressed as if for a round of golf. Captured while traveling, or on a day trip? He and I are on the line of prisoners along the façade, who seem to constitute the façade. Another line is parallel to it, then another, and yet others. There must be corridors between the lines of invisible cells. The row along the façade concluded with the Englishman when I arrived; as the last arrival, I have extended the line by one cube. The first arrivals must have been lined up in the distance, on the other façade. That takes away any chance of my seeing Mlle. LT.

The brown humus of the nursery down below forms a bizarre grid with bars of light. Through these gaps, bands of France appear at the bottom of the gulf. Then I see the layer of scattered stones, then the backs of the animals. Immediately beneath my feet a pink and grey pig is sleeping in mid-air. Immediately above my head, a tawny eagle with nocturnal plumage prances in the void, its yellow talons flattening out and clutching at the invisible floor of its cage, soiled with its excreta.

From time to time, one thinks that something is about to fall on one's head—but it stops, without apparent cause, in mid-fall.

And still no jailers! Invisible, therefore, or made invisible. Is it their presence that produces the odious intermittent scraping, whose sound, along with that of the flapping, is the only sound one hears here?

How do these sarvants contrive to live in the void? Is it an ancestral adaptation that permits them to exist outside the atmosphere?—the atmosphere that is as indispensable to hu-

mans as water is to fish; the atmosphere, with its warmth, its pressure and it oxygen. Are they a race of humans completely modified by the long passage of time? It's hardly probable. Our kidnappers are more likely provided with diving-suits as invisible as they are...unless it's the diving-suits that render them invisible. The diving-suit of Gyges![40] *Unless they're not human at all...but that conclusion is repugnant, although...there's the question of* classification.

All the specimens of terrestrial fauna and flora are arranged in order, but not in the order of naturalists. *One indubitable fact is that I'm an integral part of a collection of types—a museum or a menagerie....or, rather, an aquarium, since, instead of truly being like beasts in cages, we're plunged in our vital element, as fish in an aquarium are...or rather, since that element is air, we're in an aerium. Yes, an aerium as well-designed as the aquarium devised by Maxime Le Tellier for reproducing the environment of the submarine depths. And all those scraping sounds that give me gooseflesh might be a mysterious multitude admitted to stare at us— perhaps on payment of an entry fee?*

---

[40] Gyges was a king of Lydia famed for his wealth, whose name was borrowed by Plato for a moral fable constructed in the *Republic*. In the story, Gyges is a herdsman who discovers a mounted corpse wearing a golden ring in a chasm opened up by an earthquake; he removes the ring, which turns out to have the power of rendering him invisible; it gives him the means to violate King Candaules' wife and then usurp his throne. The tale was adapted into French literature more than once after being recycled by the fabulist Jean La Fontaine; Théophile Gautier's "Le Roi Candaule" (1844) is the most spectacular adaptation of it. Plato invented the fake legend to dramatize the question of whether a man who need not fear the consequences of his actions is likely to act morally—a question inherent in almost all literary accounts of invisibility, including H. G. Wells's *The Invisible Man*.

243

This hypothesis occurred to me in the first minute; its obsessive horror still imposes itself upon me. It came to me as I looked at all those frightened faces directed toward mine. There were shouting, questioning me. I heard nothing, but I saw them crying out. The exceedingly low sun is illuminating us at an upward angle, putting us in the glare of theatrical footlights, brutal and livid. Our shadows can only be projected on ourselves. All of us, all of us are Peter Schlemihls.[41] *All of us are men without shadows!*

The Sun set into the aerial sea. The surface of the Air was scarcely discernible, and only at the horizon, as a flat, diaphanous, visionary ring. The immense Earth, deep and blurred, became golden in the twilight. There was a blue ribbon between the terrestrial horizon and the horizon of the aerial sea, a circular ribbon, and, as my eyes made a tour of that ribbon—when I was given my binoculars, which I found a little while ago—I was able to pick out regions.

From here one can see the Balearics, half of Sardinia, and as far as Leipzig, Amsterdam, London and Rome. From here one can discover a European circle fifteen hundred kilometers in diameter, a geographical carpet spread out in the form of a cup, which is much wider than the square screen made by the nursery on the ground floor. The seas look like dark plains. There is a great deal of mist, especially in the distance.

The Sun set abruptly, but the day had lasted longer than on Earth, and I saw nightfall darkening Germany while the Atlantic Ocean was still sunlit.

In the fearfully dark sky, the stars were shining with incomparable brightness. The atmospheric sea gleamed serenely. Here and there, in the dark Earth, vaporous phosphores-

---

[41] The protagonist of Adalbert von Chamisso's classic *kuntzmärchen* [art fairy-tale] "Peter Schlemihls Wunderbare Geschichte" (1814; tr. as "The Shadowless Man") makes a deal with the Devil, who takes his shadow, and is subsequently shunned by his fellow men.

cent patches revealed the sites of large cities. The valves were flapping in a sepulchral silence. My courage failed; I was afraid of these unknown and formidable individuals who have captured me, afraid of this frightful place. I was ashamed of no longer being anything but a number in a collection, an item doubtless labeled...the beautiful stars no longer appeared to me as an oasis in the desert of darkness...a nameless fatigue wearied me, and I went to sleep in the invisible world, after having experienced a singular relief in closing my eyes— which is to say, in finally no longer seeing what could not be seen.

I thought I was mad when I woke up this morning, July 4. Ah, my poor companions in misery, by the rays of that exceedingly low sun, in that light from beyond the tomb! The Earth was a greenish expanse, muddled and dappled by clouds; from time to time, the Alps threw forth a white flash. But the aerium, with its detainees in all the postures of misery, despair and malady, sustained in the air as if by invisible strings!

During the night, my binoculars and my photographic apparatus had been returned to me, doubtless in order to see what I would do with them. The camera is broken; I mourn it! With the binoculars, I began make a review of the humans. Salad leaves, carrots and beautiful water affecting the form of its invisible jug—flattened at the top and bottom—had been slipped into the cage of every prisoner in the aerium, and every animal too, during the night. It was a droll spectacle. My neighbor was devouring his salad. Underneath him, a sheepdog was lapping up its ovoid water.

With the aim of communicating with my neighbor, I wrote Do you speak French? on a page of my notebook and showed it to him. He shook his head and went back to devouring his salad—but then another young man, very thin, who occupied the next cell along attracted my attention by his mimes. He replied to the question in my notebook by means of gestures, having neither paper nor a pencil. I thought I understood that he was a reporter and that he had been abducted *in the vicinity of Culoz. He seemed to be afraid of something that I could not grasp.*

An incident interrupted this conversation. To the north, I saw a black dot rising up from the Earth. Through the binoculars, I saw that it was a man. He looked as if he had been launched by a ballista. He stopped five kilometers away from us in the horizontal dimension, at the place where I had arrived the day before—the dock. We saw him lifted up by the crane, then shuttled along the side of our hill—perhaps through invisible streets and boulevards? My co-detainees studied him attentively. They seemed glad not to recognize him. He was hoisted up to my level, but he was not established as my immediate neighbor; a space about two cells wide was left between him and me along the façade. (This break in continuity is repeated on all the floors and marks the middle of the aerium on the side of the façade.) He was a bewildered ruddy-faced peasant in a smock. I noticed, at that moment, that a number of birds had arrived during the night: a barn-owl, a short-eared owl and an eagle-owl. The infernal humming trap has been busy since yesterday.

I continued scanning the crowd. This time, I discovered someone: Raflin, Fabienne d'Arvière's rejected suitor: Raflin, in his dressing-gown, with a cotton night-cap.

Above the heads, right at the back, on the side of the first arrivals, is a larger head than the others: the head of a statue, a Watteau gardener[42]...and also a tall hat coiffing the head of a manikin. Ah! The statue from Anglefort and the scarecrow! What? With the humans?

At intervals, one of our cells is coated with frost, causing a resplendent cube to appear. The prisoner falls unconscious. One sees him come to after the thaw. It's probably no more

---

[42] The idea of a "Watteau gardener," on which the stolen statue is supposedly modelled, actually derives from a popular engraving of *Le Jardinière fidèle* by Gabriel Huquier, who abstracted the figure in question from one of Antoine Watteau's elaborate paintings of "*fêtes galantes.*"

than a temporary breakdown in the functioning of the valve-flaps. The cold and dryness of the void that surrounds us are certainly frightful.

Thanks to a large slot made by the invisible sustaining wall in the checkered humus almost directly beneath me, I have been able to take advantage of a gap in the clouds to pinpoint my position. It wasn't easy. The aerium must be a little to the south of Mirastel. With Monsieur Le Tellier's telescope, one could see it...but what hazard might guide his curiosity to a place where there is nothing to attract astronomers? It is so barely credible that the missing persons are up in the air!

At about half past ten, the Sun emerged from the atmospheric ocean, which began to sparkle. It described its curve in the black sky, like a large orange scarcely furred by a flamboyant halo. The shadow of the aerium was projected on to the cloud layer. Then at half past one, the Sun re-entered the gaseous horizon.

A little later, the statue of the Watteau gardener and the manikin filed in front of me! They glided along inclined planes, one after the other, down to the first floor, the quarter of inanimate things. There, they were placed among the agricultural implements, the hands of a clock, a tricolor flag and a large yellow ball, all properly aligned. And a few minutes later, a golden cock waddled down from the bird floor, and went to join the two simulacra amid the bric-à-brac on the first floor. It's perfectly evident that errors of classification are being corrected—but that leads one to think along strange lines...

6 p.m.. A monkey has arrived: a large ape of the orangutan family. Escaped from a menagerie, in all probability, and captured in the forest by the sarvants. They've put it next to the red-faced peasant, with the humans. In a few days, they'll take it back down, like the statue, the manikin and the cock—but what can these individuals be, who can be mistaken in such matters? These humans so ignorant of humankind, so

247

*different from us—so evolved, probably—who botanize pop-
lars, collect pebbles and treat their brothers below as livestock?*

July 5. *I couldn't continue writing yesterday; my valve-
flaps stopped. I was obliged to use up my reserve supply of
oxygen, but I fainted all the same, numbed by cold in a cube of
ice. I only recovered consciousness at night, during which I
reflected. These are my conclusions:*
*This invisible ground that supports us is not an island.
It's not an island in the atmospheric sea—for then it would be
a floating island, a sort of errant buoy. But it's fixed; we must,
therefore, be on an invisible* continent *that envelops the entire
Earth, letting the light and heat of the Sun pass through: a
continent in a single block, like a thin hollow sphere englobing
the Earth and its atmosphere, upon which its rests; a continent
in a single block, but doubtless ragged, perforated by holes
where, in spite of the laws of our human science, the 50-
kilometer-deep atmospheric sea is in free and direct contact
with the aerial void, with the imperfect ether of the upper atmosphere.*
*Yes, it can only be a world concentric to the Earth, a
kind of spherical continental raft, a thin membrane on the
surface of the Air, as the Earth's crust is, according to some,
only a thin membrane on the surface of the interior fire. It's a
light globe surrounding the planet; gravity, acting on all its
points at the same time, maintains it at an equal distance from
the Earth, and the centrifugal force released by terrestrial
rotation doubles that effect by acting in the opposite direction.
Each molecule of the invisible continent is solicited by two
opposite forces, each of which tends to immobilize it relative
to the center of the Earth. Thus, it is as if the invisible world
were riveted to the visible one.*
*An invisible world! Like the planets that science has an-
ticipated—and, like them, inhabited by an invisible population! A very light world, to be sure—all the lighter because it
is a long way from the Earth. Here, things must have the same*

relationship with the air as things down below have with wa-
ter. This region is an Earth for which the void serves as an
atmosphere, so to speak, and in which air plays the role of the
sea. The aerial sea bathes its coasts. Perhaps there is only one
sea, one single hole pierced in the invisible world. Yes! Yes,
that's it! That's why the superaerian beings, the so-called sar-
vants, dare not venture anywhere else in their machine but
Bugey: the Bugey that is evidently directly beneath that unique
sea; the Bugey that is the bottom of their lake! *They're afraid*
of getting lost, rising up again underneath their continent and
choking for want of vacuum—*they, for whom the void is as*
indispensable as air is to humans and water to fish!

For these people have invented a sort of diving-bell—or,
rather, a sort of submarine. Eh? That's the word: a SUBAE-
RIAN! It permits them to go prospecting at the bottom of their
sea and to visit unknown plains. They're doing oceanography,
after their fashion. Perhaps they're governed by an invisible
Prince Albert, and perhaps it's him who has set up a pretty
little museum of oceanography, with creatures from the great
depths, in imitation of Monaco!

The cylinder that I have seen white with frost, as it rose
up, is the well of air in which the netted fish are placed; it's
merely a part of that subaerian, *which is itself formed like a*
cigar, as our own submersibles are, and also our dirigibles!
That's what Maxime saw in the fog; or, at least, it was the
space that the strange balloon-boat displaced in the fig, and
which appeared so confusedly that one could see things
through it—*which Maxime attributed to its speed! It was the*
subaerian, too, that we saw in the cloud, and for the same
reason, on the day when we thought we were seeing its mo-
tionless shadow!

I've got it! I've got it! This boat is 'full of void,' if one
might express it thus. That's why it floats so well in the air, as
a boat filled with air does in the water. It's equipped with 'air
ballast' instead of 'water ballast', in order to descend or as-
cend within the void—which is to say that it's the lightest thing
in the world, the zero of weight, when air weighs 1.3 grams

*per cubic meter and hydrogen 0.07! The void, which all aero-
nauts would employ instead of hydrogen if they were able to
have envelopes both solid enough and imponderable enough
to resist the pressure of the ambient air without their own
weight canceling out the ascensional force of the void.*

*Truly, though, all that is glaringly simple! Water and air!
They're two twin elements, governed by the same essential
principles. Hydrostatics is the twin sister of pneumatics! The
aquatic sea and the atmospheric sea—how many times has
one been compared to the other? In fact, neither one of them is
terminated abruptly by a precise surface. The water of the sea
extends into the air by means of briny vapors that we cannot
see; in the same way, the atmospheric sea extends into the
aerial void by means of degraded effluvia that I wouldn't be
able to perceive! They both have their lunar tides, and the
gaseous ocean even has its solar tides. They have their whirl-
pools! Here, however, the birds take the place of the superior
fish, and we humans, creatures of the deeps to which our hea-
viness attaches us, are the poor crustaceans that drag themselves along wretchedly!*

*The atmosphere!—which weighs upon the Earth as much
as a layer of water ten meters deep, enveloping it completely
would weigh upon it. The atmospheric sea, in which the mountains are the shallows! Shallows more accessible to the sarvants because they are closer to the surface; because, to reach
them, they do not need to let as much air into their ballast
tanks—which explains why they go fishing there so preferentially!*

*For we have been caught, hooked and netted! Then they
place us in their receptacles, in these tanks—which must be
transparent even to the sarvants—before the eyes of an indiscreet public, in this display-hall, this monumental museum,
doubtless in the middle of a large city on the shore of the sea!*

*And we have never divined its existence! Deceived by the
invisibility of this universe, which does not inhibit telescopic
vision at all—which the bolides falling on the Earth go
through as a rifle-bullet goes through the bark of a tree, and*

shooting stars leave far beneath them—we never guessed that that a world vaster than our own, having a radius fifty kilometers larger, was set above us, turning on the same axis as the terrestrial mass. And we would never have suspected that an active population was laboring there, that, in all probability, it was thinking, inventing and manufacturing, that it was launching increasingly-improved boats on to the atmospheric sea, that it was undertaking—blindly, I believe—maritime soundings, and that it would eventually arrive that that rightly fêted, glorified and acclaimed prowess: the construction of a subaerian.

It's more than probable that the first one to be launched suffered a serious accident. Ineptly navigated by apprentices, carried far away by the wind, as if by a submarine whirlwind, it was, I believe that aeroscaph that caused the celebrated collision in the month of March. First it must have collided with the French steamer, then, a second later, the German destroyer, or vice versa. *That day, the invisible matelots had a lucky escape, having been dragged so far, and the subaerian must have sustained heavy damage, whose repair explains the time that elapsed between that accident and their depredations in Seyssel. Prudence enabled them to gain experience.*

Perhaps they've been watching us for centuries through the sky; perhaps they've been waiting impatiently and avidly for the moment when their progress would allow them to descend as far as human beings and study them; perhaps the subaerian is only a copy of our dirigibles, espied through the sarvants' telescopes—but I don't believe that. Their errors of classification suggest to me, rather, that they had not yet observed the ground on which we live. I would wager that the air, in its considerable thickness, is for them a non-transparent substance, as the sea is for us; that their ground, invisible to us, is opaque to them, and that they cannot distinguish through it, beneath them, either the ocean of air that supports it or the terrestrial depths of that ocean. I would even wager that they have no eyes. *What use would eyes be to them in an invisible world? No, no eyes—so that all that I have just said applies to the sense that, for them, replaces sight. No, no eyes! Light and darkness have no more influence on their perception of the external world than the presence or absence of odor has on ours. Indeed, on the one hand, they don't possess any artificial light to illuminate the darkness—any such thing would have made them known to humanity a long time ago, and I didn't see the slightest glimmer last night—and on the other hand, they navigate admirably in the depths of their sea in our deepest darkness, which proves that our obscurity is not theirs, and is not obscure at all to them.*

If one considers that their misdeeds are accomplished more frequently by night, it's even possible to suppose that that their perception is improved in darkness, that it's at night that their means are most powerful, and that obscurity is as favorable to their sense of direction as light is to our sight. What fools we are, poor creatures submerged in the ocean of gas, who believe that we are masters of the Earth! We don't suspect that another humankind, more considerable than ours, exists above it, knowing little or nothing about us, attributing to us the intelligence that we attribute to crabs! Another humankind, which evidently believes itself the sole monarch of the planet! Another race, on a world exterior to ours, which the astronomers of Mars and Venus might well take for the true Earth, if our atmosphere is not transparent to them and if, on the contrary, they can see that which our eyes are powerless to distinguish. Didn't we, the astronomers of Earth, for a long time, mistake the photosphere—the dazzling atmosphere of the Sun—for the surface of that heavenly body?

An adolescent has just arrived among us. He's next to the ape. We watched him advancing without movement, in that extraordinary progression, suspended in space. A woman of a certain age began to cry, holding her arms out to him...

Maxime Le Tellier has recognized me. He is signaling to me from afar.

My hypothesis of the raft-continent explains why the noise of loud explosions is heard, on Earth, at seemingly-improbable distances—a phenomenon that meteorologists have only been able to explain by mean of some sort of 'sonic mirror,' by admitting 'a reflection of sound in the upper atmosphere' at the limit of two zones of different density, and hence of very different composition. *That limit is not a gaseous vault but a solid one, constituted by the superaerian would.*

My hypothesis will also facilitate the explanation of crepuscular red lights. It will also explain why bolides that do not arrive perpendicularly to the Earth always ricochet from something that was believed until now to be an atmospheric cushion, and are then lost in space...

In truth, it seemed that this final sentence, relating to bolides, had never been read by the Duc d'Agnès, for, at the moment he began it, an unanswerable instinct made him and Monsieur Le Tellier leap forward, taking them away from the invisible mass against which they were both leaning.

That mass, silent until now, had just produced and unpleasant scraping sound directly behind Monsieur Le Tellier's back.

"Go on!" said Monsieur Le Tellier. "Go on reading the journal! It's urgent—most urgent!"

But it was necessary to expect further delays.

While the contents of the red notebook were being read, the audience had been swollen by firemen, municipal guards, scientists, civil servants and—most numerous of all, unfortunately—by steel-workers who were working at that time at the rear of the Grand Palais in the Avenue d'Antin. They had been attracted by curiosity and had not understood anything of the journal, of whose first part they were ignorant. The brave steel-workers imagined—God knows how or why—that there were prisoners of their species inside the invisible mass. When the scraping sounds began, one of them—a journeyman named Virachol, nicknamed Gargantua because of his giant stature and obesity—proclaimed that it was "a bloody shame" to "leave those men inside." And he started swinging an enormous crowbar, with which he wanted to break open the invisible object.

Virachol was restrained—but every time the scraping sound started again, Virachol started again too, with the result that we cannot reproduce all the interruptions that disturbed the conclusion of this public reading without composing an indecipherable rant.

XIII. The Conclusion of the Journal

July 6. These indications must be forwarded to someone who can save us—but by what means can they be forwarded? By what means? Escaping? How? And then, it would be a frightful death. Here in our cells, it's warm, we breathe sufficiently moist air, and our bodies are subject to the normal pressure of 15,500 kilos[43] that they need—but outside! All the same, these sarvants must be quite clever, to have calculated all the elements necessary to our life, and to have grouped them together...

This morning, there were new inmates of every sort. It's definitely by night that the sarvants prefer to operate. Is that for the reasons set out above, or is it simply because they know that darkness weakens us?

From time to time, there are people who hurl themselves head first against the invisible walls. One sees them hurt themselves.

The more I reflect on what I've discovered relative to the world where I am, the more convinced I am that I'm right. I've discovered something else: I think I know why the aerium contains so many representatives of the human species and so few, proportionally, of each animal family. It's because the sarvants imagine that clothing is a pelt, which marks as many varieties in the species as occur naturally. One fact corroborates this: that is the great quantity and great diversity here of

---

[43] Atmospheric pressure is nowadays measured in units of force—such as kiloPascals or millibars—but in 1911 it would routinely have been rendered in units of weight per unit of surface area; the mean weight of the atmosphere above a square meter of the Earth's surface at sea level is approximately 10,200 kilograms, and the measurement is not difficult to make, so Renard's figure is mistaken.

animals of the same sort but with different patterns of fur or plumage, like rabbits, ducks and so on. The sarvants—aristocrats, in their fashion—believe that frock-coats and blouses are different breeds. That's what justified the system I devised of dressing like one of the missing persons in order to escape the Blue Peril, Madame Le Tellier was disdained by the sarvants for no other reason than that. Under the horn-beams, they remembered that they already possessed a black-bodied and yellow-haired specimen of the inferior-adherent-pawed subclass of the vertical class—and they released her, instead of carrying her off with Maxime and the calf that they had just confiscated in the vicinity...

One may conclude that all the sarvants resemble one another, and that they go naked.

A little while ago, the Englishman, my neighbor, had a fainting fit. He exhibited all the symptoms of being placed under the bell-jar of some pneumatic machine; then he gradually recovered consciousness. But the walls of his cell weren't coated in frost; in consequence, the pressure must have weakened without the temperature being lowered.

Was it an experiment? I don't like it. I've said 'cell;' I should have said 'padded cell.' My neighbor is mad—and others too!

O joy! O joy! I definitely seem to have glimpsed, in the far distance, a certain grey dress... and not far away, I recognized Henri Monbardeau, although with difficulty. How thin he is!

July 7. It's always at night that they bring us food, without our being able to see anything. It's also by night that our cabins are cleaned. Found, on awakening, my ration of carrots and my ration of water.

By searching the aerium with my binoculars, I've discovered the provision-store on the ground floor—a heap of vegetables stolen from Earthly kitchen-gardens—and the cistern of pure water, perhaps from a spring on the Colombier or extracted, one drop at a time, from the atmospheric sea.

What a horrible penned herd we make! A thousand filthy details...a house of glass in which no one has any privacy...and then, the mortal terror of modesty...

About eleven o'clock, through the gaps in the humus, perceived something like a little pill, which soon disappeared. It could only be a balloon.

Having taken out my revolver to examine it, what imploring gazes I saw directed towards me! Some pointed to their foreheads, like targets, one opened his shirt to show me the place where his heart was. Do they even know whether my Browning's bullets could reach them?

The sarvants: what can they be? Haunted by that question.

At half past three, again saw a balloon moving down below. Dirigible. It must be extremely high, for I could see it quite clearly with my binoculars. What does that signify? Has the spot been seen, and are people trying to get close to it?

These hours of idleness, lulled by the sound of the valves, are desperately long. I'm raking my brains with regard to the sarvants...

These beings, living in the void where the presence of a liquid is impossible, can't have any blood! These people are invisible and dry. They must be more different from human beings than the inhabitants of a planet that is unimaginably distant from the Earth, but which is endowed with a similar atmosphere. The substance of this invisible world must have nothing in common with that of our central world. The sarvants have souls united with bodies that are not made of the old traditional matter. They are forms of ether, or electricity, or of God knows what, which is doubtless concentrated...

Why not? We humans always think of ourselves as paragons! We always imagine that there is nothing beyond us in the scale of living beings! And we think we know everything, can foresee everything, can imagine everything! If a creature were made of water, would we be able to see it in the water? *Well then, if a creature were made of air, could we see it* in the air? *Creatures the color of water, or the color of air...but in fact, that's simply a phenomenon of mimicry! Besides, since it's possible, and even probable, that invisible planets exist, this world even becomes, by virtue of that fact, perfectly natural.*

But how are the sarvants conformed? What contours would they present to our eyes in becoming visible?—they and their vegetables, their animals, and this entire universe over which they seem to reign? I've looked hard at the humus in the nursery, searching it for their footprints, but I haven't seen any. Oh, how much progress we poor humans will have to make in order to get up here, to live here, to observe here!

It's still necessary that I inform humankind, that I reveal the existence of the superaerian world...and that, I still don't know to do.

The grey dress is no longer visible. Time drags so slowly. Are we all going to die here? Was my sacrifice futile?

July 8. *Yesterday and today, the invisible fishers only brought animals.*

Yet more balloons. 'A balloon is a buoy,' Nadar said.[44] Never has that seemed more true to me. They can only make very tiny leaps toward us! But doesn't that prove that the aerium has been sighted?

Midday. *Certain animals, now, are paired up; the sarvants are undertaking experiments in breeding. They've differentiated the sexes, but they're still mistaken with regard to species. Thus they've put a fox in with a wolf, which made haste to devour it. The unfortunate carnivores are on a vegetarian diet, and the wolf wasn't displeased with the little snack. That must have astonished the invisible biologists!*

2 p.m. *Saw Floflo, Madame Arquedouve's pet dog. He seems to be in good health.*

---

[44] Nadar was the pseudonym used by the flamboyant caricaturist, photographer and pioneer of aeronautics Gaspar Félix Tournachon (1820-1910).

3 p.m. *Revolting! The invisibles are treating us like animals. There are now cells inhabited by human couples, which they have paired up. The prisoners thus united are chatting to one another sadly, but one can see that being able to talk about their distress has reduced its bitterness. Unfortunately, there are mad people, and the sarvants seem to be incapable of understanding madness and the dangers that one might run in being brought into its presence...*

These singular marriages are multiplying. It's obviously dresses and trousers that serve as a basis for the learned experimenters to determine femininity and masculinity; have they not coupled Maxime with a venerable curé in a soutane? Maxime and the priest are conversing in a very animated fashion.

4:20 p.m. *The sarvants have installed Madame Fabienne Monbardeau with her old admirer, Raflin! An unexpected coincidence! The unfortunate Raflin has lost his dressing-gown—otherwise, I think, they would have taken him for a woman. He's in his underpants and makes a dismal sight, so gloomy and skeletal. He's taking no notice of his companion except for trying to steal her ration of beetroot. Henri Monbardeau, who is sharing the cell of a peasant-girl, looks at them like a man intoxicated...*

Myself I'm still alone in my invisible cabin. O little grey dress I glimpsed the other day...! Yes, but I'm the only one who remains a bachelor in the sarvant mode...except for—terror! There are still the mad! And—oh my God!—there's the great ape!

6 p.m. *I've just this second perceived the face of Mademoiselle Suzanne Monbardeau. When I recognized her, and the very back of the groups, I searched for the grey dress.*

July 9. *Seen many more balloons again, minuscule particles of ash. So what?*

3:15 p.m. *One of my cell's valve-flaps has slowed down. Is it about to stop? An experiment? That's a dire possibility. Multitude of scraping sounds on the wall and in the corridor...*

[From this point until the end of the red notebook, Robert Collin's handwriting becomes unsteady, undulating and jerky, each page becoming increasingly laborious and irregular. The next page is covered with illegible arabesques.]

July 10. *It was an experiment in rarefaction. It left me with a general numbness akin to paralysis. I can't stand up, and I've been trying to write, without success, for several hours. Just as long as I have the strength to do what I have to do!*

The wolf that killed the fox is dead—also, killed, I believe. Retribution? Justice? Don't know where its corpse has been discarded.

Spent ten hours writing these few lines.

July 11. *The sarvants have been coming up from the Earth all night. The ground floor of the square is getting bigger.*

July 12. *Have not been calm since that semi-paralysis. Dirty, lonely, anguished, impotent. Egoism, save for Marie-Thérèse. Tedium, tedium. Enervation. And yet, I'm the one who's brought useful objects: toilet-bag, binoculars and this blessed notebook! The others have nothing! They envy me when they see me combing my hair, writing, observing the Earth. Oh, the good old Earth!*

July 13. *Made inspection of the walls of my cell—in the insupportable anguish of being seen by some invisible guard. Impossible to scratch anything whatsoever with a knife; nothing pulverizes it; like glass. Located the valve-flaps quite easily. At the base of the wall, two orifices of pipes, and one above them, making a triangle, one to let out the vitiated air, the others to let in pure air; one can feel the currents. I don't understand the mechanism. The flaps are quite far back in the pipes; can scarcely touch them with fingertips.*

July 14. *Veritable eruption of aerostats today. A spherical one came up very high; I diverted myself by following it through the gap at the nadir, which permits me to see Bugey.*

Nightfall interrupted my observation. I'm writing by starlight, because I can see incomprehensible glimmers beneath us. Ah—fireworks! July 14! National holiday! We're here, in the sarvants' realm, and our fellow citizens are holding pyrotechnic displays!

July 15. *We have new comrades: four men wrapped up in furs. Near the Anglefort statue—the Watteau gardener—the gondola of a balloon, rigging, a flaccid and torn envelope on which I can see letters, a name half-hidden by a crease in the rubber-lined silk:* LE SYL...*probably* Le Sylph.

I no longer experience any surprise in seeing people suspended in mid-air, nor things that move by themselves. The ink-black sky and its excessive stars, the degraded crown of the aerial sea...I'm indifferent to it all; the fate of my co-detainees is irrelevant to me. And yet, what a nightmarish horror, this exposition of my peers! I understand now why I've always found wax museums repugnant—it's because they evoke the idea of a human museum.

July 17. *Among other things, last night enriched the aerium with an acacia branch. Now, that branch hasn't stopped moving. An invisible pocket-knife cuts into it, splits it; the bark and pith are carefully scrutinized.*

July 18. *No more balloons. Henri Monbardeau has quit the peasant-woman's cell for another, which I can't see. Bad luck has ensured that throughout these exchanges Mademoiselle Marie-Thérèse has remained behind the mass of individuals. Thought of the treatment to which she might be subjected makes me more anxious than ever.*

I've seen her, I think. That blonde hair with its silvery iridescence can only be hers.

By virtue of the empty spaces between the internees, one can quite easily imagine the architecture of the aerium, its corridors. Quite symmetrical. I search in vain to explain the purpose of the large gap in the middle of the façade, next to my cabin. Are there cabinets left vacant on every floor? If so, why? Is it a cavity in the building? Again, if so, what purpose does it serve? Is it a great hall whose floor is on the ground floor and whose ceiling is on the top floor? A conference hall?

The sarvants are growing crops. The square of humus they added the other day is a field of carrots—for our use, presumably.

The sarvants have been disabused with regard to our clothes. This is how: a madwoman took her clothes off. A few minutes later, others were stripped. *Oh, the poor folk—what distraught faces! They were allowed to get dressed again. In the final analysis, though,* by whom? *In consequence of this, that ape has been taken down to the animal floor; I even saw them trying to take off his fur. Oof! I can breathe again...*

This is better still: the four aeronauts from the Syl..., *who haven't taken off their furs, have also been taken down a level. The sarvants didn't even take the trouble to see whether their goatskins and sealskins were immovable! They assumed without further ado that they were monkeys.*

July 20. *It's becoming increasingly difficult to write. This notebook! Which needs to be so complete! In the final analysis, the essential thing is that it's sent.*

[Nothing for July 21, 22, 23 or 24. Several pages filled with calculations, unskillful and awkward drawings. The word Marie-Thérèse written everywhere, in all directions, sometimes crossed out. Then a drawing that is surely an attempted portrait of the young woman.]

July 25. *I know the purpose of the empty halls.*

July 26. *Yesterday, I was still shaking too much to write. It's frightful, what I've seen. I saw, there, right next to me, a naked man, lying down at my height. I saw, imprinted in his pale and shivering flesh, the red tracks of invisible bonds immobilizing him.* They want to know how we're constructed! *Oh! Sudden gashes! Abrupt injuries! The appearance of wounds that open without the instruments of torture being perceptible! And that screaming mouth! And all the blood! All the blood! I couldn't watch any longer; I turned away...*

Then I saw the others who were watching that, *fascinated, their eyes wide with horror—but in that petrified crowd, something black was moving. It was Maxime's old priest, making large signs of the cross. He was moving his arms in benediction. The crowd of prisoners knelt down in front of him. Our eyes no longer left his lips, which moved with a suggestion of eloquence, pronouncing words—words that Maxime alone could hear...*

The old priest kept his arms extended in the form of a living cross, and he began to turn round and round, so that all of us could contemplate the crucifix, instead of the hideous spectacle that was shedding blood beside me.

Maxime was livid, at the old curé's feet. I saw him once again, in his laboratory at Mirastel, covered in blood: covered in the blood of animals, the construction of which he wanted to know! *Alas, what do we do to animals? Cain, what hast thou done with thy brother?*

*They butchered that man alive...*alive, *and therefore* in breathable air...*so they have diving-suits of some sort in order to vivisect fish in their aquatic element...*

I no longer look in that direction.

The sarvants cannot be creatures larger than us. The dimensions of the corridors, the height of the floors, proves it.

July 27. *The unfortunates! The unfortunates! The frightful torture! It has continued. It is continuing...*

On the lower floor, the pig has been transported into the empty chamber beneath the tortured man. It has begun to suf-

fer those unparalleled agonies that will augment the science and the importance of the sarvants.

Scraping sounds swarm about my cell; the crowd is jostling to get a better view of the operation...

July 28. *They're little cuts...little cuts made by little blades...careful, scrupulous work...*

Down below, a large snake is in the process of suffering...and after that, which animal next? And after the man, who? Which woman? Oh, my God, which woman? It's enough to drive one mad!

Blood—the blood they don't possess, that vital liquid forbidden to their anatomy—seems to intrigue the sarvants. They gather all the different kinds of shed blood together in a single invisible jar, and, curiously enough, have already found a means that prevents them from coagulating.

A white heifer is next to pay her debt to the science of the Invisibles. The column of blood mounts within the jar. The man is still alive.

It's not possible that the sarvants understand how much suffering humans undergo.

The serpent is in pieces. Thus, in their classification, the serpent is at the very bottom and the bird at the very top. They have given the first rank to those that are able to approach them most closely and most easily. Come on! They aren't much more intelligent than we are! (Haven't I said that already?)

July 30. *The man isn't dead; the white heifer is in agony. In the operating-room on the bird floor, a bat is dying. A bat with the birds!*

July 31. *I no longer sleep; I dread too many things. I always keep my hand on my revolver.*

Last night, beneath the Moon, which made the ring of the atmospheric sea shine from afar, I witnessed the removal of the remains of the heifer. They were taken to the aerian port, and thrown down from there.

The jar of blood is like the shaft of a column made of rubies. From time to time, invisible things plunge into it. For an hour, the mixture has been continually agitated by a stirrer; while I've been writing, bottles have been filled and taken away—to be studied. I can see red liquid in various forms being taken away in every direction.

Thus, for the Invisibles, we're crustaceans. They catch us and study us as we catch and study them—but does the parallel stop at that resemblance? We eat crustaceans...and when I think about an American lobster...

August 1. *Today. For 16 days—since the arrival of the Syl...—the sarvants haven't captured any humans. It's quite plausible, on the one hand, that the Bugists no longer go out at all, and that, on the other, the sarvants have completely risking themselves beyond the depths of their sea.*

The man is dead. Whose turn is it next? *Whose turn?*

August 2. *They're continuing the dissection of the poor wretch's limbs. That might last for some time yet.*

August 3. *They threw him away this morning, in broad daylight. They've thrown his remains into the sea. And they've also thrown away all the blood, under the influence of God knows what inexplicable idea, perhaps superstitious...*

August 4. *I've been here a month, impotent, seeing this world bathed in light, a prisoner of a world like a strange night without darkness, as if in dazzling shadow.*

I, who so wanted to see Marie-Thérèse at closer range, now dread nothing more than that—seeing her at close range!

It's a madness: they're cutting everything up, butchering everything. Branches quiver and lose their leaves one by one, then break and are divided into a thousand cuttings. Stones split, with an apparent spontaneity. Birds, mammals and fish are covered with gashes. But the operating theater for humans is empty, for the moment.

It isn't any longer. If there's a Providence, I need to give thanks; it's not Marie-Thérèse—but I can no longer look in that direction.

August 6. *Raflin has died. He has been placed in a separate cell. I'm certain that he died in the course of an experiment with compressed air. The solidity of our crates is truly admirable, to be able to resist such internal pressures with no equilibrating pressure on the outside. Then again, how the devil are they made so as to avoid the mist that ought to condense on the surfaces of our walls, as on the windows of a warm room when it's cold outside? A mystery.*

August 7. *Raflin's corpse has disappeared, but I didn't see it thrown in the sea. Three women and a man—my English neighbor—are also dead, I don't know how. I saw the Englishman and two of the women thrown away. Where's the other?*

August 8. *It's certain that the cadavers are no longer of any interest to them. Life is of paramount attraction to them. They throw the dead away with their clothes, without paying any further heed to them. When an animal dies, though, I don't know what they did with it. Living animals are still arriving—but no more humans.*

August 10. *Nothing new; still the same horrors. I've seen the blonde hair again, and later I saw the grey dress. One or the other doubtless belongs to Marie-Thérèse, but not both; they weren't in the same place—unless there was a change of cell between my two observations. How lonely and sad she must be!*

August 11. *Event: for the first time, a prisoner has been taken down to Earth—and it's Maxime! With what purpose?*

He looked like a condemned man when they grabbed him. His plunge was vertiginous. It was very early.

8 p.m. *Maxime hasn't returned. There's a woman who is laughing incessantly...*

August 12. *Maxime not back. And yet, last night, the invisible fishers brought up animals. Thus, as I'm certain that there's only one subaerian, only one aeroscaph, the aforesaid aeroscaph must have come back up without Maxime. Now, if the sarvants have abandoned him, it's because he's no longer anything but one of those cadavers they disdain. Maxime is dead! What's happened?*

August 13. *This morning, no animals, nor stones, nor plants, nor humans. That's never happened. What's up, then? Hazard might have chosen me instead of Maxime, and then I would surely have found a way to transmit my notebook to someone. If it were discovered on my inanimate body...*

11 a.m. *We've been given water, as usual, but the salad was scarcely fresh.*

2 p.m. *Finally, they're annoying me, these sarvants! They don't know what I'm capable of. I'll show them. I'll do them a bad turn. I'll...*

[These last few lines, in an incoherent hand, were crossed out—badly, since one can still make them out. A few more lines follow, these completely obliterated. The next seven pages have been torn out. Then there are 15 lines masked by cross-hatching. Thus, nothing from August 13 to 24. Finally, it resumes as follows.]

August 24. *I've destroyed all the insanities I scribbled. For ten days I've been subjected to the cruelest experiments. Without being taken out of my cell, I've been subjected to all sorts of pressures, all sorts of decompressions, all sorts of mixtures of gases. I've passed from the most frantic overexcitement to the most profound prostration; breathed superox-*

ygenated air, supernitrogenated air. They've also forced nitrous oxide on me, I'm sure of it—for an hour I couldn't stop laughing, and I understood why that woman was laughing so much the other time. At one time, I remember trying to shatter my prison with a revolver bullet—but the bullet flattened against the wall—then trying to stop the flap-valves by means of my knife—so those weapons have been confiscated. The scraping sounds never stopped being audible. Finally, it's over! I've recovered. Fortunately! What would have become of the notebook, then? They'd had thrown me in the sea without it!

The vegetables they're giving us are rotten, and the water we're drinking tastes foul. The level in the cistern is decreasing. By connecting these facts with the facts that no prey has been captured since the twelfth, it's easy to deduce that the reprovisioning boat has been lost. The aeroscaph has been shipwrecked. I can't think of a better explanation.

August 25. I'm wondering whether it's any more than a hallucination due to some new experiment that I haven't noticed. Down below, twenty meters from the façade of the aerium, at ground floor level, isolated in space and as motionless as a statue: Raflin! The late Raflin, whose death I witnessed! But who's the rigid woman who's emerging from beneath the nursery and advancing toward Raflin? Oh, it's one of the women who died at the same time as him...

She's motionless beside him, and—this surely can't be anything but an illusion—all those stiff, rigid animals are emerging from the same place, in procession, and are being arranged not far from the couple, the horrible human couple! My binoculars!

No, it's not a fever-mirage. They're stuffed animals, packed with something invisible. The sarvants have stuffed a specimen of each Terran species! There's a taxidermist's studio in the cellars of the aerium!

268

[On August 26, 27, 28 and 29, Robert Collin abstained from recording his impressions in the red notebook.]

August 30. *For four days I've felt my reason totter. Moreover, I can hardly hold the pencil. If I want this journal to be rational, and if it's to be of any use, it's time to take stock.*

The water is better, but it's no longer the same. The sarvants must be obtaining it by some other means. The vegetables are now quite fresh, because they've begun to harvest the ones in the plantation.

Many empty spaces among the humans. The abomination of the aerium is nothing compared to the macabre museum facing it, perhaps on the other side of the road: that sinister museum of aerial oceanography annexed to the Institute where we are. With its invisible display-cases and its mummies it bars an even closer resemblance to some foreign wax museum. If I live a thousand years, I shall see that stuffed man and woman every day of my life.

August 31. *It's vital that my journal, which now contains all the necessary indications, reaches Monsieur Le Tellier, or someone capable of getting it to him, without further delay. If I'm vivisected, or only dissected, the notebook might be lost. If I stay here,* ditto. *If I'm asphyxiated before I've taken my precautions,* ditto. *But if I die in my cell, with the red notebook under my clothing, I'll be thrown away like that. It's the only way in which I can be useful to Marie-Thérèse. I no longer have a knife; I have nothing that I can use to block the valves. I have, therefore, to do it myself.*

September 1. *Like a coward, I hesitated all night. What! Shall I abandon Marie-Thérèse here? And abandon here forever? That's also a frightful death. There's still that journey through the void, which will deform my poor corpse...and that fall, about which no one can think without shivering on his cadaver's behalf!*

Marie-Thérèse! If I could only see her once more, be it only her blonde hair or the hem of her grey dress! But it's a long time since I've seen anyone I know here. They've been put back in their original places, behind that human wall. I'll never see Marie-Thérèse again.

September 2. *I'll fasten the notebook under my shirt, tightly secured with my belt.*
6 p.m. *There are too many scraping sounds. I'm afraid of being spotted, stopped in my work and having it made impossible for me to start again. The frost will be seen immediately, at the outset, since the warm air won't be coming any more. Just so long as the sarvants...*

September 8. *There are no more scraping sounds. The stuffed specimens, down below, are oscillating and whirling around. It's obvious that they're being manhandled. It's even possible that* they're being inaugurated, *for the sarvants appear to have deserted the aerium. The unfortunates they've tormented in a hundred different ways have a respite. Our torturers have departed in a crowd toward the gallery opposite. It's time. I'll block the valve-pipes with my clothing, and I'll put all my weight on them.*

I'm not writing any farewells; time's pressing, and I don't need to become maudlin.

I'll attach the notebook to my breast."

[Sixty-six blank pages follow.]

XIV. The Aerial Wreck

"Gentlemen! Citizens! Friends!" cried Monsieur Le Tellier. "I beg you to wait!"

He threw himself in front of the metal-workers who had broken through the circle with a single thrust. The journeyman Virachol, alias Gargantua, the French steelworker who displaced the greatest volume of air, advanced at their head, waving his crowbar like a drum-major's staff. "Enough humbug, my old astrologer!" he said. "Me, I only understand one thing—that there are brothers and sisters to free. We can hear them scraping. Let's go, then, lads—get in there!"

"Stop! For the sake of your life, stop—or I'll have you thrown out right now! And listen to me. If I've let you stay here, instead of having the whole lot of you sent back to your workshop, it's because I consider your special skills to be potentially useful—but I demand rigorous discipline from you. The first time you get out of line, goodnight! I insist that you allow yourselves to be guided in your work by the scientists and officers around me, and I demanded the same submission to me. For the moment, listen to me. Come closer, guards and firemen! And don't worry about those scraping sounds, damn it!"

The astronomer accelerated his speech: "Gentlemen, you ought to be grateful to me now for having apprised you of the contents of Monsieur Collin's journal before touching this invisible object. Thanks to my lamented secretary, who has so cleverly deduced the unknown from the known, we now know what machine it is with which we have to deal. It is not a matter of a machine from another world, as rumor has it, but an apparatus fallen from an invisible land superior to our own, which is part of our planet; it is neither a *uranoscaph* nor an *etheroscaph*; it's quite simple an *aeroscaph*. It's a subaerian, which travels in the air as our submarines travel in the bosom of the ocean—which further accentuates the oft-remarked re-

271

semblance between aerial and submarine navigation, and that between air, the common form of gas, and water, the common type of liquid.

"This invisible boat has been freighted by an unknown, invisible, superaerian people. Without any doubt, it is manned by invisible matelots. One can affirm, furthermore, that it is equipped for prospecting the subaerian depths—or, to put it another way, our ground—with the aim of doing what is, for our neighbors above, 'oceanography.' If you compare that to the studies of His Highness the Prince of Monaco, you will agree with me that this vessel, whose shape recalls our submersibles even more than our dirigibles, is an invisible and submersible *Princess Alice*, a diving yacht designed to fish at the bottom of the sea: a *Princess Alice* and a *Nautilus* rolled into one. We possess nothing analogous…"

"Pardon, Monsieur!" objected the captain of a frigate, who was listening attentively. "There is a submarine for collecting sponges, invented by a priest.[45] It functions perfectly."

"In that case, the sarvants are not such original inventors as I thought," Monsieur Le Tellier went on. "However, they are certainly not stupid, for, given the evident lightness of their constitutive substance, they have had to overcome singular difficulties in order to descend to the bottom of the atmosphere. Imagine natural humans trying to dive to the bottom of an ocean of water 50,000 meters deep! The sarvants have had as much trouble descending to our depth as we would have had in rising up to theirs. The material of their vessel must be to their individuality what lead is to our flesh…

"The unfortunates, moreover, have paid for their audacity with a catastrophe. It is martyrs to science that we have before us, for—listen to me gentlemen; this is of the utmost importance for the success of the enterprise we are about to undertake—as Monsieur Robert Collin has admirably sus-

---

[45] This reference remains enigmatic; the most famous submarine inventor who was a priest was George Garrett, but his experiments date from a much earlier era.

pected, we are witnessing the epilogue of a drama parallel to those of the *Lutin*, the *Farfadet* and the *Pluviose*, which we all recall, and which put the French fleet in mourning.[46]

"In the course of a dive effected on August 12 by this aeroscaph—this aerial submarine—a breakdown occurred in its mechanism, at a moment when it was still in the most elevated regions of the atmospheric ocean. From that day on, it has been sinking slowly. Gently impelled by the south-east wind that was blowing until Wednesday, the aerial wreck has finally run aground in Paris, after three weeks of uninterrupted submersion. It is, therefore a *shipwreck*, which would be terrifying, if its victims were not *the ferocious enemies of humankind*. Do you understand, Monsieur Virachol?

"Everything indicates that some of the mysterious matelots are still alive. Those scraping sounds are evidence of their activity. In the same way that the crew of the *Lutin* or the *Farfadet* survived for long hours at the bottom of the ocean, with their provisions of air, the crew of the aeroscaph is surviving at the bottom of the air with their provisions of void, the latter doubtless being less exhaustible than the former, since no respiration can be taking place—in my opinion, the Invisibles must be exempt from lungs, just as they are deprived of hearts.

"Yes, based on the revelations of Monsieur Collin's journal, I affirm that this is a shipwreck. A point of the utmost

---

[46] The *Lutin*, the *Farfadet* and *Pluviose* were French submarines; the first two were commissioned together and were stationed at Bizerta in Tunisia, off which they both sank, the *Farfadet* in June 1906 and the *Lutin* in October 1906; the *Pluviose* sank in the English Channel in May 1910. All the crews perished, but members of the *Farfadet*'s and *Lutin*'s crews were reportedly still alive and trapped inside their stricken vessels when the initial attempts to raise the vessels were made. Sensational press coverage of the three disasters helped to make the French public acutely aware of the dangers of submarine navigation, and added a useful dimension of dramatic plausibility to Renard's story.

importance, gentlemen, for, in consequence, we do not have to fear that this descent by the aeroscaph might be a ruse aimed against us. It follows from this that we are the masters of the moment. We may act, albeit with the most extreme prudence.

"There are creatures of the void in there, which are not dead. Therefore, there is still a vacuum inside; the air whose infiltration provoked the descent has not invaded it completely—far from it. That might do us harm—not to mention that this substance is so hard...

"In conclusion, to facilitate our task and our understanding of the question, let us suppose that we are about to handle something that has sunk to the bottom of the sea—for everything applicable to bodies plunged into water is applicable to bodies plunged into air, all proportions being taken into account. Be wary, too, of the tricks that invisibility might play upon you. In sum, in this respect, what is happening is the opposite of what the red notebook recounts—instead of there being a collection of a few exceptionally visible individuals in an invisible world, there's a single exceptionally invisible object in a visible world.

"Patience Monsieur Virachol! And prudence! Let's not risk our own lives to extract two or three brutes *who will die as soon as they are in the air*. That's what you'll never understand. Like fish, Monsieur Virachol! Like fish! Do you get it?

"Now, if everyone will follow my instructions..."

At this point, the indescribable discovery of the aeroscaph truly began.

Under the direction of Monsieur Le Tellier, with the Duc d'Agnès serving as his secretary, everyone did his best to obtain a tactile impression of the thing. Monsieur d'Agnès carefully noted down Monsieur Le Tellier's findings. Ladders were brought, which were stood up against the invisible. They gave the impression of being magical ladders, leaning in unstable equilibrium. Those who employed them seemed to be marvelous acrobats toying with gravity to the point of annulling it. Having reached five meters above ground, they set foot on the nothingness; then, with a thousand precautions, they went forward in mid-air like novice gods. Some walked; the soles of their shoes could be seen from below. The majority got down on all fours and proceeded in that manner. Everyone experienced difficulty in standing upright on that platform, level and resistant as it was, solely by virtue of its being invisible.

The subaerian was measured precisely. It was five meters eight centimeters tall, but 40 meters ten centimeters long. Contact revealed nothing but a surface that was both icy and smooth—some compared it to marble, others to steel or glass—with no joints, devoid of rivets or bolts, as if its hull had been sculpted in one piece from a colossal block of invisible matter. The mighty crash in the Carrefour Louis-le-Grand had not even dented it. On the sides, two lines of rounded hollows were discovered, like two rows of soup-dishes. Monsieur Monbardeau maintained that they were portholes, and he frightened everyone with the notion of the grimacing faces possibly installed at these bull's-eyes, staring at the crowd in a frightful manner, grinding their teeth in that exasperating fashion that never ends.

Monsieur Le Tellier told him, correctly, that it was necessary for the sarvants to scrape the hull in order to make themselves heard, since they were in a vacuum. At the same moment, a sequence of five slightly raised disks was discovered on the flat top of the aeroscaph, arranged along the median line. The middle one was four meters in diameter, the others only fifty centimeters. Everyone wanted to feel them. It was agreed that they had to be lids: panels sealing hatchways.

Meanwhile, an animated group stood at the rear and set up several double ladders, tightly bound together. The invisible propeller was the reason for this. Its shaft was two and a half meters above the ground. It could easily be turned by hand, without making any sound—which proved that the workings of the machinery were still functioning in the void.

The propeller astonished the Duc d'Agnès. Short and broad, cleverly curled, multiple, mobile and susceptible to banking, like the shaft of a hirsute and jagged corkscrew, it was, in sum, a much-improved Archimedean screw. There was no need to look elsewhere for the involuntary siren that had hummed its soft and somber song in the fearful nights, the ventilator whose wind had added to that of the aeroscaph's passage to shake the trees and made Mirastel's weathervane spin when the aeroscaph described its approaching spiral around it.

One by one, the men of science came to play with the incomparable propeller, with the result that one of them—Monsieur Martin Dubois of the Institute—was rudely smacked on the head by one of the blades when one of his colleagues rotated the helix. After that accident, Monsieur Le Tellier decided to ameliorate the inconveniences of invisibility as much as possible, by effecting a delimitation of the aeroscaph. For the time being, it was circled by ropes—the very ones that had served to support it. They then had before their eyes an extraordinary carcass, somewhat reminiscent of the skeleton of a whale modeled in string: a skeleton that only had ribs; a thoracic cage of hemp, in the form of a cigar squared off in the middle. Poles were set up around the propeller.

Then, to the great satisfaction of Gargantua, they attacked the hatches. It was hot; the workers bared their chests.

"Not too soon!" Virachol muttered. "He says it's just like the *Lutin*—at that time, I was a skinny quarter-master myself." He could not conceive that, if the aeroscaph really had contained "skinnies," he would have been able to see them through that ultra-diaphanous envelope as clearly as he saw his fat Pantagruelesque belly expanding before him, already streaming with a sweat of anticipation.

The hatchways resisted crowbars. Pick-axes rang out, buckling on the substance that had flattened Robert Collin's bullet and withstood two opposite torrents of automobiles without flinching. A bizarre emotion gripped the spectators. In a few minutes, they would know what the sarvants were! The last enigma would be solved; the last veil of the monstrous Isis[47] was on the point of falling.

But the hatches refused to open, and the inconvenience of unstopping them was further increased because Monsieur Le Tellier had forbidden anyone to get closer to them than a meter, for fear of the void, in case of an abrupt perforation.

The works being carried out behind the Grand Palais necessitated the employment of a steam-powered winch; it was fetched. Hooked on to the aft hatchway, however, it lifted the entire aeroscaph, in spite of the counterweight of a hundred men hanging from the ropes. The void beneath the panels kept them sealed by the enormous weight of the atmosphere. Essentially, it was a variant of the two famous hemispheres of Magdeburg,[48] of which every schoolboy retains an affectionate memory.

The winch was withdrawn. Monsieur Le Tellier mounted the aeroscaph to feel the invincible lids again. A numerous following joined him there—and now it is necessary to know what had become of Virachol.

Beside himself, his humanitarian instincts in revolt because of the slowness of the "rescue," he had recruited his comrades for the execution of a deadly project. He had noticed

---

[47] The legendary veil of Isis was placed on a statue of the goddess at Memphis, and subsequently became a significant mystical symbol of barriers to enlightenment. It was repopularized in that context during the 19th century occult revival by W. Winwood Reade's *The Veil of Isis; or, The Mysteries of the Druids* (1861).

[48] The hemispheres of Magdeburg were manufactured by that town's mayor, Otto von Guericke, in order to demonstrate a new air-pump of his invention. They were made of copper, and fitted together to form a sphere 50 centimetres in diameter. When the pump created a vacuum between the hemispheres, holding them together, 30 horses were unable to pull them apart. The original demonstration was mounted in 1654, but it proved so striking that it was repeated many times over.

that the scraping sounds were coming from a part of the subaerian situated low down in the bow. He decided to attack there, directly, and to scuttle the ship in order to "get air to the victims." While the hatchways were distracting attention, Virachol pin-pointed the scraping sounds: directly behind the last "porthole," beside the prow. Then he tried to draw a chalk circle on the invisible aeroscaph, in order that the perforating blows could always be aimed at the same spot—but the chalk made no mark, either on the "porthole" or the hull. Then he folded his meter rule into the shape of a pentagon and had a journeyman hold it up in the right place, between two ropes.

There were eight men supporting Virachol-Gargantua's huge pointed crowbar. For a moment, they swung it rhythmically back and forth; then aiming straight into the pentagon, they struck. The ram rebounded...the impacts sounded with the regularity of a pendulum and the timbre of a bell.

At the first blow, the astronomer guessed what was happening. "Stop them!" he ordered, from the top of the platform. "Quickly! It's madness! Stop them! The void! The void!"

Gargantua breathed out, grunted and spat out phlegm. "Courage, by God! Get a move on, lads!" He was in front of the others, and shoved the crowbar with all his phenomenal weight, sweating, reddening and exhaling savage noises.

"Stop it!" implored Monsieur Le Tellier, hastening to get down. "You're going to..."

But he was too late.

A prodigious hiss was heard, brief, sharp and deafening. It was followed by a dull, flaccid sound and a piercing scream. Virachol had let go of his crowbar, and was waving his arms; it was easy to see that he was stuck to the subaerian. He braced himself, in vain; his alarmed friends tried to pull him backwards, in vain. The desperate man could not detach himself, and he look down fearfully at his immoderate belly, from which a swollen excrescence had suddenly begun to extend.

A crowd pressed around him. Monsieur Le Tellier calmed them down: "Don't pull; it's futile."

"The sarvants have got him!" someone said.

278

"No," the astronomer replied, hotly. "It's the vacuum, and nothing else."

The workmen explained what had happened. "The crowbar suddenly got away from us. One might have thought that it had decamped voluntarily. There was a whistling sound, and Gargantua's stuck there in mid-air, as if he were trying to follow the crowbar!"

Indeed, everyone could see the stout iron bar *inside the vessel*. It seemed to be perpetually on the point of falling, sustained as it was by an invisible opposing force. As soon as it had pierced the flank of the aeroscaph, the vacuum had absorbed it avidly—or, if you prefer, the entering air had drawn it in—and then it had aspired Gargantua who was now blocking the airway that he had opened with his own abdomen. His elastic flesh was being sucked in by the formidable cupping-glass; the apoplectic appendage was elongating, swelling and bleeding. There was a dreadful possibility, it seemed, that the entire man would end up being sucked into that little hole.

The panic-stricken Virachol took out his knife; he preferred to cut off a part of his paunch rather than adhere for one minute more to the sucker of that gigantic artificial octopus...

Monsieur Le Tellier stopped him. "It's simply a matter of letting air into the vacuum-chamber."

Another battering ram was already attacking the sonorous hull. The hearty fellows maneuvering it had passed cables around their waists, and fifty firemen were holding them back.

The second ram departed like the first, but no man was cupped, in spite of the air that was whistling louder than a steam-engine in distress.

Virachol was able to disengage himself. He was carried away unconscious.

The scraping sounds had ceased.

"Dead!" whispered Monsieur Le Tellier, in the Duc d'Agnès's ear. "The invisible matelots are dead, *drowned in air*!"

"Then there's no more void in the subaerian?"

"Oh, yes. We've only forced an entry into a single compartment—the blast of the whistle didn't last long for us to suppose anything else. My God! I'll simply have the hatchways staved in, after all. The void will assist us. Too bad about the damage—I'd have preferred to open them."

Gathered around the aft hatchway, six athletic metalworkers working as a team plied six long-shafted twenty-kilo sledgehammers, and began to strike it resonantly, as if chiming an invisible bell.

While they were hammering, the Duc d'Agnès took Monsieur Le Tellier aside. "I might seem stupid to you, but—invisibility? I still don't understand. And many others are in the same boat, who dare not admit it. Robert Collin seemed to find it perfectly natural that invisible worlds and invisible beings might exist..."

"Since ancient times," Monsieur Le Tellier replied, "people have admitted that there might be invisible entities. The gods of paganism hid themselves from mortal eyes; they were granted the Olympian faculty of *aorasie*,[49] which is nothing but invisibility. An ancient legend, retold by La Fontaine in 'King Candaules,' relates the story of Gyges, the shepherd who became a king thanks to a ring that rendered him invisible. I also remember a certain turban in the *Thousand-and-One Nights*, which one only had to put on in order to disappear..."

"Mythology! Fable! Literature!"

"Certainly. But are we not surrounded by invisible entities? *Real*, but invisible? Energy, sound, odor and the air that bathes us—and the wind, the invisibility of which you are so well aware that you have equipped your airplane with an instrument to render it visible? You recognize that these are in-

---

[49] I have retained the French form of this Greek-derived word, because it does not appear to have been adapted into English; as the text states, it refers to the particular ability that the Greek gods had of rendering themselves invisible to mortal eyes.

visible entities. Well, that's sufficient to strip all implausibility from the conjecture of invisible worlds that are formed entirely of similar entities..."

"All right, then—things. But living beings?"

"Oh, living beings. Let's see—what is a living being? Let's go as far as possible: what is a man? A soul and a body. Perfect. But the soul itself is always invisible; you've never seen a soul wandering about by itself, have you? Good. As for the body, an abstraction made by the soul—my God, the body is nothing but a certain quantity of matter, neither more nor less estimable that a certain quantity of atmosphere. In consequence of that, I can't see why one would refuse to one any property that one grants to the other, including the property of being optically imperceptible, for...

"For, don't forget that invisibility is only that; it's the quality of that which makes no impression on our retina. For an object, therefore, it's no more extraordinary to be invisible than to be odorless or tasteless, given that we admit without difficulty that it doesn't smell of anything or leaves the taste-buds indifferent. Do you think it prodigious that we don't hear the clouds gliding past? Then why are you surprised not to see the sarvants passing by? Why are you, who admit impalpable objects, so reluctant and astonished to recognize the existence of invisible objects?

"Our amazement in the presence of the Blue Peril originates from the fact that these newly-revealed entities are *solid*, and that invisibility and solidity are two qualities of matter that are not found together in the habitual conditions in which we exercise our senses of sight and touch. However, even before our first contact with the invisible world, we had already witnessed instances of the combination of those two qualities in the same object. A solid body, animated by a rapid movement, can no longer be seen. Examples: a bullet in its trajectory; a propeller turning in the shade. Another, quite different example of an invisible solid is that of a colorless crystal vase plunged into pure water has the same refractive index. *Colorless*, I said—but a colorless entity is already invisible, and you've doubtless admired panes of glass so colorless, so *aerian*, with respect to visual perception that closed windows still seem wide open.

"Now, take note, please, that of all these substances we're talking about, some are at least as important in the universe as the perishable clay of our bodies."

"Even so," retorted the Duc d'Agnès, instinctively, "one is tempted to deny the reality of that which is invisible."

"Yes, because among our senses, sight is the one that has the vastest domain; it's the sense that we deem principal—and that's why you contest the existence of entities that it does not appreciate in any fashion. Imagine a creature, though, endowed with but a single sense—the sense of smell, for example. Such a creature is not absurd; there must be one among the multitude of living things. Think, then, of the infinity of things whose existence it would deny. Everything that has no odor! That blind creature would deny the reality of any visible thing that had no perfume!

"We resemble that creature. With respect to the aeroscaph, sarvants and the superaerian world, we are just as blind. Since the commencement of life, we have been playing a terrifying game of Blind-Man's-Buff with the sarvants, and we're the ones whose eyes have been bandaged! Moreover, they aren't the only invisible enemies we've had for all that time. Think of treacherous carbon dioxide and its poisonous accomplice, carbon monoxide, and many others! We're blind in confrontation with the sarvants, I tell you—that's all; it's a question of words. We can only perceive them by means of hearing or touch. For Madame Arquedouve, who cannot see at all, they're exactly like other creatures, since they merely lack a quality that she is incapable of perceiving. Were she to touch that aeroscaph, the impression she would obtain would be the same as if it were a matter of a visible craft, unless her touch, perfected by experience, informed her that the object possesses some special characteristic that, for the sighted, translates into invisibility—a characteristic that would only exist for the blind. A man born blind would be unable understand that, from his point of view, there is any difference between the metal or the aeroscaph and our flesh. Are you still astonished, then, Monsieur, by an exception to what seems to certain people to be a general rule, which reason seems to impose as such with all its omnipotence?

"Would you like to break the spell of the invisible? It's not difficult—close your eyes!"

"Rhetoric, Monsieur, rhetoric! Furthermore, admit that the objects you cite as being invisible are merely temporary and occasional. The bullet only becomes so once it is fired, the propeller when it turns and the vase when it is immersed in water. As for *permanently invisible* things, they're gases, impalpable and very far from..."

"Who says that palpable gases cannot exist?"

"They would no longer be gases, by definition. Air only becomes palpable when liquefied under high pressure—when it metamorphoses from gas into liquid."

"Bravo, young man! But tell me: this very liquid, this 'honorary gas' may be frozen. Why should that gas, having become a solid, necessarily lose its property of invisibility? *It would only require one not-very-exceptional exception!* It's a simple question of the index of refraction. Does not opaque sand, Monsieur—sand, which is a kind of solid liquid—become transparent when it is transmuted into crystal? Why then, if you please, should an invisible gas not remain invisible on adopting another consistency? In the present case, is it not much less arduous to *remain* than to *become*?"

"All right. And what about the invisible worlds to which Robert Collin made allusion?"

"You'll recall that the planets, including the Earth, don't describe circular orbits around the Sun of which the Sun is the center, but ellipses, of which the Sun only occupies one of the focal points. What is at the other focal point—the second center, if I might put it thus—where there must be something powerful enough to counterbalance the action of the Sun and to contrive that the orbits of the planets are elliptical instead of circular? Some worthy intelligences maintain that there must be other Suns, invisible to human eyes, at the second focal points of the planetary ellipses. Have you read what the pamphlet on this subject by Jean Saryer has to say?[50]

"The Sun and the other invisible Sun, actual focal points of the ellipse, seats of two equal forces coupled in the immensity...draw the Earth along with an influence constant in direction.... Perhaps the other star radiates cold light and illuminates creatures invisible to humans.

"A world of the same contexture as the one that envelops us on high! Creatures similar to the sarvants! Sight has no purchase on them; they are endowed with absolute transparency; light goes right through them."

"We are stupidly trusting of the evidence of our sight," said the Duc d'Agnès. "First, we mistook the victims for the kidnappers—remember the flying men—and then the prisoners for the prison—recall the square patch!"

"And the inexplicable flying fish—which was, in reality, writhing on the floor of the invisible cylinder!"

"Ah, they're..." Monsieur d'Agnès broke off to plug his ears. A skull-splitting whistle, accompanied by a sudden blast of wind, had just replaced the beat of the hammers. Under their repeated impact, and under the pressure of the air, the invisible hatch-cover had finally given way. It had caved in with surprising brutality. They heard things breaking, which it demolished as it went through the subaerian from top to bot-

---

[50] Renard's narrator inserts a footnote here giving an incomplete reference to Saryer's text, whose full title is *Réflexions sur le second foyer de l'orbite terrestre: Essai sur l'invisible* [Reflections on the second focal point of the terrestrial orbit: An Essay on the Invisible]. It was published by Chacornac in 1909, presumably just before Renard began writing the novel, and probably helped to inspire it. The hypothesis—derived from a misunderstanding of the implications of Newton's law of gravity—never had any appeal to the mathematically competent and it has now been effaced from the history of science, along with its author.

tom, and, as a hole was suddenly formed in the ground, they knew that it had gone clean through the bottom of the hull, in the manner of a bullet from an air-gun.

To avoid the suction, the six hammer-wielders had dropped into prone positions, forming a human star radiating around the orifice. One of them, whose head was on the very edge and who was hanging on to it, quickly got up and shouted: "Something brushed against me as it came out violently, immediately after the whistling! It went past me…"

Scarcely had he expressed his surprise when they heard a sound of breaking glass high above. In the expectation of an invisible collapse, everyone ducked. After a second or so, a rain of broken glass fell on the audience. That was all. The roof of the Grand Palais had just been split open; no one knew how or why.

"It's the body of one of the matelots!" Monsieur Le Tellier explained. They must be very light! As soon as the air had flowed in, equilibrium having been re-established, the body rose up again toward the surface of the Air, like a cork, just as one of our bodies would rise up from the bottom of the sea, with incalculable force. That's one of them lost. Let's try to safeguard the others—those that were scraping in the bow."

And he thought: *They're not human—that's impossible. So light! No hearts! No lungs! They can't be human, damn it, even adapted. Transformation has its limits. What are they, then?* His imagination forged frightful and fabulous creatures. The idea of Marie-Thérèse was inevitably mingled with these infernal evocations, and the astronomer felt himself becoming increasingly tremulous the closer they came to full knowledge.

A naval cadet, Monsieur Rigaud, slid into the invisible breach. He went down into the aeroscaph, taking every possible precaution. He reported out loud on the shapes he encountered. He went back and forth in mid-air, in a miraculous fashion, His circumspect footsteps were audible, along with the tick-tock of his fingers tapping the walls. His voice became gradually fainter. He moved upwards and downwards, and turned corners, seemingly opening doors and hatches, crawling through invisible tubes and turning sideways to follow narrow corridors. His voice could no longer be heard, nor his footsteps, nor his stumbles. He continued the exploration of the fantastic labyrinth, but suddenly went pale and made frightened gestures. *He was lost!* He was visible a few meters above ground; it seemed that they could reach him with a single bound, and yet he was a captive in an inextricable jail. Foremen holding hands formed a chain through the labyrinth as far as Monsieur Rigaud. He came out, saying that he would only go back in with a coiled thread that he might unroll like Ariadne.

It was, in fact, by means of that ancient method that they were able to explore the whole of the airtight part of the aeroscaph to which the first hatchway gave access. Then they stayed in the others, except for the fifth.

The vessel was divided into numerous very small cavities. There were no staircases, only inclined planes. Monsieur Martin-Dubois of the Institute discovered enclosed sections that had to be air-ballasts, and from the fact that the majority were full of air the deduced that the cause of the wreck was that the expulsion pump had broken down; the sarvants had then found it impossible to restore the void in the air-ballasts and, in consequence, impossible to regain the surface of the aerial sea.

In the middle, a broad chimney occupied the entire height of the aeroscaph. It was the unforgettable cylinder, which a momentary frost had caused to appear to Robert and which served as a temporary aerium for the sarvants' victims. They were taken in at the base, whose double bottom could be slid open. At the top, sealed by the largest of the five hatches, they were transferred to their final cells.

It was Monsieur Le Tellier who was the first to palpate the terrible pincer mechanisms, complemented by a metallic chain-mail basket, with which the Invisibles cut branches, seized their prey and deposited it in the cylinder. Mounted on the end of long articulated arms, which were extended at the appropriate moment from the inferior opening of the chimney, this pincer-basket constituted a mechanical masterpiece, at least so far as could be judged blindly with mistrustful neophyte hands.

The sliding floor elucidated the miracle of the English cock. When the trap had opened so that the pincer could collect the cock from the bell-tower, a real cockerel, already captured, had become excited, and the opening had permitted the old lady to hear its cries of fear. In the same way, the dwarf from Ruffieux had slipped out on the summit of the Colombier at the precise moment when floor slid aside to allow the passage of the unfortunate reporter-photographer. Some unknown cause had prevented the sarvants from re-seizing their prey— probably the unexpected arrival of some remarkable quarry.

It still remained, however, to penetrate the anterior chamber of the aeroscaph, where the scraping sounds had been manifest. So interesting was the machinery that had been discovered that everyone had been diverted by other attractions when Monsieur Le Tellier announced that it was time to break into the last stronghold, where the mystery was entrenched.

The astronomer had forbidden the staving in of the hatch of that final portion for fear that the bodies of the invisible matelots might return skywards like the first. They had not felt objects resembling cadavers anywhere; the sailors had doubtless take refuge in the bow, in the subaerian's most secure shelter, leaving one of their comrades behind. Dedication? Punishment? Accident? Chance? They did not know.

Drills, at the end of flexible cords, pierced aeration holes in the forward bulkheads. There was still a vacuum in the upper compartments. The others were found to be accessible by means of flexible metal doors that unrolled in the manner of our roller-blinds, like the shutters of our shops.

There was a series of small, very low-ceilinged spaces. Monsieur Le Tellier and Monsieur d'Agnès advanced into them prudently, bent double. Their hearts beating strongly, they arrived near Virachol's crowbar. The Duc, bending down, moved it through the air with his hands.

"We'll have to look for them on the ceiling," the astronomer told him. "Hold on! Ah!"

Five inert bodies, stuck to the ceiling by their astonishing lightness, were palpated one after another and recognized as *five human corpses*. As was only to be expected, the enormous abnormal pressure had deformed them cruelly; they were bloated and bulging, due to the frightful death that so horribly swells up cadavers drowned in the depths of the sea. What was surprising, though, beyond all expression, was that the sarvants were human—exceptional humans, it goes without saying, but humans nevertheless! These creatures of the void, these invisible, almost imponderable creatures deprived of circulatory systems and denuded of respiratory apparatus, these collectors and torturers of humans, were human themselves!

Without wasting time in vain reflections, Monsieur Le Tellier had them laden with heavy chains, in order that they would not fly away. Zinc coffins full of ice were brought, in which the dead invisibles were laid. Then Monsieur Le Tellier entrusted them to Dr. Monbardeau, with orders to take them to his laboratory in the Boulevard Saint-Germain, in order that autopsies might be carried out. He promised to rejoin him there in due course, in order to begin the work.

Having said that, and overriding the protests of a few physicians who complained about the monopolization, Monsieur Le Tellier groped his way back to the machines. He realized then the strange disproportion that seemed to exist between the medium height of the invisible men and the narrowness of the aeroscaph's cabins, where even the smaller matelots would have been unable to stand upright or lie down full-length.

The machines occupied a dozen tiny chambers, only separated by slender columns. You can imagine the difficulties they had to surmount in order to count all these housings and to draw up an approximate plan of them, without being able to see anything. There were many learned men there who, although stumbling because of vertigo, adapted themselves ardently to contours they could not see. They were nourished by an avid curiosity with respect to the machinery and the motive force employed by the Invisibles to activate the propeller, the pumps and perhaps even the cylinder's heater. The majority were sure that they were about to discover an electricity-capture mechanism even more advanced than the *Epervier*'s.

When they arrived at the end of the machine opposite to the propeller, they found a great many boxes regularly separated on shelves. Mobile pieces of metal connected them to the transmission apparatus. These seeming accumulators or piles were opened easily enough....

Each one contained the cadaver of a squat and baroque animal: a kind of exceedingly muscular toad, imprisoned in a rotating drum that its mission was to put in motion and which, each one turning by virtue of the force of all the rest—obliging the animal to run within its hollow wheel, under threat of being harshly shaken, thus contributing to the general labor. This energy, communicated by little crank-shafts to the central axle, was transformed in a thousand ways within a mechanical jumble.

Thus, the civilized beings of the world above—these people whose science seemed to be advanced—were still making use of animal power! Their toad-slaves were turning in their drums like squirrels rotating their round cages and horses operating threshing-machines moving in endless circles. They were mechanized animals, brute-instruments, reminiscent of the drum-regulated rowers of the triremes of old; they were galley-frogs!

The lightness of these domestic batrachians was extraordinary. They tended to rise up like animals inflated by hydrogen. Compression had damaged them severely. There were 130 of them, which caused Monsieur Salomon Kahn to say, jokingly, that the aeroscaph was a 130-toad-power machine.

This demonstrated the superaerian existence of an entire void-based fauna, invisible and of a constitution analogous to that of the sarvants.

Monsieur Le Tellier set aside a few of the new victims of asphyxiation. Weighted down and packed in ice, they went the same route as their masters.

In the meantime, the engineers caressing, tapping and rubbing the machines could not help admiring their ingenious complexity. Nevertheless, the sphere played a role therein so ludicrous and preponderant that the most earnest technologists burst out laughing on finding so many marbles, globes, balls and pommels beneath their fingers. They were laughing, but also groaning, for the accursed invisibility prevented them from getting a firm grasp of the mechanisms. Several young blind people, chosen for their intelligence from among the inmates of an institution, rendered them valuable service with their enhanced sense of touch, but that was no more than a half-measure, and Monsieur Le Tellier soon perceived that it would be indispensable to render the aeroscaph and its details visible if they wanted to study it effectively.

Oh, if only they could coat it with something! But the aeroscaph resisted any kind of daubing. Nothing marked it, any more than Virachol's chalk had done. From distemper to gloss, all the paints in the world were tried, one by one; they might as well have been trying to paint glass with water-colors.

This inconvenience incited the astronomer to have fragments of the subaerian taken away for chemical analysis, in the hope that the analysis might lead to the invention of a paint capable of attaching itself to the invisible material, and, in consequence making it visible. While awaiting this fortunate eventuality, Monsieur Le Tellier contented himself with summoning a crew of workmen equipped with sacks of plaster. They set out to make molds of the simplest pieces, including the pincer-basket and the propeller. That way, they would at least have molds of the invisible objects.

Dusk fell.

"Come on," said the astronomer to the Duc d'Agnès. "We'll go dissect the sarvants now. When I think about my daughter, it seems to me that I'd gladly have butchered them alive. Come, Monsieur. We'll take that blind man you can see over there; his name is Louis Courtois and he knows anatomy. The director of the institution recommended him to me warmly. Go fetch him, please."

When the trio left the Grand Palais arm-in-arm, the white plaster helix was emerging from its mold, unorthodox and implausible—a faithful reproduction of a marvelous propeller that had not yet been conceived by those who, until now, had been the only ones to call themselves *human beings*.

XV. The Truth About the Sarvants

Dr. Monbardeau was waiting for them impatiently in the laboratory in the Boulevard Saint-Germain: a fine painter's studio on the sixth floor of its building, which Monsieur Le Tellier had fitted out for all sorts of scientific investigations. The doctor was pacing back and forth there under the harsh glare of electric arc-lamps. On a table, he had set out gleaming steel implements and liquids with chemical tints, borrowed for the occasion from Parisian colleagues.

The five zinc coffins were lined up side by side, and the refrigerated boxes containing the toad-motors were lined up with them.

The Duc d'Agnès and the astronomer set about opening one of the coffins; in the meantime, the doctor, without ceasing to march back and forth, questioned the blind man and summoned him as a witness to the horrific turn of events.

"Human beings, Monsieur! What shame! Humans! Macrocephalic bipedal bimanes, like you and me! Beings who have the honor of resembling Claude Bernard,[51] Pasteur and...Tolstoy!..and who fish for their own kind as if for gudgeons. And who collect them! Oh, a wretched humankind, Monsieur!"

"Bah!" replied Monsieur Courtois. "We'd do the same if we could. Under the pretext of ethnography, savages have

---

[51] The choice of Claude Bernard (1813-1878) to head this brief list of paragons of humankind is ironically significant; he was the physiologist famous for demanding the rigorous application of the scientific method to medical inquiry—a policy subsequently employed, fervently and with considerable success, by Louis Pasteur. It was, of course, that methodological imposition that led human scientists to begin extensive series of animal experiments involving vivisection, acting in exactly the same fashion as the sarvants.

been exhibited in the Jardin d'Acclimatation in a manner reminiscent of the sarvants' aerium. And consider, doctor, the perverse enjoyment people seem to obtain from watching a woman through a keyhole without her suspecting it; it's simply the passion of the collector!"

"A wretched humankind, I tell you!"

"Come and help us, Calixte," said Monsieur Le Tellier.

The lid of the coffin was removed. Amid the chains and the melted ice, a void confusedly marked out the "three-dimensional silhouette"—to coin a phrase—of a human being, neither fat nor thin, neither tall nor short.

This temporary and imperfect visibility suggested to the Director of the Observatory the idea of having the cadavers molded the following day, like the propeller, and permitted the sarvant to be grabbed by the feet and under the arms without groping. Its buoyancy neutralized the weight of the chains; the whole ensemble weighed zero grams, centigrams and milligrams.

It was laid out on a hurdle, and the four operators began to palpate it, not without aversion.

Impulsively, the sighted men looked at the places where their hands were, as if their gazes had the power to render things visible, and the appearance or non-appearance of objects were simply a consequence of visual attention. They quickly perceived, on the contrary, that their touch was more sensitive when their eyes were closed. The blind man with the wise hands held his head up, and his fingers moved in the air with a prestidigitatory agility. There were four blind men then, of which three were voluntarily blind—with the aim of enlightenment!

After a silence, Monsieur Le Tellier opened his eyelids. He was troubled by the bewilderment painted on the usually-impassive face of Louis Courtois. "Horribly deformed, isn't it?" he said. "I can't feel the eyes or the mouth."

"No, no eyes," the other confirmed, excitedly, "and no mouth. But there's worse—the face...the features...are so coarse, so rough...and tell me, gentlemen...it seems to me that this man is wearing clothes?"

"Damn!"

"Undoubtedly!"

"Yes indeed..."

"Very well—but feel this: there's no difference between the skin of the face and the fabric of the costume...or the skin of the hands..."

"Hands, those!" protested the doctor. "Those grainy vestigial stumps, which are revolting to touch!"

Monsieur d'Agnès repeated, in a tone of disgust: "What a vile contact! Mamillated, viscous..."

"Ah yes!" said the blind man. "But they're not clothes. They're part of the individual's body. They have the same consistency, the same substance! One might think it a sort of soft effigy, made of coarsely agglomerated pads. These pads...these pads...ah! I've got one!" His fumbling fingers were seen to grasp something in the emptiness, on the invisible breast. "I've got it...I'm detaching it...with difficulty...it's coming. Here it comes! Good, I've freed it!"

There was an abrupt click from the ceiling.

"It's risen up and stuck there, like the sarvant in the Grant Palais which went through the glass," Lois Courtois continued. "Now there's a cavity in the breast where that bubble came away."

"We have to recover it," the astronomer decided. "With a step-ladder..."

But the blind man's white hands clenched for a second time. "No need," he said. "I've got another...which won't get away. There! God in Heaven!"

"What's up?"

The other three watched the hands, then the face of the blind man. His fingers moved frantically, and horror tinted his face. A quivering gesture caused him to recoil in an attitude of the most invincible repulsion; his hands opened. There was a second abrupt click on the ceiling.

"Ugh!" He shivered as if he were cold. "*It's a spider!* An immense short-legged spider, the size of a hen's egg. A dead spider…"

They drew away from the invisible cadaver.

Monsieur Le Tellier summoned up all his strength and immediately returned to the hurdle where the chains sketched out the configuration of the terrible sarvant. "Come on! Show some guts! We need to know. All this…"

He resumed the hideous manual work on his own. Then, formulating his discoveries as he made them, he pronounced words whose enormity will remain for centuries to come: "No, no…you're right, Monsieur; it's not a human being that I'm touching…*it's an agglomeration of creatures aggregated in human form, and those creatures are definitely spiders*…yes…or large lice, if your prefer…"

"I prefer the spiders!" whispered the Duc d'Agnès.

The astronomer went on: "They're tightly bound together in a compact mass, in the position in which the aerial drowning surprised them. They're mingled in the fashion of little garden-spiders whose gathering on their mother's back makes a horrible swarming fleece—but here, it's a creature entirely constituted by animals…animals grouped in human form…and the form of a human wearing clothes. It really is!"

"So," said the doctor, slowly, at the height of excitement, "our children's torturers are spiders!"

Monsieur Le Tellier broke the ensuing silence by remarking: "Robert anticipated that when he said: *the creatures of the void must be more different from human beings than the inhabitants of a planet that is immensely distant, but which is endowed with an atmosphere.*"

A short while before, Monsieur Monbardeau had been indignant to think that the sarvants were human; now he wished wholeheartedly that they were. Spiders! Intelligent and civilized, perhaps—but spiders all the same! Could one imagine anything more sordid?

Their repugnance increased further when the Duc, having donned his gloves, detached another invisible arachnid from the body, which he had the inspiration of coating with powerful glue fortified with red ink.

Entirely immersed in red-stained secotine,[52] the little monster stood out, bloody and gelatinous. Its hideousness was so unbearable to those who knew about the abominations of the aerium that someone threw it out of the window. Weighed down by its sticky burden, it rose up slowly toward the stars—toward the superaerian world—and was soon lost in the fallacious darkness, treacherously flourishing with exquisite lights.

The courageous blind man palpated the remains of the sarvant for a second time, his agile hands now seeming to be two five-legged spiders, living their own lives, busy with their mysterious task.

"That human form!" muttered the doctor. "But why? Why?"

"I've got it!" Monsieur Le Tellier suddenly announced. "We're confronted by a *phenomenon of mimicry*! It's a defense-mechanism—a stratagem of war! When they found themselves in our power, these spiders thought that we might respect creatures similar to ourselves, and that's why they agglutinated in such a manner as to represent human beings! It might be purely instinctive mimicry, or rational mimicry; in either case—it's mimicry!"

Three exclamations burst forth in unison.

"That's what it is, my boys! And that's why the spaces in the aeroscaph were so confined. Compared to the stature of the matelots who lived in them, they were large rooms. For the sarvants, the aeroscaph is a huge liner, proportionate not to its crew but to the prey that it was charged with capturing and transporting."

"We're not gudgeons, doctor," said the Duc d'Agnès. "We're sperm whales."

"Small consolation, Monsieur. However, I confess that…miserable dwarfs…spiders though they are…"

---

[52] Secotine was a kind of glue manufactured—as many of the most effective glues of the period were—from fish-guts.

"Oh, extremely skillful dwarfs! Exceedingly clever spiders. What a monument the aerium is, in those circumstances! An aquarium for whales!"

"Pass me the scalpel," said Courtois. "This cohesion seems bizarre to me."

"You've found something else?" Monsieur Le Tellier asked him.

"Wait," said Monsieur Courtois. "Let me work. It really is! I expected it. Oh, these spiders...they're not simply united by the enlacement of their legs; they're also held together by nervous tissue. Each presents two external nervous papillae, connected to a center—a brain, medulla or ganglion—which fulfill the function of electrical contacts, or power-points, as you prefer. *The spiders connect themselves to one another by means of these nervous contacts!*"

"Heaven and Earth!" said Monsieur Le Tellier. "But if they can weld themselves together in that fashion, the entire arachnid species can form a variable quantity of collective beings, as it pleases, or become a single immense animal endowed with a single mind, a single will and a single sensibility: a gigantic ball, or rather an interminable cordon, a chaplet..."

"Like a tapeworm!" said Monsieur Monbardeau. "That's also composed of organisms arranged in sequence..."

"The sarvants resemble water," said the Duc d'Agnès, "which scatters into innumerable droplets, but can form a single ocean. We're no longer sperm whales, doctor; these people are titans, when they wish to be."

"Yes, titans," said Monsieur Courtois. "Multiform proteans! These elected to borrow our stature in order to try to deceive us; they had a choice between all possible conformations; they were able to amalgamate into any plastic combination, and thus become several large colony-creatures, many small social beings, or remain a host of separate individuals."

"These spiders are nothing, in sum," Monsieur Le Tellier observed, "but units of construction, like the cells of our own bodies—since after all, a human being is only a collection of elements. The difference is that our cells have no personality, no independence, while among the sarvants, each free element is an individual. This biological type realizes a social chimera: the co-operative State. The superaerian people enjoy the ideal republic: one for all and all for one. It's admirable."

"It's disgusting!" said the Duc d'Agnès.

"All modes of life are admissible," said Monsieur Courtois, "and this one, which subordinates the preponderance of a race to the practice of solidarity, isn't without grandeur."

"Bah!" said Monsieur d'Agnès. "Preponderance over toads!"

"That's true!" said Monsieur Monbardeau. "We're forgetting the toads! Shall we study them a little now? I'm curious…each one of them, remember, was doing the work of an ox, and that's an accessory mystery, in which, in spite of everything, I suspect the involvement of a science…"

He ran to the motor creatures then, and experienced the regret of observing that their decomposition was proceeding with an unfortunate rapidity. An odor of formic acid,[53] given off by the ice, pricked his nose and made him weep. Bubbles of mephitic gas were making glug-glug noises in the water of the melting ice. The lid of one of the boxes was thrown off, with a bang and a stink.

"The sarvants must be brutes," declared the Duc d'Agnès, "to have treated God's creatures like that!"

---

[53] Renard's narrator inserts a footnote: "*Formic acid.* Perhaps the scientists did not give sufficient thought to that odor of formic acid. It is not the commencement of a proof tending to demonstrate that the invisible mechanized toads drew their bovine force from themselves? The extraordinary strength of the most minuscule ants is well known. A guinea-pig consubstantial with an ant could carry loads whose weight would astonish the reader. Now, a toad being the same size as a guinea-pig…" The note is superfluous, the strength of ants relative to their size having nothing to do with their secretion of formic acid.

"First of all," Monsieur Le Tellier said, by way of contradiction, "you don't know whether these toads might have been delighted to find protection, shelter and subsistence, at the price of a labor doubtless proportionate to their strength. Personally, I think that the sarvants *are not evil*, since they thought that we would do no harm to creatures that resembled us…"

"Oh, certainly!" mocked the doctor. "The most obtuse animal knows perfectly well that wolves don't eat one another!"

"Of wolves, that's true. Not of humans."

"In any case," murmured the Duc d'Agnès, "the sarvants don't stop at martyrizing those who don't resemble them!"

"And what if they don't know what suffering is?" replied the astronomer. "Have you thought of that? We, who suffer, claim that some animals are ignorant of pain. In the end, what do we know?"

"Perhaps," suggested the blind man, "they adopted our appearance knowing, on the contrary, that there is nothing humans fear more than other humans? But let's hurry—putrefaction is taking hold of these remains."

"Which is annoying," sighed Monsieur Le Tellier. "I would have liked to submit them to experiments in radiography and make molds of them."

"You won't have the time."

"Let's at least try to find out how they make up for the lack of blood circulation and respiratory function, by disaggregating that human simulacrum."

The rising Sun found them bent over the little corpses—which were invisible, light and repulsive, and difficult to retain, liable to flatten themselves against the ceiling at the slightest false move. The results of their night's work, however, are much too technical to report in this popular account—whose clarity, besides, would not be reinforced in the least.

Thus terminated the memorable night of September 6 and 7, 1912, the worthy sequel to a Friday forever to be celebrated in the annals of science.

XVI. De Profundis Clamavi [54]

The morning papers vanished as soon as they appeared. Everyone was expecting to read a full explanation of the phenomenon of the grand boulevard—the previous evening's papers having related it in confused and irrational terms—but had the disturbing experience of only buying, even in the best papers, a surplus of incoherent ramblings and contradictions. They gave a passable account of what had happened at the Grand Palais, but they followed that information—already very frightening—with inept commentaries and highly fantastic explanations. In the excited public mind, everything concerning the aeroscaph became a little clearer, but the notion of the superaerian world remained tenebrous and ghostly.

The instinct of the people warned them that something serious had happened. Paris was in a ferment. The shops were deserted. Crowds besieged the ministries one by one, without knowing to which of them they ought to have recourse, in the circumstances. People imagined that the government was keeping secrets and mounting pretences, electing to remain silent; they wanted the truth. To the bobbing of Chinese lanterns in front of the Chambre des Deputés, a hundred thousand people demanded it.

A delegate was sent to Monsieur Le Tellier to ask him to instruct the nation. At four o'clock, there was a gratuitous distribution of a bulletin printed in haste, which included the astronomer's response (*item 821*). It did not conceal anything, but merely undertook to be stoical.

It was then that the Blue Peril became manifest in all its horror and all its formidable implications—when it was clearly stated that above humankind, on an invisible globe more

---

[54] These are the opening words of the penitential prayer conventionally recited in the Latin mass for the dead; they translate as "From the depths I cry."

immense than the Earth and enveloping it everywhere, lived another race of intelligent beings, which seemed to have attacked us; a race redoubtable by virtue of its location, its might, its way of life, its genius and its invisibility, which put a metaphorical blindfold upon us.

All humankind shared the same fear, and its excitement was bizarrely aggravated by the fact that the two known forms of the creatures of the void exactly duplicated those of the most repulsive terrestrial animals—a repulsion to which centuries of daily acquaintance had not been able to render humans insensible.

The fate of the prisoners ceased to interest public opinion; people feared too many calamities for themselves. The repulsive meddling of toads and spiders in our affairs preoccupied everyone's thoughts—for it is important to note that, at the outset, the popular mind did not differentiate between the sarvants and their dynamic livestock. In spite of the information provided by Monsieur Le Tellier, the assurance of an imminent invasion persisted for a long time; the army expected to be mobilized at any moment.

Within 24 hours the panic became worldwide. An avid thirst for science developed everywhere, even in the most backward tribes. The ignorant had themselves initiated in the rudiments of optics and meteorology; clerks extended their knowledge to the remotest arcana. Displayed by bookshops, Jean Saryer's *Essai sur l'invisible* sold out in multilingual editions. *Le Journal*, the *Daily Mail*, the *New York Herald*, the *Novoye Vremya* and the *Gazette de Cologne* offered Monsieur Le Tellier fortunes for authorization to publish the red notebook, but he refused.

The end of the world, feared for several months, seemed suddenly to have arrived. The churches, temples, synagogues, pagodas and mosques were overflowing with horrified multitudes moved to instinctive fervor, and the taverns produced drunkards by the dozen. The banks, silent and abandoned, could not attract a burglar. There were unanimous prostrations, followed by universal overexcitement. One might have

301

thought that the nervous systems of all humans were in communication, like those of the Invisibles. The despondency extended throughout the family of Eve, prey to that unjustified fear of extermination. People admitted that the time had come.

Everyone told himself that it was the sad termination of so many efforts and victories, and knew again the incessant distress that gripped the hearts of our ancestors when human beings were nothing but feeble mammals perennially exposed to the monumental aggression of mastodons, which they feared without respite and the obsession of which never left them. That terror, suddenly awakened from a 20,000-year sleep, must have been as supreme in prehistoric times as love, for to experience it was to recognize it. More numerous than in any time of eclipse or cometary visitation, gazes fixed on the apparent void, where the fall of humankind was inscribed in invisible characters. But the human tenants of Earth had not even been dethroned—they had never reigned! They had believed themselves to be masters, while another race—industrious, ingenious and absurd—remained their superior, to the point of fishing for them!

Humiliation of humiliations!

Man, no longer being MAN, bowed down, gripped by stupor. He accepted his lot. He felt a great compassion for himself, in confrontation with the iniquity of which he thought himself the victim. And the priests in the pulpits preached in the following fashion:

"From the depths of the abyss we have cried to Thee, Lord, our desires, our suffering and our love; and we were like subterranean beasts. Yes, all the more profound in being beneath an unsuspected world. Were those to whom Thou hast given the kingdom of the Earth, not therefore the sons of clay transfigured by the breath of Elohim? Our prayers, in rising to Thy glory, to the highest of the Heavens, have traversed the universe that it has pleased Thee to interpose between us; but more than ever, O Lord, we cry out to Thee, from the utmost depths of the abyss, our keener desires, our rekindled suffering and our magnified love!"

The evening spider signified chagrin, like that of the morning; both were crushed as soon as they were perceived.[55] Furious pursuers hunted them and stamped on them senselessly. Fear made the non-existent urge forth. Everywhere, people saw *faucheux* and *phrynés*; hallucinated Mexicans saw *atocalts*, Africans imagined that the stars were luminous galeodes, and Victor Hugo's poem was realized in reverse, for the radiant sun paradoxically evoked the dazzling shadow of some titanic Sisyphus: *Et l'homme, du soleil, faisait une araignée.*[56]

---

[55] There is a French superstition, expressed proverbially, which goes: "Araignée du matin, chagrin; araignée du soir, espoir" [Morning spider, grief; evening spider, hope]. It means that a spider encountered in the morning is supposedly a bad omen, while one encountered in the evening is a good one.

[56] The wordplay in this passage poses acute difficulties in translation, and must have challenged Renard's original readers. *Faucheux* are long-legged hunting spiders; their name is adapted from the verb *faucher* [to mow] and is suggestive of the Grim Reaper. Atocalts and galeodes are also intimidating spiders, the latter being a general term for fearsome-seeming solifugids, or "camel spiders." The Victor Hugo reference is to *La Légende des siècles*, specifically to the early section entitled "Puissance égale bonté" [Power equals generosity], in which God and Iblis (the Devil) engage in a creation competition, in which Iblis' *pièce de resistance* is the spider—but God turns the tables on his adversary in the last line: "*Car Dieu, de l'araignée, avait fait le soleil*" [For out of the spider, God had made the Sun." In Renard's transfiguration, it is, of course, Man who makes the Sun into a spider. The reference to Sisyphus also has an arachnid connection, *Theridion sisyphium* being known as the mother care spider—because the mother feeds her newly-hatched young—as well as the Sisyphus spider. The odd term out is *phrynés*, a common noun improvised from the name of an Athenian courtesan famed for her success in her chosen profession, but whose name is derived from a Greek word for toad.

In all the rural regions of the five continents, toads and frogs were massacred, from the delicate green frogs of our meadows to the ignoble *pipas*[57] of Brazil, which are hopping abscesses.

And then, suddenly, there was a turnabout. Humankind pulled itself together, with an abrupt surge of energy. Lay and religious preachers alike cried that, after all, nothing certified the superiority of the sarvants; that their technology, at the end of the day, was less advanced than ours in certain respects, with its risible spheres and its toad-motors; that it was necessary to defend the surface against their incursions and to mobilize all the engines of destruction that our science had constructed and would construct.

It is well-known that human beings in herds are strange beasts, lunatic, sheep-like and Panurgian.[58] The reaction took effect swiftly. An exaggerated confidence supplanted the excessive demoralization. The basilicas emptied, to the profit of the theaters; fashionable shops welcomed an influx of customers and rethreaded needles ran competitively through pongees, shantungs and other silken fabrics. Everything started again. Following the example of a first syndicate for the defense of the territory, others were formed; posters were stuck up in profusion. Public meetings were added to conferences. The world's capital cities seemed lacking in illumination when it was announced that in France, the Council of Ministers was

---

[57] *Pipa* is a genus whose only species is the Surinam toad, which is not actually found in Brazil; its eggs are carried on the mother's back until the tadpoles are released, although that hardly licenses its description as a "hopping abscess," especially as the species is entirely aquatic.

[58] François Rabelais' Panurge actually derives his name from the Greek *panourgos* [cunning], and it labels him as a trickster figure, but the name is easily misconstruable, as *pan* signifies "all" in both Greek and Latin and the Latin *urgere* gives rise to such French words as *urgence* [urgency], so that he becomes a seeming model of reckless instinct.

about to deliberate in combination with the Academy of Sciences—an eminently salutary measure which all other States proposed to imitate.

We shall briefly recall the French mixed session: that historic assembly, model of future parliaments, anticipating the day when scientific experts will replace politicians completely. It opened at the Elysée on Wednesday, September 11, and began with a discussion. (Official record, *item 943*).

Reflecting the national conviction, which he shared, the Minister of War proposed to examine without circumlocutions the surest, most expeditious and radical means of destroying the superaerian continents. He added that it was important to do so as soon as possible, before the sarvants had constructed further aeroscaphs. He mentioned colossal mortars and explosive projectiles—but his speech was cut short. The Minister for the Colonies interrupted him and demanded what right he had to bombard this country, which could, in time, undoubtedly be conquered, perhaps annexed, and might, at the very least, be rewarded by a protectorate. The worst that he could permit himself to foresee was the massacre of the indigenes, although it would be preferable, in his opinion, to enslave them. But to devastate the invisible land from top to bottom?—never! There must be very appreciable unknown riches up there. On his own account, he nursed the hope that France would one day be augmented by this beautiful possession, more extensive than the entire surface visible on maps of the world.

The physicist Salomon Kahn tried to intervene then, but the Minister of Labor entered into the discussion. After a compliment addressed to his two colleagues—admiring them both for having shown, for once, the spirit of his own department, and congratulating the Minister of War for being bellicose and the Minister for the Colonies for being a colonizer—he announced that he, the Minister of Labor, was about to voice the sentiments that ought to have emerged from the mouth of the Keeper of the Seals, the Minister of Justice. And he proved that the idea of colonization was not admissible, from the triple viewpoint of the law, jurisprudence and justice, because the plains of the void already belonged to human beings. (*Prolonged sensation.*)

"You know," he said, "that any landowner is the owner not only of the ground but also the subsoil of his property. Since the extension of aerial navigation, you will recall, the upward extension of property has been symmetrically recognized—the ownership of that portion of the air that is above the ground. All the space that is above my field belongs to it; thus, I am the owner of a portion of the superaerian territory. If my field is round, I own a circle of the invisible continent on high—but that circle is slightly larger than that of my field because, gentlemen, that which we possess when we possess a terrain is not a surface but a volume. To buy a round field is not to buy a circle of land; it is to buy a limitless cone of fire, rock, soil, atmosphere and void, the apex of which is at the center of the Earth—where all properties, coming together, decline to nothing—and the base of which is at infinity. The planets and stars, gentlemen, can only gravitate by passing from one of these conical divisions of the ether, of which we are the possessors, to another. In the same way, to sell a square field is not to sell a square of arable land; it is to sell a regular four-sided pyramid..."

The President of the Republic said nothing.[59]

"I demand the floor," said Monsieur Le Tellier.

It was ceded to him; silence fell.

"Gentlemen," he began, "before annihilating or colonizing the invisible world, scientific France has decades of work to do. No bomb can reach a height of 50 kilometers, at least usefully—for, if it got that far, its explosion in the void would only produce insignificant damage. On the other hand, in falling back to Earth with the force of bolides, its unexploded shrapnel would provoke irreparable misfortunes. So much for annihilation.

---

[59] The President of the French Republic from 1906-1913 was the aging radical Armand Fallières (1841-1931). The conservatively-inclined Renard disapproved of him strongly.

"Let us look at colonization. The technology at our disposal cannot transport us to such a height; above a height of about 25,000 meters from the surface, the air is too rarefied to sustain our balloons, airplanes or helicopters. Trying to fly there is like trying to swim in fog—folly.

"Even if we knew how to build a ship as light, precise and resistant as the aeroscaph—or if the refitted aeroscaph were taken back into service—it could only take up six men at a time. And it would be necessary to know how to maneuver it! In any case, the aeroscaph cannot be repaired, we are powerless to reproduce it, and any motor we put in place of the bufonic dynamos—if you will pardon the barbaric neologism—would be too heavy.

"Then again, gentlemen, how would we survive up there? I know that we have respiratory apparatus to counter asphyxia, but what diving-suit has been invented to counteract decompression? What hermetically-sealed and yet articulated suit of armor?

"No, no, we cannot think of demolishing the superaerian continent—which might perhaps, in any case, play a fundamental role in the economy of the planet. It might be a precious condenser of solar heat, whose disappearance might perhaps be followed by that of the terrestrial fauna, including a certain degenerate, tyrannical and vicious orang-utan that is very dear to our egotism.

"And we can no more think of colonizing that world, since it is beyond our reach, given that it is only in utopian dreams that we possess Jules Verne's *Columbiad* and H. G. Wells's *cavorite*.

"What shall we do, then? Yes, what shall we do? Are we going to allow ourselves to be fished, to the last man? They will colonize us, if we don't colonize them?"

The President of the Republic said nothing.

"Just a minute! A few more words, I beg you!" Monsieur Le Tellier said, overriding the exclamations. "All of that's irrational. Which of you has ever planned to mount a peaceful invasion of the world of fish? To colonize the submarine steppes and liquid pampases? You know full well that the sarvants profess nothing for us but *simple scientific curiosity.*"

"The rest will come!"

"Certainly not. Or, at least, only in the far future, when we ourselves are entertaining dreams of conquest with regard to the sea-bed—and by then, we shall be ready to receive the Invisibles.

"For the moment, what is at stake is no more than a matter of defending ourselves in case further explorations threaten us—or threaten unfortunate Bugey, which all evidence suggests is at the bottom of the sarvants' sea. That is the question. Now, I claim that, if we give it a little thought, the question will no longer seem urgent!"

(*General movement.*)

"Convinced by reason that the spiders do not at this moment—and doubtless never have had—any but *oceanographic* motives with respect to a world in which they can only survive awkwardly clad in isolating armor or cloistered in subaerian diving-bells, as we can in deep water, I declare that years will pass before they recommence their attempted museum—and I can prove it.

"Come on, gentlemen—do you think they attach any great importance to human fishing, this *immense* invisible population which has, for that purpose, only constructed *one single* vessel? Yes, only one! You are not unaware of the fact that, since the wreck of the aeroscaph, *there have been no further abductions.* We are, therefore, dealing with a rather modest enterprise by a group of sarvant scientists—some of those which, I assume, play the role of brains in their singular assemblages. Well, tell me, have the results of that campaign been encouraging for them? It has failed completely. On the one hand, the subaerian has been lost, with all hands; on the other hand"—here the orator's voice was hampered by restrained sobs—"on the other hand, gentlemen, their captives...excuse me...their captives are dying with fr...frightful rapidity. The members of the government are better placed that anyone to tell you with what horrible frequency cadavers are now falling from the sky on to poor Bugey…

"Blinded by my own tears and deceived by my own grief, I was briefly able to believe in the enormity of the Blue Peril; I was able to believe that it threatened all humankind henceforth—but I am edified. The sarvants are not about to renew an attempted aerium *that has fallen victim to a naval catastrophe and the lack of success of the breeding program.*

"What shall we do? Let us prepare for the future, however distant it seems—and let those whose relatives are in the spiders' claws wait courageously for their bodies to fall!"

Monsieur Le Tellier sat down heavily, like a traveler at the end of his journey. His colleagues surrounded him and shook him by the hand. Amid the noise of their compliments, the Minster of War was heard to say, obstinately: "The sarvants must be destroyed!"

The President of the Republic, emerging from a reverie, then said in a heavy Gascon accent: "Hey, tell us something, Monsieur Le Tellier. You, who are the Christopher Columbus, the Vespucci of this America—or better still, the Le Verrier of this Neptune—tell us something. These territories superimposed over ours, these people beneath whom we have been living all this time…tee hee, isn't that sentence absurd…?"

"Everything seems absurd, Monsieur le Président, when it is entirely new and very strange, and when we suddenly perceive it, unexpectedly, without a chain of events or reasoning having led us to it progressively, by way of successive faint surprises or gradual small enlightenments, whose sum nevertheless constitutes an extreme amazement and a more profound knowledge.

"There's also a question of vocabulary. For instance, what if you had declared to a Roman of yesteryear, to the most intelligent and poetic of Romans—Horace for example—or to a Greek, the wisest of the Greeks—Aristotle, if you like—the simultaneous lyrical and scientific statement: 'One day, O masters, lightning will be employed to propel galleys?' At those words, Monsieur le Président, I can now see Aristotle smiling and Horace shrugging his shoulders...however, the sentence that you claimed to be absurd just now will be as simple and natural in a few years time as saying today, 2000 years after Horace and Aristotle: 'There are electric boats.' "

The President of the Republic resumed his Elysian reverie

"The sarvants must be destroyed!" intoned the well-known minister.

The session continued, and was ended with an order of the day "inviting the Chambers to vote funds for the study of projects to combat a new arachnid expedition, however improbable."

XVII. A New Message from Tiburce

The astronomer left the Elysée overwhelmed by fatigue. He had had to make a violent effort of self-control in order to appear optimistic at the conference session. His parental grief and scientific reason were at war. It is a noble action, but a torture, to paint the future of others in pleasant colors when the future confronting oneself is like a black hole.

He went home demoralized, considering that his task was finished, and no longer thinking of anything but seeing Mirastel again, where Dr. Monbardeau had preceded him. Monsieur Le Tellier wanted to be there—what an infernal torment the thought was!—when, in the rain of cadavers falling upon Bugey...

Oh, that hellish thought, which kept coming back to him unrelentingly, and which he never found the horrible courage to complete...

Monsieur d'Agnès was waiting for him in the Boulevard Saint-Germain. The sight of him was not calculated to cheer the poor man up, so sharp was the memory of thwarted cherished plans, and so somber was the Duc's expression...

He opened up his despair to Monsieur Le Tellier. No engineer had left him the slightest illusion. The invisible world was impregnable, according to the Faculties. It was driving him to neurasthenia. By night, nightmares frightened him with superaerian visions—vivisections, scandalous marriages, workshops of human naturalization, etc.—and his thoughts remained imbued with delirium by day. He had not escaped the phobia of the invisible that tormented all impressionable people at that time and made them grope their way alone in broad daylight, so that the streets everywhere seemed full of blind men. And when the Duc d'Agnès watched the agitation of passers-by from his window, he thought he was looking through the panes at a collection of fish in an aquarium! "If there only remained the tiniest chance!" he said, suddenly, with an ashamed half-smile...

Monsieur Le Tellier raised his arms and let them fall back, as a sign of helplessness, and the Duc d'Agnès went on, stammering: "Yes, I know full well...one would have to be mad, wouldn't one? As mad as...ahem!...as Tiburce, for example. Ah, nothing disconcerts that one! Hmm..."

He took out a letter, with an emphatic gesture. "I got...ahem!...he sent me this."

"No—don't make me look at that letter. Ah! I scarcely think about him anymore, your Tiburce. It's true—one would have to be an imbecile still to believe in these benevolent chimeras! Ah, the enviable cretin! Fold up your piece of paper, my friend—it would make me feel ill."

"Evidently!" conceded the Duc d'Agnès. Even so, he re-read Tiburce's insane message, for his own benefit.

(Item 845)
Bombay, 3 August 1912.

I still have every hope, my dear friend, although I have a great deal of bad luck against me, and the cleverest man in the world: Hatkins.

You will recall that I embarked in pursuit of a certain Hodgson and his daughter, whom I suspected of being Hatkins and Mademoiselle Le Tellier. I found them in Singapore with surprising ease. *They were an old protestant pastor and his elder sister! The ostentation with which they were not hiding immediately alerted me to a trap; the two old people were accomplices that Hatkins had disembarked at the same time as him and who, from then on, had taken the borrowed names under which the American and Mademoiselle Le Tellier had been known on the ship. While I occupied myself with them, Hatkins and his companion were fleeing. They were still fleeing; it was, therefore, increasingly certain that it was them.*

By deduction, I discovered the route they had taken, Since their arrival, only two steamships had sailed, one for Calcutta, the other for Madras. My familiar spirit whispered

"Calcutta" to me. I went there and I learned, by means of bribery, that no one disembarked therefrom resembled, at close range or from afar, the person whose resemblance I wanted to find.

Having smoked a few pipes, I recognized my error, and thought I would pick up the trail in Madras. I therefore set out to sea again, after a considerable delay, In Madras, however, I had the satisfaction of realizing that my intuition had not been mistaken; two young Moldavians of the masculine sex had just taken a train for Bombay, under the name of the brothers Tinska, after having stayed for a few days at a hotel. It is true that they had not come from the east, from Singapore, by sea, but from the north, from Hyderabad, by land—but what did that matter? Is not Tinska an anagram of Hatkins, minus the H?

I had them!

Without dawdling, I leapt on to the express to Bombay, where I counted on finding Mademoiselle Le Tellier dressed as a boy—but there, in the confusion of the city, it was impossible to pick up the trail of my pseudo-Moldavians. This morning, however, after a thousand false steps and setbacks—for I do not have Sherlock Holmes's ability to command admiration and deference—I discovered at the Cook Agency that a Greek party composed of four individuals—two young couples, the Yeniserlis and the Rotapoulos—had just embarked for Basra at the far end of the Persian Gulf. From Basra, they intended to travel overland through Mesopotamia to Constantinople, in order to return from there to Greece.

I'm sure that the Monbardeau-d'Arvières have rejoined Hatkins and Mademoiselle Le Tellier, and that the other Greeks are them! They have furnished the agency with a wealth of unnecessary details about what they intend to do and not to do. They've said to themselves: "Tiburce will never think that it's us, since we're not hiding anything." And, indeed, they're not even trying to hide the fact that they're two men and two women! Anyone else but me would have abandoned that excessively clear trail—but a good cat catches a *good rat! I have the better of them, and I'm heading for Basra tonight.*

A superb chase! Via America, Japan and Indochina I've gone more than half way around the world. Before they've looped the loop, I'll have caught up with them. I'm conscious of having been hot on their heels, tracking them so implacably that they haven't been able stop where they wanted to, and that I'm forcing them to return to Europe, where we shall be their masters! Sursum corda, *my dear friend!*

To you in all affection; and in the hope that Mademoiselle d'Agnès might care to find homage to her devotion herein.

Tiburce

When the Duc d'Agnès had finished reading this preposterous missive, Monsieur Le Tellier glimpsed a slight gleam in his eye. "Ah!" he said, folding his arms. "Do you, by chance, retain any doubt on the subject of the stupidity of this amateur policeman?"

Monsieur d'Agnès blushed. "Doubt? Alas, how do you expect any doubt to remain? I know from a reliable source that Mr. Hatkins is in New York. I've read Robert Collin's journal, who saw the person we're already mourning among the sarvants. After that, how can you believe that I have any faith in letters from Tiburce, who claims to be following them around the world? I realize, however, that...yes, momentarily, that joyful tone, that nimble assurance...and then again, Monsieur, we are always tempted to believe that which causes us grief, and, you see, when I think that Mademoiselle Marie-Thérèse might have gone with Hatkins..."

"You'd like it better if she were in the aerium," said Monsieur Le Tellier, bitterly.

"Oh, Monsieur, what are you saying! Have pity on me. All my anxieties, all my jealousies, all my eternal martyrdom, rather than one tear on your daughter's eyelashes!"

And the Duc continued in that vein for some time, confessing his love and his illness in an enervated, raucous and vacillating voice, with the melodramatic emphasis that causes the exaltations of the finest life to resurface in the tone of bitter tirades.

XVIII. The Appearance of the Invisible

The departure of the scientist whose authority had dominated the Parisian phase of the Blue Peril permitted a project that the astronomer had always opposed to be put into execution—we are referring to the admission of the public to the Grand Palais. Monsieur Le Tellier had not opposed it on principle, but he had argued, with reason, that admission ought to be free and that, in any case, it was necessary to wait for the aeroscaph to cease to be invisible, at least in part, by virtue of the intermediation of paint or some other procedure.

Unfortunately, the public complained—which is to say that three or four publicists caused them to complain. The moment was foreseeable when the question would become an election issue and, even though the subaerian still refused to accommodate any coating that would render it visible, it was decided to give the public access at five centimes a head, the profits going to the Bugist disaster-victims. The entry fee was only imposed to prevent overcrowding.

From the first day, Sunday, September 22, Monsieur Le Tellier's predictions were fulfilled. All that the crowd could see was a high and solid barrier defending an unoccupied enclosure, with policemen guarding the interior. It was a clear case of paying to see nothing. In the obtuse soul of the multitude, the idea took shape that "one ought to be able to see, somehow, that the damn thing was invisible!" They wanted to see! And they were furious at seeing nothing for their ten *sous*.

A riot broke out. "It's a trick! It's theft!" The existence of sarvants was no more than a confidence trick designed, in the final analysis, to cheat the taxpayer yet again. All the workers in their Sunday best recalled the enormous sums sent to aid Bugey from all points in France and abroad, of which the distribution committee had only paid out 3,746.95 francs. Even those who had accepted the invisible object in the Carrefour Louis-le-Grand no longer admitted it now that they had paid out their five-centime piece in order to contemplate it.

In response to an order, the policemen struck the resonant aeroscaph.

"Ooh! Ooh! Conjuring tricks! Robert Houdin! Ooh! Ooh! Conjuring tricks! Enough! Enough! Shameful!"

Carrying out a second order, the policemen readjusted the ropes around the subaerian...

Then the officers went up on to the occult platform, and walked up and down on it, without support, like the stars in the infinite subtlety...

Then someone went to fetch the molds of the propeller and the pincer-basket...

Then a dozen citizens were invited to come and touch the aeroscaph...

But nothing could convince the crowd, which saw conjuring tricks everywhere. The Grand Palais was filled with an incredible racket. The public was seething like a fermenting puddle; if it had believed in the reality of the vessel, it would have attempted to smash it into pieces. Scuffles broke out here and there; a few brats were crushed. It was necessary to refund the money.

The prestige of the Blue Peril had been struck an irreparable blow. The following day, the opposition's newspapers claimed that it had not only been a swindle, but a stratagem to distract civic attention from the ever-worsening social situation. The ruling party had made use of this unworthy distraction as it had sometimes made use of the threat of war, as fallacious as the menace, or the very existence, of invisible lands. And when the chemist Arnold, of Stockholm, announced triumphantly to the world that he had found the much-desired paint and thus caused the fragment of the aeroscaph that France had entrusted to him to become invisible, democracy refused to see anything therein but a further item of Machiavellian charlatanry. "What a hoax! They're going to put a new coat of paint on some old decommissioned submarine and exhibit it as the invisible aeroscaph covered in the celebrated *arnoldine*! Bravo, Tartuffes! But we know what you're up to!"

Thus was born the legend of the Blue Peril—which was, however, actual and genuine history.

Arnoldine, meanwhile, really had been discovered. The Swedish chemist came to Paris without losing a minute. He brought the fragment of aeroscaph on which so many compounds had proved their inefficacy before the victorious amalgam. Arnold had been careful only to paint half of it; it was, therefore a bar half-invisible and half-yellow—a magnificent canary yellow. The first disappointment, however, was that the Chambers refused to vote it the slightest subsidy. Secondly, an attempt to establish a limited company with a capital of 400,000 francs for the painting of the aeroscaph failed miserably.

Arnold showed himself to be nobler than an entire population. He took responsibility for the considerable expenses— for the paint was worth more than 3000 francs a liter—and manufactured arnoldine in quantity.

Normally, painting hides things; now, painting was about to display things.

When everything was ready, Arnold convened a scientific congress around the vessel to witness this new kind of varnishing, such as the Grand Palais had never seen before. Belloir set up his scaffolding, surrounding the invisible apparatus with a circle of planks...

On the appointed day, which fell on October 5, in front of a gallery of cosmopolitan celebrities, the Scandinavian donned a white smock and applied the first brush-stroke. The cinematographers and snapshot-takers described a great circle; pots of arnoldine were distributed in all directions; an orchestra played a heroic march, Little by little, the invisible became visible.

As if the cream-charged brush had the gift of creating them, all the details of the vessel surged forth in mid-air, one by one. First there were the terrible pincers, the frightful secaturs and the terrible basket in the form of a landing-net, with its mesh of mail—all three at the ends of articulated shafts extending by means of sliding sleeves. The machinery then exhibited its complications of finesse and entanglement, its countless peculiar spheres, and its deserted boxes in which mechanized batrachians galloping on the spot had produced the vessel's motive force. The drive-shaft was seen to elongate, become a long tube, and crown itself with a propeller as yellow as itself, as yellow as the machinery and the pincer-secaturs. Arnold's brush was seen to paint, in the same atmosphere, the round protuberances of disorderly instruments, some elementary and voluminous in appearance, others infinitely complex and multiple—whose delicacy, alas, was coated over by the arnoldine.

Suspended in the middle of the empty space, Arnold crawled, slid and slithered through the invisible layout of the cabins. Having painted the body of the aeroscaph, he joined his assistants and continued his magical work.

The pincer-secaturs and their basket disappeared into a saffron tower that resembled the chimney of a steamboat. The audience shivered; its members had recognized the cylinder in which so many captives had been abandoned to so much terror...

But the air was partitioned by walls, ceilings and floors; cells accumulated around the machinery and the equipment. The aeroscaph was reminiscent of a vessel that had been constructed in reverse order to others, commencing where one would normally finish; the hull was still lacking. To coat it, Arnold and his assistants, mounted on ladders, spread arnoldine around in broad strokes. Piece by piece, the entrails of the subaerian were hidden behind the rigid and bulbous sulfur curtain that they deployed in a magical fashion.

Finally, the layer of arnoldine being complete, a long canary-yellow cigar stood within the scaffolding. Faced with a resemblance that the citrus tint further accentuated, everyone was violently astonished.

Arnold went back into the subaerian to daub the bottom of the hull, and when he re-emerged through one of the

319

hatches—to the strains of the Swedish national anthem—in order to stand alone in the middle of the arena on the back of the aeroscaph that he seemed to have defeated, it seemed to be his apotheosis.

Color! Color! Principle of visibility without which our eyes would be useless marvels! Color, which justifies in itself the existence of the sense of sight! He had given color to the clandestine matter, and now the whole world could *see the invisible*!

Arnold bowed. The stains on his smock bathed his gesture in sunlight, and drops of gold fell superbly from his arnoldine-soaked brush.

The crowd withdrew, regretfully. By the time the last spectator had quit the Grand Palais, the paint was dry and a moonless and starless night had fallen, so black that one might have thought that the aeroscaph was still invisible, lost in the darkness that abolishes color and nullifies our eyes.

At the heart of that shadow, while a 15-cent-a-head banquet was alimenting the congress of scientists and celebrating the victory of humans over the invisible, an obscure, inexorable endeavor was being accomplished—an incomprehensible endeavor of unknown, infinitesimal forces; a labor of atoms and corpuscles at work, perhaps in conflict...

It happened in darkness and silence. No one knows how it happened.

Belloir, who came at the crack of dawn to dismantle the scaffolding, found the subaerian no longer there, but merely, in its place, a carpet of canary yellow dust—a very thin carpet of dust refined to the ultimate degree.

They ran in every direction, groping in the air and beating the empty space with long poles. The aeroscaph no longer existed. The Swedish paint, corroding the invisible surface, had consumed it in a matter of hours. The chemist's glory foundered in ruin and ridicule. He tore out his hair; he did not understand how the aeroscaph had been pulverized, when the specimen, excised from the vessel itself, which he had used in his experiments, had resisted the attack.

Finally, the truth dawned in Arnold's mind. Among all the treatments to which he had subjected the specimen before succeeding, one bath had undoubtedly possessed the virtue of immunizing it against the harmful action of arnoldine—whereas the aeroscaph itself had not benefited from any such preliminary operation.

One bath—yes, but which one? He had tried so many! Then again, what good would it do to identify it, now that the aeroscaph was no more?

In the meantime, Arnold tried to manufacture the invisible matter, to synthesize that bizarrerie, the analysis of which cost him a thousand torments—only to remain incomplete, the compound producing extravagant reactions with acids. He only succeeded in dissolving several specimens in a demoniac mixture enfevered by alternating currents, and so effective that he destroyed all of the inestimable metal that still remained on the surface by that means.

The unfortunate inventor lost his mind in consequence. His fatherland hospitalized him. He is still in Gothenburg. Sometimes he wants to set off to paint the superaerian continents, in order to reduce them to dust—and sometimes, believing that he has found the antidote to arnoldine, the madman talks about vanishing that transparent vault in order that night should extent forever over ingratitude and irony.

It was in that fashion that the invisible appeared and—hey presto!—disappeared again.

XIX. Tiburce Abandoned

In her white and pink bedroom, very bright in that morning sunlight which makes young ladies' bedrooms more "young ladies' bedrooms" than ever, Mademoiselle d'Agnès had just finished dressing. Her maidservant was tidying up a confusion of baubles.

Mademoiselle Jeanne d'Agnès looked at her face in the depths of a mirror, and addressed a little sad grimace to herself, because it was none too beautiful. Then she drew a perpetual calendar closer to her, and pressed the switch that set the day. The calendar marked WEDNESDAY, OCTOBER 16—and the English carriage-clock chimed 10 a.m.

Almost simultaneously, Mademoiselle Jeanne thought that it was past time for the postman to come, and that for a whole month, Tiburce the fool, Tiburce the madman, Tiburce the reckless had not sent her any news...and that she was 20 years old today.

With her forehead pressed to the window-pane, she watched the chestnut-trees in the Avenue Montaigne shedding their leaves.

Three discreet raps on the door disturbed her reverie.

"Who is it?" she said.

A man's voice replied, muffled and obsequious. "It's Monsieur le Duc, Mademoiselle, asking whether Mademoiselle would care to come down to his study for a moment."

"...?...!" Without saying a word, utterly icy, with her breast quivering, Mademoiselle d'Agnès went to see her brother.

He was standing up, waiting for her; although the light was behind him, she made out his red eyes and his defeated expression. He said to her, point blank, in an extraordinarily gentle and affectionate tone: "Listen, Jeannette...first, listen: you're still in love with Tiburce, aren't you? You're all a-tremble, poor thing! Don't think..."

"Yes...I love Tiburce..."

"Well, my Jeanneton, you shall marry him. Yes, my little one, you shall marry him anyway. Before, you know, I was silly to oppose your marriage; and afterwards, making it conditional on Tiburce's success—making your happiness dependent on mine—that was unspeakable egotism. You shall marry him, my child."

"I thank you with all my heart, François." She took his hands in hers and spoke timidly. "He...has not succeeded, then? You say that I shall marry him *anyway*? And you're weeping!" She embraced him. "He hasn't succeeded?"

"Damn it!" said the Duc, tremulously. "It's quite certain that he'll come unstuck. I don't know how I was idiot enough to latch on to that hypothesis—but the other, that of the sarvants, was so frightful! I've seen another two engineers this morning, and my correspondence...there's nothing but engineers' replies. All of them despairing! We'll never get up there—never, never, never!"

"Do you have a letter from Tiburce?" asked Mademoiselle d'Agnès, softly.

"Yes—here it is. I asked for you in order to let you read it, and to reassure you at the same time."

She unfolded the letter.

(Item 934)
Ankara, Turkey, 11 October 1912
> *My dear, oh, very dear friend, forgive me!*
> *Forgive my stupidity! The people I have been pursuing around the world were not those for whom I was searching!*
> *I can see clearly now. Pain has washed my eyes with so many tears!*
> *I was tricked several times into following various travelers, driven by my obsession, less guided by circumstances than by a delusion that I extended myself before my own steps!*
> *Oh, these last weeks! That feverish journey, on horseback, from Basra to here, that gallop through Mesopotamia, along the Tigris, in which I gained ground every day on the*

Yeniserlis and the Rotapouloses. They were not in any hurry themselves, visiting ruins, dallying over landscapes, making a detour via Babylon, returning to Baghdad, exploring the rubble of Nineveh after dropping in on Mosul. They had a fortnight's start...

I caught up with them between Diyarbakir and Ankara...and I established that they were not Hatkins, Mademoiselle Le Tellier and the Monbardeaus, but two actual young Greek couples, authentic Yeniserils and true Rotapouloses—nice people, in sum, to whom I confided my disillusion and who did their best to console me.

We arrived here together. Ankara is the terminal point of the railway to Constantinople. One day's journey separates me from the Turkish capital, but I'm worn out by fatigue and annoyance and I intend to stay here—for how long? I don't know—to rest amid the flowers and the sunlight, thinking of my stupidity as some illness from which I am convalescing. To make a novel of reality! To become Sherlock Holmes! Poor sick fool that I was, alas!

But now, François, I beg you—don't leave me in despair with regard to Mademoiselle Jeanne. Promise me that perhaps...in time...

Forgive me; I shall finish.

When I think of that, my vision clouds over.

Adieu!

Tiburce

Mademoiselle d'Agnès looked at her brother. "I too, François, am in need of forgiveness. I knew perfectly well that Tiburce would not find Marie-Thérèse, and if I let him go, it's because I counted on his determination to weaken your resolution. But now that my plan has finally come to fruition, it seems to me that the machination was not very honest..."

"Oh, my love, it's your diplomacy that has defeated my prejudice! Anyway, calm down—Tiburce would have gone even if you had forbidden it; he was so convinced!"

"That's possible, and I feel strangely relived in knowing that he's disabused. Such a fine fellow in such error! But I wonder, François, how you, knowing the truth, let yourself fall prey to his nonsense?"

"Since I learned what the aerium is and what the sarvants are, and that Marie-Thérèse is the sarvants' prey, in the aerium…that's what my mind could not support, not mad ideas and encouraging follies!"

"Courage, brother. I love you too. Courage."

"I shall have it. I have had it. But I'm exhausted…I'll try to get some sleep. Leave me, my child, will you?"

When his sister had withdrawn, the Duc d'Agnès felt an isolation more absolute than he had desired. Would he not be as alone everywhere, henceforth, as he was in this room? How could one not be alone in the eternal absence of Marie-Thérèse?

He extended toward the sarvants' sky the threat and the vanity of his fists—and was suddenly overcome by a bitter intoxication, an irresistible desire to suffer and to sob. *Ah! Fate considers me a spoiled child. It wants me to be unhappy, does it? Well then, I'll be unhappy! More unhappy than it wants!* Thus humans always pretend to have reasoned with their destiny.

To make his frightful solitude even more mournful, therefore, the Duc thought of enveloping himself in the black shroud of darkness—but such was his aberration that he had forgotten the time. He flipped the electric switch, intending to put out the sun, which he took for a lamp. A ceiling-light came on, yellow and strange in the daylight, like an owl's eye. Monsieur d'Agnès got a grip on himself again.

"My compliments!" he said, aloud. "That's how spoiled you've become. Oh, no—none of that, my lad! Even if it's only to see her one last time, dead and disfigured—to carry her amid flowers and put her in the grave—you must live! And live wholly, body and soul! Come on! Have some guts!"

XX. The Disappearance of the Visible

Tiburce's letter, which had upset François d'Agnès so profoundly, did not have any effect on Monsieur Le Tellier when he received it at Mirastel, by courtesy of the young Duc. The astronomer and his entourage had known the truth of the matter for a long time, and all of them—Maxime, finally cured; Madame Le Tellier, white-haired and blonde at the same time but scarcely thinking about elegance; Madame Arquedouve, somewhat shriveled up, and so very thin; and the poor Monbardeaus, old and at a loss—were only thinking about two things: examining the base of the aerium through the telescope, with the tiny movements produced in the void by the agitation of the prisoners; and identifying the cadavers as they fell into the abyss, one by one.

It was always by night that they fell. As Robert had hypothesized, the sarvants were obviously more active and more at ease in darkness; and no night passed without the whistling sound, no morning without a peasant coming to the château to tell them that a corpse had fallen in his vineyard. The country folk were finally reassured; from dawn to dusk they worked the land fattened by human flesh. Sometimes, when they arrived, they found animals that had fallen by night, sometimes men and women. In response to their summons, Maxime, his brother and his uncle would come running. Now, the cadavers no longer bore the traces of anatomical investigation—no more vivisection or dissection, no more torture. They were complete, honorable, but exceedingly thin. Autopsies showed that diseases had ravaged them without the sarvants having been able to do anything about it. The captives were only dying for lack of care, of treatment, of fresh air and nourishment.

But they were dying, in increasing numbers.

A record of the missing persons had been made, and the cadavers were checked against it. By October 10 or thereabouts, Monsieur Le Tellier was certain that no more than 25 unfortunates remained up there, among whom were Marie-Thérèse, Henri, Fabienne and Suzanne.

It was a terrible discovery. At the rate things were going, it would all be over in twenty days. The four exiles would be dead. Mirastel resounded with lamentations.

The next night, two whistling sounds pierced their hearts…but it was only the fall of a billy-goat and a jenny-ass.

Those who were awaited did not fall in the following days.

At the zenith, the dark patch did not move and did not change, save that the animation of the slots diminished, becoming rarer and slower. By October 18, nine humans and a dozen animals had fallen since October 10; there were still 16 condemned individuals in the aerium.

Sleep deserted the château. At night, by virtue of the strain of listening, everyone suffered strange auricular disturbances. At 2 a.m. on October 19, the darkness resonated with a peculiar sound that was not the usual whistle. One might have thought that a discharge of particles of lead was peppering the nocturnal peace. The noise was repeated several times in succession. Monsieur Le Tellier and the members of his family went out on to the terrace. The Moon had just set; its light was still visible in the west as a diffuse clarity. There was a slight fresh breeze.

The noise began again, while a sort of dark cloud, hissing like lead shot, crashed into the marsh in the direction of Ceyzérieu. A second followed immediately, then a third and a fourth. They landed heavily, one after another, in the same place, slapping the damp ground. They counted as many as 32. The 33rd fall made a quite different sound, rattling like pieces of scrap-iron, and not having the appearance of a cloud. All of it manifestly came from some invisible harbor, only falling to the south by virtue of the slight breeze.

What were these consignments from the upper world? Neither men nor animals, certainly; their manner of announcing themselves was too familiar. What were the sarvants up to now?

They waited for the sun with anxious impatience. It arrived, revealing a number of very obvious mounds in the middle of the marsh—but it was necessary to renounce any thought of approaching them, in the center of that unstable and dangerous plain. Nothing seemed to be moving there.

The astronomer decided to study them with his best telescope. They went with him to the observatory in the tower. The optical tube was there, mounted in the terrestrial bracket, having been aimed at the square patch for weeks.

Monsieur Le Tellier put his eye to the ocular lens. "Hey!" he said. "Who's touched my telescope? I can't see the aerium anymore." He examined the apparatus. "But no, nothing has been disturbed...and yet the aerium is no longer in the visual field. It's disappeared!"

"My God!" said Madame Monbardeau. "What now?"

"Disappeared? Could they have moved that immense exhibition-hall?" Maxime suggested.

"A catastrophe?" the doctor put in. "A superaerian earthquake?"

"We'd still be able to see something...there's nothing left!" affirmed the astronomer. "Nothing! At the exact point where I saw it yesterday evening above the air...ah! Wait a moment!"

He lowered the little telescope and aimed it at the mounds in the center of the marsh. The magnification showed them in detail. On the olive-colored expanse there were heaps of brown earth, and in that earth, three-quarters buried, there were many disparate objects: dry foliage; grey branches; a shapeless mass of various colors, in which one could make out the gilded silhouette of a cock...

"The aerium's there!" said Monsieur Le Tellier, straightening up. "Or rather, the things that rendered it visible. It was clumps of earth that were falling last night. The sarvants have jettisoned it, one wagon-load at a time. They've dismantled their oceanographic museum!"

White faces surrounded him.

"What about the...the living beings?" demanded Madame Arquedouve. "The 16 prisoners?"

"Henri?"

"Suzanne?"

"Marie-Thérèse?"

"Fabienne?"

"There's nothing alive out there—nor anything dead, either...and up in the sky, there's nothing at all."

"The sarvants have taken them to another part of their world!"

"Don't say that, Maxime!" cried Madame Le Tellier, all her limbs trembling. "I beg you—not that!"

"But what are you hoping for, then, Mama?"

"How do I know?"

Maxime had taken possession of the telescope. He studied the mounds. Everyone was silent.

At that moment, among all the murmurs of the dawn chorus, a dog yapped.

Madame Arquedouve pricked up her ears.

The yapping drew closer.

The blind woman pressed both hands to her heart. The others looked at her curiously. She was listening to the dog as if she were admiring the splendor of the reconquering light. She was too overcome with emotion to be able to say anything.

"Mother, mother!" whispered Madame Le Tellier. "*Is that really Floflo coming home?*"

Madame Arquedouve lowered her eyelids, and everyone interrogated her with their gaze. Floflo? Floflo, whom Robert and Maxime had seen in the sarvants' realm? Floflo alive? Floflo coming home? The grandmother must be mistaken...

It was, however, really him.

He arrived, an interminable pink tongue hanging out, jumping with joy in spite of his fatigue, licking hands, faces and even shoes. But how thin he was, poor thing! And dirty, too! The dust of the road was sticking to his long hair, which was still soaked...

"It doesn't require a magician," Maxime reasoned, "to see that this dog has been plunged into water before accomplishing a long journey—before or during. He's taken a bath along the way, in some spring—but where has he come from? It isn't the mounds; we'd have seen him crossing the marsh, and he wouldn't be so exhausted, nor covered with so much dust. Anyway, it's inadmissible that the sarvants have thrown him from the height of…"

The bell at the main door rang, preventing him from finishing.

The emotion that overwhelmed them made them go pale; it was a contradictory mixture of hope and anxiety, which produced a physical sensation of sudden weakness and icy cold.

Disappointment awaited them; the visitor was a bumpkin on a bicycle. But there was another surge of emotion; the bumpkin had brought a letter for Monsieur Le Tellier—and then there was a delirious joy, for the letter came from one of Monsieur Le Tellier's friends, in Lucey, on the Rhône, 18 kilometers from Mirastel, and it said:

(Item 988)

Come quickly. This morning, the surviving missing persons were found on an islet in the river between Lucey and Massignieu-de-Rives. None seems to be injured. The authorities have put them in quarantine.

In spite of the bizarrerie of that final sentence, their joy assumed such proportions that it was frightening to behold. It seemed to them that the atmosphere had suddenly been transformed. The astronomer told us: "It was as if I had been relieved of a straitjacket that I had been wearing for six months!" Laughter was reborn in the depths of their throats, but their faces had lost the habit and their cheeks opposed it. They made an infinite number of futile movements, marching right and left with groans of delight. Finally, they calmed down.

Maxime interrogated the bumpkin.

330

At daybreak, a laborer on his way to work had spotted a group of people on an island in the Rhône, in a very poor state—badly dressed and in poor health, most of them lying down—in company with an incredibly various population of animals, some of which were trying to get over the water. When the man arrived, a little black dog was swimming across, heading northwards, and the current was carrying away two or three emaciated animals, betrayed by their lack of strength in mid-stream. An eagle was apparently making relentless attempts to take off. The mayor had forbidden anyone to approach the island for fear of some ruse on the part of the sarvants, and had put the escapees in quarantine.

They piled into the large white automobile, as on the day of the abduction—but how the faces had changed since then! And how their cheerfulness contrasted with their wrinkles and their emaciation! And they were laughing! They were laughing! They seemed to be deceiving themselves, laughing so heartily with such faces. It would not have taken much to make them break out into song.

As they passed by, Monsieur Le Tellier shouted to the peasants: "They've come back! They're here! My daughter has come down!"

"And my children too!" rectified the doctor, in a comical tone, feigning sensitivity. "My children too!"

The same altercation was renewed at every encounter. The brothers-in-law were amusing themselves wholeheartedly, slapping their thighs, and the others were laughing with their mouths wide open.

They arrived.

The road ran along the Rhône, which forked at that spot through an arid and bare archipelago. A host of villagers was crowding both banks level with the escapees' island. The later, like the others, projected a bank of livid earth from the robust flow, strewn with a few bushes. It was quite a long way from the shore.

Monsieur Le Tellier wanted to unhitch a boat, but the local policeman stopped him "by reason of the quarantine." The astronomer became angry, but to no avail. Wrathfully, he gazed at the wretched survivors of the aerium lying on the ground amid hares, chickens, wild pigs, foxes, buzzards, guinea-fowl and other wild or domesticated creatures that did not seem much less self-conscious than their overlords. The eagle was running back and forth, from one end of the islet to the other, occasionally leaping up with its wings employed, then slumping back again, devoid of strength. They were all dying of consumption; hunger had sapped the strength of the men and women, and an imbecilic ruling was preventing anyone from helping them!

At a distance, Monsieur Le Tellier could only recognize Fabienne Monbardeau-d'Arvière to begin with; then it seemed to him that Suzanne…but he was distracted from his examination by a terrible scream behind him.

Everyone turned round. Madame Le Tellier, standing on the seat of the car, proclaimed dismally: "Marie-Thérèse isn't there! There are only 15, instead of 16! And my daughter's not there! Not there! *They*'ve kept her! She's the only one they've kept! Oh, my God!" She collapsed on the cushions.

Monsieur Le Tellier aged 100 years in a second.

And nothing was truer. By some means as yet unknown, the sarvants had repatriated all the inmates of the aerium—except Marie-Thérèse.

Henri, Suzanne and Fabienne sketched hasty gestures of recognition from time to time. Madame Monbardeau looked at them longingly.

But the relatives of the other escapees had come running, curiosity-seekers were massing incessantly, and everyone was murmuring in opposition to the quarantine. There is no way of knowing what havoc might have been wrought upon the mayor and the local policeman, if Maxime and three young men from Massignieu had not landed on the island with the aid of a punt that they had discovered upstream.

When it was seen that nothing disagreeable happened to them, the quarantine was lifted; a flotilla of boats accosted the lazaret, and the company took possession of the 15 inert, famished and wrinkled, voiceless and seemingly unconscious bodies. Monsieur Le Tellier's friend lent his limousine to Monbardeau; the inn in Lucey opened its doors to the revenants that had not yet been reclaimed.

As for the animals, they were killed, for no particular reason, with no considerable necessity or humanity. In doing that, does it not seem, strictly speaking, that the killers showed themselves to be *inferior* to the sarvants, who had not killed them? Is it not reasonable to suppose that the Invisibles had finally perceived the existence of pain? Having discovered that subtle, atrocious and marvelous thing—foreign to their world—in the creatures from below, had they not stopped the vivisections?

For it must be admitted—the state of the cadavers bearing witness to it—that the vivisections had suddenly stopped, and the only valid reason that can be given for that is the mercy of the sarvants, awakened by the discovery of suffering. And if they had not immediately repatriated the poor wretches whom they had begun to pity, was it not necessary to attribute that delay to the time it took to construct a second aeroscaph or some other invisible apparatus designed to take the down again? On that subject, the most likely hypothesis is that of an automatic machine, driven by the wind, which had set down on the island by chance; a trigger-mechanism would have made it rise up again automatically, after unloading. Nothing authorizes certainty on this point, but it is not impossible. The reality is that the sarvants returned our people to us as soon as they could, and everything leads us to believe that they were motivated by intelligence and generosity.

It is, in fact, rather monstrous, logically speaking, that the poets and philosophers who have imagined intelligent beings other than humankind have always made those creatures bloodthirsty and malevolent. To be certain of affecting the reader and to forge civilized beings that are as different from humans as possible, these utopists have refused their chimerical individuals the virtues that pass for our own. They have tried, by this expedient, to demonstrate independence with regard to anthropomorphism, and they have sacrificed themselves in a servile fashion, without being aware of it, by depriving their hypothetical nations of merits and qualities of which humankind, in crowds, is similarly deprived.

The sarvants are, I believe, as superior to us in morality as in altitude—and that opinion cannot be so very worthless, since it imposed itself on the eminent mind of Monsieur Le Tellier at the very moment when he was wondering, furiously, why the Invisibles had kept his daughter.

For they had kept her; that much was certain. The census taken of the cadavers had been too assiduous for Marie-Thérèse's to have escaped it. Thus, she was still up there. *Why?* Her beauty explained nothing, having no currency among the sarvants, any more than the grace of a spider has among us. Why, then?

"Why Marie-Thérèse?" wondered Monsieur Le Tellier. "And why her alone?"

They went back. He squeezed his wife's hands as she lay unconscious on the floor of the car.

In front of them, the Monbardeaus' limousine was moving along the road; within it, leaning over his daughter's plaintive face, the doctor murmured: "Suzanne, Suzanne! I've forgiven you, you know."

A smile passed lightly over the violet lips. Then Monsieur Monbardeau occupied himself with Henri and Fabienne—but as he had nothing to forgive them, he never succeeded in smoothing their expressions. Their distress surpassed all apprehension.

"Henri, do you know why they've kept Marie Thérèse?" asked Madame Monbardeau.

"Shh! Calm...silence," advised the doctor. His son's physiognomy had indicated a vague expression of ignorance. "Let him be, Augustine. We can interrogate him this evening—this evening or tomorrow morning."

The two automobiles slid along the bed of the celestial ocean. They left behind them a trail of dust similar to the opaque clouds with which marine octopodes conceal their flight.

XXI. The Triumph of Absurdity

That same day, at 5 p.m., as the Duc d'Agnès—who was wandering through Paris like a soul in torment—was crossing the Boulevard Bonne-Nouvelle, 30 or 40 newsvendors launched themselves forward at a run, shouting at the top of their voices: *"L'Intran! La Presse! La Liberté!"* They were selling them on the wing to all the passers-by.

Monsieur d'Agnès bought *L'Intransigeant*.

(Item 1037)

UNEXPECTED RETURN OF MISSING PERSONS
Their state of exhaustion
Mademoiselle Le Tellier alone not among their number

The joy occasioned by the first line did not last long, but it was sufficient to cast a darker shadow over the frightful disappointment of the last. And he learned that on the Boulevard Bonne-Nouvelle! No, such bad luck was not possible, not permissible! It seemed to him that the misfortune must capitulate in the face of his incredulity.

One by one, he bought *La Liberté* and *La Presse* (items 1038 and 1039) and, in spite of the fact that their information was identical, sent the following telegram to Monsieur Le Tellier:

Is true Marie-Thérèse not returned? Reply by return telegram, Avenue Montaigne.
D'Agnès

Then, in the fury of his helplessness, he started marching straight ahead, his eyes fixed and his teeth clenched, telling himself that the three newspapers could not be mistaken on this vital point, and that his misery was now worse than he had

335

ever imagined, even though he had thought that it was the greatest misery of all time.

It was while he was returning on foot to the house in the Avenue Montaigne that the Duc d'Agnès formed a resolution to kill himself. Mentally, he visualized the ultimate scene of his life, from the writing of the will to the final revolver shot...

His sister was watching out for his return. She had read *La Presse*. The Duc had never felt fonder arms around his neck. He embraced her more tenderly than usual. He had touching words for the domestics, full of benevolence and tact. He wanted to die in generosity—which is the best way of departing in beauty.

Mademoiselle Jeanne watched him anxiously, and when the anticipated telegram was brought in—whose text he knew without having read it—Monsieur d'Agnès had a smile so tearful, an expression so profound, that his sister, understanding fully, turned away to weep.

The roar that she heard interrupted her sobs painfully, with a spasm of terror. She whirled around and saw her brother transformed, straightened up, uttering burst of ferociously joyful laughter, shaking the open telegram and eventually crying out, after a moment of delusion: "Jeanne! Jeanne! This telegram is from Tiburce! Tiburce has found Marie-Thérèse! Tiburce has found Marie-Thérèse! Tiburce! Tiburce! He's found her! By chance! In Constantinople!"

The Duc sank to his knees, his hands joined, to utter some unknown prayer. He kissed the sheet of blue paper over and over again, laughing and sobbing, sobbing and laughing— it was impossible to tell when he was laughing and when he was sobbing—and stammered, in a soft and tender, slightly breathless voice: "Marie-Thérèse! My darling! My darling! Oh, my beloved darling!"

His sister mopped his handsome, excessively cheerful face, whose long eyelashes were empearled...

But the doorbell sounded again in the twilight, and a few moments later a second telegram as brought in—the one from

336

Monsieur Le Tellier, his time, which did not say what Monsieur and Mademoiselle d'Agnès had expected at all, but this:

Yes, is true Marie-Thérèse not returned, but Henri Monbardeau has revealed Mari-Thérèse not abducted with him and Fabienne. Was Suzanne that was kidnapped with her brother and sister-in-law. Had gone to join them in secret near Don on day of abduction. Marie-Thérèse has never been with sarvants. Hope, therefore. We hope.
Jean Le Tellier

"Monsieur le Duc," said the valet, his empty tray in his hand, "there's a man who rang at the same time as the second telegraph boy, who asks to see Monsieur le Duc. He says that he has an urgent communication to make and says that his name is Garan."

"Garan! Show him in!"

That old friend came in, his moustache combat-ready and his eyebrows like tusks. "Good news, Monsieur le Duc! Guess what! Mademoiselle Marie-Thérèse has been found!"

"I know."

Garan was disconcerted, but continued anyway: "You know? Ah yes! The telegram, of course! Well then, if Monsieur Tiburce has already brought you up to date, that does no harm—and I've still arrived in time."

"In time? Why?"

"Here's the thing, Monsieur le Duc—it's a funny story. You'll understand. I've been sent here by the government to give you a word to the wise and ask you not to advertise certain details. They chose me because they know that I'm acquainted with you and played a part in the events in accursed Bugey! Show me Monsieur Tiburce's telegram, if you please...let's see: *Have found Marie-Thérèse safe Constantinople, by chance. Arriving Marseille Wednesday. Very best wishes to your sister. Regards. Tiburce.*" After a pause, Garan continued: "I suspect that laconic prose is due to the collaboration of Monsieur Tiburce with the Ottoman authorities."

"What do you mean?" cried Mademoiselle d'Agnès.

"Listen, Mademoiselle—this is how it is. A little while ago, Foreign Affairs received a long dispatch from the Sublime Porte, via the Turkish ambassador, in which the story is told in full. But I must ask you urgently—as Monsieur Tiburce has been asked, out there—not to divulge anything, lest it compromise the memory of a highly-placed individual, a former vizier and cousin of the Sultan. In a word, Monsieur le Duc, this concerns Abdul Kadir Pacha, *who abducted Mademoiselle Le Tellier!*"

Mademoiselle d'Agnès and her brother, the Duc, were amazed.

The policeman continued: "Yes, it was that barbarian! A vicious, corrupt man, Monsieur, by virtue of an excess of this, that and the other! When I learned that—ah, the Blue Peril was less blue than your humble servant! Just think! Never in my life would I have believed it!

"After asking for Mademoiselle Le Tellier's hand in marriage, and being refused, that demon Abdul Kadir swore that he would have her in spite of everything. He had her abducted—as I told you—in an automobile, in the vicinity of Mirastel, on the fourth of May last, while she was on her way to Artemare to have dinner at Dr. Monbardeau's house... *and I saw the place*, Monsieur and Mademoiselle! The trampled grass at the intersection of the little path and the road! I saw it, *and noticed it*! I showed it to Monsieur Tiburce, telling him that it might well be a place where...and a place which...and a place of which...! Imbeciles that we were, both of us!

"The automobile rejoined Abdul Kadir in Lyon, where he caught a train to Marseille that evening with his 12 wives, in order to board a ship there. *The animal had had one of those 12 martyrs killed*—the oldest—by a eunuch from his seraglio, in order to substitute Mademoiselle Marie-Thérèse for her. The dead woman was stuffed in a sack, naked, in the Sultanic fashion, and—for want of the Bosphorus—was thrown into the Rhône in the fog as they went over a bridge. It even appears that Monsieur Le Tellier went to Lyon when the body

338

was discovered and was admitted into its presence. Isn't that a coincidence? One can't say different.

"During the car journey, Mademoiselle Le Tellier was forced to dress in the costume of the 'disenchanted,' and beneath the black veil that covers their faces, which is called a *burkha*, she was tightly gagged. How did they get her into the reserved carriages at Lyon-Perrache station? Skillfully, for sure. A fifteen minute stop, the crowds, the confusion augmented by that troop of fezzes, turbans and burkhas coming along the platform, public curiosity, the evening twilight and the fog…with all that, I, who was in charge of the police escort, saw nothing but the smokescreen. Anyway, I was only thinking about protecting the Turk from thieves, and not about protecting others against him! All was in order, wasn't it? Twelve veiled women embarked, twelve veiled women disembarked…that would have been the count, if I'd taken it into my head to count them…

"In Marseille, I did observe that one of the women was making efforts to remain; two others were holding her. But what about it? It was an inviolable matter, no concern of mine! We were in a hurry, moreover, to get that inconvenient individual embarked.

"The steamer raised anchor, and I returned to Paris, to have the honor of making your acquaintance, Monsieur le Duc."

"Very good," said the latter, "but out there in Turkey, Mademoiselle Le Tellier…and on the ship, Garan, on the ship!"

"Out there, shielded from view in the impenetrable harem, as in the cabins of the ship, she was unable to say anything or to do anything. But it's here that she had a stroke of luck—an unexpected stroke of luck! Abdul Kadir, worn out by alcohol and depravity, was already ailing on his departure. The Mediterranean put him in no state to do any harm to anyone, of any kind, and he arrived in Constantinople seriously ill. Afterwards, he got gradually worse, and never left his sick-bed again—which became his deathbed yesterday. Mademoiselle

Le Tellier had not even caught a glimpse of him during her entire imprisonment.

"Meanwhile, Abdul Kadir has snapped his *hookah*, if you'll excuse the expression, and here come his nephews and heirs to invade the old palace in Stamboul, spilling into the harem and finding, in the midst of all the Fatimas and *ferid-jees*—guess who? Mademoiselle Marie-Thérèse Le Tellier, a trifle pale, in the process of looking at the sky through the holes in a moucharaby—is that what they call it? Young Turks brought up in the European manner, speaking French fluently, they had her taken out with a thousand and one *salaam aleikums* and a thousand and two excuses. And on the threshold of the palace, who should she meet but…?"

"Tiburce! Go on!"

"Yes, Monsieur le Duc, Monsieur Tiburce! Come from Ankara and on the point of leaving for Marseille, he was sadly visiting the Stamboul quarter and admiring the faïences on the gateway with a cavernous eye!"

"So," Monsieur d'Agnès remarked, laughing—he was laughing at everything—"Tiburce has gone almost all the way around the world to discover the person he was searching for! He went in a direction directly opposite to the right one! He reached Constantinople all the same, without knowing that that was where he had to go. Ineffable hazard! Ineffable Tiburce!"

"He's made the grand tour, that's all!" said Mademoiselle d'Agnès, indulgently.

"You see," declared the inspector, with facetious gravity, "that Sherlockism has merit!"

"I have to send a telegram to Mirastel right away!" Monsieur d'Agnès went to his desk.

"If you wish, Monsieur le Duc—although Monsieur Tiburce has undoubtedly already done so, on in his own initiative. But you won't say a word about Abdul Kadir, will you? The Commander of Believers implores you, with my voice."

"All right. Since Mademoiselle Le Tellier has escaped from the misadventure unscathed, we shan't say anything about Abdul Kadir."

The inspector rolled his large eyes and said, in a whisper: "The Sultan, Monsieur le Duc, is offering 500,000 francs for a promise of silence."

"What!" said the Duc, in an irritated tone—but he calmed down all of a sudden. "Five hundred thousand francs? Well, that's all right too. The disaster victims of Bugey will be grateful to receive them—and I'll add another 500,00 more, to make a round figure. Only I'm the one who'll distribute the million, *without any distribution committee*, you understand, Garan? Tell that to the Sultan of the Turks and the Sultan of the French!"

"You're an admirable man, Monsieur le Duc!"

"That's not all, Garan. I certainly intend, for my part, to say nothing about Abdul Kadir, but I intend that the State should take the initiative, tomorrow, in a national subscription for the erection of a statue of Monsieur Robert Collin, whose intelligence, courage and sacrifice have set us such a fine example in unveiling the secret of the invisible world."

"Bravo!" exclaimed Mademoiselle d'Agnès.

"You're right, Monsieur le Duc."

There was a pause.

"And to think," the inspector resumed, in an emotional voice, "that poor Monsieur Collin was only sustained up there, in the aerium...by blonde hair and a grey dress...which were not those of Mademoiselle...Oh, pardon me, Monsieur le Duc!"

"Grey dresses have played an important role in this affair," said Mademoiselle d'Agnès. "It was also a grey dress that led the innkeeper at Virieu-le-Petit to confuse Marie-Thérèse with her cousin Suzanne. Do you see how it happened, François?"

"I see it all. On the day of the abduction, Marie-Thérèse left Mirastel at about 10 a.m. It was, therefore, at about 10 a.m. that she was abducted by the pasha's followers. In the meantime, Henri and Fabienne were climbing the Colombier. They'd organized a secret meeting with the unfortunate Suzanne. Do you recall, Garan, the letter from her that Henri went to fetch from the *poste restante* on the eve of May 4? Suzanne, therefore, had come on the train from Belley, and was to take the local train to meet her brother at Don at about ten-fifteen. They did, indeed, meet up, and the three of them continued climbing. The innkeeper at Virieu, who recognized Henri, only saw the two women from behind, without paying much attention to them. She did, however, notice that the grey dress was a town dress, not a tourist's dress. It's probable that Suzanne Monbardeau had no intention of letting herself be dragged very far up the mountain, but the opportunity—so rare—of a nice family outing... and that's everything."

"Everything."

"Everything."

Speaking to his sister, Monsieur d'Agnès concluded: "Which doesn't affect the fact, my Jeanneton, that Tiburce has won you fair and square, since he's found Marie-Thérèse!"

Which Mademoiselle Jeanne completed by adding: "He's won me, above all, by regaining his sanity!"

In Monsieur Le Tellier's dossier, the four telegrams mentioned in the present chapter are items 1040, 1041, 1042 and 1043.

Items 1044 and 1045 are invitations to two marriages celebrated on the same day, one of the Duc d'Agnès to Marie-Thérèse Le Tellier, the other of Tiburce to Jeanne d'Agnès.

Item 1046 is the rough draft of a letter sent by Monsieur Maxime Le Tellier to the Prince of Monaco. The former naval officer begs His Highness to accept his resignation as an employee of the Museum and a member of oceanographic expeditions, for the reason that, having been fished himself, put in a sort of aquarium and lowered down on the end of a line as a piece of bait, he would experience an indomitable repugnance in subjecting others to the fate to which he was subjected by the sarvants.

"I do not deny," he writes, "the importance that such research has with respect to humankind, and I wish Your Highness's dedicated work every success, but for my own part, I am incapable henceforth of taking any part in it."

And it is with that final item in the dossier that it would be necessary to bring our popular history of the year 1912 A.D. to an end, if we had not omitted, voluntarily, to mention a report that ought, according to its number, to be placed between the testimony relating to the disappearance of the aeroscaph and Tiburce's letter from Ankara, and which it is necessary to mention now.

This document...

Epilogue

...Is the list of the molds of the aeroscaph.

As everyone knows, they were taken to the Conservatoire des Arts et Métiers, along with the photographs of the aeroscaph appearing thanks to arnoldine. They can be visited every day of the week, except Mondays. In the material order, they are all that remains of the sarvants' first incursion into our territory.

Few people go to look at them, and some persist in seeing them simply as the vestiges of an enormous hoax. The terror was so great that they are glad to forget it, to believe that it was irrational and that it will never return. The year 1912 A.D. seemed unforgettable while it was in progress; once it had elapsed, people did not even want to remember it. The prayers of believers rise once more into Heavens where nothing any longer exists, since nothing is perceptible. In France especially, people are pleased to maintain that there has only even been one Blue Peril: the Prussian Blue Peril. Bugey does not like to think that its limits coincide with the superaerian littoral; in a few months, it will contest the fact.

Truly, if the former Minister of War, now a mere deputé again, did not brave the Chamber's mockery by terminating all of his speeches with the Catoesque[60] declaration, "The sarvants must be destroyed!"—if the unfortunates escapees were not here to tell the story of their martyrdom; if the memory of the Blue Peril did not resonate tunefully in the magazines; if Monsieur Fursy had not composed an immortal "chanson rosse" in which the respectable is no more than "*un p'tit bou*

---

[60] The Roman statesman Cato (232-147 B.C.) used to end every speech in the Senate with the declaration that Carthage must be destroyed.

344

d'Ain" (a *petit boudin*—that's rich, all the same!)[61]—one might imagine that we had dreamed that nightmare, or, at least, in accordance with a vulgar expression singularly appropriate to the circumstance, that for half a year, people had had "spiders in the ceiling."[62]

That is the kind of scatterbrains we are. Our thoughtlessness is no excuse. We only think about rising river levels when the flood-water surrounds us.

Certainly, there is anxiety regarding sarvants; work is being done to ward off new attacks, but indolently, and there is less and less of it, the risk having ceased to spur us on with the stimulant of its presence.

It must be said too, that if the sarvants were to return, they would find wiser adversaries—not braver, but more resigned. For, disturbingly, *people had begun to get used to the abductions*, to those disappearances whose bizarrerie was eroded by their frequency, to that increasingly familiar scourge which, after all, sacrificed far fewer victims than *microbes*, which are similarly invisible, albeit in a different manner. Fewer victims than the least bacterium! Fewer victims, too, than disastrous *war* or *alcoholism*, those exceedingly

---

[61] Henri Fursy (born 1867) was a prolific composer of popular songs; his *chansons rosses* carried forward a sturdy French tradition of satirical songs dealing with topical issues, to which Félix Bodin, author of *Le roman de l'avenir* (1834; tr. as *The Novel of the Future*, Black Coat Press) had been a prominent early contributor. The translation of "Un p'tit bou d'Ain" depends, even for a French listener, on whether the ambiguous phoneme *bou* is construed as *boue* [mud] or *bout* [end]; the Ain is the department in which Bugey is situated. A *petit boudin* is a small black pudding or any other object commonly twisted into a torus, but the words also occur in a slang expression meaning "to fizzle out."

[62] The equivalent English euphemism for craziness would be "bats in the belfry," but that does not retain the same "singular propriety."

murderous epidemics which we nevertheless unleash at will (have not the plague and cholera been put at the disposal of human beings?) Assuming that these abductions were to be multiplied indefinitely, they would become for us an endemic affliction of Bugists, or even of human beings, and we would finish up accepting them, as an individual accustoms himself to a chronic illness.

Some such inertia, some such cowardly and vague resignation, is the reason why the peoples of the globe have not nobly confederated a United States of the World, in order to resist the common enemy, the Invisible—as sublime dreamers might have hoped.

In our eyes, in spite of everything, the sarvants have remained fishers of individual men, although they are in truth the assailants of humanity. That insupportable idea has been driven back into the darkness of times to come, but one day, these beings who share with us the empire of the Earth might take it into their heads to enslave us, or even to exterminate us, just as we might one day occupy the ocean bed. They might surge forth again, effect a descent, and say to us: "How about a 50-50 split!"

A half-share? Only *a half*? That's modest. What do we know? This adventure has allowed us to glimpse the immensity of what is unknown to us. After this, it would be a grave and puerile mistake to limit our world to the world of sarvants, which is really only the most recent of our discoveries, and not the final step of our science. A half-share? What if it were a third, a fourth, a fifth or a sixth?

We do not know much more about the ocean depths than the atmospheric heights. Perhaps there are social creatures in the Pacific, at the bottom of the Tuscarora Deep, which is 8500 meters deep, or the Caroline Trench,[63] which extends to

---

[63] The West Caroline Trench is nowadays known as the Yap Trench; the deepest part of the world's oceans is located at its junction with the Mariana Trench, but it is not as deep as Renard's estimated figure suggests; the figure for the Tus-

9636 meters: malicious crustaceans, unable to scale the submarine mountains, whose centuries-old dream is to rise up through their dense altitude toward the secret of the culminating waters. One fine evening—who knows?—an incredible machine might emerge from the sea: a boat that ought to be called a balloon, laden with monsters, suspended from some enormous bubble filled with artificial air fabricated *in profundis* as we fabricate the hydrogen of our aerostats, wrapped in a network of silk woven from unknown seaweeds. That ascent of crabs, future invaders of our shores, would be the counterpart of the descent of the invisible spiders, reaching us in a pocket of void. Perhaps their aquatic realm is strewn with prodigious curiosities. I can imagine strange lakes of enigmatic fluids heavier than mercury, stagnating as our dormant ponds do at the bottom of the air, and as somnolent air does at the bottom of the void, and I can imagine these abyssal lakes populated by moving animals, which the fish call "fish."

Let no one protest! *Our scientists know less about the fauna of the ocean depths than about those of geological periods.* We still do not know whether the giant reptiles of bygone eras might still be living in the murky depths, and whether the great sea serpent might be the ancient plesiosaur. In fact, the aerial precipice, the marine basin and the compact gulf of the soil are equally unknown to us. No physicist is in a position to affirm that the terrestrial crust does not allow the passage of certain solar radiations, dark and cold, whose action is sufficient to sustain the life of subterranean races, in the same way that the pellicle of superaerian continents does not intercept any of the warm and luminous radiations that sustain the activity of nature on the surface of the Earth.

Then again, perhaps the middle of the ball contains populations that have no need of the Sun to exist. One can easily imagine all these superimposed creations around the same center...and nothing prevents us from arguing that the

---

carora Deep is similarly overestimated, also by approximately a thousand meters.

world of the sarvants is not the most exterior of these concentric spheres, since it is only at the surface of the first atmospheric layer and there is a second. Perhaps there is a second invisible universe, a supreme Earth of Jovian dimensions, at the surface of the latter, between the relative void and the absolute ether…

Thus, we might imagine our planet composed of a sequence of globes, one within the other, but nevertheless isolated and without intermondial exchanges, each with its inhabitants, animals and plants. It would resemble Dante Alighieri's Inferno, whose circles enclose circles. Would it, then, be a great stupidity to develop that parallel? Considering the torments of our days, calmed by pleasures so paltry and so brief, is one not tempted sometimes to doubt that our life really is *life*? Could we not believe, effortlessly, that our real existence has been accomplished, that we are all dead, and that the space that we see, in the form of glabrous and morose bipeds, is merely a purgatory: a median circle, a sphere in the midst of others, in which we are expiating, in a state of mediocre suffering, the venial sins of an anterior life? Might one not go so far as to claim that sarvant existence was our initial condition, and that their descent constituted a descent into Hell? But that hypothesis carries a strong stain of metempsychosis, and we must revert to the innocent agitation of more fertile lessons.[64]

Oh! I have not made allusion to one fine example of generosity that the sarvants have given us. It is too obvious.

---

[64] The phrase I have translated as "innocent agitation" is "*secousse bleue*" [literally "blue agitation"]; its meaning is a trifle enigmatic. I have assumed that "*bleue*" is being used metaphorically to refer to callow innocence (as "green" is sometimes used in English), as well as contriving an untranslatable pun with reference to "Blue Peril." The reference to the possibility that humans might be reincarnated sarvants is an echo of the thesis of cosmic palingenesis, which was employed by several French writers of scientific romance, most notably the astronomer and spiritualist Camille Flammarion.

Their invisibility also reveals to us that, without seeking populations 50 kilometers up in the air or 50 kilometers down in the depths, we might conjecture as to the presence of invisible and intangible creatures in the very midst of humankind. The might be molded in gas or formed of X-rays, as we are made of carnal substance. Our restricted senses might be unable to perceive the slightest sign of them.[65] The souls of these subtle beings would have some imponderable matter for support—which is, I think, more acceptable to reason than belief in a soul without any support, which is, however, admitted by all the partisans of eternal life, who are legion among intelligent men. These ungraspable individuals might perhaps inhabit our surface and live here without our knowing it. Perhaps they do not suspect our existence and more than we suspect theirs. Perhaps they pass through us and we pass through them as we walk; perhaps their cities and ours overlap; perhaps our deserts are full of their crowds and our silences of their cries...

But perhaps we are their unconscious slaves. In that case, our unsuspectable masters are installed within us and direct us according to their whim. In that case, there is not a gesture of our hand that they have not desired us to perform, not a word from our mouth of which they are not the prompters. At that thought, the mind rises up in disgust...and yet it would be sufficient that these beings, invisible, intangible and all-powerful, combined their other monstrosities with that of being individual or collective at will, like the Sarvants, to unite merits that are revered everywhere, under other names: the sacred.

Vital concurrence is, therefore, undoubtedly much greater than is presumed. That is what the discovery of the sarvants tells us, first and foremost—but that is not all.

---

[65] Renard was to return to this hypothesis in several later works, including "L'Homme truqué" (tr. as "The Doctored Man"—in which he acknowledges its earlier development in J.-H. Rosny aîné's "Un Autre monde" (1895)—and "Eux" (tr. as "Them"), both translated in volume 4 of this series.

If we consider the adventure in a wider context, it teaches us a truth that it would be wise to remember—even if the Blue Peril were nothing but a fable, so prodigiously possible would that fable remain. It is that, at any moment, unexpected cataclysms of an analogous sort, might befall us, our children, or their descendants.

Humankind only possess a small number of peep-holes to the universe: our senses, which perceive only a derisory fraction of it. We must always expect surprises, issuing from the vast unknown that we cannot contemplate, emergent from the immeasurable sector of the immensity that is *as yet* forbidden to us. Let us, therefore, armor ourselves with abnegation and arm ourselves with science in order to sustain the impacts and meet the challenges of the future. But without any truce, O sensitive, nervous and valiant Humankind, let a smile flourish on your innumerable mouths as that prestigious arsenal is enhanced, before which the unknown retreats further every day! And say to yourself firmly, in spite of your misfortunes and your grievances: "It was, after all, an unparalleled gift that Destiny gave to human beings, in placing them in the bosom of an infinitely admirable and various world, and affording them the joy of discovering everything for themselves, little by little, marvel by marvel, by means of strokes of genius and the rewards of toil."

That is why it would be a bad thing if the history of the Blue Peril were to be envisaged as a delusory legend, and the photographs and plaster casts in the Arts et Métiers scorned. Even if generations to come are persuaded that they are fakes, the evidence of a hoax, and even if they refuse to believe in the Blue Peril—that it still menaces us, and that it might begin to rage again tomorrow—they ought, if they are wise, take their young people to the Conservatoire and say to them, in front of the molds and the photographs: "Look. Then think. Then imagine. *That* isn't impossible."

Then, like all fables, the fable of the sarvants—a grain of bitter philosophy rolled up as a golden pill in the sugar of an apologue—will have borne its fruit.

Monsieur Le Tellier knew that, so he wanted a popular account to be rendered of *The Blue Peril*.

And all is said, now.

Afterword

Le Péril bleu seems in some ways to be a more conventional work than *Un Homme chez les microbes*, whose first version was written immediately before it, but its reversion to something much more closely akin to a mystery/thriller format was by no means a retreat to safety. It is, in many ways, the most ambitious of all Renard's works, and is rightly considered, at least from the viewpoint of scientific marvel fiction, to be his masterpiece. Like his other early novels, it can be seen as a calculated variation on themes previously developed by H. G. Wells, employing narrative templates that Wells had adopted himself, but the fact that it fuses two such ideas and two such templates together—those found in *The Invisible Man* and *The War of the Worlds*—adds a vital extra layer of complexity to it.

The mystery presented in *The Invisible Man* was always heading for a relatively trivial solution, like almost all previous literary accounts of invisibility—which go back, as Renard conscientiously notes, to the tale of Gyges fabricated in Plato's *Republic* and had been previously co-opted into scientific marvel fiction by C. H. Hinton in "Stella" (1895). Renard goes far beyond that, providing a solution to his mystery in which the puzzlingly invisible intruders originate from an entire invisible world. Unlike Wells's Martian invaders in *The War of the Worlds*, however, they are no mere would-be colonists anxious to relocate because they have depleted their own resources and prepared to use the human-standard genocidal method in order to facilitate their task. The journey that Renard's intruders make is every bit as difficult, in physical terms, as an interplanetary voyage—in spite of being much shorter in terms of mere distance—but it is even more difficult in conceptual terms, as illustrated by the conceptual leap that the central characters are forced to make in trying to figure out exactly what it is by which they are confronted.

The fact that Monsieur Le Tellier ends up, in one sense, looking in a mirror—as a scientist contemplating other scientists, embarked on an equally awkward mission of discovery—is, of course, sharply and ironically subverted by the discovery that the seemingly-humanoid form adopted by the disaster-struck "sarvants" is a mere matter of mimicry, and that they are very different indeed in terms of their own mysterious biology and mentality. Renard's brief sketch of the biology of his aliens clearly has Wells's account of the Martians in mind, but Renard's immediate reaction to his model was not to imitate it more crudely—which was the reaction of so many other writers that *The War of the Worlds* has become the archetype of a vast subgenre of stories of monstrous alien invasion—but to challenge its assumptions.

Like Wells, Renard modeled his aliens on Earthly creatures that humans find innately repulsive—spiders, in his case—but he deliberately echoes Victor Hugo's *Légende des siècles* in questioning that unthinking reaction. His alien arachnids are, indeed, thoroughly alien, existentially as well as physically, as a result of having the capability of linking their own neuronal apparatus to the neuronal apparatus of their fellows to former larger thinking aggregates of varying dimension and capability. Because they live in a world in which liquids cannot exist, and which is devoid of oxygen, that apparatus and its physiology has to be very different from ours—much more akin, in fact, although Renard did not have the analogy available to him, to the inorganic bodies and "brains" of computers, which are similarly networkable. Inevitably, liquid-based organic physiology, and such corollary phenomena as blood, are very difficult things for them to comprehend—but when they do so, they evidently obtain sufficient understanding to be able to engage their moral sensibilities quite rapidly, releasing all the specimens they have gathered that have not already fallen victim to their scientific inquiry. This makes them, as Renard is careful to argue explicitly, not merely morally superior to Wells's Martians and their myriad clones, but also morally superior to us and ours.

The aliens themselves are, of course, only one facet of an entire world, which, although much closer to the Earth's surface than Mars or the Moon, is equally inaccessible to our technology. It is interesting to note that, although *Le Péril bleu* has little else in common with Jean de La Hire's unauthorized sequel to *The War of the Worlds*, *Le Mystère des XV* (tr. in a Black Coat Press edition as *The Nyctalope on Mars*)—which was presumably running as a serial in *Le Matin* when *Le Péril bleu* was published—it shares exactly the same fascination with new technologies of flight, and with the competition that had developed in 1909 between winged aircraft and dirigible airships, in terms of speed and maneuverability. Both novels have an acute sense of the significance of technologies of flight as a watershed in human progress—Renard explained why in the 1909 essay reprinted in volume one of this series—and both celebrate it.

While La Hire imagined such technologies as the prelude to an imminent gigantic leap that would produce viable spaceships virtually overnight, however, thus allowing the French to colonize Mars—Wells's technologically-sophisticated vampire Martians notwithstanding—just as they had once colonized Algeria, Renard was much more acutely conscious of the small step that aerial flight really was, by comparison with the actual magnitude and probable strangeness of the universe beyond the Earth's surface. When the politicians who are confronted with the idea of the world of the sarvants are absurdly unable to think of it in any other terms than as a target for wars of destruction or conquest, the mere impracticability of such quests pales into insignificance beside their conceptual inadequacy—an inadequacy further represented by the willingness of the world at large to put the world that remains conveniently out of sight and entirely out of mind.

Renard was slightly unfortunate, from a modern viewpoint, in that he found a justification for the notion of an invisible world in a recent pamphlet by Jean Saryer, whose pseudoscientific nature was not obvious to him, although perhaps it should have been. His quotation of Saryer's allegation that

355

there must be an "invisible sun" at the second focal point of Earth's elliptical orbit inevitably makes the logical foundations of his central conceit seem unsound. From the viewpoint of the present day, though, we can see a much better justificatory strategy that was not available to him at the time. We now know that the greater part of the mass required to hold galaxies together and to maintain the broad structure of the universe is "missing," in the sense that it is undetectable to our conventional astronomical instruments, which rely on electromagnetic radiation as a transmitter of information. It is commonly called "dark matter," although that does not adequate distinguish it from matter that is detectable, but does not shine in the visible spectrum; scientists, in consequence, tend to prefer the label "non-baryonic matter." It is, in fact, *invisible* matter, which possesses mass, and presumably has energetic relations of its own, of which our senses know nothing, but which remains transparent to electromagnetic radiation—much like the alternative matter envisaged by Renard.

Renard thought sufficiently deeply about the possibility of invisibility to realize that there was a fatal flaw in Wells's depiction of *The Invisible Man*, which he dramatized in his own story "L'Homme qui voulait être invisible" (tr. as "The Man Who Wanted to be Invisible" in volume four of the series), but he must have been pleased to realize that his own invisible aliens were immune to the criticism in question— which is that an invisible man would be unable to see, because his invisible retina could not intercept light. Being creatures composed of "alternative matter," the sarvants are, inevitably, equipped with senses appropriate to that state of matter, doubtless relying on some sort of "alternative energy"—plus the sense of touch, which they share with us simply by virtue of being material.

It is worth noting that this notion of alternative matter is coherent with the extension of the Cartesian dualism fundamental to *Le Docteur Lerne* that Renard deployed in *Un Homme chez les microbes*, which imagines the microcosm not in terms of material "atomic solar systems" but in terms of different kinds of substance, into which ours might be alchemically transmuted as the climax of a process of "diminution" initially manifest as shrinkage. The idea that there might be worlds "adjacent" to our own—both within and without—but composed of an alternative kind of matter, was to be further developed by a small number of subsequent speculative writers, but never attracted nearly as much literary attention as the notion that there might be adjacent worlds made of the same kind of matter, but displaced in a fourth spatial dimension.

Worlds of the latter sort have the convenience—like Wells's Mars and billions of other "Earth-clones" scattered through the galaxy—of slotting into the ready-made conquest/colonization narrative framework that Renard's imaginary world is designed to deny and defy, thus lending themselves to conventional narrative exploitation. The whole purpose of *Le Péril bleu* is, by contrast, to expose not merely the ridiculous absurdity but also the wretched pusillanimity of such carbon copies of *The War of the Worlds* as *Le Mystère des XV*. It is, therefore, no wonder that variants of its central notion have been left relatively unexplored and unexploited by other writers. Coincidentally, the science fiction novel that provided the most adventurous and intriguing variant of it, *A Wreath of Stars* (1976), was the work of Bob Shaw, who had previously "rediscovered" the central speculative motif employed in Renard's later novel, *Le Maître de la lumière*.

In his 1909 manifesto for scientific marvel fiction, Renard had observed *en passant* that Edgar Allan Poe had invented both detective fiction and scientific marvel fiction, but had made such a complete job of the former that he had only left room for imitators, while he had been so sketchy in the latter regard that he had left a vast unexplored wilderness for the use of "disciples." *Le Péril bleu* rams that opinion home in no uncertain terms in its merciless caricature of Tiburce, whose attempts to mimic Sherlock Holmes—considered as a mere carbon copy of Auguste Dupin—are so absurd as to qualify as madness. Tiburce's counterpart within the plot is Robert Collin, a disciple of imaginative thought, who even-

357

tually does solve the mystery—although he has literally to go out of this world to do so, without any means of coming back alive.

Unlike Dupin or Holmes, both of whom were confirmed bachelors, Tiburce and Robert are both motivated by the seemingly-hopeless love of a woman—which, in the latter case, can only lead to fatal self-sacrifice, thus continuing a fundamental pattern in Renard's early work, in which unbridled love leads only to disaster and death. Even conventionally-bridled love had usually led to loss prior to the denouement of *Le Péril bleu*, but the pattern is broken there when Tiburce does find a happy ending, in a chapter titled "The Triumph of Absurdity," while the object of Robert's desire falls into the tender arms of the Duc d'Agnès—whose attempts to tackle the problem by building a better airplane have been just as hopelessly ineffectual as Tiburce's crazy detective work. There was, of course, a moral in this, although Renard probably did not realize the full extent of its horrid implications at the time: in order to survive in the long term as a writer, he eventually had to abandon writing determined challenges to conventional thought in the form of scientific marvel stories, and settle down to writing blandly imitative mystery stories dealing with perfectly vulgar crimes, in which the hero would inevitably get the girl. Fortunately for posterity, he was slow in accepting that realization—unlike the vast majority of writers, who not only realize it before they start, but never have the slightest inkling of the possibility of doing otherwise.

Another frequent feature of Renard's early work that is shown off to particular effect in *Le Péril bleu* is his use of specific dates. This can be an awkward tactic in futuristic fiction, partly because it can disorient readers slightly to be reading a book in 1911 that refers to events occurring in 1912 as if they were familiar history, and partly because it ensures that the book will go very rapidly "out of date," in the sense that readers picking it up belatedly in 1913 will know that major events attributed to specific dates, which would have been universally evident if they had happened, actually did not happen. Most novels, of course, follow the policy that Renard had adopted in *Le Docteur Lerne*, of specifying the month in which events happen by month, but not by year, and of dealing with events on such a small scale that they could, in any case, pass unnoticed by the world at large, thus constituting episodes of "secret history." *Le Péril bleu* flatly refuses any such compromise, grasping the nettle of proffering an "alternative history" rather than a secret one.

Nowadays, of course, many readers are perfectly familiar with the idea of alternative histories and have no difficulty in dealing with books that were set in the future when they were written but whose settings have now been relegated to pasts that never were. In Renard's day, by contrast, the idea of setting a story in the future without the benefit of a preliminary expository sequence explaining that the author was about to do it was quite new. (I have searched hard, but I cannot find a single 19th century instance of a future-set story that is not equipped with a preliminary expository "essay.") By the time Renard read *The War of the Worlds*—which is set in "189-," although it did not appear in book form until 1898—it must already have been a manifest alternative history, set in a past that never was, and he must have realized immediately that leaving the last digit of the year of its setting unspecified had been quite unnecessary—but, even so, the decision to take the extra step must be counted a bold one. Indeed, even though it was published in 1911, Renard must have assumed that *Le Péril bleu* would be taken to be an alternative history even then, and that must be regarded as an essential aspect of its address to the reader—as is made explicit by the final remark that whether the events described in the story really happened or not makes no difference to their significance as a cautionary lesson for the human imagination.

Le Péril bleu was sufficiently widely-read to have some influence on later works of French speculative fiction, although it is perhaps unfortunate that it was not translated during the 20th century, and thus had no influence on English-language works. The influence it had, however, lay mostly in the belated encouragement of a few works deploying exotic neighboring worlds—like the invisible moon featured in Léon Groc's *La Planète de cristal* (1944)—for the sake of bizarrerie. Despite its publication as a *feuilleton* serial in *L'Intransigeant* after the Great War, and its subsequent reprinting in book form, it did not encourage any significant revival of interest in the larger ambitions of scientific marvel fiction. It remained an unanswered knock on the part of opportunity—but it is, nevertheless, a loud and spectacular knock, which fully deserves to be recognized as a *tour de force*.

SF & FANTASY

Guy d'Armen. *Doc Ardan: The City of Gold and Lepers*
G.-J. Arnaud. *The Ice Company*
Aloysius Bertrand. *Gaspard de la Nuit*
Félix Bodin. *The Novel of the Future*
André Caroff. *The Terror of Madame Atomos*
Didier de Chousy. *Ignis*
C. I. Defontenay. *Star (Psi Cassiopeia)*
Charles Derennes. *The People of the Pole*
Harry Dickson. *The Heir of Dracula*
Sâr Dubnotal *vs. Jack the Ripper*
Alexandre Dumas. *The Return of Lord Ruthven*
J.-C. Dunyach. *The Night Orchid. The Thieves of Silence*
Paul Féval. *Anne of the Isles. Knightshade. Revenants. Vampire City. The Vampire Countess. The Wandering Jew's Daughter*
Paul Féval, *fils. Felifax, the Tiger-Man*
Arnould Galopin. *Doctor Omega*
V. Hugo, Foucher & Meurice. *The Hunchback of Notre-Dame*
O. Joncquel & Theo Varlet. *The Martian Epic*
Jean de La Hire. *Enter the Nyctalope. The Nyctalope on Mars. The Nyctalope vs. Lucifer*
G. Le Faure & H. de Graffigny. *The Extraordinary Adventures of a Russian Scientist Across the Solar System* (2 vols.)
Gustave Le Rouge. *The Vampires of Mars*
Jules Lermina. *Panic in Paris. To-Ho and the Gold Destroyers. Mysteryville.*
Jean-Marc & Randy Lofficier. *Edgar Allan Poe on Mars. The Katrina Protocol. Pacifica. Robonocchio.* (anthologists) *Tales of the Shadowmen* (6 vols.) (non-fiction) *Shadowmen* (2 vols.)
Xavier Mauméjean. *The League of Heroes*
Marie Nizet. *Captain Vampire*
C. Nodier, Beraud & Toussaint-Merle. *Frankenstein*
Henri de Parville. *An Inhabitant of the Planet Mars*
Polidori, C. Nodier, E. Scribe. *Lord Ruthven the Vampire*
P.-A. Ponson du Terrail. *The Vampire and the Devil's Son*

Maurice Renard. *Doctor Lerne. A Man Among the Microbes.*
The Blue Peril
Albert Robida. *The Clock of the Centuries. The Adventures of*
Saturnin Farandoul
J.-H. Rosny Aîné. *The Navigators of Space. The World of the*
Variants
Brian Stableford. *The Shadow of Frankenstein. Frankenstein*
and the Vampire Countess. The New Faust at the Tragicomi-
que. Sherlock Holmes & The Vampires of Eternity. The Stones
of Camelot. The Wayward Muse. (anthologist) *The Germans*
on Venus. News from the Moon
Kurt Steiner. *Ortog*
Villiers de l'Isle-Adam. *The Scaffold. The Vampire Soul*
Philippe Ward. *Artahe*

MYSTERIES & THRILLERS

M. Allain & P. Souvestre. *The Daughter of Fantômas*
Anicet-Bourgeois, Lucien Dabril. *Rocambole*
A. Bisson & G. Livet. *Nick Carter vs. Fantômas*
V. Darlay & H. de Gorsse. *Lupin vs. Holmes: The Stage Play*
Paul Féval. *The Black Coats: The Companions of the Trea-*
sure. Gentlemen of the Night. Heart of Steel. The Invisible
Weapon. John Devil. The Parisian Jungle. 'Salem Street
Emile Gaboriau. *Monsieur Lecoq*
Steve Leadley. *Sherlock Holmes: The Circle of Blood*
Maurice Leblanc. *Arsène Lupin: The Hollow Needle. The*
Blonde Phantom
Gaston Leroux. *Chéri-Bibi. The Phantom of the Opera. Roule-*
tabille & the Mystery of the Yellow Room
G. Marot & L. Pericaud. *Nick Carter vs. Jack the Ripper*
William Patrick Maynard. *The Terror of Fu Manchu*
Frank J. Morlock. *Sherlock Holmes: The Grand Horizontals*
P. de Wattyne & Y. Walter. *Sherlock Holmes vs. Fantômas*
David White. *Fantômas in America*

CPSIA information can be obtained
at www.ICGtesting.com
Printed in the USA
FSOW04n1443110617
35118FS